Like Adam and Eve
Leaving the Garden,

they had stumbled down the hall to her chamber, as she leaned her weight upon him. His arm clasped her waist tightly, his tears dampening her brow as he laid his head against hers. They had not spoken. When they were inside, Kit had helped her to her bed, where she lay down without undressing. Kit said, "I have truly been wicked, and there is no excuse. I could say I was not awake, but I was. No dream could be as lovely as you. Now I shall be free, but you must suffer the vengeance of that—"

"That awful father of mine," she finished for him, more humiliated by Edgar Cochran's behavior than by her own.

"I shall come back for you, never doubt it," Kit swore. "I'll return soon. My father and I will consult a lawyer. We'll find what can be done. If you were not so very young . . . if only . . . if only!"

ROMANCE LOVERS DELIGHT

Purchase any first book at regular price of $4.95 & choose any second book for $2.95 plus $1.50 shipping & handling for each book.

_____ **LOVE'S SECRET JOURNEY** by Margaret Hunter. She found a man of mystery in an ancient land.

_____ **DISTANT THUNDER** by Karen A. Bale. While sheltering a burning love she fights for her honor.

_____ **DESTINY'S THUNDER** by Elizabeth Bright. She risks her life for her passionate captain.

_____ **DIAMOND OF DESIRE** by Candice Adams. On the eve of a fateful war she meets her true love.

_____ **A HERITAGE OF PASSION** by Elizabeth Bright. A wild beauty matches desires with a dangerous man.

_____ **SHINING NIGHTS** by Linda Trent. A handsome stranger, mystery & intrigue at Queen's table.

_____ **DESIRE'S LEGACY** by Elizabeth Bright. An unforgotten love amidst a war torn land.

_____ **THE BRAVE & THE LONELY** by R. Vaughn. Five families, their loves and passion against a war.

_____ **SHADOW OF LOVE** by Ivy St. David. Wealthy mine owner lost her love.

_____ **A LASTING SPLENDOR** by Elizabeth Bright. Imperial Beauty struggles to forget her amorous affairs.

_____ **ISLAND PROMISE** by W. Ware Lynch. Heiress escapes life of prostitution to find her island lover.

_____ **A BREATH OF PARADISE** by Carol Norris. Bronzed Fiji Island lover creates turbulent sea of love.

_____ **RUM COLONY** by Terry Nelson Bonner. Wild untamed woman bent on a passion for destructive love.

_____ **A SOUTHERN WIND** by Gene Lancour. Secret family passions bent on destruction.

_____ **CHINA CLIPPER** by John Van Zwienen. Story of sailing ships beautiful woman tantalizing love.

_____ **A DESTINY OF LOVE** by Ivy St. David. A coal miners daughter's desires and romantic dreams.

A Breath of Paradise

CAROL NORRIS

Exclusive Distribution
by
PARADISE PRESS, INC.

This book is for Willo,
always our inspiration,
and for nine loving critics:
O'Shirley, Emma, McShirley,
Ann, Ellen, Helen, Carolyn,
Virginia, and Mabel

This novel is a work of fiction. Names, characters, places and
incidents are either the product of the author's imagination or are
used fictitiously, and any resemblance to actual persons, living or
dead, events or locales is entirely coincidental.

Book I

Prologue
1870

Christopher Westcott stood gazing into the latticed summer-house set in the gardens of the estate called Blue Downs. It was October, shooting season, and he and his father had just arrived in Victoria from the Fiji Isles, as they did each year at this time.

White clematis covered the fragile summerhouse, which was surrounded with beds of pink and white roses, and bisected by cobbled paths. Kit had been drawn here across the lawns by the sound of a woman weeping. There, covering her face with tear-streaked hands, was Camilla, the last Cochran child left at home.

Kit hadn't seen her for a year. Those coiling red-gold curls could belong to no one but Cammy. Last year she'd only come up to his chest, and had freckles on her nose and a body like a chunk of steamed pudding. Today she was totally changed. When his boots sounded on the parquet floor of her vine-covered hideaway, Camilla reared back, letting him see that her waist had slimmed to nothing, and she'd filled out above. Even in her misery, all wet-faced and no more than sixteen, she was very desirable. She was adorable.

Her gown was white, sprigged with yellow flowers, and the fluted brief sleeves were transparent. He managed, with effort, to worry about the cause of her sorrow and not to contemplate his own male urges.

"Whatever has made you cry so, Cammy?" he asked cautiously, trying to remember how once he'd lifted her into her pony cart, years ago when she was a mere child. Things were so different this year! The Cochrans' marriage had been wrecked by some unnamed tragedy, and their hostess of so many seasons, Minnie Cochran, was gone. Edgar Cochran did not mention his wife; his temper was nothing less than foul. Kit's father already spoke of departing, and they had scarcely arrived.

"Mama's gone off, and I'll never see her again!" Camilla confided, before she even bothered to wipe her eyes and ascertain who was speaking to her. Then she noticed him and cried, "Kit! You're back!"

"So it's your mother who's making you weep. Where has she gone? Whatever has happened?"

Cautiously, he came close to her and put his arm around her shoulders, just as he would have comforted a child who had bruised herself. Now such comforting brought him exquisite torment. He was twenty-three, auburn-haired, smooth-skinned. As an admiring aunt once said, he was a perfect colonial gentleman, but at this particular moment, his impulses were not gentlemanly. Camilla's dark, coppery curls, unruly as always, brushed his shirtfront. He longed to put his hand into their luxuriance, to bury his face in the shimmery loveliness, kiss her brow, her neck . . .

"Mama said Papa was unbearable," she murmured. "Cold and cruel. She went off with her cousin Stephen from England and wanted to take me with them, but Papa said I may never see her again!"

"That is shocking," Kit responded with a frown. Indeed, Minnie Cochran had been one of his favorite people. She was such a sweet, chattering, always agitated woman. Kit recalled that she would ask him the hour and never hear his reply, and she'd hang on his arm and praise his every deed, and then feed him sweets. She was the most delightful woman, and Cammy promised to be much like her. Some man had carried Minnie off? The idea disturbed him greatly. He sat down beside Cammy and tugged her onto his knees. She settled against him with a sigh.

"Tell me every detail, Cammy. Sweet child, you must come up for air!"

She pressed her damp, pink-flushed face into his shirtfront, gasping with tears. She was seven years his junior, and how he wished that she were younger—or older.

Camilla swayed against him, sweet-smelling and as tender as an infant koala. He wanted to cuddle her, and to ravish her. He stroked her shapely arm and waited for her to catch her breath. Pointed breasts, enticingly prominent, pushed out the front of her gown. Her small weight upon him caused him wonderful pain, but the closeness of their bodies did not seem to trouble her at all. Trembling, he restrained himself from speaking. He could only think that her downy white neck close to his lips looked delicious enough to devour.

When she finally raised her head, her eyes brimmed with tears. Not blue eyes like his, but an extraordinary yellow-green, almost those of a kitten.

"Believe me, Cammy," he said softly, "I too thought the world of your mother."

He should never have used the past tense. Cammy shuddered, sucked back sobs, and gazed up at him. Her scent was captivating. Honeysuckle or sweet pea, he could not tell which.

"Tell me about this cousin Stephen."

"He came over from England last Christmas. Mama kissed him, and Papa saw. Just one kiss, but without any mistletoe."

Kit suppressed a smile at the naive remark.

"She said Papa reminded her every single day since. She was losing her senses. So Stephen came back one day a month ago when Papa was in town, and took Mama away."

Kit gritted his teeth. Damn Edgar Cochran, so smug. Whatever he did to drive away a wife so much like Cammy was insanity. No wonder the bald, pinched-face man had been sour and silent and had not once spoken his wife's name.

Kit wanted to wrap Camilla tight in his arms, to comfort her as a brother would. Her own brothers and her sister, Charlotte, were all grown and had moved away from home. Minnie had wed a man much older than she, a man with little charm. Now she'd deserted him.

Cammy looked up at Kit. Sprinkles of gold dust across her small nose and her flushed cheeks had once been freckles. Her wet eyes enlarged like opening flowers, petal-fringed.

Kit felt dizzy. Contain yourself, he cautioned his impulses.

Suddenly, the child-woman lifted both hands, jerked his head down, and pushed her soft lips against his. The intimacy stunned him into paralysis. Her eyes remained staring earnestly into his, her brows furrowed intently.

"There!" she exclaimed. "Now I'm no better than Mama!"

"What do you mean?" he demanded, his heart racing.

"Mama kissed Stephen, and I kissed you! I wish Papa had seen. Then maybe he'd send me to live with Mama."

"You kissed me only for that?" he asked. "Not because you like me?"

She flushed and looked away.

"Cammy," he began, his better nature still in control, "you must never kiss a man with your lips parted. You must close them firmly. Like this."

He showed her, barely able to hold himself in check. He pulled his head back before she did and swallowed the groan rising in his throat. She squirmed upon his lap, her eyes very wide.

"Kiss me when Papa is looking," she begged. "Oh, please!"

"Kissing signifies love," Kit said with some exasperation. "Your father would more likely lock you up and never let you out of the house again if we did that. It isn't a kindness to kiss a man merely to spite your father, Cammy."

"Oh, Kit!" she cried, terribly upset.

"I feel worth very little to be kissed as a means to an end," he reiterated.

She sprang off his knees and stood gasping in the doorway of the summerhouse, tears again springing from her gold-green eyes.

"Christopher Wain Westcott!" she spluttered, "how can you think that! I want to go to Mama, but I didn't mean . . ." She bit her lip. "To say I don't . . . Kit, my dearest Kit. I've loved you since I was ten years old!"

Kit sat staring at her. He'd come to Blue Downs every year from Fiji. Had he had her devotion for six years? While he was teasing or ignoring or tolerating that little girl, while he made approaches to her older sister Charlotte, and talked of events at the university with her brothers?

Kit's heart swelled with pride and he could not, dared not, move. He perched on the edge of the bench, and just stared at her.

He viewed his life before him. For the first time, he could see his future.

He saw Camilla, all in white a year hence as his bride, and

then Camilla holding pink babies, laughing, looking merrily up at him. A dream of pretty perfection. His wife, his beloved. They would grow old together, sharing everything they had. They'd die peacefully in each other's arms after a full and satisfying life.

His lips parted, and his eyes blurred with tears as he recognized the same perfect dream reflected in Camilla's eyes.

He was suddenly filled with shame for his lustful thoughts. He must wed a virgin Cammy, not offend her maidenly innocence. She was yet a child at heart. Granted, to wait would be terrible, for his nature was not cold. In Fiji, he had already tasted pleasures of the flesh. But while he had amorously toyed with many island girls, Camilla Cochran had faithfully waited for him to learn of her love.

She embroidered and dreamed, here at Blue Downs, and he had never suspected. Instantaneous revelation shook him to his very soul and made him dizzy.

Now she whirled out of the summerhouse, stumbling over her many petticoats. He plunged after her to prevent her from falling, but she recovered herself, hiked up her skirts, and ran away from him up the long, sloping lawns. Laughing, he followed in hot pursuit. Some day, she would be his.

Chapter 1

Things changed after she said she loved him. Since that first moment when he sat there stunned into silence, everything was different. She had run away, half hoping he would love her in return but not sure at all that he cared. It was scandalous of a girl to kiss a man and say she loved him.

But it was so wonderful, and each kiss she shared with Kit aroused new feelings in her, which led to more kisses and then . . .

For the next month, everything was colored with a rose hue for Cammy, as she and Kit grew to love one another more each day. She constantly marveled at this beautiful man who was now hers. She loved to look at his golden body. From childhood, he had gone swimming in the lagoons without clothes, shaking himself dry in the hot Fiji sun. England did not have the power to turn his limbs fish-white again. He'd been raised by native women when his mother died, and spoke two languages from birth, which Cammy greatly admired. His English was oddly accented and it gave her nothing but pleasure to hear him speak. She adored him and wanted to become a Fijian like him and go about in thin, white cottons and wide-brimmed hats, barefoot in the sun.

6

He told her of his homeland as they lay together on the lush grass in the fields beyond her father's estate. But they did more than talk.

Kit's lips would rest on the side of her neck, moving from her soft earlobe to the exquisitely sensitive curve where neck joins shoulder. His hands would span her waist, thumbs touching over her spine and fingers touching in front, hands sliding up her sides, cupping her breasts. He made her moan, but she loved the sensation and begged him to continue.

He soothed her as if she were a restive filly, and his arms and hands, strong and careful, wound about her. She felt his heart pounding against her when he pressed her to him and talked into her ear when he was not kissing it. Her ears were like perfect pink seashells, he said. His breath was sweet, his sea-blue eyes so clear and merry and tender that her love, which was limitless, grew greater and deeper each day. His eyes crinkled with pleasure the moment he saw her each morning.

He was no longer the lanky boy of seventeen who once kindly harnessed her pony to her cart and exclaimed over the kangaroo-tail soup and the bush chutneys Cook prepared. Cammy had watched Kit grow up.

Never had she leapt from her bed so eagerly, afraid she'd miss a moment of him. Once a late and lazy sleeper, lounging in her canopied bed till midday, she was now a student of early morning bird life, up with the kookaburras, the laughing jackass birds with their aboriginal name.

She had learned the art of kissing from Kit, and now they could not contain themselves for love. Every morning they slipped away, riding over the paddocks, under the towering, pale-barked, fragrant gum trees, meeting in the bushland full of noisy pink and gray galah parrots and sulfur-crested cockatoos. With Kit she could almost forget Mama's going away. Papa had been so inattentive lately, he did not notice where she was and with whom and for how long.

The old dry dam had been their favorite hiding place from the others around the property: the gardener, the grazier's boy, and swagmen who happened by and asked for work.

Kit would hold her leaning back against him, sitting on the rough stone barrier that contained the small lake for the English coots and grebes and the black swans. The dry stream below the dam was bordered with wattle and willow that shielded them from onlookers. The tiny overflow ran into a sagging old trough where their tethered horses drank in the heat.

Kit would cuddle her against him as he leaned his own back on the end of the wall, propping his knee up so she could admire his fine strong leg in the tight riding pants and tall boot. Under her long-skirted riding costumes, she wore thin lawn blouses now growing too small for her, she was so puffed up with love. But Kit seemed to like the buttons straining down her front between her breasts. She also wore a touch of scent, from the bottle that Mama left behind when she left in such a hurry.

Cammy could forget about Mama's leaving only when she lay in Kit's strong arms, so she sought his arms for shelter and his lips for sweet refreshment.

Together they half-reclined, mouth to mouth, breathing each other's quickened breath.

Papa never noticed them, blind as he was with infuriation at Mama. Cammy's father had never been an affectionate man, but now he was brooding or angry all the time. Her only recourse was to stay out of his way.

The shooting season was drawing to a close, and the Westcotts were due to return to their plantation in the Fiji Isles. Kit swore that he would come to her this autumn with a proposal of marriage. He had confided their dreams to his father and had his approval. At seventeen, he said, Cammy could become Kit's bride; Kit would be twenty-four by then, well on his way to managing the family plantation. His father desired a quieter life, saying that Fiji planting and Fiji politics could be left to the younger generation. And to assist Kit, said Mr. Westcott, an energetic, adaptable wife would be a great boon.

"Move yourself a bit to the left, dearest," Kit said. "Do have pity on me, Cammy. You don't realize what you can do to a man." But then he disarranged her hair and her collar, kissing her until she went half mad for more.

"What do I 'do to a man'?" she asked innocently. "This is very nice."

"I do not wish to ruin you. I expect to wed you, Camilla."

But she always made him relent. She'd twist herself around so she could nuzzle his fine smooth chin and pull down his head as she had that first day, and kiss his soft eyelids closed.

She'd rub her nose against his, giggling until he laughed, too, narrowing his eyes and tightening his arms about her. How could she bear it when he left for the Cannibal Isles to tend their canefields? She feared she would die of the loss.

"Let me come with you," she pleaded. "I'm sixteen, a grown girl. You have money, or your father does. Let us wed now and be happy forever."

"Father wouldn't hear of it," Kit replied firmly, still holding her close. "In our family, at least a half year's betrothal is tradition. I have duties on the estate. I must prove myself worthy of a wife and able to care for a family. I'll come back for you, Cammy, I swear it, and next year we'll marry."

He did not dare to put a betrothal ring on her finger, but secretly he had sent for a garnet ring from Melbourne that had been his dead mother's. He gave it to Cammy who wore it on her right hand. She never told Papa where she got it. Mr. Westcott probably knew, but he said nothing.

When the days grew fewer in number, Cammy began to beg Kit to come to her room at night, but he always refused. He said it was not proper.

On the evening of the Westcotts' departure, Camilla became frantic. She begged Kit to come to her chamber just that last night. They would stay up together to see the dawn. They would hold each other through those final hours.

"My father and I are guests of your father. I do not wish to add to sorrows already suffered," Kit said slowly.

"But how could sweet love bring trouble to anyone?" she asked, ignorant as a new-born rabbit. Kit was too much of a gentleman to explain. Why, even Mama, who said everything that came into her head, used to turn away Camilla's questions, urging, "Ask your husband, Cammy, once you're married."

The night before the dawn that would take Kit Westcott away, she had slipped out of her bed, garbed herself in her prettiest floral brocade wrapper, and brushed her curls until they shone. If he would not come to her, then it was her duty to go to him. She'd carried some chocolates up to her room, and arranged them on a cut-paper doily on a silver tray.

For weeks they had enjoyed blissful play, kissing and stroking and caressing, both of them dressed in all of their clothing. Hands fondled bodies through layers of fabrics, touching very little bare flesh. She did not know what she would gain by insinuating herself in her nightclothes into a young man's bedchamber. Kit knew everything, he claimed, but he would not inform her. He only told her what a wonderful bride she would prove, for she was "warm," and few British girls were. She could not imagine how any girl could be near Kit and not feel warm all over. He'd playfully pat her bustle, and bid her run away before she killed him.

How could she do that? she'd asked. He was far larger than she, and so strong that he could lift her with one arm.

So that night she took the chocolates on their tray, and a candle balanced in the middle of them, and left her room. Kit's door was unlatched. She came around to the side of Kit's bed with her hair falling around her neck and her wrapper sliding off her shoulders. Her blood was in a tumultuous boil when she gazed down at her lover, so angelic in sleep. Instead of the Prince awakening Sleeping Beauty, it would be the other way around. She sat carefully on the side of his bed.

In the candlelight, his tanned profile against the white linen was sharp and perfectly set off by his dark brows and lashes and the brown hair curling around his ear.

She wanted to be kissed for once in a soft bed, not outside in the hot wind among flies and horses and possible onlookers. She leaned over him and touched her lips to his cheek.

Kit awoke suddenly, and for once did not smile. She had no time to do anything but set the candle and tray on the bedside table. Then his mouth was on hers. He caught her to him, burying his face in her bosom, his eyes glazed. By the time he jolted awake, she was returning his kisses with violent passion, and he was lost. He tumbled her down on top of him, murmuring one surprised cry. But in an instant his nightshirt was off, and she could feel all of him sliding against her, so smooth, warm, and hard-muscled that she almost swooned. Her nightdress vanished from her.

What Kit did next astonished her. At first it hurt, and then it excited her. They both were naked, eagerly wrestling.

How strange and wonderful this was! The two of them lay there gasping, body to body, their legs and arms entwined, lips claimed lips. Cammy was awestruck by the astonishing tool with which Kit teased and prodded her. It did not fit where he wished to drive it, and his face became grim in the candlelight as he bared his teeth. Then suddenly she gave a little scream.

Beneath his weight crushing her into the bed, she held his head between her hands. He grasped her hips and lifted them. He pushed, and she cried, "Stop, stop!" but he would not.

Kit was not himself. He was a man possessed, and she felt invaded. Then for a moment he lay still and soothed her. She decided that she liked being joined to him. She kissed him, and then he began to rock. He pushed his face into the pillow by her head to muffle his groans. Camilla endured all of this, clenching her teeth, her eyes wide open, her fingers splayed tensely apart. The bed creaked loudly.

Then she thought surely she'd killed him, because he bit into the pillow and almost screamed. He fell back on her as if he were dead.

"Kit? Kit?"

He lifted his head, shook it, and seemed to see her for the first time.

"What have I done to you, Camilla?" he cried, stroking her face with one finger.

"You hurt me a little," she whispered. "Then I hurt you very much, didn't I? Oh Kit, what happened?"

"There must be no child," he groaned into her tumbled hair.

"Child? Of course not! We aren't married!"

"My God, do you know nothing?"

"I love you," she said, kissing his hot face.

"I tried, but I could not cease," he said, touching her everywhere. "Oh, Camilla, I love you."

She slipped her hand down between their two bodies to find the thing that had hurt her so mysteriously and relentlessly. As she touched it, she jerked her hand back because it stiffened instantly.

"Don't do that," he said, drawing her close.

In a moment the sweet invasion started again, and this time it truly was sweet. She lifted her knees and held him very tight, marveling at the sensation of swimming, of whirling around in a pool of heated honey, of sinking and drowning in it. His weight on her lightened, and she arched her back and dug her fingers into his shoulders. She could not help exclaiming aloud. Kit quickly covered her mouth with his, and all her insides exploded like fireworks, showering sparks from her toes to the roots of her hair.

What happened next Camilla tried to shut out, but to no avail.

Someone had come into the room.

It was her father. Edgar Cochran opened the bedchamber door she'd never thought to latch. He was standing at the foot of the bed. They peered at him, horrified, over the edge of the coverlet.

Camilla ducked her head under the covers and pressed it upon Kit's wide, smooth chest. She might be smothered, but she would no longer see the furious, lined old face glowering above her and the mouth twisting with words hateful to hear.

"You have ruined my daughter!" he hissed.

Kit interrupted him, rearing up on one elbow and announcing, "We shall be married, sir, within the week! I swear it. We already are betrothed, in secret. I love Camilla, and my family welcomes her."

"No Westcott shall be my son-in-law! You and your father get out of my house before the sun rises, or I'll see you both in hell!"

"Father!" Camilla cried aloud, but she did not emerge from the darkness of her sanctuary against Kit's strong, warm body.

"Your unholy sin was committed with noise enough to wake the dead!" Cochran ranted. "And your own father collaborates in your sin!"

Camilla heard her father pound the wall.

"I shall bring him here to witness this," cried Edgar Cochran. He pounded again. "Come in, Westcott!" he shouted. "Come in and see!"

"This is my fault entirely," Kit was saying, "not Cammy's."

Mr. Westcott arrived hastily, drawing his robe around him. Cammy peeked out long enough to see his uncombed hair standing straight up, his face a wretched mask of sorrow.

"Now!" Edgar Cochran began again. "You see? Your son has ruined my last solace, my innocent daughter!"

"You cannot believe such nonsense!" Mr. Westcott protested. "My son shall immediately marry Camilla. They have been devoted since childhood. This unfortunate folly must only hasten their union."

"You have never warned me—" her father raved. "Marriage? You think my child can simply be stolen away? In truth, man, are you insane?"

"The question is what Kit and Camilla desire," Mr.

Westcott said patiently. Kit kept trying to interject a word in her defense, but neither man heard.

"Let me finish!" roared Edgar Cochran, nearly apoplectic in his rage. "You shall not hang your vile name on my daughter, sir! I have treated you as my friend for years," her father fumed. "But then, you were always more solicitous of my wife. You took Minnie's part against me over the years. I should have known."

"Sir, you act deranged," Mr. Westcott said, shaking his head. "Kit, put on your clothing. See what your folly has caused. Certainly you and Cammy shall wed. There is no other way. Come to my room. I wish to speak with you. In the morning we shall all be calmer."

Cammy shivered beneath the covers.

"I shall marry Camilla and give her the protection of our name, Mr. Cochran," Kit said manfully, hugging her close. "If you'd please leave us—"

Kit shifted his body and Camilla peered out. His arm came around her and held her tightly, defying her father.

"Whore. Daughter of a whore!" Pushing Mr. Westcott ahead of him, her father stomped out of the room.

Camilla collapsed into sobs, praying that she'd dreamed all this. She raised her tear-stained face to Kit. "My father has gone mad!"

"He sees evil in everyone, but no sin in himself," Kit growled. "I am sorry to say it, Cammy, but your mother did well to escape him."

"I believe you are right," she replied, forcing her arms into her nightdress and then into the wrapper he scooped off the floor. She could scarcely sit up, and when she put her feet down on the carpet, she almost fainted. There was blood on her gown.

Camilla groaned and turned over in bed, burying her face in the sweet, down-filled pillow. Kookaburras were laughing in the trees outside, but now it was well past their bedtime and hers. They laughed at her endless sorrow. She brought her right hand to her lips and kissed the little garnet that Kit had given her. At least she had something of Kit's to keep.

She lay there without sleeping, wishing Kit were beside her to nuzzle his face deep into her neck and stroke her sides, sides bare of any corset or chemise. She knew the taste and scent of his body: his temples salty after he'd been riding, his hair smelling with the hint of the aromatic oils of gum trees, his hands of leather reins and saddle. He was clean and beautiful and good. She'd die before she accepted a kiss—no, even a glance—from any other man.

At last, unable to stand the lonely bed, she arose and dressed. Tomorrow she would learn what was to become of her.

Chapter 2

Camilla stood by the tall window overlooking the south lawns of Blue Downs, straining her eyes toward Melbourne. Kit had gone. Her midnight-blue gown swept in a severe princess line from the carpet up and over her bosom to push a bouquet of pale lace against her chin. She wore no ornament, not even a trace of powder on her white face. She dared not speak or raise her eyes.

She was in mourning. She was a disgrace.

Kit and his father were exiled, and it was all her fault! The servants made light of it, saying that two young people so much in love and so beautiful might be expected to . . . err. Their glances were sympathetic.

Did they all know?

Father shouted horrible things. "I'll shoot him on sight if he comes in range of my gun!" "No grandchild of mine will claim Westcott as a grandfather!"

Father's older sister, Rina, had come straight up to Blue Downs the next morning, to preserve Father's sanity, as he said. Rina would keep the estate going in their absence, for Father was taking Camilla around the world, "away from that island politician and his son, the ravisher!"

"You are extremely fortunate, Camilla," Aunt Rina said

when she heard the story, "that your father is so generous as to forgive you. Girls in India are betrothed at three years of age, and by sixteen they have several children. In some lands you would have been stoned to death, and him with you. Here in Victoria you might have been driven out upon the streets to bear a child under a bridge while you earned your bread in the vile profession you seem most fit for."

Camilla blinked and shuddered at this. The phrases were silky smooth, but the savagery in them was evident. To escape Rina's scorn and her father's cold stares of bitter resentment, Camilla attempted to ignore them. For two days she had tried to close her ears to condemnation. Her small, black-haired aunt and her balding, wizened father constantly harped upon "sin." She knew, though, that it was not sin in intention. It was a beautiful, pure thing, though it confused her. What did they mean that she was ruined? Even Kit had said that.

It could not be ruinous. Nothing had ever felt more glorious! Yet they persisted, and now, until her father took her away, she was a prisoner at Blue Downs.

Tonight the English garden was in full bloom. Camilla knew that no other prison offered such lovely vistas, with Melbourne a tantalizing glow on the horizon. Melbourne where Kit and dear Mr. Westcott had gone, propelled by her father's rage and accusations. If only her mother had been here when it happened! She would have taken their side against Father.

Mother now lived with Stephen toward that sunset in South Australia, their neighbor colony. She had written two letters since she'd run away. Father insisted upon reading the one addressed to Camilla, and Camilla had to submit her answering letter to him for perusal before it could be posted. This requirement left her with little she dared say to Minnie Cochran. She wished that she and Mama knew some secret language, some exotic code, and then she would be able to write all about wonderful Kit. But Father would be sure to burn any suspicious missive.

Now Kit was gone, and tomorrow she, too, would be gone. He could not write to her, nor she to him.

"The young bounder is lucky I do not send him to prison!" stormed her father. "Corrupting my daughter! I let those two live in my home when no one would expect hospitality of me at such a time! When I myself had only recently suffered a loss."

"You said it was my fault, Father. Please don't condemn the Westcotts," Cammy begged.

"True, true. You had your wicked mother's example before your eyes, and quickly you repeated her sin. Her bequest to you is a taint in the blood. Had I but disciplined her more severely, she might have overcome evil inclinations. But I shall not be mild in your case, Camilla. You shall go away from here tomorrow. You shall not mention the name of your seducer ever again. You shall be as loyal and obedient to me as your mother was not. I shall not have another of my dearest possessions stolen!"

The tickets were immediately obtained, and space was reserved for three persons to sail to England. The third member of their party would be a chaperone her father had hired to guard her day and night. She would have to bid farewell to her home of sixteen years.

Kit would not even know when and where she'd gone.

Camilla stood on the dew-damp grass, hugging herself, watching stars coming out like chips of ice in the blue-violet sky. In fantasy, Kit was suddenly there with her again, putting his hands around her waist, kissing her neck as she bent it for the sweet touch of his lips.

She had acted very young—silly and giddy and ignorant! She had no idea, Kit had told her, what strain she caused a young man. Kit always seemed to have a smile quirking the corners of his wide mouth, and lights dancing in his eyes like stars in the bluest of skies. He was a merry, happy, calm, entrancing person. His gentle whimsy had deceived her into thinking him not much older than she or much troubled by things they wished to do but shouldn't. Her father had called these lovely things "sins." Merely to go to Kit with her heart filled with love and devotion, that was one sin. To kiss him awake was another. For him to hold her tightly, without his nightshirt on, was another.

No, she could not believe they were wicked. After all, they had done almost the same during the weeks of his visit at Blue Downs, and his father knew and only smiled.

Was it the injury he'd done her? The blood? The ache that lasted until now? He had spoken of a child. No one ever told her how a child entered the world. Was this the way? She knew now, of course, of the strange difference between men and women, but she did not have all the answers and had no one to ask.

After their discovery in bed together, Kit had covered himself as if ashamed, had helped her dress as well. Like Adam and Eve leaving the Garden, they had stumbled down the hall to her chamber, as she leaned her weight upon him. His arm clasped her waist tightly, his tears dampening her brow as he laid his head against hers. They had not spoken. When they were inside, Kit had helped her to her bed, where she lay down without undressing. Kit said, "I have truly been wicked, and there is no excuse. I could say I was not awake, but I was. No dream could be as lovely as you. Now I shall be free, but you must suffer the vengeance of that—"

"That awful father of mine," she finished for him, more humiliated by Edgar Cochran's behavior than by her own.

"I shall come back for you, never doubt it," Kit swore. "I'll return soon. My father and I will consult a lawyer. We'll find what can be done. If you were not so very young . . . if only . . . if only!"

He struck the heel of his hand against his forehead, and tears started up again from his eyes. "I love you, Camilla. I adore you. I shall never cease loving you. You shall be my wife."

"You have won me, but I'm my father's prisoner," she said, suddenly seeing her future. She'd seldom known her father to show mercy. Mercy to an errant servant, perhaps, or to a drunken workman or a lazy scullery maid, but never to a Cochran. "Cochrans do not make mistakes," her father had said. Cochran sons do not disobey, Cochran daughters are pure. Minnie Cochran had once been "the best of wives."

All the other Cochrans were now scattered, and now Camilla understood why.

Charlotte, whom Kit had courted for several years when Camilla was still an awkward child, was now married and living in Queensland bearing children of her own. Michael was studying to become a lawyer in Sydney, and Jock ran his own sheep farm in New South. Richard, too, had married young and lived in New Zealand now. Bernard, whom Cammy hadn't seen in many years, was well ensconced as a printer in Salisbury, England. They had all fled the nest but her. Even Mama. When Mama was there to kiss her and plan gay parties and fetes, to take her to the city for shopping and treats, Cammy hadn't noticed how empty the house had become. She scarcely knew her papa at all. She knew Mr. Westcott better, and the other men and ladies who came for

the shooting or on Papa's business when he still owned
factories and went to an office in Swanston Street. Everyone
made much of Minnie's "baby," and she enjoyed everyone.
Now no one was left but Papa and sour old Rina with her
dyed black hair. Now Cammy must sail to England with Papa
and a new lady's maid she'd never seen. Kit would be left
behind. All the servants would be sacked because of her
shame.

Chapter 3

When they reached the busy metropolis, Cammy managed to scribble a letter for Kit, telling him she was being taken away, but she knew no address for the Westcotts in Melbourne. In the Fiji Isles the name "Westcott" would be well known, for white men there were rare, and rich white men even fewer. She'd post it to the Isles, confident it would eventually reach him.

Melbourne was dazzling, full of beautifully dressed and coiffed ladies in spring dresses with hats to guard their complexions. She saw tearooms, fine shops, and Chinamen with poles across their shoulders. There were smart gigs and landaus on the wide streets. Swanston Street, made completely of granite blocks, had omnibuses drawn by three horses abreast. There were dogcarts and wagonettes, bridges over the Yarra River covered with bright boats, and the tall cathedral by the Flinders Street Station.

When the maidservant Father had obtained was introduced to her, Camilla was disappointed. She was not young and lively, but a full-bosomed woman with a lined face. Was she over forty? Under sixty? Her name was Mrs. Finch, and she'd accepted the position of lady's maid for Camilla in exchange for passage to England.

She was better than Aunt Rina, of course, but no comfort to a lovesick girl of sixteen.

If she asked Mrs. Finch to post a letter for her, would the request be honored? But there was no other way. They would travel this very afternoon on the railroad to the Sandridge docks. Father did not allow Cammy out of his sight or out of her hotel room where she had been permitted to wash after the dusty buggy ride of the morning. When she'd changed into warmer garments for the sea trip, she'd thought twice and at last put her letter to Kit stealthily into Mrs. Finch's small, gloved hand. It was only an hour before their scheduled departure.

"Ah, certainly I'll hasten to the post office, child," the woman said with a smile. She understood immediately. "Never fear. I'll post your billet-doux."

This sudden friendliness disarmed Cammy. She had to trust this woman, for she had no one else.

Mrs. Finch came back promptly, patting her small hands together, rapidly clicking along in her worn, buttoned boots. She really was aptly named—just like a little round finch or robin redbreast, bright-eyed and busy.

"I've done it. Your father will never know."

"How did you guess that my father must not—"

"I can see it. Any half-wit would see there's no love lost between the two of you, Camilla. And you may call me Letty, though you're the age of my grandchild."

"Grandchild? But you're—"

"We marry young in this land, if ye didn't notice," Letty interrupted. "And so did my own girls. I was a grandmother before I was thirty-three, and a midwife in the bush where precious few saw a doctor. If I hadn't married an emancipist, if I'd waited for a free settler I could trust, why I'd be a wife in my own cottage right now."

Camilla nodded, wide-eyed. Poor Letty had wed a freed felon sent over from England for some crime.

"Your father had to pay well to get these cabins on so short notice, I daresay. Not many could manage that. He's in a great hurry to take you out of the colonies, that's for certain."

"Away from the man I love," Camilla whispered, barely able to hold back tears. Despite herself, she was excited about the huge ship. This was her first voyage anywhere! If only it were her honeymoon trip! Would Kit receive her letter? she wondered anxiously. And what would he do about it?

"Now we're bound for Salisbury, your father says, to visit your brother there," her confidante told her as she unstrapped their cases and placed items in the net hanging over each bed. "I hope you get on with your brother. It'll be hard enough when the baby arrives."

"What? What are you saying, Letty?" Cammy was shocked.

"I reckon he'd not take you away so quick, so far, and in secret unless the lad had got you with child. Isn't this the way with rich folks? Hide the gehl until she delivers, and no one is the wiser. Though it'll be more difficult for you to find a good man, once you're a mother."

"I am to be a mother?" Cammy marveled, pressing her hands on her stomach. "How can you be certain?"

"Well, there's one sure way to discover it. If your monthly episode comes, then you're not. If not, then you are, for dead certain."

Camilla sat on the leather couch in their trim, wainscoted cabin with its green carpet and latticed doors and washbasin beyond a screen. She frowned and contemplated her future. Was it possible that she really was with child? Dear God, that *did* give Father some reason to be outraged. A baby? Mama said babies came after the bride asked her husband about babies, and he told her. But evidently, Mama was mistaken.

The sea voyage was awesome across the great Port Phillip and between the fortified headlands, but in the Bass Strait the wind arose and made the deck rise and fall with the running tides. Camilla suddenly fell ill. She scarcely remembered the first half of the voyage. She lay on her railed bed and groaned and tossed, wishing herself dead. Dear Letty, however, drew a chair beside Cammy's bed and endured the motion of the ship like a champion, applying damp, cool cloths to Cammy's face, and offering her food she could seldom devour or keep down.

Rather, she lost all she had in her, and slept, when she could sleep, with her arm crooked around a tin basin. She grew thin and gaunt and yellow, and thought she surely would die. The "monthly episode" did not come, but Letty thought it might be because of her severe seasickness. No girl so sick and wasted could be filled with life, she said. Or if she was, perhaps she'd lose it. But none of this meant anything to

Cammy. She hardly knew that Christmas came. She could buy no gifts, but she wept over the red and gold cloth that Letty gave her.

It was not until the Suez Canal was traversed and they sailed the quiet waters of the Mediterranean Sea that Cammy came to herself again. It had been over six weeks now. She had lived on gruel and coddled eggs and lots of dry toast, thanks to Letty Finch. She had wept gallons of salt tears upon the salt sea and soaked Letty's broad bosom many times.

"I am lost! I cannot live without him!" Cammy had sobbed. Kit was always in her thoughts—beautiful, laughing, loving Kit, Kit so wonderous and enticing, and gentle with her except on that one night. Their final night.

"It is called breeding," Letty confided to her. "Not that it's just like the animals do it, mind you, but the act's the same and with the same consequences. A pity that gently reared gehls aren't told such things. That's the way babies are made. The man plants the seed, and the leddy grows it."

"It was so *wonderful!*" Cammy sobbed. "After the first, I mean."

"Hush, m'darlin," Letty crooned, rocking her like a child. "God makes it be wonderful, so folks will be wanting to do it, and then babies will come. Wonderful for lads, at least, and lucky gehls who like it. Me, I was a lucky one. I loved my man, though he was flighty and flew away from me. I'd marry again if I could. There's less chance of marrying in England, however, than in the colonies, where womenfolk are so scarce."

"Are you going to England to see your family?" asked Cammy, finally able to take an interest in something beyond her own survival.

"I've not seen my dear father and mother in London for near onto nine years. I plan to persuade them to come out to the colonies. They're old now, and the weather's much kinder to old folk in the southern climes."

A few days later, Camilla was able to walk the decks or sit out with a woolen rug over her knees. She wore a rust-colored traveling cloak, and a matching bonnet tied firmly under her chin against the Mediterranean breezes. The sea was blue, and the land gray-green, dotted with olive trees. It looked rocky, and Cammy could see goats at play. Hundreds of white fishing boats bobbed around their great steamer.

After her walk, she returned to her cabin to find her father waiting. He told her to sit down and listen to him carefully. He wore a dove-gray suit and sat holding his tall hat on his knee. Cammy had no desire whatsoever to talk to him. Watching him prepare a speech frightened her, and she felt ill again.

"Camilla, I am, of course, going to divorce your mother." Camilla pressed her lips together and could not breathe.

"You realize she will never have a shilling from me. I do not forgive."

"I've noted that," she said somewhat sarcastically.

"If you bear a child, Camilla, you shall give birth in secret and never see it. I shall give it to some decent family. But one thing I vow is that you shall never wed. You shall serve as my hostess at Blue Downs, and I must confess it is very generous of me to suggest this. Few men could survive two such terrible blows one after the other. First the desertion of a wife of thirty-one years, and then the ruination of a daughter. You should be glad I am not out of my mind with grief. Now, have you anything to say for yourself?"

"I shall always love Kit. If someone had told me about making babies, I would never have gone to his bedchamber," she said with a cold determination that surprised even her.

Her father sat up straighter in his chair. "Highly improper words to come from a girl raised as you were."

She wanted to say much more. She longed to tell him about love, about mercy, and about Letty Finch's kindness as compared to her father's cruelty. But she remained mute, and stared at the floor.

"In a few days we shall be past Gibraltar and shall dock at Southampton," her father said in a raspy voice as he fidgeted with his hat. "I have telegraphed ahead to Bernard, and he will meet us at the docks. You shall say not one word about your sin or your likely condition. The ostensible reason for our visit is that we have not seen Bernard in years, and he won't take the trouble to visit me."

"What of Mother?" Cammy asked. "Does Bernard know about her?"

"If she is mentioned, say, 'Ask Father.' They will know the truth eventually, but in the meanwhile, the most important thing is seeing to your own business."

"My business?"

Her father cleared his throat. "If you are with child, I shall send you away to the country for your lying-in. No one shall know your name there."

"I think you wish I were pregnant," she said in a whisper.

"That would be no more than you deserve."

"I don't think I am," she said. "Letty says I cannot be—"

"Don't speak of such things," her father interrupted crossly, springing up. "A doctor will presently examine you."

Four days later, they tied up at the Southampton docks. Bernard was there with Beatrice, and seeing them smile lifted Cammy's spirits. They hugged and kissed her and promised her a view of Stonehenge and of their famous cathedral. They laughed gaily about the chill of England in autumn after the warmth of the colonies in spring.

The doctor came to the hotel where they stopped for the night, and did no more than to listen to Cammy's heart and take her pulse and look down her throat. He went away after speaking a few words with Letty. The next morning, Letty took the railroad train to her family in London, promising to write.

In a week Cammy knew for sure there was no baby, and rejoiced. But the thought of a baby who looked like Kit gladdened her heart. Might that be all she would ever have of Kit? No. Father would never have let her see her baby in any case. He would have stolen it from her and given it away before she even knew its sex or saw its face.

Bernard did not know about Kit, but he easily fathomed the truth about Mama's running off. He didn't seem surprised.

"Each of us runs from Father," he said harshly, over his third glass of port in the library of his fine house near Salisbury. It was raining and cold, and Cammy was sitting by the fire, warmed by golden flames while Beatrice played Chopin on their grand piano. Edgar Cochran had retired to his room for a nap before dinner.

"I can see why he'd rush away from Blue Downs," Bernard said.

He was bearded and becoming stout, even at thirty. Cammy adored her oldest brother, and had missed him. They ate teacakes, and she had port wine, too, at Bernard's urging. He stood a good half foot taller than Papa and spoke down to him in more than one sense of the term.

"The old man cannot bear to lose a thing he possesses," he

explained. "All of us Cochran children find reasons to leave Victoria. You'll marry young, if Papa permits it, Cammy. I can't say I judge Mama for bolting."

Cammy liked the word he used: "bolting." That's what convicts did; they bolted from prison.

"Father thinks Cousin Stephen plotted to take Mama away," Cammy ventured. "But you've met Stephen. It wasn't wicked of them, was it?"

"Cammy, it's rather shocking to speak like that," cautioned Beatrice.

"I've always liked Stephen," said Bernard. "Barely knew him, but he seemed a solid chap. Poor as a ragman, with all the children he had from his former wife. Then she died and he was alone, poor man. Good place for him, the colonies."

"He's not a close cousin, is he?" asked Beatrice, again interrupting her piano playing.

"Not at all," Bernard reassured her. "Second or third cousin, once or twice removed. Very much on the up-and-up. He's a year or two younger than our mother, I believe. No, I could never condemn them, and as the eldest, I shall speak for our brothers and sister, eh?"

"For me, at least," agreed Camilla with a smile. Then she thought of Kit, and running away with him. Now he could write to her if he'd received her letter. If he knew they had sailed to England, would he expect them to be in Salisbury? He surely remembered where Bernard lived.

"Wretched weather. Winter coming on already," said Bernard, peering out the window at the rain. "Only the glasshouse will remind us of home, eh, little sister?"

He had allowed himself the luxury of a gas-heated conservatory where he was nurturing flowers to bring a bit of Victoria to foggy England. Cammy and Bernard left the library and went in to enjoy the flowers. They walked between pots of boronia and callistemon, bottle-brushes due to bloom in spring, and the brilliant cylindrical Banksias named after Joseph Banks, their first Australian botanist. Bernard had also grown several tall, potted tree ferns with green lacy fronds. One stood in each corner of the cozy glass house.

"I wonder you are not a botanist by profession, my dear brother," Camilla said to him, "instead of a book printer."

But she loved to smell the sweet printer's ink and walk between the ungainly, noisy machines in his shop. Bernard

was able to spend his money on his business and become a
success quickly, due to the fact that Edgar Cochran had
financed his house. Bernard's workers loved him, and the
man from whom he bought the business came in occasionally
to work beside him, just for old time's sake. Camilla received
beautifully bound volumes of verse and flower sketches as
free samples of their craft. Her brother took her to tea near
the cathedral, laughing, as did she, at Englishmen who would
not dirty their hands in trade. A colonial had to labor, bend
his back, become familiar with grease and dirt, said Bernard,
and such free-spirited men could then come back to their
motherland and make a fortune among soft Englishmen who
remained too "propah" to sweat.

Cammy felt so comfortable here with Bernard and Beatrice. She longed to talk to them about Kit, but she dared not.
Bernard had offered to keep her with them and educate her in
England. Although it was tempting and a way to escape
Father, she did not want it. She'd lose Kit forever if she lived
half a world away. Bernard would have to content himself
with amusing his strangely pensive baby sister while she
visited him, and keep her father out of her way.

"Why so sad?" he asked Cammy once and got no answer.
He remembered her as always full of smiles.

She was afraid to tell him the cause of her melancholy. If
her father got wind of it, he might lose all control and beat
her.

Chapter 4

Winter set in with force: black skies, icy winds, heavy fog during the day and sleet at night. Cammy had never experienced such cold, nor had she ever needed heat in every room and piles of comforters in bed.

She could only weep for the comforter she most wanted, he who was so far away.

Bernard's and Beatrice's friends did not interest Father. He took no one with him when he rode off to visit an old friend of his, Riclef Torandor, whom he had known years ago. Cammy did not recall the name. Her father returned from that expedition in better spirits, saying the man was his sole acquaintance south of London, and he enjoyed his company. Mr. Torandor, a very rich and cultured world traveler, had promised to visit them in Blue Downs the next time he came out to the colonies.

"A man like that would curb your vile appetites and make of you a dutiful wife," said Edgar Cochran to his daughter in the privacy of her boudoir as she sat at her writing desk. "If ever you wed, you would be lucky to find a rich, older man."

"How much older, Father?"

"Twenty years, at least. With an estate to manage and a

husband who would rule you like a daughter, you would not run wild."

"I do not need another father, nor does wealth attract me," she said softly, staring straight into his eyes. "Someday I shall wed Kit Westcott, whether you like it or not."

"We shall just see about that, miss!" he cried, his face going livid.

Father grew gloomier by the day, apparently disappointed that she was not expecting a child. Bernard returned barb for barb with his father. Beatrice was a proper daughter-in-law, but reserved her affection for Cammy alone. It became clear that Edgar Cochran was not happy in his son's house, but that he dreaded a return to Blue Downs and to the inevitable humiliation of being a cuckold, a deserted husband, and, eventually, a divorced man. As hostess of his house, Rina was a poor substitute for Minnie Cochran.

One bright day in February, Beatrice allowed Camilla an unchaperoned outing to Stonehenge. Delirious with her temporary freedom, she rode north across the Salisbury Plain on the west side of the Avon that flowed from Stratford. Past Old Sarum, nearly to Amesbury and then bearing west again, she rode sidesaddle on Bernard's gentlest mare, Rosemary. She wore at a rakish angle her velvet toque hat, her boots were polished, her tight wool coat was stylish but thankfully warm.

How wonderful to be out in the air on a day almost as warm as a winter's day in Melbourne, listening to the larks and to the small animals scurrying into the hedgerows. The trees were bare, but that seemed only fitting beside the bare, towering megaliths standing in a circle. They had stood on this ground since antiquity.

Cammy reined in the mare and stared in awe. How she'd yearned to see Stonehenge, particularly since she lived in a new colony among houses no older than the last century and a half. But this monument was thousands of years old, built by Druids before the Christians came to England.

It was tea time when she rode up, and no sightseers were in evidence. She felt almost happy as she dismounted, although it occurred to her that she'd have trouble remounting without aid. She tied Rosemary to a shrub, and picked up her skirts to walk over the circular ditch and ridge as she approached the gigantic gray stones. Some stood free; some pairs supported

lintels, making great squared arches. The surfaces bore
grooves and dimples, the work of men and weather. Many
had tumbled down, leaving deep depressions in the yellowed
English grass. Of all the sights in England, Cammy had most
wanted to see this. She loved the legends of the Druids, and
had never been frightened by the notion of their human
sacrifices.

Letty Finch said it was morbid. Letty longed to see the
cathedrals and parks of London. But Cammy wished nothing
more than to be alone. Even in Salisbury there were too
many people, and she could not stop herself from searching
the crowds for Kit.

Now she was alone, no longer under her father's scrutiny,
not buffeted by seas or crowds. With only her horse for
company, she might have been at the old, rugged dam at Blue
Downs.

But suddenly she noticed a man was standing with his back
to her among the ancient stones.

He wore a fine suit of brown merino and had a gray cloak
slung over one shoulder. Though his hair was a lighter color
than Kit's, from the slenderness of his back he seemed about
Kit's age, tall like him. He held his hat in his hand and stood
there, unaware of her approach, staring up at the highest
stone. Camilla stopped and considered the propriety of being
alone with a strange man, but she had as much right to be
there as he.

Her heart caught in her throat, and she put a gloved hand
over her lips. She stood there watching him slowly pivot to
stare at another one of the stones. Had he come on foot?
There was no horse or carriage in evidence.

In profile, she could see that the young man wore a pale,
drooping mustache. For one brief moment, she had been able
to believe it might have been Kit. But indeed, on closer
inspection, she realized he looked nothing like Kit.

"Miss?" he said, suddenly noticing her. She hastily spun
around, pretending not to have been staring at him.

"Miss? May you say to me the age of these stones, yes?"

She almost smiled at the hesitation in his voice and his
halting English. He was German, she thought. His plea
touched her sensitivities. She turned back to him with a smile.

"I think they date from Druid times. Very long ago, when
my ancestors were great builders. No one is sure where the
stones came from. Far away, I gather."

"I see," he said in a soft voice, looking at her now instead of the stones. "Have you arriven . . . arrived here by foots? I heard nothing of your coming."

"My horse is tied just over there, outside the circle."

"I see. I see."

"You are not English," she commented. It was a novel sensation, being the hostess here to a foreigner. His accent was appealing. He was a perfect gentleman, and that reassured her. He must be at least twenty-one, she thought.

"I come from the Netherlands," he explained. "My father and me, we visit our home in Amsterdam for the winter, and then we sail to Java soon. The weather, it is too cold in Europe."

"I have thought the same thing myself," she agreed. "A lovely day like this is rare."

He gazed down at her from Kit's height with eyes as blue as Kit's, but she felt only a mild curiosity about him, nothing at all like the excitement Kit generated in her. She wore Kit's garnet ring beneath her glove, the gem turned toward her palm so she could rub it like a magic stone. No man could move her heart but Kit; no one ever would.

"I have walked to here," he said. "I left the coach at Amesbury. I think this is a wonderful thing to see. My father prefers other entertainments."

"Oh, is your father . . . ?" she began, suddenly feeling a kinship with him. A note of distaste had been evident in his voice when he mentioned his father. Did they also not get on together? She'd had no person her age to talk to since she left Blue Downs, so this conversation was a welcome change. On the ship she'd been too indisposed to notice other passengers, and at Bernard's house she was by far the youngest.

"I came out from Victoria with my father," she volunteered to the young Dutchman. "This is the first I could slip away by myself to take a ride. Do you ride much in Java?"

"Yes, I do. Our plantation is large. It must be supervised, and so I learn to be my father's heir."

"Do you grow sugar?" she asked, unable to stop herself from thinking of another father and son on a far smaller island.

"No. Coffee."

"I see," she said with a sigh. This man was not Kit, but he was pleasant to talk to. And she so desperately longed for a good friend, male or female, within half a dozen years of her age. She smiled at him, but got only a bow in response. He was a very serious-faced young Dutchman.

"I am Hans Van Beek. May I inquire for your name, also?"

"Camilla Cochran."

"Would you like to sit?" he asked, taking out his handkerchief and brushing off a place for her on the largest fallen stone. "Do you ride from Amesbury to here, miss?"

"No, all the way from Salisbury," she said rather proudly. She had come the eight miles all alone, without incident.

"Most girls in the country where I live have horses," she told him by way of explanation when he appeared surprised. She sat down as bidden and knew he would sit close beside her, eyes glowing over his fresh new mustache, white as baby's hair.

They talked of Victoria, where he'd never been, and of Java, of England, and the Netherlands. He was quite a world traveler, having sailed to Europe for his schooling and returned again several times during recent summers to visit his cousins. Usually he came alone, but this time his father insisted upon accompanying him, he said. Hans didn't seem happy about that.

He told her that he was twenty-two, and because he was too polite to ask, she admitted that she was sixteen.

"Is it rude in your country to note that you are very beauteous?" he asked, his English improving as he relaxed with her.

"It is not rude, but it is impulsive," she replied, smiling.

Camilla found that she was able to entertain this young man without actually trying. His fair, blooming complexion flushed when he spoke to her, and not only because he was unsure of the language.

"Miss Cochran, I have much . . . much joy in talking with you. I can almost see the house of your family, and the gummy trees—"

"The gum trees. Eucalyptus," she corrected him gently.

"I think . . . I know you are a wondrous person," he said.

"Thank you," she said, inclining her head. It was so good to hear that! As if it might be possible to start over afresh, two hemispheres away from the scene of her sin?

"Now comes others to see Stonehenge," he observed, rising somewhat nervously. "I think we must not sit here. It is a sacred place."

"Yes. It surely once was sacred." Cammy decided she

would like to marry Kit in this place. To make it sacred by their everlasting love.

But it was good to talk to Hans. They had a lot in common. Gradually, she gained a view of his saturnine, sarcastic father, and let him glimpse Edgar Cochran, though she said not a word about Mama's desertion or about Kit.

They walked slowly, still talking, to her grazing horse, which she untied. Hans quickly assisted her into the high sidesaddle. "May I walk beside you to Salisbury?" he suddenly asked. "It is no distance to me. I can make you safe on the journey, and then I will find a coach back to Amesbury."

She saw no reason why not, and they started off slowly. At the fifth mile, however, with Rosemary growing eager for her stable and some hay, and therefore difficult to rein to a staid walk, Cammy jokingly asked Hans if he could sit in a sidesaddle.

"I would try if the horse would not be angry."

She actually laughed! It was the first peal of laughter to pass her lips for months.

"She's a large mare. Together we would weigh no more than one very fat man, I think. But please, you must be tired after your long walk."

It was shocking to ride with a strange man like this, but there was no one to see them. One stirrup had to be lengthened for his leg, and his other boot swung free. Cammy decided to sit behind him, but with no pad under her, she had to hold him around the middle with both her arms, sitting sideways on Rosemary's broad rump.

They had three miles to ride, and they went quickly. Unfortunately, her father was the one to glimpse them before she slid off, ungracefully, into the hawthorn hedge. Her behavior was quite unseemly, even if Hans had been an old friend or cousin.

"I see you have brought home a friend?" said her father in a surprisingly mild tone. He gazed avariciously at the elegant costume of the Dutchman. She could see wheels spinning in his scheming old head.

"Mr. Van Beek was seeing me home safely, Father. He is from Java."

Hans was off the horse by now, and after he had arranged his rumpled suit, he drew himself up straight and looked down with wry interest upon Cammy's bald father.

"My greetings, Mr. Cochran. I am delighted to be meeting your fine daughter."

"Hmmm," said her father. "Yes. A planter, are you now?"

Papa smelled money. Cammy could almost see his nose quiver. "She lives a lonely life here, so recently come from Victoria," said Father. "Will you be staying long in England?"

Hans was not sure of their departure date, but said that they'd sail to Java sometime in the next month, when his father finished with his business with the coffee traders.

That started Mr. Cochran on a discussion of wheat and British colonial trade. Camilla gave the mare over to the care of Rodney, the stable boy, and listened wonderingly to her father monopolize the newcomer. Hans' attention kept coming back to her, his eyes glancing at her over her father's head. When Papa suggested that Hans remain for dinner, she was not surprised when the Dutchman acquiesced. "Oh, yes," he said, "that would be full of delight!"

Camilla suddenly saw just what was going on. Her father was not a subtle man. Father did not care a fig for Dutchmen or for Java planters. He was suddenly matchmaking.

Bernard seemed approving as well as amused, as they all sat together over dinner. He praised his baby sister's mind and wit, pitting himself against Father in a competition. Which could make her seem the finest? Hans nodded at each of them, agreeing.

By the time they had finished the jellied tongue and loin of mutton along with the baked cauliflower and orange carrots, currant cakes and tea to top off the meal, Hans was almost a member of the family. Camilla's mind kept running from point to point, from Kit, to Mama, to Fiji, to Victoria, to her "wondrousness," to her fallen state. Perhaps her father had decided to make the most of a bad situation. He had vowed, after the night with Kit, that he would never permit her to marry, but now, finding that this ingenuous and wealthy young man was enthralled with her, he would sell her off like valuable property!

Beatrice had been the one innocently to ask Hans if he was as yet betrothed.

"Oh, no. Certainly not," he'd exclaimed.

"Are there many European ladies in Java?" she'd then asked.

"Very few," he'd said. "I meet many in Amsterdam, but . . . my cousins, their friends, but . . ."

"Dutch young ladies tend to grow fat, do they not?" said Bernard as Camilla scowled at him.

Papa and Bernard did not lure Hans away to the library to drink brandy and smoke, but instead urged Cammy to show him the Australian flora in the conservatory, and left them alone together. Hans, keeping his arms rather stiffly at his sides, bent his head when she spoke to him, and blinked rapidly when she looked into his eyes.

Hans stood over her, gazing. This admiration was less appealing to her than his frank speech at Stonehenge. Despairing of gaining only his friendship, she led him back to Father, who offered him Bernard's carriage to take him back to Amesbury for the night. At least, Cammy thought with relief, he was not invited to sleep over.

"A fine young man. Going to be quite rich," Edgar Cochran exclaimed gleefully as soon as Hans had departed. "Propertied. And smitten with you so quickly," he added, fairly strutting around the room. She took the opportunity of Bernard's presence to fight back.

"You know my affections are otherwise engaged, Father," she said pointedly. "With Mother gone, I thought I must be your spinster housekeeper."

"One does not shun a fortune when it presents itself, you ungrateful child!" Father cried. Bernard cocked his head. Beatrice turned hastily to face her and was the first to respond.

"You've not breathed a word about love, Cammy!" her sister-in-law exlaimed. "There's a young man you favor?"

Camilla looked at her father and said nothing.

"Well, she's no child, Father," Bernard remarked. "Remember that our mother was scarcely seventeen when you wed her."

Edgar had no apt response and retreated with a scowl and went up to his chamber. His son and daughter-in-law immediately rounded on Cammy.

"Stay here with us, Cammy," Beatrice begged, seizing her hands. "We cannot endure seeing you and your father fence with looks and frowns. Now that your mother's left Blue Downs, it's no place for you. Aunt Rina is a horror. Live with us. You can attend a young lady's school, you can make a

circle of acquaintances that you would never find, so isolated
at home in the country."

"He's bound to see you married to Hans Van Beek, that's
obvious," Bernard murmured, pipe in hand. "If you prefer
not to wed him, take this chance and dwell here. You brighten
the house."

"That's kind of you to say, dear brother, but—"

"Of course you do!" Beatrice exclaimed. "So kind and
helpful, so interested in everything. I'd love to take you
around and show you Salisbury and have you meet my
friends. Please, Cammy."

"I . . . I feel convinced that you want me," she replied.
"Thank you. I love you, but—Oh, I admit your offer is
tempting. I do not enjoy Father, and as you can see, he does
not like me much. He has even said I may not visit Mama—"

"Not surprising," said Bernard. "His chief amusement
seems to be brooding on how to keep our mother from every
joy, now that she's gone off. It's not fair to you, Cammy."

"Think how dull it will be for you at Blue Downs until you
do wed, whomever it might be, and you shouldn't hasten into
marriage only to escape your father," Beatrice added.

Cammy smiled at them. She did so love her freckled,
bearded brother in his smoking jacket, and his tall, sweet-
faced wife, dressed all in green. They pressed Camilla's
hands, urging her to stay, making her want to weep.

Should she tell them about Kit? But saying a little would
not explain her tortured state of mind. Revealing every detail
would lose her their respect and perhaps also their love. If she
merely said that she cared for a boy in Victoria, of whom her
father disapproved, they'd point to all the Englishmen in the
Isles, even to Hans. If she admitted she felt already married
to the lover who'd taken her maidenhood, then what? To
what decent gentleman could they offer her as a bride?

The enormity of her problem staggered her. She tore her
hands from Beatrice's and spun away from them. "Oh, I
cannot explain myself!" she cried. "I would give all I have to
live with you here and not see Papa ever again! But I must go
back. I must return to Victoria. There's something I must
do!"

From the corner of her eye she glimpsed Bernard and
Beatrice sending each other anxious gazes.

"Sleep on it, little sister," Bernard said at last. "Say yes,
tomorrow."

Chapter 5

Cammy did not sleep well that night. She dreamed of Kit as he was the previous year, before he ever saw her as his sweetheart. In her dream she remembered that summer day when her mother, brother Michael, and she had journeyed down to Melbourne to watch Kit play polo. Michael wanted badly to take up the sport.

When Kit, five years Michael's senior, led his pair of ponies over to them, the Cochrans had exclaimed over the beautiful bays. That day Kit wore a white shirt and riding pants, which made his skin darker, and his sun-bleached hair near to golden. She was desperately in love with him even then, but received from him only the broad, careless smile that told her she was nothing special to him. He seemed much more interested in her sister, Charlotte.

When the three Cochrans took their seats behind the railings, Kit vaulted into the saddle of one pony and saluted them with his mallet. He rode with his team onto the field, and almost immediately Camilla was transported out of herself.

She was only fifteen then, but now in her dream, she realized what she'd felt that day when the six men and ponies surged into battle over the small white ball. Quickly, the

37

galloping, swerving ponies turned dark with sweat, their panting rising over the men's shouts as their riders twisted to swing their mallets and wheel their mounts from one side to the other. Kit was so skillful! He moved with such violent force and speed it took her breath away.

Michael kept muttering to himself. "Got off a clean shot, there!" "He tipped it!" The muffled thud of hooves on grass, the squeak of leather, the click of mallet on ball sent her into a fascinated stupor. The sun beat down on her lightly covered shoulders. She recalled Mama, fanning herself with a Chinese rice-paper fan. But Camilla sat with her lips parted, her eyes always on Kit, that marvel of muscle and speed. His skin was glistening with sweat, his white shirt molded to his body, his thighs gripping the pony while his teeth flashed white in a grin of triumph.

To think that only one year later, that marvel of male beauty and power would hold Camilla Cochran, kiss her, promise to wed her, take her into his bed . . .

She awoke in a sweat, alone in Bernard's house, and began to cry.

Oh, if only she could live here, and lure Kit to come to her! Or if she could steal away to Fiji, without going back to Victoria. If only Kit had a brother or sister or some close friend through whom she could trace him. Of course, she might ask Bernard how to find Kit's father through a sugar growers' association, but then the whole story would surely come out.

More than anything, she wished to confide in her mother. She'd written her a long letter several weeks ago, but at the last moment decided not to add her troubles to her mother's and Stephen's. Receiving divorce papers would cause enough pain for Minnie Cochran.

One thing Camilla was certain of was that if she could not find Kit or go to Mama, she would not live her life with her father or wed a man he chose for her. Instead, she'd find something useful to do. What that might be, she did not yet know, but it would come to her.

The following day Camilla was whisked off to the finest shops Salisbury could offer to be fitted for stylish costumes. The only problem was what to buy. Summer was approaching in England, but Victoria was welcoming autumn. Costumes here would be up-to-the-moment in style, and some designs came straight from Paris. Australian ladies had to wait for ships sailing halfway 'round the globe, and therefore their styles lagged by half a season.

Camilla did not care what she wore if it was not to please Kit. But the new fabrics in these shops were so delightful in color and texture—pink-coral grosgrain, violet foulard, grenadine, gauze, pongee—that for a day she let herself sink into luxury, examining designs and materials, then turning for her measurements. Beatrice glowed with the pleasure of seeing her look so lovely. Those who wished her married—everyone did, it seemed—said she must look fashionable.

She did not like garments made of wool and yak hair, or the new puffy look. Overskirts pulled up into balls and bundles and hung with all manner of passementerie trimmings made her laugh. She chose simple designs, although she ordered these decorated with ruchings and fringe and many rows of bows and buttons, and wound with silk scarves. The weight of the gowns was enormous on her small frame, but at least their skirts were wide and not terribly off balance to the sides or the back. Cammy chose half winter and half summer costumes, and also selected pearl beads, two Swiss muslin and lace fichus, and a basque-waist to go along with the walking, house, and evening dresses.

Camilla sighed over the pictures of 1870 bridal dresses, simpler in line than previous confections for that special occasion. She wondered if she could wed Kit in white, now that she was no longer his virginal bride but rather his lover. The word gave her shivers. She would never speak it aloud except to Letty Finch, who understood. Or, naturally, to Kit.

The following evening, Mr. Van Beek and Hans came to tea. Camilla fretted that Papa had not informed her, or even informed Beatrice. Their cook managed to accommodate the larger group very well, and produced a high tea as sumptuous as a holiday dinner.

"The gentleman has not come to eat, but to make Camilla's acquaintance," she overheard Papa say to Bernard. Her brother saw nothing wrong with this, since he had no idea of her heartsickness.

The elegantly clad Hans, in a gray suit and blue cravat, flushed and paid her compliments as he gazed down on her, while she felt he could be only like a brother to her.

Mr. Van Beek proved to be a quiet man who spoke occasionally in Dutch to Hans and in painfully correct English to her father. He was of middle height, brown-haired, lean, and excellently costumed in black. His heavy-lidded eyes, smooth as eggshells, watched everyone closely. When he spoke, he kept them half-closed, which gave him at the same time a shrewd and a lethargic look. As for Hans, he seemed shy as a schoolboy in his father's presence, and Camilla pitied him.

"My son has not been often with young ladies," Mr. Van Beek told her in a loud voice. "You must excuse him."

"We very much enjoyed his charming and animated company the other evening when he dined with us," Beatrice replied instantly.

"I am glad. I hope that Miss Cochran shares the same opinion as yours, Mrs. Cochran."

After tea, Mr. Van Beek asked permission to smoke his deeply curved tobacco pipe, and after a moment of sucking upon it, he began asking Camilla one question after another. What were her tastes in books, in music, did she enjoy stitchery or singing? Was she like her mother, and where, in fact, was her mother?

"Ask my father," she said with a glance at Mr. Cochran, who hemmed and hawed and avoided the truth. Mr. Van Beek allowed him to escape with the excuse that Minnie hated travel and preferred Australia. Indeed, the Dutchman countered that his own wife was too delicate to accompany them to England.

"We shall sail home to Java in a month or so," Mr. Van Beek announced. "Before mid-April. To arrive by June." He and her father exchanged a long look that puzzled Cammy.

"Camilla will remain here with us, I'm sure, even when Father sails," Bernard cut in.

"I think I cannot remain, dear brother," Cammy said, "though you invite me so kindly." She dared not give her reasons. "Mother" and "Kit" were both forbidden names.

Edgar Cochran threw up his hands. "You see? I cannot command my youngest daughter. She has a will of her own. She will dwell here, she will dwell there, she will have her own way, regardless of me."

"Spirit is admirable in young women of intelligence," said Mr. Van Beek, "and surprising in one so young and beautiful."

At that, Camilla excused herself and retreated upstairs, but was aware of Hans gazing after her with the wistful expression of a lap dog abandoned with no parting caress.

Pulled one way by Bernard and Beatrice, another way by her love for Kit, she felt she would burst. She was growing fonder of England each day, but still yearned for the tropical shores of Fiji and the even warmer embrace of Kit.

Eventually, seeking guidance and comfort, she begged permission to visit Letty Finch in London.

"You obtained her for me, Father," she cajoled Edgar Cochran one sunny morning. "We are dear friends now, and besides, she has invited me. Here, this is my second letter from London inquiring why I have not yet come to see her and her parents. Do permit me to go."

"You cannot travel alone," he said firmly. "That solitary excursion to Stonehenge was shocking, though I said nothing because of your fortunate meeting with . . ." he paused to scrutinize her face, "a rich young man to take you off my hands and save you from future sin. Only if Beatrice will accompany you, may you travel to London."

Beatrice agreed in a moment, and she suggested they also visit Windsor, the palace of the widowed queen, Victoria. How exciting, Cammy mused as she readied herself for the trip. What an era it was! Their wonderful canal at Suez, the Thames Embankment no older than just last summer, war raging in Paris. She was young, fed and protected, even by a parent who despised her. "Think of the poor, the soldiers," she told herself, steeling her mind against self-indulgent tears. "Think not of yourself, but try to find a way to help others." At the very least, she would be away from her father, and that was a blessing.

She straightened her back, forced herself to smile, and packed her bags for a trip to the greatest city of the Empire.

They traveled on a luxurious Pullman that featured tiny beds complete with curtains, and a magnificent dining salon on the rails. All this was as new to Camilla as their great ship from the colonies had been. She glued her nose to the train's window, absorbing the wonderful panorama of downs and fields, deserted hamlets, then the backsides of grimy tenements, black-faced miners, rubble, and finally swift rivers and lush forests. The railway coach jerked from side to side, and the noise was tremendous. Their sleeping and sitting compartments were shared by people of the greatest respectability, however, and Cammy marveled at the luxuries reserved for the wealthy. She wondered where the poor, tattered souls rode, and if they had to sleep sitting up on plain wooden benches.

They descended at the Victoria Station in Belgravia at dawn, and deposited their luggage at an elegant hotel beyond the railway district. But Beatrice would not let Cammy rest. She insisted on taking her arm and marching her northward to Buckingham Palace. It stood before its lovely gardens, distinguished. They did not stay long to admire it. Instead, they went on through Green Park to St. James' Palace where the Queen did her state business, and then southeast to Westminster Cathedral, so covered with industrial soot that Camilla did not recognize it from pictures she had seen. Things were not so black in the colonies, nor the dawn so bitingly cold on the first of March. The women had to muffle themselves up to the ears, and Cammy wished she had a hot potato to put in her ermine muff. Her new myrtle green corduroy suit with fur trimmings was covered by her heavy mantle, and still she was not warm enough. Beatrice hugged Cammy's arm and urged her to tramp along more hastily, because it would surely get her blood moving.

Under the soaring, jagged spires of Parliament they marched, out upon the new Embankment by the cold, slow Thames River. Cammy found herself laughing at the spectacle of Englishfolk of all ages and stations hawking their wares or hastening to their employment. It was so different from life at home. At last, by ten o'clock, there was a burst of warm sunshine.

"Now we shall see which is the younger, you or I!" jested Beatrice. "Have you as many miles of streets in all of Melbourne as I have taken you over this morning? Tell me, is Victoria so fine as this?"

After lunching on oysters and giblets served on toast, topped off by a golden custard under cream, they struck out for St. Paul's Cathedral. From the Strand they crossed over to Fleet Street, past the dark, narrow pubs that Dr. Samuel Johnson used to frequent, past newspaper offices, Christopher Wren churches, and memorials. When they passed several colonial offices, Cammy immediately thought of Kit, and the crucial issues that obsessed kind Mr. Westcott and took more and more of Kit's attention away from the growing of sugar cane. This London government said that British subjects owed loyalty to the United Kingdom, and owed no fealty to King Thakombau, who could not rule the Fiji Islands without it. This was a terrible dilemma, and both Westcotts were caught in the midst of it.

She was shaken out of this mood when she saw the towering, domed cathedral at the end of the street on Ludgate Hill. St. Paul's seemed to sit astride London. After they had climbed its many stone steps, Camilla entered the Great West Door and gasped.

The interior of the cathedral was so enormous that it almost drew one's soul up past its giant arches. Marble statues stood all around them, as well as tombs and stained glass. Circles upon circles of gold and alabaster rose to the interior of the hollow dome. Camilla, staring up so fixedly, nearly tumbled backward, but Beatrice caught her arm.

Camilla burst into tears.

"What is it? Oh, my dearest sister, has this place affected your senses?"

"It's . . . it's . . . Oh, Beatrice. I feel so small, so unworthy to stand here," she whispered.

"Then let us walk quickly out into the unsanctified world," her sister-in-law suggested.

"No. It does me good," Cammy replied, looking around again in awe and wonder.

Beatrice led her down the south choir aisle to the effigy of John Donne. This was the only surviving memorial of the Old Cathedral that had burned in 1666. Camilla reached out a finger to touch the smoke stains upon the statue of the Dean of St. Paul's, wrapped in his winding sheet. Poor Donne. How she loved reading the sermons he had written centuries ago. He'd stare scornfully out of those marble eyes if he knew what sort of girl presumed to revere him.

"I must find some good work to do, Beatrice," Cammy said solemnly as they made the long walk back past the Wellington monument and the font, and the Dean's staircase that circled the interior of a tower. The experience of being inside this holy place had truly affected her.

"You're only a child!" Beatrice laughed. "Only an innocent schoolgirl of sixteen! Why have you such solemn thoughts? What sort of good work do you have in mind? Would you go into a nunnery? Be a missioner to darkest Africa?"

"I don't know," Camilla brooded.

"Pish! You enjoy yourself! You'll be a wife and mother too

soon if your father has his way. Enjoy your youth while you can!"

A housemaid opened the door when they rang at the address in Westminster that Letty had sent her. The parlor was full of pictures, mostly photoengravings. The small frames stood on the tables, on the mantelpiece, and hung on all the flower-sprigged walls.

Letty rushed in and embraced Camilla before clasping Beatrice's hand. She was promptly joined by an elderly man and woman, so bright-eyed that they seemed far younger than their white hair and lined faces and the age of their daughter must make them.

Then a most extraordinary thing occurred. Letty began gesticulating with her hands in a deliberate manner. Her fingers formed every shape imaginable—castles and butterflies and darting birds, as Cammy watched amazed. Letty did not speak one word aloud. She pointed to Cammy and Beatrice in turn, then smiled and raised and lowered her eyebrows and shoulders.

"My parents cannot hear," she explained, "because they have both been deaf since childhood. I am introducing you in their language. Whatever you say, I shall make visual for them. Cammy, Beatrice, allow me to introduce Katherine and Lawrence Shrader."

"You never told me about them!" cried Cammy.

"Did I not? Oh, I'm sure I did. Perhaps you were too desperately ill on the sea voyage, poor child, to take anything in. Food or information, either one!" She paused, spun a few more ideas off her fingers. "You see, I forget that they're not like everyone else." Then she turned back to them again.

"Mother is very sorry you were ill, and hopes the return voyage won't be so bad."

"She said that?"

"Didn't you see her?" Letty laughed.

Beatrice was shaking her head in astonishment. "It is a very pretty exercise," she commented. "Truly a miracle!"

Cammy sat forward in her seat, her eyes glowing. "Oh, Letty, I do wish you . . . that they could teach me!"

"My mother wishes to know what you want to learn," said Letty.

"To talk silently." Cammy listened to herself and feared she was being presumptuous. But a spark had been lit within her. Here was something useful one could learn and with which one could help others. Camilla knew neither French nor Latin, nor anything a cultivated young Englishwoman should know. Kit was expert in languages of Fiji, she recalled.

"Few people are able to use hand language," Letty translated for her father. "You could learn from us and teach little deaf children."

"I could?" Cammy gasped, noting that Beatrice was interested but amused.

"We're planning to sail for Victoria in one month's time," Letty went on. "I've persuaded my parents to move to a warmer clime. If you're bound for home then, and choose the same ship, Camilla, we could make you expert before you reached Victoria."

"Do you mean that? Oh, I would love to try!"

"A school for deaf children has just been built in the St. Kilda Road," said Letty. "You might find a way to be helpful there, aiding the graduate teachers."

Letty's parents responded to her dreams as if they were playing pianoforte keys in midair. The old man with white side-whiskers and black brows smiled warmly upon Camilla. His wife was not so round as Letty, and did not have Letty's rosy cheeks, but she was so keen-eyed that Cammy felt they both could read her mind. But somehow she felt comfortable with them.

Cammy demanded to know the Shraders' life stories. What was the old gentleman's occupation?

"I kept the books for a chemist in Wardour Street," said Letty as her father's mouthpiece. "I did the accounts until only a year ago, when I retired. Now we are free to emigrate."

"Do all your children hear?" asked Cammy.

"Yes. We could hear when we were born," explained the old lady. "A fever made us deaf before we could walk and talk. But we can read and write, and our handicap has never stopped us from having ever so many friends."

The Shrader family then took Cammy and Beatrice to the dining room for a sumptuous luncheon of roast fowl and savory pasties and pudding, and then insisted that they lodge with them for the night in London. When Beatrice and Cammy departed the following morning, they could speak of nothing but their kind and capable host and hostess.

"Such handsome, lovely people! One would not have

dreamed they could say so much without uttering a word," said Beatrice. "I think it might be grand for you to sail with them and learn their hand language, Cammy, but we shall have to see. Your father's temper is foul these days. He speaks bitterly of you, although I cannot fathom why. Perhaps it is because you and your mother look so much alike."

Cammy wanted to tell Beatrice all about Kit then, but she held her tongue. It was still not the time for confessions.

Chapter 6

At the Windsor Station, a boy they hired went ahead to
Salisbury with their luggage. Beatrice and Cammy went on by
themselves, like schoolgirls on holiday, climbing the steep
street under the very walls of Windsor Castle. The fortress
was tall and very rugged, but Cammy was undaunted. She
loved castles. Windsor was ancient, made of great, gray
stones covered by a thick growth of ivy.

The two women had tea in the High Street and then walked
past the walls of Windsor, up Castle Hill by the King Henry
Gate and all the famous towers to the Long Walk, which ran
straight as an arrow between elm trees from the castle to the
immense Copper Horse in the Great Park. Camilla turned
and stood staring at the castle.

The Round Tower rose just to the left of center, flying the
Royal Standard, which signaled that their widowed Queen
was in residence in her private apartments, possibly just now
peering out a window at them. To the east and west the
castle's turrets stood in a line, round and square, pearly gray
and cream in the noon sun. The beautifully cropped sward
was turning green again, and a few carriages moved on the
smoothly paved roadway. Only a few horsemen passed them
by.

"I think I see a friend of ours," said Beatrice, tapping Camilla on the shoulder.

"Not—" she blurted out, but before she could hazard a guess, she saw that the man approaching them was Mr. Van Beek. He reined in beside them and gazed at Cammy for a long moment before saying a word. He raised the silk hat from his head with a black-gloved hand. He wore a cravat, even though he was on horseback.

"How did you find us here?" Beatrice asked ingenuously. She must know this was no coincidence.

"You mentioned that your journey included a stop at Windsor on the return," he replied coolly. "How did you find London, Miss Cochran? Mrs. Cochran?"

"It was truly wonderful," Cammy said in all honesty.

"I would like you to be my guests for tea. Would you care to see the Tudor White Hart Inn, Miss Cochran?"

Camilla was certainly hungry from all the tramping up and down hills and along the three-mile road to the park, so she nodded politely at Beatrice, who inclined her head. Mr. Van Beek dismounted, and walked his shiny roan beside them as they trailed the stylish trains of their dresses down the Long Walk.

At the inn, Cammy was grateful to remove her mantle and uncover her pretty walking dress. It was a new one, made of velvet and mohair with a pinched waist and contrasting tunic. Mr. Van Beek treated them to a wonderful feast of poached turbot and all manner of delicious side dishes. When their host ordered wine, Cammy gave Beatrice a startled look. At midday? But Beatrice gave a little shrug, and made no objection.

Cammy drank perhaps too much madeira, and was rather light-headed by the end of the meal. When Mr. Van Beek politely but coldly requested an interview alone with her, she had no recourse but to agree. Beatrice gave her a look, but got no response, and therefore offered to walk around the old town of Windsor and wait for them at the Town Hall.

Camilla sat numbly in the inn dining room and stared at the Dutchman. He lost no time getting right to the point.

"Miss Cochran," he began, "you have captivated my son. I must tell you that he has excellent prospects. He is my only surviving son, my sole heir. He is good, brave, intelligent. But, you see, his mother was too pure. She wished Hans to be perfectly pure as well. Do you understand what I am saying?"

"No. I do not," she answered bluntly, wishing to leave at once.

"Excuse me," he said, shaking his head apologetically. "I have not total command of your most interesting language." He drew his chair closer to hers in the now deserted dining room. "Miss Cochran, you have worked a magic upon my son. With you, he is as I would want him. He speaks his thoughts and can laugh and be at ease. It is very good."

"And so?" She knew exactly what he was about to suggest, and yet she could not believe that a father would do this to his son.

"And so," he continued, "I wish to confide in you. I took Hans to Amsterdam and Rotterdam, to cousins and young daughters of my friends, and all of them think Hans could be a wonderful husband. Do you understand? But with them he is shy. With you, however, he is not shy. You do not seek in him a husband, so he wishes to win you. Do you follow?"

"I do not wish Hans to court me, Mr. Van Beek. You flatter me, but I am not ready to think of matrimony," she said nervously, looking away.

"Your father thinks otherwise. He says you are 'ripe,' in his words, for a husband, and he encourages Hans' suit. I understand from him that there is no other suitor, that you are a pure young woman perfectly right for my son."

She was about to call her father a liar, but she could not. This man would report to Father all she said. What was Father thinking of? Did he imagine Hans to be so stupid and innocent that he would not notice? Yes, very possibly he did!

She would never marry Hans, this she knew for a fact. She sat there under the Dutchman's heavy-lidded gaze and pondered carefully before she spoke.

"I am sure that Father would not force me to marry a man I do not love," she said quietly, "and Hans would never presume. He deserves a bride who cares for him. He is a very kind boy."

"A boy is exactly what my son is! I believe you would make him become a man."

She rose from her chair, insulted by his bluntness.

"Be seated," he snapped. She sank back, her teeth clenched, before his hand could close around her wrist and hold her.

He was an outrageous old lecher!

Why did she not have a father to protect her against such demands?

"Each person in your present household," the man continued, almost as though he could read her thoughts, "has encouraged my son to seek your hand in marriage, Miss Cochran. You can surely see why I am surprised at your response!"

"But I am a person in my own right, Mr. Van Beek, and I shall make my own decisions!"

He watched her with an amused expression. When she averted her face, he was bold enough to take her by the chin and turn her face toward him again.

"Sir!" she cried, slapping away his hand.

"I am concerned for my son," he said. "Hans shall be a rich man someday. He will not seek other women. He wants children, and will prove a worthy father. What more can you require?"

"I require a man that I love." She gathered up her bag, and snatched her mantle from the hook where it hung before hastening out of the White Hart Inn. The man was insane to make such a suggestion. This was not the sixteenth century!

Yet, in Father's eyes, she was merely chattel, to be disposed of at his will.

She found Beatrice outside, but refused to describe her conversation with Mr. Van Beek. During their wait for the coach to take them back to Salisbury, she paced around, hands stuck into her muff and brow knotted, much to the distress of her sister-in-law. Head bent, Camilla marched back and forth pondering her situation deeply. Could two fathers, working to conspire on a marriage, legally overcome her? Was her own father so eager to be rid of her, or was he trying to marry her well for her own sake? At first he'd said she'd never marry. Wasn't this a far better revenge, to make sure she'd never have Kit?

Even best allies, Bernard and Beatrice, could not aid her if she did not confess her reason for declining this Dutch boy's proposal. Unless she confessed her sin with Kit and made them forgive her, taking Kit's part against Father, she was doomed. But she realized that Bernard could do nothing legally.

The coach ride back to Salisbury took the rest of the day. Cammy sat with her chin stuck into her fur collar, her fists in her muff, and her brows deeply furrowed. Beatrice sighed and shook her head, biting her lip, wondering what the nature of Cammy's ailment was. But Cammy simply could not tell her the bitter truth. To lose Beatrice's love would kill her. The one thing valued above all else in England and its colonies in this noble era of Victoria's reign was female purity. All women were expected to take as their example their Queen, and follow her precepts. Of course, Cammy had never been taught how one remains pure. And what did purity consist of? There was a great, gaping darkness in her mind between the first kiss of a maiden and her beau and the arrival of the first baby after the marriage. She and Kit had strayed in that darkness, and now she was ruined.

They had no sooner returned to Salisbury, been helped from the carriage, and gone upstairs when she received a message. Rodney, the stable boy, had met the man who'd delivered it, but could not come into the house, so the parlormaid sent the chambermaid to greet Cammy with the information she had received.

"Miss Camilla," the girl whispered, her eyes bright, "there's a young gentleman wishing to see you, and would you please come out o' the house and talk to him in the lane?"

"What young gentleman?" Camilla asked, her heart sinking.

"He didn't give his name, they say. But he's fine lookin' and tall and was ridin' a horse. He says it's a private talk, and there was somethin' about his father or *your* father—"

"His father!" Cammy moaned irritably. "Had he blue eyes and an accent?"

The girl ran downstairs to ask the parlormaid to ask Rodney, fairly quivering with excitement. She returned a few minutes later.

"Yes'm, Miss Camilla. He's got blue eyes, they say, and he's got an accent, to be sure."

"Rodney should tell him to—" Cammy began angrily. But then she realized that the servants were not proper emissaries for messages between herself and Hans. Imagine! He had hardly given her enough time to get out of her mantle and bonnet before he came courting. His father dares to lay siege to me at Windsor Castle, and the son lies in wait for me here!

She decided not to go down, since she'd had enough of the Van Beeks for one day. Her opinion of Hans was falling, not rising. He was clearly a mother's boy, still tied up in his parents' apron strings, one who sent his father or a servant to speak for him because he could only stammer his love for her. Cammy began to feel revulsion for him, as well as indignation. Of course, he was handsome and clean and kind and well-spoken. But what use were those qualities if he were so childish and shy and secretive?

"Wait, Priscilla," she said to the maid. "I shall pen him a note, and you shall carry the message to the gentleman."

"Oh, yes," the delighted girl cried. "It is the most romantic thing!"

"Don't make too much of it," Camilla cautioned her. "Pray, do not gossip about this. Wait outside, please. The letter may take me some time."

She sat down at the writing desk in her tiny boudoir and chose the nicest writing paper available. It was thick and white with wiremarks on it and had a soft feel. She would be as gentle as possible. Hans was, like her, the child of imperfect parents, but there was no reason why he should not have accepted her often-repeated wish that he be her friend and no more. No, the only way was to drive Hans off, so he would never be peddled to her as a choice property. He would gather up his dignity and tell his father to desist. Hans would not want a wife who did not love him.

When Cammy had finished the letter she read it over. It seemed rather long, but she felt pleased with it.

My Dear Friend,

I am sorry to have to tell you this, but I am not interested in a continuation of our friendship. Forgive my bluntness but our relationship must end. Believe me, although you yourself have always behaved most kindly, my feeling for you cannot at the present time be called love, and I am very sure I could never love you in the future.

My father's wishes are clear to everyone, but I am not my father's slave and can make my own choice of friends. On my own behalf, then, I say that you must cease to take any interest in me as a friend or as a fiancée. Please, end your suit, for your own good.

I do not wish us to meet ever again. I do not regret our

relationship, but by seeking me out you will cause distress and sour the truly pleasant memories I have of you.

Sincerely,
Camilla Cochran

She reread it and decided that it was firm without being cruel. Let Hans show this to his father or to hers. She would not be sorry. The strength of her convictions was something to be proud of, she felt.

She summoned Priscilla again and gave her the message, which she had folded, placed in an envelope, and carefully sealed with wax.

"There," she said. "Deliver this into the hands of the gentleman. Take care that he and he alone receives it. Promise me, though, that you will not speak a word of this to anyone. I am trusting you, Priscilla."

"Oh, miss, it is so very exciting!" the servant girl gushed. "You are so beautiful, and I understand the young gentleman is handsome. I do so hope that—"

"Please," Cammy interrupted her. "No more. Do as I say." Cammy felt as though she had grown up very quickly in one brief day. There was wisdom and maturity in her actions now. As she lay down on the bed to rest, she did not have a twinge of regret. Hans would survive. His broken heart would heal. As for hers, well, that was another story entirely.

Chapter 7

Kit Westcott unfolded Camilla's letter and read it once again.

He was sitting beneath the bare boughs of a tree, and his horse grazed behind a nearby hedge. His gloved hands smoothed out the paper. His eyes slowly scanned each line, though he'd long ago memorized the words. The paper was worn almost through at the creases and resembled the gauze dresses that Camilla had worn at Blue Downs, the pink and cream and violet gowns he had wished to take off her eager body. If only they had not destroyed everything! Damn!

He put the letter to his lips and kissed it. To have come so far, and to have this as his reward!

At first, he'd tried to see her at Blue Downs. He'd ridden there less than a week after he and his father were evicted, and was met at the door by a ferocious tiny woman in black, her black hair coiled and pulled back tightly from her lined face. This, he learned, was Camilla's paternal aunt. Camilla was ill, Aunt Rina insisted, and Mr. Cochran was not at home.

Kit went again, four days later, against his own father's wishes. Mr. Westcott thought it best to let Cochran calm himself in solitude. Edgar had threatened to kill them both, and the very sight of Kit at his front door might have driven him mad. He might have gone for his rifle, as he'd promised to do.

Yet Kit went nevertheless. This time the same reply would not satisfy him. He tried at the rear entrance, only to find that all the servants he had ever known at Blue Downs had been dismissed and new ones hired. The new gardener did not know the reason, but Kit needed no explanation. So great had been his sin that a dozen innocent people had lost their employment. Fortunately, servants were very much in demand in the Australian colonies, and they would have no difficulty finding work.

The gardener informed him that Mr. Cochran was not at home, nor was Camilla. They had "gone off." No one was sure where. Kit was furious and at a loss as to what he should do next.

He made ready to search for her at all the border crossings of Victoria, to scour the passenger lists of sailing ships, and to hire detectives. But these dire methods would come only after he had sought her at her brothers' and sister's homes.

Michael was about to graduate from the King's School in Sydney and go into a law office. Kit rushed by coach north to New South Wales only to find the tall, sweet-faced, dark-haired boy unaware of what had happened. He had no trace of Edgar Cochran or Cammy. Michael was harshly critical of his father, and he vowed to be of any assistance when the time came for a confrontation.

Another week wasted. Kit managed to locate Jack Cochran in the same colony, in the western bush near Dubbo, and Charlotte in Queensland. Neither had any idea of what had occurred or where Cammy currently was.

Should he next try Richard in New Zealand, or Bernard in England? Kit had not met Bernard, who'd left home before the age of twenty, and he had only a faint memory of Richard. Of course, they might know nothing, and he would have wasted more weeks of search.

So he took the Cobb's Coach to Melbourne, had lunch with his father at his club, and set out again. It was five long weeks since he and Cammy had made love and declared themselves. He simply *had* to find her. Hoping against hope, he went to the steamship offices. He was too weary to walk straight by the time he arrived, after the long days and nights in the unsprung coach, rattling south over rutted roads, but he refused to be defeated by a man like Edgar. Even the man's own children and wife had deserted him. Camilla must be saved. He was her love and he would not abandon her. Although he chided himself that he was seven years her senior and should have known better, he could not deny that he would do it again, had he the opportunity.

That was when they received Camilla's letter, this fragile sheet of paper now dissolving in his hands. It had been sent first all the way to Fiji, addressed to "Mr. Christopher Westcott, Suva, Fiji Islands," and had been forwarded to him at the Scott's Hotel. When he staggered home from a vain mission to the coastal steamship company, there stood his father holding the envelope in his hands, saying it was all he could do not to unseal it himself.

How frantically had Kit torn open the letter inscribed in her dainty hand! Tears stung his eyes as he read. It was dated a mere three days after their bedchamber tryst, yet ages had passed. The little letter had sailed to Suva and back. Now where was his love?

He was astounded to find that Cochran had taken her to England! Kit would follow them there, and quickly. His father would simply have to do without him for a while. Henry Westcott said not one word in objection, although a busy time for them both was approaching in Fiji. He gave his son several errands to perform in London in regard to convincing the Colonial Office that they reevaluate their opinion of King Thakombau. Kit agreed at once to take care of this, although his mind was only on Cammy. He would contact Bernard. Although Cammy did not mention him in her note, surely her brother would know of her whereabouts.

Again, Kit read the precious letter.

My Dearest,
  I blame myself for this terrible separation. If I had been wiser, we would be married in a year. I fear that Father will never hear of it now. I have a dear woman to be my companion, known as Letitia Finch, of London. How long I must stay in England, I do not know. Father will tell me nothing. He believes vile things of you, but will never convince me of their truth. Do wait for me and love me, and someday I shall return to you. I must write in haste since we sail this very day, possibly to Southampton. I do not know the ship or the line,

unfortunately, because Father is determined to keep me
ignorant. Do love me.

Your faithful,
Cammy

The scribble became more difficult to read near the end.
The ink on this one sheet of thin paper was spotted with
teardrops, so some words were almost illegible. Now he held
her letter against his lips, praying that she had not been
abused, and that she still was his.

Cammy had blamed herself!

Any other man who loved her as he did would have been
better to her and for her, Kit had told his father, fighting
tears. The older man had read the letter and looked away,
holding back his own desire to weep. Cammy's warmth and
happy recklessness were delightful. She'd loved Kit since
childhood, and had trusted him. He sadly recalled the days of
his tropic island youth, before school in Victoria, before the
Westcotts met the Cochrans. The native women had been like
mothers to him, they had fed him, bathed him, praised his
dark golden hair and his skin, which was so much lighter than
theirs. He recalled their gentle hands upon his body, their
teasing, their comfortable manners. Oh, yes. They covered
themselves in flowing dresses, and the men wore the *sulu*, the
knee-length skirt, to be decent, but how quickly girls' dresses
could come off, when he was a grown boy and amorous!

He knew that sailors and others did harm to the dark-
skinned girls, threw them down and attacked them and left
them to swell with babies, but he and his father were appalled
at that. The dark people were intelligent and gentle, and Kit
was always a favorite with the young girls. He would lounge
in his bed until the little maids would slip in to bring him
pawpaws and tea. He would laugh with them as they sat upon
his bed and taught him the art of kissing. Never once did he
force his attentions on one, and never did he get one of the
girls with child. No, he would wait until he was married to
have children and Camilla was his destined bride.

He could not cease thinking about her. To see her so
securely wrapped in yards of fabric, in cruel, tight corsets and
stiff stays, stockings, shoes, gloves, he never dreamed she
might feel the same passion as a Fiji girl. Father had warned
him of the differences in customs. There were few young

ladies of breeding in the Australian colonies where they went
for supplies and for his early schooling. He would be extremely lucky to find a bride so close to home. A suitable European
girl did not so much as kiss her young man until they were
betrothed. The slightest hint of desire would drive her off. A
good girl was never supposed to admit to feeling anything but
dizziness upon having her hand pressed or her costume
complimented. So naturally, Kit was not prepared for
Cammy.

Camilla was intelligent. He had taught her to play chess
when she was fourteen, and they used to sit for hours and talk
of serious subjects like war and peace and the modern poets.
She loved to read, and would always come to him with a book
and read aloud in a clear, high voice, before she ever uttered
a word of conversation.

Then she grew up and told him she loved him. Cammy
came to his bed, and crawled in beside him, and he had taken
her.

He cursed aloud and almost crumpled the fragile sheet of
paper, which he folded again and carefully put away. He
raised his eyes to the linnet singing overhead in the lime tree
as if to attract a mate. The grass was dampening the costume
he'd chosen to look appealing for Cammy. He'd dressed in
fawn-colored woolen coat and riding trousers, had polished
his boots to a sheen, had combed his hair briskly, and
brushed his hat.

He'd reconnoitered the neighborhood and talked to people
who knew Bernard before searching out his house. Then,
when he found it, he stood out of sight and watched Edgar
Cochran on the road to the settlement. He walked alone, his
anger still written on his face, but unaware that he was being
observed by his daughter's lover. Kit sighed again as he
thought of that night. In all his youth, playing love games of
all sorts with the Fiji girls, he had never pulled one of them
under his larger, stronger body to force himself upon her. No,
he had done that only to Camilla, his delicate, devoted,
intended bride. He had gone mad with love for her and
ravished her. The first virgin he had ever encountered! He
shuddered to think of how he had pierced her, hurting her,
causing blood to flow. And then he wanted to make it good
for her, too, so he'd done it again, and she'd loved it. And
that was what grieved him. She loved him so much, and was
so ignorant of men, she did not know what he'd done.

Suppose she were pregnant? Was that why they kept her within? He had not glimpsed her in these two days he'd avoided Cochran and lurked about the place, not daring to approach the front door. Warm, loving, forgiving Cammy.

Had he possessed enough sense to tell her he would be going to Scott's Hotel after he was driven away from Blue Downs, then she could have run to him. They might have escaped together to West Australia, or to her mother in Adelaide, or even home to Fiji. Now it was four long months since they had seen each other. Who could tell what might have happened to her in that time? Did she speak to any other men? Did her father mistreat her? What of Bernard, who might be a grim-faced bigot like Edgar Cochran himself? Did he know about her situation? Her lover, her possible pregnancy?

Caution was essential. Kit had come first to Salisbury, right from the slow ship that docked at Southampton. Then he had bought a horse and obtained lodgings in the city, slurring his name in the book so the hostler inscribed "Weston" instead of "Westcott." Edgar Cochran was fully able to spirit Camilla away from him again, he knew that, but he had to see her, beg her forgiveness, kiss her gently. Then, together, they would try to plan how to overcome the obstacles her father set in their path. Kit had money, youth, strength, and some English friends here from his Cambridge days. He wondered whether Cammy had any allies in this fine house.

At last he took courage. Next time the stable boy appeared, he signaled to him and asked if he might see Camilla. The boy returned some time later through the hedge, holding a piece of white paper in his hand. A message from Cammy!

"We done told her of you, sir," the boy said, beaming. "The maid says Miss Camilla knows you and was expecting you'd come. She sat down and wrote you a letter, and here 'tis."

Kit paid him two shillings for the errand. His hand shook when he turned his back on the lad and tore open the envelope. "My Dear Friend," it began, "I am sorry to have to tell you this, but I am not interested in a continuation of our friendship."

Kit's eyes flew down the page. This was written in her hand. It exactly matched the first letter, but the tone was as different as night from day. He walked to the tree and leaned his back against it, feeling suddenly weak.

". . . your father . . . my feeling for you cannot be called love . . . never love you in the future."

He felt his heart sink. ". . . father does not rule me . . . end your suit . . . cease to take any interest in me . . . sour the pleasant memories I have of you . . ."

"Wait!" Kit cried to the boy, running after the messenger. "Did you tell the lady . . . I mean, can she have known—?"

"She asked Priscilla was you blue-eyed, with an accent, and we done told her yes," said the lad.

"Has she . . . do other men call on her?"

"Oh, yes. One done ride with her home from the Plains, both of 'em on one horse. She met him at Stonehenge, the big stones, y'know? She was a'holdin' him 'round the middle, and he 'et dinner here, and he's been visitin' since."

"Are you lying?" Kit demanded of the boy, wanting badly to shake him for the information he had just imparted.

"No, sir, I'm not. She's just come back from London, and they had 'emselves a fine time."

With whom had she gone?

"Is Miss Camilla—" Kit could not phrase it. He could not think or talk, or swallow the bile that rose in his throat. "Is she—" And then he remembered that it had not yet been four months. If she were carrying his child, would one yet be able to see it?

But this letter! She had disowned him, rejected and rebuffed him. Already she had another suitor.

Kit was desolate. He had ruined Camilla, and now she had done just as her father predicted. She was familiar with another man, intimate with him, perhaps right in her brother's house!

Kit dismissed the boy and walked slowly to his horse, scarcely able to lift one foot after the other. He slung his arm over the saddle for support. He wanted to kill someone, or better, to kill himself. He dug his boot heel into the spring-green grass. He should not have come to England. He should not have let Cammy show herself as fickle and unfaithful.

He mounted, wheeled the horse, and gave him his head. Kit rode at a hard canter in the direction the horse chose to go. For himself, he cared not a whit where they went, as long as it was far away.

Chapter 8

Camilla woke up only long enough to have her maid undress her. Then she sponged her face and arms over the basin. She snuggled back into her bed, where a light supper of scones and jam was later served to her on an enamel tray.

A good night's sleep put Camilla into passable spirits, and in the early morning she sought out her father who always breakfasted before her. Edgar Cochran never retired after ten o'clock at night or rose after six in the morning. Cammy usually avoided his company at breakfast, but today she rose early to speak with him. After delivering that firm letter to Hans, she felt totally in control of her life again.

"Father, I know you enjoy England," she began after the servants had poured their tea and retired, "but I wish to return to Victoria, if that is amenable to you. Mrs. Finch is taking her parents, sailing out of Southampton to go to Melbourne in a month. She has invited me to come with them. Please may I? With your permission, sir?"

"Without my accompanying you, you mean?" he frowned.

"Well, if you wish to remain in England for a while, they'd be ever so good as chaperones. Three decent old people. Ask Beatrice if they all were not lovely."

"And what do you propose to do in Victoria, without me?"

"I could dwell at Blue Downs with Aunt Rina, or wait in Melbourne with Mrs. Finch, or—"

"You'd be more likely to leave the ship at Adelaide and run off to that mother of yours, if not something worse."

She looked away from him, but not in time. Her guilty expression betrayed her.

"You would seek out that despicable Westcott creature, that's what you'd do!" her father exploded. "Why do you think I brought you all the way to England, at great expense, in a first-class cabin with a servant, eh? Not to keep you here for a short spell and see you rush right back into riot and shame."

"I would not do that, Father," she whispered, but her tone did not convince him.

"I would like to see you dressed nicely by the hour of six this evening, Camilla. We have a dinner engagement," he said, rising from the table. Evidently, the subject most on her mind was not anything he wished to discuss.

Camilla had a notion of what was afoot, and felt a certain amount of trepidation. Father invited poor Hans? Hans would surely refuse any enforced association with her now, after receiving her dismissal letter. But if he *did* come, what an awkward evening *that* would be.

Cammy spent a lethargic day indoors, reading, for it rained quite hard without a break until three in the afternoon. Tea, luncheon, and tea again were her sole distractions. Throughout the day, Father paced upstairs and down, like a barrister brooding over a case. He made everyone anxious, and forbade even a little music as a respite, for his head ached. Camilla watched him polishing his spectacles, gazing nearsightedly at the rain, and she wondered how she had the bad luck to be the daughter of such a man. She played a hand of whist with Beatrice, but her mind was not functioning. She was curious to know where they would dine and with whom, but no one would tell her. All she knew was that she and Father were going out alone.

At five o'clock in the evening, she bathed in perfumed water in a plungebath, and slowly donned her silken undergarments, building up layer upon layer of lacy rich fabrics, ending with the blue *peau de soie* gown that trailed behind her and dropped rather low in front. Father had specified that she was to wear this dress, saying, "I paid enough for it. You might as well get some use out of it."

Father soon would be storming about her tardiness. Punctuality was something he insisted on. Cammy added a blue velvet hat with a ribbon cockade on her red-gold hair, and then she was ready to go downstairs.

Father took the precaution of meeting their friends at the hotel where they were to dine. But Camilla was not at all surprised when Hans Van Beek and his father bowed them into the dining room.

The elegant room with its gilt- and red-flocked wallpaper, Aubusson carpet, and crystal chandeliers was lost on Camilla as she studied Hans' face. He did seem embarrassed. He was shy and flushed, but that was usual for him when he was with his father. Still, Cammy was amazed that he possessed even this degree of composure. She totally ignored his father, sending her gaze past his ear, or staring at his blue cravat instead of his face. His smug expression led her to believe that Hans knew nothing of their Windsor encounter. And Hans was surely too ashamed of his rejection letter to speak of it to his father.

She suffered through the fine dinner, finding little pleasure in the soup and sauces, the rarebit, and the many courses of fowl and meat served on fine Staffordshire china. She was allowed several glasses of sherry and drank it to blur her senses. She managed to laugh and seem at ease, chiefly to ease her fellow sufferer, Hans. How awful it must be for this harmless lad to be served up as a potential suitor after she had dismissed him forever from her life. She did feel compassion for him, but that was all.

When Hans ventured to compliment her upon her toilette, however, she began to wonder. The light in his eyes was rather warmer than should be expected. Could the servants have lost her letter en route to him? But that was impossible. Though it passed through three pairs of hands, they all had judged it a love letter, and would therefore be quick to deliver it.

She forced her attention back to the dinner conversation. The talk was of the coffee plantation in Java, of steaming fields of wet black soil under green leaves, with men dressed in white moving slowly down the rows. Of wide, airy houses with open porches and insect netting where one drowsed in the heat of the day. It was not much cooler at dark, said Mr. Van Beek. But the wealthy had their mountain retreats, with weather as cool as England's in summer.

The Van Beeks were undoubtedly rich, in search of a bride who'd bear many heirs, and her father was carrying out a transaction. She was the gift-wrapped parcel he offered them. Camilla frowned and stabbed at her sculptured ice that sat before her in a silver dish. The great bells of her sleeves dragged on her arms, stays stiffened her spine, and the leather corset was too tight around her middle. She wondered if her father knew of the meeting at Windsor, but doubted that he did. There were many secrets! The Van Beeks, naturally, did not know about her lost virtue, though she wished they did. She should stand up, right here and now, and announce she was no virgin. That would surely kill Hans' devotion, and infuriate both of their parents. But her pride would not let her tell that secret and bear that scorn unless she absolutely had to. It would be a last resort to save Hans' heart from shattering completely.

By the time the dinner was finally over, Camilla could no longer bear the constant implications that she should marry Hans. While they were awaiting their wraps in the entryway, she drew him aside and whispered, "I'm sorry my letter was so blunt, but I meant it, and I have not changed my mind. I have been polite this evening for our parents' sake."

"Your letter?" said the tall Dutchman. "You have written to me a story of your feelings? When was this letter posted?"

"It was not posted," she said with growing anxiety. "It was put into your hands when you rode to our house yesterday at dusk and asked for me."

"But Camilla, I was not out riding then," he said, shaking his head. "What a pity. I would treasure a letter inscribed in your hand."

"It was not one to treasure," she protested, her voice now shrill. "I was asking you not to—Hans, did my servant not deliver—? You were not near my brother's house?"

"Yesterday? No. I met with the train to bring my father to this hotel, Miss Camilla. I was nowhere near your brother's house."

She stared at him, horrified. Was it a servants' trick? Who, then, if anyone, had received her letter? Had she known this two hours earlier, she would have sat frozen, and never touched her dinner.

In the morning, she was up at the first call of the lark, though she'd retired very late the previous night. She donned a velveteen walking dress striped in maroon and cream, and slipped down the carpeted stairs, skirting the dining room to avoid her father. She found the parlormaid sitting in the servants' quarters, eating cheese and bread.

"The letter that Priscilla gave you," Cammy began hurriedly, "to give to Rodney, the stable boy. Did you not deliver it? It was for the gentleman who had sent me a message." The other servants in the hall looked at her in consternation. She was so upset, she was nearly babbling. "Was my letter delivered to a man on a horse?"

"It came through me hands, yes, miss," insisted the parlormaid who had sprung up at Cammy's approach and almost overturned her tea. "Is there something amiss?"

"Yes, yes, there is," Camilla said fretfully, wringing her hands.

"I will call the boy. Oh, I hope it is not somethin' tragic!"

"No, please. Finish your breakfast," said Camilla. "Only tell me where to find him and I'll go myself." She was half out of her mind with worry.

"He lives over the carriage house, miss. He must be up at this hour feedin' the horses."

Camilla rushed out the back door and dashed across the brick court to the stables. She hastened past the woodstores and coal shed, to the stalls. The boy was busy at work currying one of the mares when she found him.

"Rodney," she gasped from the door of the stables. "Come out immediately."

He came at once, respectfully. He was no more than fourteen, but still he was taller than she. "Yes, ma'm?" he asked.

"Rodney, did you deliver a letter for me yesterday?"

"I did, ma'm. I took a letter to a gentleman like I was told."

"And what did the man do when he read it?"

"He was angry, like, and turned pale as a turnip. He asked was it truly fer him. I said yes, 'cause of his eyes and his accent."

"He was the same gentleman who came back with me from Stonehenge?"

Rodney looked blankly at her.

"Speak to me!" Camilla cried, restraining herself from grabbing him by his thin shoulders and shaking him. "Say your piece. It was the same man, wasn't it?"

"No, miss," he said, very puzzled. Her distraught face seemed to mesmerize him. "No, miss, it were a different man."

Her mouth went instantly dry.

"But he had blue eyes and an accent. You said so! A Dutch accent, wasn't it?"

"It weren't a Dutch one, miss. More like . . . like from the colonies. Like to yours, miss," he said, brightening as he thought of the comparison.

She put her hand on the stable wall for support, not daring to believe that she now knew who the man was.

"But more stronger an accent, like," Rodney added.

"My letter was given . . . to him?" she whispered, but now she was not really talking to Rodney. Then she came to her senses. "Was he tall?" she demanded. "Was he handsome? Well dressed? Describe him. Oh, quickly, please!"

"He was all that, miss. He was real posh, and dressed in fine togs."

"Was there no mustache on his lip?"

"No, miss. Nor beard, neither. He was older than the Dutchman, and stronger lookin'."

She wanted to scream. "What did he say to you?" she asked in a choked voice.

"He asked was you entertaining young gentlemen here, and I said . . ." he lowered his gaze, "I didn't say yes or no."

The boy backed away from the sight of her ravaged face.

"Then where did he go?" she persisted.

"I walked back through the hedge, there, and didn't see him go off. I'm truly sorry, miss."

Her throat was closing, suffocating her. She knew who had come here yesterday and received her letter of dismissal. Kit Westcott.

Chapter 9

Camilla left the house, telling no one where she was bound. Actually, she was not sure herself. All Cammy knew was that she needed to walk and think. She took her alpaca mantle against the cool of morning, and without even a cup of tea to fortify her, she set out.

Oh, why had she made that foolish journey to Stonehenge, and once there, why had she chatted with Hans? Loneliness was no excuse. Think of how desperately lonely Kit was for her! To have come halfway around the globe only to be handed a rude letter would have to be the worst blow imaginable.

Against all odds, she checked the post box, but there was no letter from him. Why should there be? To seek hoofprints in the muddy path was hopeless. Oh, why hadn't she asked before writing the letter if the stranger wore a beard or mustache? She'd not even addressed the letter's recipient as "Hans." And now Kit believed that she no longer wanted *him.*

She would ask at all the hotels in Salisbury, all the lodging places where Kit might have stopped. Women searching for men who'd abandoned them were legion, but she had abandoned Kit, or so he must think.

"I am Kit's wife," she said aloud, believing it with all her soul. "We are wed, and it is wicked to keep us apart."

That morning she trekked from hotel to hotel, trusting to her pretty costume and innocent face to win her sympathy. Every hostler she asked allowed her to look at their register books for her "visiting kinsman." His name was Westcott, she said, and he was a tall young man from the colonies. She tried to appear blithe and carefree so they'd think nothing was amiss.

Kit was not registered in the hotel where she and Father had dined last night with the Van Beeks. Well, that was a comfort. After five more hotels, she found what she searched for. A friendly fat man at the desk opened his book for her, and in his guest register she found the name "Christopher Weston." She knew that he was here. It had to be her Kit! Pausing only briefly to thank the man, she flew up the dark stairs to the floor above, found the room number listed, and pounded on the door. She feared she'd faint from love and terror if he did not open quickly.

Cammy rapped again, waited, and rapped louder. She laid her cheek against the paneling and listened, then tried the doorknob. The lock held. If only she had the eyes of a spiritist and could pierce the wooden barrier to see her lover. Kit, her mate, her beloved, forever.

Camilla dragged herself away from the unyielding door and retreated slowly down the stairs. But she knew he was here, she felt it. The sound of crockery attracted her to the dining room, where breakfast was being served. She stood there in full view of the door, carefully studying the men's profiles and backs. Kit was not in the room. She no sooner turned away when suddenly a tall silhouette in the open door of the lobby caught her attention. The shape, the posture—it was so familiar! The young man carried a folded newspaper under his arm and his head was bare. He went to the desk for his key, spoke in low tones to the fat man, who gesticulated and grinned, and then the man went to the stairs and took them two at a time. She saw his face come out of the shadows. It was Kit!

He looked far older. His face was set in hard lines, and his expression so grim, she might not have known him. His light-colored spring coat hung open over his waistcoat. He was thin and drawn.

She ran up the stairs behind him, but before she was in

sight of him, his room was unlocked, and the door slammed shut. She couldn't force a sound from her throat to get his attention, try as she would.

At last, she tiptoed to his door and tapped on it lightly.

"Who is it?" he asked suspiciously, and still she could say nothing in reply. She heard his boots as he approached the door. He flung it open.

Cammy stood gazing up at him, her fingers knotted together. Unbidden tears cascaded from her eyes, and she was unable to prevent a sob from escaping her lips.

"Oh, Kit! You came! You came!"

Hundreds of emotions warred in Kit's face. His eyes narrowed, and he clutched his hands into fists at his sides. But then his arms jerked of their own accord toward Camilla, and he embraced her. They did not kiss, but stood holding each other. He crushed her in his arms and buried his face in her hair as she clung to him. The moment seemed to go on forever. Then finally he released her, and she fell away from him by force of gravity.

"Cammy?" he began hoarsely, "I came all this way, only to get a letter of dismissal!"

"But that is why I had to find you. The note was not meant for you! It was a terrible error, Kit! I was sought after by another man, and that letter was written to him."

She heard passersby in the corridor behind her, so she quickly came in and pushed the door shut behind her.

But as she looked at him again, she gasped. If he had struck her, she'd feel less pain. There was no trust in his grim face, and she staggered away from him, seeing nothing, her eyes swimming with tears.

"Oh, Kit, why did you not come straight into the house?"

"You have so many suitors you cannot tell them apart?"

"I do not have any . . . this Dutchman does not interest me. He is all my father's doing. Oh, if only I had addressed Hans by name in the letter! Then you'd believe me!"

"You rode horseback with him, two of you upon one horse. The stable boy told me. You and I never shared that pleasure, Camilla." His voice was bitter, but his eyes continued to sweep over her longingly. She could almost feel the heat of his gaze.

"We met at Stonehenge by chance. He feared for my safety on the return, so he walked beside me. But Kit, it was eight miles, so I gave him a ride."

He seemed not to hear her explanation. "I do not own you," Kit said, his tone like steel. "I did not realize how very young you are."

"But I want to be yours. I have looked at no one else!"

"It was stupid of me to come here," he muttered. "You're only sixteen, you are not ready for a permanent alliance with a man. But I needed to see for myself if you were—"

"If I am with child? No. I am not." She noted the relief in his face.

"Have you seen this Dutchman since you sent the note?" Kit asked very slowly, as if he was testing her.

She nodded her head. "But I want to marry you, Kit. I adore you, and you alone. Can you see me and not know that?"

"Say if you have broken with him."

"I have! I have!"

His face paled. "Camilla, you are lying to me. Last night you were dressed in the most ravishing gown I've ever seen. I walked into that hotel to take my supper there, but when I saw you, I left promptly. You were not under any cloud of despair. You smiled and chatted, and a man at your table flirted with you. That was Hans, correct?"

She threw up her hands. "Yes, it was. But I acted that way because I must please Father, and his father, who watched me. I thought poor Hans had read my letter and was pretending not to be hurt."

Kit considered her answer, but his face was more dour than she had ever seen it.

"My darling," she said, reaching for Kit's hand. "There is nothing to this relationship. I wanted a friend my age to talk to. Then Hans began to feel more for me than I—"

"Of course he did. Holding a man around the waist for a long ride on horseback! Oh, Camilla!"

"Strike me, if you will," she said miserably. "I am your love, and ever will be. I've never betrayed you." She looked into his eyes, and her face was so intense, he had to believe her. "I love you."

"Camilla," he sighed. "I loved you." He reached for her and snatched her light frame off the floor, unable to stop himself, and embraced her tightly. "No . . . I love you. I love you!" They kissed with a fierce hunger, their lips pressed together, her hands in his hair.

When he bent and let her toes touch the rug again, he was

shaking his head in wonder. "I want you whether you are true or not, Camilla. A goddess like you—"

"I am true! You taught me all I know, and I've kissed no other man."

"So very passionate," he mused. "That can be dangerous if I do not wed you. But how can we wed?" he asked anxiously.

"We must. I have to leave my father. He has accused us of—"

"You are beautiful, Camilla," Kit interrupted, stroking her luxuriant curls. "Temptation will always be at hand, and you will have suitors flocking from here to Victoria, like bees to honey. How can I keep you and not suspect you? We cannot marry for five more years until you are of age."

They kissed again, and held each other against all the problems they would have to face.

Chapter 10

Kit stood watching Cammy. Solemnly, not looking up at him, the youthful beauty in her white- and red-striped gown busily unfastened her bodice. Her pale fingers trembled down between her breasts as she struggled with the buttons. Her pink, tear-streaked cheeks were shadowed by her dark lashes.

But he could not manage to stop her. He wished to see her beauty, to hold her, devour her alive, and she wished it, too. The damage was already done, and they were hopelessly lost in love together. Did he love her? He desired her hellishly. Yes, he *did* love her. If she were honest and faithful . . . he so needed to believe she was. They had been apart so long! He was hot with need, starving for her, and if she was driven by passion—No!

He himself had taken her maidenhead and taught her the joys of love. He would have to protect her and believe in her, no matter what. She said she'd never lied to him, and that was good enough for Kit.

What was he to do, standing over his beautiful Camilla with his eyes shining as the striped fabric slid off her slim white shoulders and dropped to her waist? She untied the strings of her chemise and lowered the lace straps down her arms.

Her bosom was now almost bare, those wonderfully

smooth globes arching beside the chasm between them. Kit gritted his teeth, a man under torture. Only a fringe of lace now covered her above the vase-shaped corset that compressed her middle. Now Kit was frantic with desire. He could not take his eyes off her slim but rounded arms, her lovely body. On her finger winked his mother's garnet ring, proving again that she was his.

"Cammy, don't do this!" he begged. She was still weeping, but she did not cease undressing. Her gown was constructed to go over her head, not down over all her petticoats, but she was too impatient. She shoved the fabric of her outer and inner garments down to her hips, and then discovered that she couldn't reach the laces in the back of her tight corset. She finally dared to raise her eyes to his, her green eyes full of indignation and passion, and raised both arms like a child asking to be lifted.

He fell to his knees, embracing her hips. His head was on a level with that precious bosom. When he pressed his face between her breasts, forcing his tongue tip into the cleft, she moaned. Then he caressed her delicate back. He freed one shell-pink nipple from its bonds and then the other, so that his lips could enjoy them. His hands dropped to the hems of her skirts and petticoats, and dove beneath, before sliding up the silken legs that quivered as he stroked them.

She kissed his hair and the back of his bent head. She held him 'round the neck, swaying with him, murmuring how she had wished for this. For months, she had desired him alone.

"I am your wife," she whispered intently. "We are mated, Kit. We must be married somehow. Some priest will do it. Like Romeo and Juliet. They found a kind priest, and neither father gave them permission."

"That was only a made-up story, Cammy." He was dizzy, inhaling the fragrance of her perfumed bosom.

"Gretna Green," she persisted. "That's the place in Scotland that lovers run to. Papa could not prevent us. Scotland must be better. I know it! And in two months I'll be seventeen."

"Are you mine truly, Camilla?" Kit asked solemnly, looking into her lovely, tearful face. "I so want to love you forever."

"Yes, yes! Oh, Kit, believe me! I would die for you. Do what you will with me. I am your bride."

She was shaking all over, her entire body pulsing with

desire for him. He moved his hands under her clothing as he drew first one breast and then the other into his mouth. Then he felt his passion rise beyond the point of safety. Suddenly, he cried out, crushing her so she lost her footing and collapsed into his arms. He tumbled on top of her, his mouth on hers. They sprawled there like mad, foolish young animals.

"You do love me! You still love me," Cammy gasped, laughing through tears at his discomfiture. "You love me, my husband!"

There were still seas of fabric separating them. He lay on her crushed clothing and kissed her repeatedly, which was sufficient for his own relief but not hers.

"You may take me like before," she said trustingly, pushing her skirts aside. "I want a baby, Kit. A boy just like you. Then Father would have to let us—" No, a child would make no difference to Edgar Cochran. He'd never let her keep it, and it would only increase his anger against them. It would only be common sense to wait until they were married.

But Kit held Cammy and drove both hands under her skirts again. Soon he saw her green eyes roll closed as her head tossed from side to side. He watched her face and her flexing silken knees while she had her own exquisite pleasure. She was his mate, his own darling. He knew that now. When she cried out, he hushed her with kisses.

Cammy lay exhausted in his arms as Kit rested his back against the foot of the bed. Neither had enough strength to climb onto the mattress. He knew that it was wrong for them to enjoy this abandon before they were wed, and yet, they were so happy, theirs could not be too terrible a crime. They had turned the world topsy-turvy, taking the harvest even before they sowed.

Kit tried to be rational. He would have to think this out clearly. When she finally reached twenty-one, he would be twenty-eight. An eternity to wait!

When he was sixteen, her age, he was a wild thing himself, a constant worry to his father. A sterner man than Henry Westcott would have flogged Kit for foolishness and license. So how could he be harsh with Cammy? If he chided her, she would be more determined then ever. He would have to be the prudent one in this delirious relationship, or else she would bear a child of his without the protection of his name.

"Kiss me again, Kit," Cammy said, moving her face nearer to his.

He did as she asked, and reveled in the kiss.

"I want to sleep every night beside you, and have your body beside mine, unclothed," she said.

Much as he loved the thought of her plan, he had to interrupt her. "We must get you out of this hotel unnoticed," he said. The hostler had jested with him about a pretty lass asking where he dwelt, and people in the corridor had seen her come into his room.

It was well past noon now, and nothing was settled. They could not remain in each other's arms all day. He was besotted with love and lust, and knew only that somehow he would manage to take her back to the islands with him as his bride. He knew little of marriage law in Fiji, but here and in Victoria, her father's permission was required. That might mean five years until they could be united. Impossible! For an instant he allowed himself to imagine Edgar Cochran pitching headfirst off a horse, or falling under a railway car, or suddenly perishing of apoplexy.

Kit knew nothing about Bernard, whether he be friend or foe.

"Cammy," he said, touching her profile with a gentle fingertip. "What of your brother? Does he know our story?"

She shook her head. "I'm afraid to tell Bernard or his wife Beatrice. I'm afraid I might lose their love. I'd tell them if I thought it would help us against Father, Kit. But with you, I need no one else."

"Everyone needs more than just a love," he reminded her. "We all need friends. But you do touch my heart, my dearest, sweet angel."

They had to find a way to marry. Only Cochran stood in their way, and Kit's anger toward the man verged on vengefulness. Cochran deserved to lose Camilla, to be gulled, tricked, and, at last, defeated.

"I don't want to go back to Bernard's house now," said Cammy. "But what can I do?"

"I must think, my darling, and ask discreet questions. You must retain your family's trust until I can come for you."

"Will you?" she asked, and the anxiety in her innocent face tore at him.

He pulled her up to lean against him. Very slowly and

tantalizingly, he began to dress her. He rearranged her fragile chemise and put her arms in the sleeves of her rumpled gown. He was sure that evidence of their recent activity would be obvious. The fabric was creased, and try as he might, he could not smooth it flat again. Her mantle would cover her, but he cautioned her that once home, she should take care to change her gown in private.

He rose, stooped, and lifted Cammy gently, holding her under the arms, her swelling young breasts between his hands. He wished she were not quite so young. If he did not let her go, it would start all over again. The bed stood there freshly made, waiting for them, a horrid temptation, and all they wanted was to spend this day in bed, alternately at play and at rest.

Camilla wrapped herself tightly in her mantle, and then with one hand tried to pat her curls into a semblance of order. Kit attempted the task himself with his comb, but her fine, curling locks knotted. Although he was gentle, the pulling made her wince.

"Your maid can do this better than I."

"There is nothing any person can do better than you," she vowed. She looked like she was about to burst out crying again, and she could not go out of the hotel with a red nose and streaming eyes.

"We haven't had time to talk to one another since Blue Downs," she insisted, desperate to stay. "Then I was just a silly child. We were so busy learning to love."

"And now I must make you depart, when I wish to know all about what you've seen in England, and what you think of this land where I went to school. Cammy, if we but had a day!"

"Let me come to you again. Anywhere!"

He pondered the idea. "Can you ride to Stonehenge again?"

"Father would not permit it. He didn't know I was alone the last time I went. Had I not made the acquaintance of . . ." She stopped, feeling wary about discussing this subject.

"Of Hans," he prompted.

"Yes. He is so set upon my marrying this milksop of a Dutch boy—" She did not have to feign a disinterested face. After Kit, Hans was an infant, a bumbling creature with no more appeal than a girl in trousers. "Of course, if Papa thought I was in the company of Hans, but if the man really was you—"

"I cannot grow a mustache so quickly," he teased. "I could not even purchase a false one, like an actor's, white-blond like his."

"I must be rid of Hans," she fretted. "Give me the letter again, and I shall put it straight into his hands myself this time."

"I burned it," Kit said. "I'm sorry, but you will have to write Hans another letter of dismissal."

She made a face when she thought of the hopelessness of the situation. "But Papa will tell Hans not to be discouraged. Kit, can he really force me to wed a man I dislike?"

"This is not India or Africa, my darling. Of course he cannot." He rested his chin on the top of her head as he enfolded her in his arms. She felt so warm, so good, that he almost forgot he was further endangering them by keeping her in that room with him any longer.

"We must part," he insisted, still holding her.

"I know, but I hate to, Kit."

"Go home to your family. When I have a plan for us, I shall write to you care of the city post office. You can reach there alone, can't you?"

"Oh, Kit. Do write quickly. You cannot live in Salisbury very long without Papa seeing you on one of his walks through town. It is lucky that Bernard went away before you ever came to Blue Downs. No," she added, "that's not so. If he'd met you, he'd love you."

"Then perhaps we should meet," he smiled. "See if he will take your part. Michael, I remember, was an open-minded lad, and I did enjoy his company."

"You were his hero," she said, suddenly thinking of the beloved brother, closest to her in age. "How he followed you 'round. I think the only thing he misses from Blue Downs, besides Mama and me, was his 'Fijian Kit.'"

"Tell me," he asked wryly, "how did a father like yours produce such excellent children? And handsome ones, too."

"Mother had something to do with it," she reminded him with a grin.

Chapter 11

Camilla hurried home on this warm March afternoon, remembering spring in Victoria only four months ago, when she'd first fallen in love with Kit. England was bursting into bloom. It was a good omen. Spring meant love, all the poets said so. Two springs in half a year meant that Fate would smile on them.

But Father met her just inside the door of Bernard's house, and her mood fell at once. "Where have you been? The maid tells me you ate no breakfast, and it's now past the lunch hour. What recklessness—?"

"I must go up to my chamber, Father," she said crisply. "Please let me pass."

"Let me pass!" he mimicked her with a smirk. "You'll earn yourself a birching if you speak to me that way!"

He blocked her path. "Remove your wrap. I wish an explanation for this mysterious, solitary excursion."

"I had to purchase something. A surprise for . . . for Beatrice," she blurted out. She was anxious to get to her chamber and remove her crumpled garments.

"Then where is it? You are not carrying a parcel."

"I couldn't find anything suitable."

She drew her sweet memories of Kit about her like a

78

protective cloak, and tried to shut out the sight of her father's glowering face. "Please," she said. "Allow me to go up. I am . . . not feeling well."

He stepped aside nervously. Any hint of things peculiar to her sex, or to sex in any sense, appalled him.

"Come down again immediately, Camilla. I must talk to you. Remember that my patience is not endless."

"I am sure it is not, Father," she muttered under her breath so that he would not hear.

She rushed upstairs, shed her mantle, the wrinkled gown, and all her undergarments. She bathed her face and arms, her flesh continuing to glow from Kit's caresses, as if, like the sun, he had turned her flesh to gold.

She must talk to Beatrice, Cammy decided while redressing. Her sister-in-law was surely the most sympathetic one in this house. Camilla would not need to say just what they'd done with each other, but only confide that the man she truly loved was now in Salisbury. Beatrice, tender and sentimental to a fault, would understand everything and help them. But Beatrice was powerless, Cammy realized suddenly. No, it would be far better to go to Bernard at his print shop. She would blush to tell him, but he did have some power. He was Father's firstborn, and he was past thirty years old. Father liked Bernard better than the rest of his sons, and showed it. Certainly, he was fonder of Bernard than of Michael, his youngest son, not yet of age. Edgar Cochran had been free with the rod in rearing Michael, Cammy recalled.

"Are you coming down, Camilla?" The voice echoed through her door.

"Yes, directly, Father."

She must face him alone. Beatrice was out in the garden, supervising the gathering of daffodils and crocuses for the table. Bernard was at the shop. With a sigh of resignation, she descended the stairs.

Her father was waiting for her in the morning room, crouched like a lion, and he nearly sprang at her when she entered. She stood her ground, and tried to concentrate on the ferns cascading from their wrought iron stands, which made patterns on the scarlet carpet in front of the bay window. She loved this room with its window pushing out into the garden, but somehow it seemed less pleasant with Father in it.

"I have considered your request to sail on the *Hawkshead*

out of Southampton on the fourteenth of April," he said, all his information correct and precise. *Oh no,* Cammy moaned inwardly. He could not have decided to give her permission to sail!

"If you were accompanied by the Finch woman and her parents, I feel that plan would be agreeable. I do not yet know whether I shall leave with you. The weather is moderating here in England, and I wish to see more of this country."

Yesterday, she would have been delighted by this turnabout, but now she was dreadfully upset. She tried to conceal her consternation.

"Otto Van Beek will perhaps also sail on that ship. Whether he does or not depends upon your coming to your senses."

"I do not understand, Father." Naturally, she grasped his meaning, but decided it was better to feign ignorance.

"Whom will you wed, if not Hans Van Beek? You soon will be seventeen, and we have a perfect husband for you in Hans. He is a child. He would not suspect that you are not pure. Take him. You shall not find another with position and fortune and a pleasant countenance and ignorance of your sin."

She looked directly at him and tried to keep her lip from trembling.

"Perhaps I should never marry. I could earn my bread in some sort of worthwhile work. After all, you do not scorn Bernard for taking up the trade of printing."

"Don't be absurd!" her father spat out. "He is a man. You are a girl, empty-headed, overly pretty, and wild like your mother. No one would allow you to teach young children, and hospital work is filthy and disgraceful. What would you do? Go upon the stage and play the role of a trollop?"

She might have wept or argued, but the thought of Kit made her strong.

"I might go live with Mama in Adelaide. Then I would be out of your sight and grieve you no more."

"You shall marry or you shall live at Blue Downs as my hostess," he said sternly, offering no other option. "And at my passing, you can play maiden aunt to your brothers' children, if they ever have any. I vow that you shall never live as an adulteress with a seducer." His voice rose and his color dramatically darkened.

"Father! Sit down! You're upsetting yourself! I fear you'll go into apoplexy!" For a moment, she felt sympathy for him.

"How you'd wish for that," he snarled. "That is why you torment me, I am well aware. You wish me dead so that you may have my money. Well, no child of mine gets a penny unless he or she does my bidding. I earned it all, and I shall be the one to say who gets it."

"I don't want your money," she said coldly, all trace of compassion dissolving at once. "Nor do I wish to continue this conversation."

To her surprise, he did not prevent her leaving. He dropped his face into his hands, looking astoundingly vulnerable, and for a moment she was tempted to stroke his shoulder, to say that his pain moved her. She could not remember ever having touched her father, but today she suddenly understood something that aroused her pity. He was an orphan, raised by an aunt and uncle, and according to Mama, they never loved him. Mama sometimes pitied him. Perhaps someday Camilla would be able to as well, but from a distance.

Evening approached so slowly, she found it impossible to contain herself. Even if she managed to steal away alone, it was too late to walk to Bernard's shop. There was nothing to do but wait until after dinner.

When the meal was finally over and the family had made themselves comfortable before the large fire Bernard laid on the drawing room's marble hearth, Camilla braced herself for action.

Bernard, squat and square in his green smoking jacket and carpet slippers, frowned at Cammy across the room. "You've seemed nervous all evening long, little sister. Is anything wrong?"

"She's eaten hardly anything at all," said her solicitous sister-in-law.

"She ate nothing until three o'clock today, and that, of course, spoiled her dinner," Edgar said in an annoyed tone.

"It must have been the hotel dinner last night, and all the wine," Cammy quickly murmured. But Beatrice, convinced that she was ill, came over to the loveseat, and sat beside her, placing a cool hand on Cammy's brow.

"I must talk to all of you," Cammy blurted out.

She bit her lip, feeling for all the world like a young child preparing to recite verses for her elders. Unconsciously, she had linked her fingers in front of her, and her back was arrow-straight.

For the occasion, she had garbed herself in a modest, high-necked, dark blue gown. "This is a matter of life and death," she said to her startled listeners.

"What can you mean, my dear?" Bernard chuckled uneasily.

"I only wish my life to include a marriage like yours and Beatrice's," Cammy continued solemnly. "If I cannot have that, I would prefer to die."

"Ridiculous!" said Beatrice. "No one actually dies for love!"

"Please listen to me!" Cammy's voice was so anguished that they fell suddenly silent.

Then her father muttered in a low tone, "Take thought, Camilla. Do not reveal ugly secrets."

"All of you think I should marry, and I wish to marry," she boldly went on, ignoring him. "You all seem to feel that I should accept Hans Van Beek as my husband. But I cannot, for my heart is already engaged."

"Daughter—" Edgar Cochran warned, rising from his seat.

"I must speak, Father. My dear brother and sister must for once know my mind and my heart."

"Recounting your past will only lose you the love of your brother," her father persisted. "But if you wish to alienate everyone here, then do go on. I take no responsibility."

Bernard looked puzzled by this interchange. "I've noted your preoccupation, Cammy, but I see little wrong with the Dutch lad. If you don't want him, I cannot imagine who'd be better."

"You left Blue Downs, Bernard, before you met Christopher Westcott."

"That name should not be spoken in a decent, Christian home!" Mr. Cochran growled.

"This is my home, Father," Bernard said sharply. "Let Cammy have her say."

"It is not yours until you pay me for it!"

Beatrice gasped, and Bernard and Cammy sat stunned at their father's remark. Then Bernard cleared his throat.

"That is uncalled for, Father. I did not ask for the money. You pressed it upon us, so we could live according to your idea of comfort. We could dwell just as contentedly in humbler surroundings."

"You may find yourself doing just that if you cross me," Edgar noted with a sneer. "But for a childless union after a marriage of five years, space is not so important. I did expect you to give me several grandchildren."

Beatrice writhed at this challenge, and Cammy threw her a sympathetic look. Could her father actually be blaming her sister-in-law for this?

"I will go on," Cammy said loudly, then dropped her voice again. Anything to get the attention off Beatrice. "I love Christopher Westcott. His father owns a plantation in the Fiji Islands, but they visit Melbourne annually, and I have known and loved him since I was a child. Kit was educated in Melbourne and at King's College, Cambridge. He is twenty-three years old, and is kind, loving, and honest. I will marry no man but he."

"Do go on, Camilla," her father invited her in a nasty tone. "If you must disgrace yourself, tell the whole truth!"

"What is your view of the man?" asked Bernard, turning to his father.

"He is a seducer and the son of a wastrel," Mr. Cochran responded promptly. "The Westcotts have no more morals than Fiji natives. It is rumored that Henry keeps a native wife.

"Westcott is no better than Stephen Plaskett, the man who ruined your mother. He had the vicious gall to condone his son's seduction of your sister in my very home! Young Westcott and Camilla were found in bed together. While I was still wracked with grief and misery over your mother, they added even more pain. That is the pair with whom Camilla proposes to go off to Fiji."

Beatrice was rigid, staring straight ahead.

"I cannot believe that two such ignoble souls as you describe would be invited so often to Blue Downs," Bernard said carefully. "I clearly recall that you mentioned their name innumerable times in your letters. You spoke well of them."

"Have you not heard of a serpent in one's bosom?" Cochran hissed.

"For six years," Camilla broke in, "I loved Kit Westcott. We all did. Bernard, if you wish proof of his good character, ask the others. Michael knew him best, and followed him like a puppy dog. Charlotte fell in love with him." She noted that Beatrice was chalk-white beneath her freckles.

"I never told Kit that I loved him until this last spring. I thought for years he would marry Charlotte, and after she moved away, I didn't imagine he would take note of me. But he came to love me. The whole thing was my fault, though. I was an idiot and went to his bedchamber the night before the Westcotts were to depart. Kit did not seduce me. If anything, *I* seduced him, although I didn't know at the time that what we did was wrong. And naturally when Father found us there, he was livid. He dragged me to England to separate me from Kit. Kit wished to wed me, and still does, and his father wants me in their family, too. I know I was bad, but you see, by now I hoped to be a wife. Our father is the only obstacle in our path."

"Are you—?" Beatrice whispered, her glance dropping from Camilla's face.

"Mercifully, I am not. Father said he'd take it from me and never let me see a baby if I had one," she added, whirling to face him.

"Monstrous!" Beatrice cried.

"I want to marry Kit Westcott," she finished in a strong voice. "I want to be his wife legally, as I am his wife in every other sense."

There was an unearthly silence in the room, not a sound except the popping of the logs in the fireplace and several indrawn breaths. Then Cammy added, "Hans would not want me if he knew that I was no longer a virgin. If you wish me to leave your house, Bernard, Beatrice, I will understand. But I will wed Kit Westcott or no man."

She bowed her head. Her hands were still knotted together in her lap so tightly that her fingers ached.

"Where is the boy?" Bernard asked softly.

Cammy could not answer. If she told Bernard, Father would find Kit and slay him. But her dilemma was interrupted when Beatrice suddenly put her arms around her and held her tight.

Cammy drew in her breath, amazed. "Oh, Beatrice, do you forgive me?"

"Yes, of course!" she cried. "Poor child! Poor ignorant children, both of you!"

"Where is he, Camilla?" Bernard asked a second time. Cammy had her face hidden against Beatrice's shoulder.

"Kit . . . . is in England," she admitted. "I dare not say where."

"He is in Salisbury this very moment!" her father stormed.

"You came back this morning with your garments in disarray, your hair messed, your face red and filled with shame. You sneaking little slut!" He came at her with his hand upraised.

"Father!" Bernard roared, as Beatrice cried out, "Mr. Cochran!"

"She has done it yet again! She cannot help herself from running to sin and her own destruction. Jezebel!"

"Calm yourself," Bernard said harshly. He rose and stood over his sister. "Camilla, answer me, did you see Kit Westcott today?"

She kept her eyes averted and her lips tightly closed.

"Silence means assent," Edgar muttered.

"I would like to meet the young man," Bernard said. "You may tell me in private where he dwells."

"You shall sail on the *Hawkshead!*" Father announced. "If not a good deal sooner. I will not have an audacious seducer following us around the globe! He will not wed her as long as I live."

"He can wed me in four years, Father!" she burst out. "Once I am of age, you will have no power over me!" She was truly angered now.

Beatrice pressed her cheek against Camilla's, whispering for her to calm herself.

"If you say or do anything at all in this business, Bernard, I promise you will be on the street within the week. Mind my words. I shall call in your debt, and I have ascertained that you are not able to pay."

Camilla could not believe her ears. The man was more vicious than a viper! "That is vile!" she exploded. "My brother is full of love, but you feel no love for anyone! Not for Mama, not for me, not for anybody but yourself."

"Hush, dear," whispered Beatrice, "he does not love himself either. He is sick with hatred."

"Cammy," Bernard said decisively, walking across the room to stand by her side. "I shall visit your young man. I must see what kind of man he is, and sort out all these conflicting descriptions."

"Shall I come with you?" asked Beatrice.

He shook his head.

"Take me," Cammy said, and before he could protest, she added, "I am going with you."

Cammy had five minutes to rush upstairs and stuff her traveling bag with a change of clothing and a nightdress. She gathered the three pounds sterling that she owned, so as not to be unprepared. She had no idea how far Bernard would go to aid them. She donned her stoutest walking boots and wrapped herself in her warm mantle. Escaping the house and Father now was essential.

But when she arrived at the foot of the stairs, the ferocious parent she expected to meet was nowhere in evidence. Bernard whisked her through the door ahead of him.

It was already half past nine, a dark, starless night. Bernard bundled her into the gig and then leaped in himself. He clucked to the horse, and they started off briskly. He did not look at her but sat frowning with his coat buttoned up to his short, stiff beard, his fierce look much like Father's. He was balding like Father, too, but everything else was Mama . . . for which Camilla thanked God.

"You do not think he would follow us?" she asked, peering out the back window of the tiny carriage.

"Tell me where your friend resides, and we will leave the gig some distance off."

When they arrived at Kit's hotel, they hid the horse and gig behind the livery stable and went in by the rear door.

"Kit saw me with Hans Van Beek last night at dinner," she confided to her brother as they walked up the stairs. She could hardly believe that only twenty-four hours had passed since then. "He assumed I was enamored of Hans, and that almost broke his heart. Oh Bernard, you must tell him I love him alone!" Then she grasped her brother's arm and gazed at him with gratitude and fondness. "I shall never be able to repay you for this."

"You've been foolish, but so have we all," Bernard assured her as they walked through the passage to the lobby. "Since your lover is seven years your senior, he should shoulder blame as well, but not so much, I think, as Father lays on him. How can I condemn you if Beatrice does not? You are my own, dear Cammy."

When they climbed the stairs and she knocked on the door, the sound of boots on the board floor reassured her. Kit asked who was there. Cammy reassured him, and when the door was unlocked, she sprang into his arms.

"I wanted Bernard to meet you, Kit!" she explained as she drew the two men together and they solemnly shook hands. Kit listened silently to her story of the family battle just concluded. Bernard let her run on as he stood examining the younger man with intense interest.

"You love my sister, then? Very deeply?" he said when Cammy had finished her story.

"Unfortunately for her, yes," Kit said with a small smile. "I've come around the world to find her, and would do it twice over if I had to."

"You're a Cambridge man, eh?"

"Yes. I read history there. A pity we never met at Blue Downs before this."

Bernard subtly checked out a few more facts, although Kit quickly realized that he was under close examination. Camilla was proud of her brother's heartfelt interest. Oh, if only Bernard were her true father and could grant his consent to the marriage!

"You are nothing like I feared," Kit confided to Bernard. "I am happy to find you compassionate." They shook hands again, this time as a gesture of true friendship. Bernard then put his free hand over Kit's and held it.

"I wish to aid you two," he told them. "You must marry, and be quick about it."

"Camilla guessed that Scotland's laws are more liberal," Kit said, "and she is correct. I've just now returned from a Salisbury solicitor who knows marriage law. If one of us will reside for twenty-one days in Scotland, we may then contract an irregular marriage, pledging our troth without her parents' permission."

"Oh, Kit! I knew it!" Cammy cried, clapping her hands in joy. "It will be possible!"

"I cannot permit you to take her away unchaperoned," Bernard put in. "If you are hiding for a length of time, she must live separately from you, of course."

Cammy bit her lip, glancing from one man to the other.

"I am grateful to accept your aid," said Kit.

Cammy took his arm. "Father threatened to beggar Bernard if he helps us," she confided.

"You would do this for us?" The other man nodded. "Then I thank you from the bottom of my heart," Kit said. "You are a brother I will be proud to claim."

"There's no time for discussion. I cannot lock my father in his room. Gather your things, man, and take her far away. Use my gig to drive north to Warminster, where I'll send one of our maidservants to meet you at the Royal Hotel. Then board the railway coach that goes through Birmingham and Manchester to Scotland. There's a train at dawn, and you three must be on it."

"I have brought a few things with me," said Cammy. "You need not have the maid bring much luggage."

"Do you need money?" Bernard asked.

"I have sufficient for us," Kit assured him. "I fear you will be in want if your father takes vengeance upon you for this kindness." At this, Kit turned and began to ravage his clothespress, flinging garments into his cases.

"He most likely will have the border watched," Bernard cautioned them. "Continue beyond Gretna Green and go into the Highlands. Do you have any friends in Scotland?"

"Yes, a few," said Kit. "Please, there is a horse in the stables, a gelding named Ben. I recently purchased him, but now he is yours."

"If my father presses me, I'll say that you are bound for Southampton to sail for Fiji, but I can lie no more than that."

Kit paused for a moment and stared hard at Bernard. "I grieve that I have caused you pain. I shall be a good husband to Cammy, I swear it. She will never regret our union."

Bernard smiled and averted his face, brushing his eyes hastily with the back of his hand. "I wish my wife could meet you. Someday, perhaps."

When they reached Bernard's gig, Camilla kissed her brother with a violence that almost tipped him over. "I love you, good soul!" she cried. "You must bid Beatrice farewell for me, and tell her to take good care of you."

"Come to us when you are married," Bernard said. "It will only be a month from now."

"Only twenty-one days, Bernard! We shall return to you as Mr. and Mrs. Christopher Westcott."

"And mark my words, Father will forgive you if you give him his first grandson." Bernard bundled his sister into the gig, and without a backward glance, Kit flipped the reins on the horse's back. They were off, into the night.

Chapter 12

They went as rapidly as the horse could be persuaded to go, Kit applying the whip until Cammy pleaded for him to cease. Soon, they were out of the city and on the moonlit highway, and they had seen no other carriage.

"This is bride-snatching, you know," Kit said, sounding worried. "I have endangered you, ruined Bernard and Beatrice—"

"Stop that!" Cammy scolded. "We're both the victims of a great injustice. And besides, anything that Bernard thinks worthy is no crime." She was pressed against Kit so closely she could feel each muscle of his thigh against hers. She pulled his wide traveling cloak around her to share his warmth. The horse's cantering hooves sounded very loud on the pebbled road, and the moon, bright above them, showed them the way.

She clung to Kit as they passed castles and large estates, content that everything had come right at last. Thanks to dear Bernard, who had inherited Mother's love for loving, her tender heart, and brave impulses.

"You do have money enough to keep us? I only have three pounds," she told him after they had been riding silently for a while.

"I've a great deal. I knew you'd prove expensive, my darling. But it was worth any price to release the princess from the high tower."

"We shall love each other forever, my gallant prince."

"We worked hard enough to be together!"

His voice sounded weary, and the night still stretched before them. It was well past midnight when they came to Warminster, and they dared not go into the hotel. They tucked the gig into an alleyway, where Kit unharnessed and watered the horse. Then they perched together on the high seat and held each other. Cammy rested her head on Kit's shoulder, and he leaned his head upon hers. They attempted to fall asleep, but it was useless.

When dawn broke, Kit harnessed the horse again and left Cammy alone in the gig while he reconnoitered the Royal Hotel. He returned several minutes later, out of breath and frowning.

"I found no lady's maid inside, Camilla," he said, shading his eyes from the brilliant sunrise. "The train is due to leave the station in thirty minutes. If we wait for her—"

"But I cannot travel with you, just us two alone, if Bernard doesn't approve!" She bit her lip in consternation.

"Perhaps he met with problems at home, and could persuade no servant to come. Your father might well have prevented it."

"I never thought of that," she murmured, shaking her head in dismay. "Oh, Kit, what can we do? Father may come here to find us. Bernard may have confided in a servant who then revealed everything to Father."

"My fears exactly," he nodded. He seemed tired, but this in no way diminished him. He looked so handsome in his trim gray coat and waistcoat, his collar only loosely closed with a hastily tied cloth the color of his blue eyes.

They watched the Royal Hotel until the six o'clock train had come and gone. Then, in despair of Bernard's success, Kit hired a man to return the horse and gig to the print shop in Salisbury. He penned an explanatory note to Bernard before hiring another carriage and driver to take them to Scotland.

Camilla was weak with relief and exhaustion when Kit handed her into the closed carriage, and their driver got up on the box. With a sigh of relief, they bid adieu to Warminster.

Spring was in retreat, as they rolled northward. The trees

showed green buds in Wiltshire, but here in Cheshire, they huddled bare and cold. All during the successive mornings and evenings, they sat bundled in their scarves and rugs, and rattled noisily through the nights, only to be faced with icy hoarfrost at dawn. They did not stop to sleep in any inn, but pressed forward, changing horses and drivers when necessary, and always continuing northward.

"I have visions of palms and sandy beaches," Kit sighed. "Even Victoria seldom has winds like this. Are you warm enough, my darling Camilla?"

They clung to each other, finding ways to caress each other under their wraps. No one could see them, for they kept the curtains drawn.

They did not stop their travel until Camilla happened to notice a square-towered Norman church by the roadside. It was deserted, and its gray stone walls attracted her. They asked the driver to halt.

Cammy took Kit by the hand, and led him up the mossy path between bare apple trees, past six rows of blackened tombstones. The step in front of the church's facade was worn into a shallow bowl, but the aged plank door creaked open when she pushed it. A scent of dust and mold rose to greet them, joined with the unmistakable musty fragrance of old kneeling cushions, varnish, and mildewed books. The stained glass was so faded it admitted streams of yellow sunlight.

She drew him up the cool, stone aisle between antique wooden pews, to the altar. As they knelt, stiff from so much sitting, a cloud passed over the sun.

Cammy had her prayer book with her in her traveling bag, and she opened it on the altar rail between them. Kit seemed to know her mind. Neither of them spoke. They did not have to.

She looked at the cross and said aloud that in her heart she was penitent. The worse she had done was to love. Then she turned to Kit. "I shall read the bride's part, and you read the groom's."

"Who shall say the priest's words?" He smiled.

"We can recite those in unison, Kit."

It was very quiet in the old church as they spoke the holy words and vows in unison. Then each in turn, Kit spoke them to her, and she to him. Lines marked his weary face, and his hair curled around his loosened neckcloth. She felt unkempt herself and half starved, and her fingers were icy cold, but

they continued, meaning every word, cleaving to one another. She shivered, whispering together, with Kit. "Those
whom the Lord hath joined together let no man put asunder."

They solemnly pronounced each other man and wife, and
Kit kissed her. His eyes asked if it would be a sin to make love
here and now. Her eyes answered yes, although she wanted
to. They could not make love in this holy place.

Their carriage waited a short distance down the hill. The
horses were cropping the grass as the driver slept sprawled
under a tree.

When the rocking carriage moved on, they flung off
inhibition and disarranged each other's clothes, fondling,
seeking, coaxing each other into passion and then sweet
release. If the driver sensed the motion of their bodies, he did
not say a word. They no longer refrained from the ultimate
union, for Cammy discovered that, sitting on Kit's lap, she
could delightfully receive him. Crouched upon the carriage
floor, they found that the jarring of the wheels on the
roadway redoubled their pleasure. If only he could always be
inside her, Cammy wished deliriously, as he cradled her
breasts in his hands, his sweet lips pressed to the side of her
neck.

In the next town, Kit bought her two ready-made gowns of
simple stuff, and they took a room, registering at the hotel
desk somewhat whimsically as Mr. and Mrs. Flyte. They
made love for hours in the soft bed, though they were starved
for sleep.

Later, they feasted on bread and cheese and drank sharp
cider from stone bottles. The next morning, they hired a new
team, which drew the carriage farther and farther north, far
away from Edgar Cochran.

If only they knew how things were going in Salisbury and
what harm had befallen poor Bernard and Beatrice. They
would be happy but for their worries about their benefactors.

Just before Hadrian's Wall and the border near Carlisle, a
dangerous crossing where Cammy's father might have stationed policemen, Kit asked the driver to take a back road. It
wound around through cold, bleak fields and ended in a
cowpath headed into Scotland. The carriage rocked like a
ship in a gale on this rough ground and barely made it through
the mire.

But at the end, no locked gate or stile barred their way.

They then drove several miles north to strike the main road beyond Gretna Green. They were sure the driver knew the true reason for their roundabout route. He knew they were not Mr. and Mrs. Flyte bound for a Scottish holiday, but two lovers bound for a marriage that was prohibited in England.

They had almost arrived at their safe haven and were optimistic enough to discuss the future.

"Tell me more of the islands," Cammy begged him. "Of the Cannibal King who is in debt to the Yankees."

"Thakombau is a great king," Kit corrected her. "His father was a wicked man-eater, but the son has converted and made himself King of Fiji, with a parliament. He's learned to pray and to read and write. Even so, not all of his people follow his example. The unconverted *tevoro,* highland cannibals, come down from the hills to vex us."

She admired the way Kit spoke proudly of his black king, though many white settlers wished Thakombau dead.

"Fifteen years ago," Kit continued, "a Yankee's house was burned—no one ever discovered by whom—and now the *kai Merike,* the Americans, demand forty-five thousand pounds in reparations."

"For one house?" Cammy asked incredulously.

"Including interest," he nodded. "They come to collect their money in warships, and the King will have to sell half of Viti Levu to raise the full amount."

"I want to live there, regardless! With you."

Then he described more cheerful things: the sandalwood and *bêche-de-mer* for China, and the *yangona* drink to make you drowsy. When cotton prices fell in Fiji, the Westcotts had planted sugar cane, which made Henry a powerful man. When ruffians enslaved the natives, Henry Westcott became an adviser to the King.

Kit taught Cammy love words in Fijian. He called her *kamikamitha,* which meant sweet, like the sugar cane, *dovu,* and named her *wati,* his spouse. She was moved to passion again as he spoke the exotic words to her, and this time they made love in a slow, languorous manner, she lying atop him, wrapped in his arms. Kit did not move within her, but shut his eyes to savor the feeling, willing it to last forever.

"Would you consume me the way the cannibals ate that missionary?" she teased him.

"That was back in eighteen sixty-seven," he reminded her, "and that was only one incidence. Beside, Mr. Burns was foolish. He insulted a chief and traveled inland where one should not go. You must recall, Cammy, that there is little animal food in the forest—"

"Kit!" she chided him. "You defend them?"

"The Tongans brought the custom to Fiji," he continued.

"Then play cannibal with me," she said, drawing his hands back to her rounded breasts.

They feasted on one another with love, and did not sleep until morning.

When they arrived in Scotland, they sent the carriage back south again. For safety, they lodged in a small inn on the least known of all the lochs in Argyll, north of Glasgow. By day they had nothing better to do than walk beside the loch and admire the shingled shore and the kelp beds. English sheep breeders had replaced Highland farmers on this land.

"The Scots want England out, and so do the Irish," mused Kit, "but we Fijians are begging the Queen to take us as a Crown Colony. Extraordinary, isn't it? Her Majesty has been holding back making a decision. So much for accusations of greedy British imperialism!"

"Fiji is so very far away, Kit," she sighed.

"Exactly half a world away," he said. "With Greenwich, England, the prime meridian, Fiji, directly below it, is cut right in two. A sailor can work all day Saturday on one side of the line, sail across, and it becomes Saturday again. There are no Sundays in a week for a shrewd ship's captain."

She loved his tales and yarns, especially the ones about the South Pacific. They seemed to warm her even in the midst of the blustering Scottish spring with gale winds blowing off the Firth of Lorn.

"I do not even feel the cold when I'm with you," Cammy said, standing to face the wind, her bonnet flying behind her by its strings. She shut her eyes, bracing her legs apart to keep on her feet. Kit stood beside her in his boots and knickers and heavy tweed coat with a wool scarf wound around his neck. She'd bought him a tartan of her mother's family colors.

"An English colonial and a half-Irish one will be wed in Scotland," he teased.

They'd clambered around ruined, deserted castles that had once been grand but now were only stone towers with the floors rotted away and stone steps left hanging around the inner walls. Together, they gazed far down the bracken-filled valleys, over the swampy, rocky Scottish moors. It was easy to imagine · hordes of Highlanders coming to get them, preceded by bagpipes and armed with cudgels and knives to assault their bastion. Camilla shivered, and Kit held her close, both of them too chilled to make love.

They perched on stone bridges arching over salmon streams, while torrents roared over rocks beneath them. They daydreamed about coconut palms and trees bright with flame-colored flowers, parrots, and the thatched houses and outrigger canoes of his islands. He bought her gloves and a fur astrakhan hat, and they walked publicly in their little settlement, making sure the laird and the police both knew they were resident here.

Fifteen of the required twenty-one days had passed. On the twenty-second day, they would suddenly throw off their false identities and take on their real names. And at last Camilla would forever discard the name of Cochran in favor of Kit's name, Westcott.

They brought food up to their cool, low-ceilinged room mostly taken up by the wide bed, with its wool-stuffed mattress. Then they would sit on the bed with a quilt wrapped around their shoulders, feeding each other haggis so peppery that Camilla winced, though the meat and grain boiled in a sheep's stomach was warm and very filling.

Kit caught fresh fish from the local streams for her, and when she begged him, he taught her to angle for her own. He offered to borrow a rifle from the innkeeper. If he shot a deer, they'd dine on the venison, he promised. But she did not want to part with him for so long.

"Shooting is for Blue Downs in spring," she said. "And that would only remind me of Papa."

"Do you realize you have been calling him 'Papa' more than you ever did before?"

"Do I?" She sat for a moment pondering. "Perhaps because I am free of him now, I can begin to feel some tenderness."

Kit snorted. "If you could imagine his feelings at this very moment, you'd feel more fright than tenderness!"

They dared not write to Bernard, because her father would undoubtedly be searching the post each day. It was necessary for them to vanish into thin air, let Papa think they were sailing through the Suez, sailing east to Fiji. He could think anything he wished except that they were hiding in Scotland, not many hundred miles from Salisbury.

"Poor Beatrice, having to put up with Papa in the state he must be in. I wish you'd had a chance to meet her. You'd like her as much as you did Bernard."

"Should I have met Hans Ven Beek, as well?" Kit teased, "And asked him face to face if ever you kissed him?"

"I did not!" Her face turned red with anger.

"I'm only jesting. I know you didn't," he proclaimed. "Now hush, or I'll say the lady protests too much."

They were both naked under the coverlet. The moonlight turned their white quilt into snowy fields and valleys around their four knee peaks. Camilla threw off the quilt so she could see all of him, the strong shoulders, the arms bulbed with muscle, the slender wrists and elbows, the wondrous, strong legs. Kit's waist was so slender and supple that she wondered he did not break in two. She sat beside him modestly covering her front, but he quickly pulled her arms aside, making a pathway so that his lips could find her breasts. He tumbled her on top of him, then dropping her breasts like fruit toward his mouth.

"These shall swell when a baby is coming," he said. "Sweet mangoes become green coconuts . . ."

"Not green!" she giggled. She shook her curls over their faces like a tent. She straddled him, but would not receive him, and he became frantic, lying on his back, pushing up with his hips in the mating rhythm. She dropped myriad kisses on his face and stroked the palms of his hands with the tip of her tongue.

"Vixen!" he gasped. "Where did you learn such tricks as that?"

"Do I please you? Oh, I hope so. I shall invent wonderful things and tempt you until you are totally blind with love."

"I am your slave already."

"But how can that be? You are stronger than I, Kit."

At that, he jerked her down to lie upon him, whipped over on top of her, and pressed her deeply into the soft mattress, sliding his body against hers. He sought the pulsing center of her and drove home, smothering her squeal with a fierce kiss.

"That is what comes of your invention, Camilla!"

"Then I shall only continue to invent and surprise you each

night and morning with any new pleasures that have occurred to me," she said smugly.

"And I shall take you now like a Fijian man, kneeling before you."

He drew her legs up over his, so her hips were higher than her shoulders. Now she could wriggle freely, and her eyes opened wide with delight. "Have you loved me long, Kit?"

"If you know how close I came to ravishing you during that encounter in the summerhouse," he said. "Camilla, you had suddenly become a woman! I expected to see a child. I had only thought of your sister, Charlotte, before she married, of course, and then I saw you again. The change was striking! You sat upon my knee so innocently. That was only six months ago, and now you are my practiced lover, my mistress, soon to be my wife. My dearest! I've stolen away your girlhood. I hope you won't regret it."

She caressed his dear, sweet face. "You're not a thief, but a fine teacher, Kit." She felt his lips curl upward in a smile. The candle was guttering in a puddle of wax, but she did not move to light a fresh candle from it.

"I thought you cared nothing for me until well after I confessed my love," she said. "I was so weary of your acting like my older brother, and never truly looking into my face. You never saw *me*."

"I know, you are right. But that is ancient history now, Cammy. Listen," he went on. "Once wed, we can travel straight down to Salisbury by railway, right out in the open, without any need to hide. We can walk into your brother's house as married people, and then sail away to Fiji, and your father can do nothing to prevent us. Think of that."

"Letty sails on the Fourteenth of April. We might by luck find berths on her ship. One berth would do for us two, don't you think? I could learn the pretty signing language from her parents, and when we live in Fiji I might find deaf children to teach."

"There are children like that in the islands, deaf of white man's diseases. You would be a welcome sight to them, my dear," he agreed, accepting her plan at once.

"Your father will welcome me, I know it."

"He certainly will, and he will welcome me back to manage the plantation. I don't think I told you, but he spends much of his time now in the capital, Levuka, on another island. To

have me back again, and a daughter he already loves, would
gladden his heart. And by the time we arrive, we may find
that a bonny bairn is coming."

She laughed at his attempt at a Scottish brogue, but her
fingers flew to her stomach as she contemplated the idea. Like
Mama, would she be pregnant at seventeen? It was five weeks
until her birthday.

At midday, when Kit kissed her awake and sat on the edge
of the bed watching her, the sun was already warming the
room, the first sunshine in three days. She threw off the quilt
and lay under the white muslin sheet, flat on her back. As
soon as she saw him, she wanted him again. They were all
passion and no talk. There would be time for talk when they
were old and the fires were damped. If they were ever
damped!

Sleepy-eyed, she began to tease Kit. "Look, I am an effigy
on a tomb in a church," she said, smoothing the fabric tightly
over her thighs and stomach and pressing it into the valley
between her legs. "All smooth white marble." She molded
the fabric over her breasts, and put her arms down by her
sides. She lay very still and closed her eyes.

"You are no effigy, but a living, breathing girl! I'll awaken
you."

Laughing, he knelt beside her and slowly slipped the sheet
down, bit by bit, kissing her all over. She had wished for this,
but lay perfectly still, enjoying the sensations coursing
through her. Slowly, her body was uncovered, flushing under
his hands, and when he kissed lower, she could no longer lie
still.

"Hark!" he cried. "She stirs!"

"I stir! I stir!" She giggled, reaching for him and closing her
arms and wrapping her legs tightly about him.

"Will a baby come from this?" she asked naughtily. "Will
you plant him deep, my Kit, my husband?"

"Deep in the moist, dark place I have grown to love," he
said in awe of her beauty and her warmth. "I think you want a
baby as much as I do."

If there were now a baby, Cammy thought, it would be
wonderful. A child would be a final pledge of their love—a
miracle they made between them.

Chapter 13

The wedding that would take place four days hence held all of Cammy's attention. She planned for it all day and dreamed about it every night. She would wear a beige woolen gown they chose together, trimmed with golden braids, and revers and tucks and graceful bell-shaped sleeves. The service would be brief and simple, and the words "I do" would be spoken by each of them with great solemnity.

Four short days before the great event, Kit went out to buy the newspaper and scones for breakfast, shutting the door quietly behind him in case Cammy wished to sleep longer.

She was hardly out of bed, her hair as wild as that of a girl from the stews of Glasgow, her feet bare, when a knock sounded at the door. She gathered her thin nightdress around her and went to answer it. Kit must have forgotten his hat or his money, and did not wish to charge into the room and interrupt her toilette.

"Kit?" she whispered through the panel of the thick door. "Is it you, my love?"

There was no reply. Was he trying to surprise her, perhaps bringing hot tea or some other gift? He'd once borrowed a kitten from their landlady for her to play with half the day in bed. He loved to see her eyes brighten with excitement.

"Kit? It is you, isn't it, Kit?"

"Yes," said a muffled voice.

She unlatched the door, thinking how odd Kit sounded. Perhaps he was catching cold. She would have to take better care of him.

The door was pushed open, and Edgar Cochran stood before her.

"Father!" she screamed, seized by a paroxysm of violent shudders. "Oh, you can't be, can't . . . can't!"

"I can," he said, forcing his way in, closing the door behind him. He took in the scene with a scowl of disgust—her body still flushed from lovemaking, the gown half off her shoulders, the large bed that clearly indicated the chief activity of this room.

Her father pointed one thin finger at the scene of her degradation and debauchery.

"Camilla," he announced, "there is no hell hot enough for you, and no heaven that would ever admit you. But I shall be kind. I shall take you home with me to Victoria, to live a penitent life."

"I shan't go with you! I'm married to Kit!"

"There has not been time. I know the laws of Scotland!"

"We were wed in church," she stammered. "In the eyes of God we are married."

"This is pure blasphemy! No minister of God would marry wicked runaways. Where is the child-snatcher?"

"The what?"

"Your lover."

"Gone out."

She prayed that Kit would be delayed. Her sweet, tender Kit, her husband, did not deserve this.

"He's a kidnapper. He has taken a child of sixteen across a border for immoral purposes. He won't be so pretty after five or ten years in prison." Her father's face was distorted with rage.

"What are you saying?"

"Kidnapping is a felony. I'll have him thrown in jail!"

"You can't do that!" she croaked at him hoarsely. "I would . . . I would *die* first! I'd kill . . ." She wanted to say "kill you," but her throat closed. Her limbs felt weak, and she staggered, unable to steady herself.

"How much do you love this man?" her father asked in a calmer but conniving voice.

"I adore him. He is dearer than any other man on earth. We could be so happy, Father. Oh, if you would only let us alone. Let us marry legally and be husband and wife. We sinned, but you force us to remain in sin."

"And you are not the only sinners. Bernard has lost his house for aiding you. The maid he was about to send after you confessed everything. She was wise enough to disobey him."

"You've taken Bernard's house away?" Cammy's eyes stung with tears.

"How dare you question me." He snarled, grabbing her arm and shaking her roughly. "A good, rich man to marry, young Hans Van Beek, and you run off with Westcott! Do you see where my mercy leads? Only to more sinning. Your inborn taint will destroy you. You are as bad as your mother!"

"You're taking double revenge on me for my mother's sake," she said, seeing the man plainly for the first time in her life. "Oh, I wish you weren't my father!"

"Considering your mother's character," he spat out, "perhaps that is the case!"

She stared at him. "What are you saying? Mama never—"

"What do you really know about your mother?"

Her brain spun, splitting with pain. Anything this man said was only the raving of a madman.

"Well?" he asked. "Do you wish to save your lover from prison? I have policemen watching outside who are most interested in Christopher Westcott."

"You're lying. It's a ruse!"

"Look through the window," he gestured, with a small, hateful smile on his face.

She did not wish to gratify him, but she could not help herself. A man stood staring up at her from the street below their upper-floor window. Another man, also not in uniform so as not to be identifiable, stood in a doorway some distance off.

"They do not know Westcott's face," her father explained as she looked down on them in horror. "If I go down and summon them, they will take him. However, if he comes here and then departs again, alone, they will not touch him."

"Please," she begged, "don't send Kit to prison. Please, Papa. He followed me halfway around the world. I was the one who first made him sin, Papa . . . it was my fault. Put me in prison, instead."

"Very touching," he said, leaning back against the window frame, smirking. "What would you do to save him?"

"Anything! You know I would. I've brought this upon him. I'll do anything—"

"Make him hate you, then," he challenged her.

"That is one thing I cannot do, even if I wished to." She swayed slightly, growing sick to her stomach. What was this evil man suggesting?

"Make him leave you. Women do it every day."

"How could I?"

"I swear to you, Camilla, if he never tries to see you again, he can run free."

"But how on earth could I deceive—?"

"That is simple. Turn to another man. That will make him leave you flat. You will never see him again, I assure you."

"What man?" she asked, staggered. "What are you saying?" The room was cool, but perspiration stood on her lip, and made her father's bald head shine. The weariness of his long journey made him look like an old man.

"Turn him totally against you, Camilla, make him despise you, and he'll cease defying me. Make him wish never to wed you. Show him how fickle you are."

"But I am not!"

"Oh?" he said, lifting one eyebrow in disbelief. "What of Hans Van Beek?"

"I never wanted him!"

"You did not pause between Stonehenge and Salisbury for a short dalliance?"

She made a grunt of shocked disgust. The suggestion was too absurd to be insulting.

"Kit and I are in love. Our hearts are linked and always were," she told him firmly.

"In that case, we will use the man I have hired."

"What man?"

"He is in the next room. Come quickly."

"I'm not dressed."

"So I notice. All the better for the scene you are about to enact."

He led her into the deserted hallway where she saw that the door to the adjoining room was ajar. A young and smiling man whom some might label handsome stood before them, his hands on his hips.

Camilla gathered her skimpy nightdress around her, as the

man ogled her breasts and hips, outlined beneath the thin material.

"Embrace him," said her father.

She could not believe this. It was a nightmare! "I shall stand around that corner, beyond the wardrobe. If your lover doubts your masquerade, he goes to prison. If he is disgusted and scorns you, he is free to return to Fiji." He stared at her ravaged face. "Do you understand?"

"I do not trust you," she said between clenched teeth.

"You have no choice but to trust me. I would not stage such a vile performance were it not to save your soul, Camilla."

She turned from her father to stare at the stranger. He was dressed in trousers and a shirt, but wore no coat or tie. He was a red-headed Scot of perhaps thirty. He was smaller than Kit, as most men were.

Her stomach roiled with loathing. "What must I—"

"He will be paid for taking a blow if your lover tries to come to your defense. But should he become violent, my man has a pistol at the ready. I will not stand by and see him killed."

"But he must not shoot Kit!" She was trembling now, unable to control her voice or her actions.

"Exactly. No one wants a killing. Therefore, daughter, you had better convince your lover that you desire this man. Pretend to make love to him and he will not use the pistol."

"Who is this man?" she demanded. "Is he a policeman?"

"Of course not. Only a discreet acquaintance. And remember, Camilla, I will be very near by. It all depends on you. The man will do nothing to you. You must do everything."

"Oh, I can't!" she cried, desperate to run from the room. If only she could find Kit and flee.

"Easy, easy, miss," the man said in a lighthearted tone. "It's just playacting. I don't plan on bein' forward, not with your father there, starin' right at us. Just kiss me a bit. She's to kiss me, isn't that right, sir?"

Edgar Cochran grimaced and nodded. Then he stepped around the corner of the wardrobe out of sight.

"You'll never lay eyes on me again, miss," the man reassured her. "I don't know your name, nor your father's. I'm only doin' this because I need the money. Your father's merely tryin' to break off your love affair without resortin' to the law."

These words partly calmed Camilla's hysteria and she

regained some power over her limbs. Slowly, the man held
out his arms to her. The door behind her was open only a
crack, but the sunlight pouring into the room through the
window was like illumination on a stage.

"Speak up. He's got to hear you as soon as he walks in,"
the Scot said, fidgeting. "I'm not keen on bein' beaten for
anything I've done, when I'm not doin' a thing."

The expectation of pleasure faded from his face, and was
replaced with anxiety.

"You won't shoot Kit? You promise?"

"If you kin prove all this is your idea, miss, then all t'will go
as planned," he promised, reaching out for her again.

At last she understood. She had no choice but to obey. If
she warned Kit, he'd land in jail. If she pretended she was
being raped, Kit would batter the man and be shot dead. Her
comfort and reputation were insignificant compared to Kit's
life. Soon, she could send a letter revealing the truth to him,
and make it right. He knew how wicked her father was.

Her face set in a determined grimace the moment before
they heard footsteps. A merry whistle sounded in the stair-
well of the inn. It was late morning, and by now the
overnighters had departed.

It's only for a moment! Perform! Camilla silently commanded herself.

They waited together, the stranger looking more frightened
than she. She flagged her brain to invention. Kit might spit
upon her, but he would never strike her. This hired Scotsman
was the one in danger, so frightened now that he was
trembling.

The fall of boots in the corridor sounded very close. Then
came the soft, merry whistle Kit used to tell her he was
coming home.

Chapter 14

In the slow, wet, Scottish spring, there were purple crocuses in the country lanes, and Kit had gathered a few in a twist of paper as a surprise for his love. It had delayed his return, but she'd forgive him.

He gave her his warning whistle at the top of the stairs, and then pushed their door open. It was shut but unlatched. Had she been bored after so many days indoors and gone down to chat with the landlady this morning? They'd go out walking this afternoon. It was going to be fine after days of rain.

"Camilla?" He stuck the blossoms into the water she must have just poured into the basin. He recalled their lovemaking this morning. How wonderful she was! He had then bathed, dressed, and gone out before she could untangle her limbs from the bedclothes and recover from their delicious wrestlings.

Then he heard Camilla's voice. At first he thought she was in the corridor. Then, curious, he walked to the east wall of the room and put his ear against the flowered paper.

"Quickly. He will be back any moment!" he heard her say.

So, she was plotting a surprise for him, as he had picked the crocuses for her. Had she planned a surprise with the landlord or landlady? She was forever doing sweet things that amazed him.

". . . thinks me a loose woman! I'm tired of his suspicions!"

Did he hear correctly? Kit stood frowning.

"He's been awful about distrusting me."

It was Camilla, and she sounded like a petulant child.

Kit stood there mute and numbed. The next voice was a man's, louder than Cammy's. "We cannot let him find us like this. He'd put blame upon me, when it's you, Camilla, who—"

"I know. Hush. Kiss me. Hold me."

Kit pressed the palms of his hands upon the wall and rested his suddenly throbbing head on the wallpaper. He was sick. He wanted to weep or to yell. He didn't know what to do or what to think. The man had called her by name. What was he overhearing? Was it a dream?

Had Hans overtaken them?

No, Hans was Dutch. That voice was Highlander. Was it all a great joke? Was Cammy teasing him this way for his foolish jealousies? Surely, she loved him and him alone. His stomach knotted, and his face grew hot as he thought of the implications of what he was hearing. But she'd led him into a church and become his bride. She could not—It was some other girl with a voice like hers, a name. He prayed that this was all a bad dream and he'd awaken in bed, holding Cammy.

Kit forced himself to creep into the corridor. These fools had not shut the door upon their tryst. Who were they? Kit forced himself to peer in.

A slim girl with red-gold curls, in a nearly transparent nightdress, was leaning against a man in his shirt-sleeves.

It was his Cammy, the sunlight setting her fair skin aflame and revealing her legs through the sheer fabric. She had her arms around the man's neck. Now the man turned his head and looked straight at Kit.

His hand lay on Cammy's back, on her fair skin above the fabric. Kit stared fixedly at that hand with its red hairs. It had blunt fingers, square nails, reddened knuckles. She had not heard him. She was kissing the man upon the neck and crooning to him.

Kit felt his brain explode, and then he was only a flash of movement. He leapt into the room as if the door were not there. He seized Cammy by one elbow, and grabbed the man by the wrist of that caressing hand. Savagely, grunting with effort, he flung them apart. His cry was a rattle in his throat. "No! No!"

Cammy regained her balance, and turned on Kit with a fierce glare. Her face was white. Rage, horror, and fear showed in her expression, but she spoke not a word of apology or appeal.

"You said you'd be away longer!" she hissed.

Kit ignored her and swung at the man.

The Scot fell, and Kit was immediately poised over him, his fist drawn back, but Cammy threw her half-nude body between them, falling full length upon the man. She embraced him, crying over her shoulder, "Stop, stop! Don't hit him! Don't hit him again!"

"I loved you, Cammy!" Kit shouted. Rage beat a terrible pulse in his temples. He was enraged at himself for his blindness. "I'm leaving you!" Kit shouted, praying she'd rise and run to him, beg his forgiveness, somehow explain.

She remained there, covering the man with her small body. She loved a craven coward! How could he believe that only this morning, she had been his!

"Go!" she screamed at him. "Get out of here! Get out! *Get out!*"

He didn't stay to hear more. Sick and enraged, he spun around, slammed the door shut on their perversity, and ran to his room.

The room that had been theirs! He tore garments out of the wardrobe and piled them haphazardly into his portmanteau. He'd had her first, to begin her life of lust, and then he'd lost her. "Cammy!" He said the name quietly, again and again, listening for sounds from the other room.

Did he hear weeping? No, that was only his imagination.

They would have been wed in four days. In four days united forever!

Well, then he'd found out about her just in time. How many other men had she gone to, when he was out of their room, she with her sanctified marriage in the peasant church?

He swallowed hard, looking down at the floating crocuses he'd placed so gently in the basin. He picked one up, dropped it on the floor, and smashed it to pulp under his heel.

Quickly he had his portmanteau in hand, his hat on his

head. He kicked the door open and went out. There was silence next door. That was a relief. He didn't want to hear their gasps and squeals.

He took the back stairs. He'd go back to Fiji, even if he had to travel steerage. In the alleyway, he walked rapidly to the next cross street and hailed a hansom cab.

Well, that was his good luck, to have found out about her before they were legally married. He'd left her perhaps thirty pounds from his wallet. His payment for nearly a month of services. For brief devotion, you pay money. You do not join with that sort of woman for life, to raise a family.

She'd marry some old fool, and lovers by the score would court her. What an actress, though! She could go upon the stage.

Wouldn't her father love this outcome, though? He was the man who had made it happen. Had they married in spring in Victoria, three weeks after she'd been found in his bed, he might have curbed her deceitfulness. If he'd have been able to keep her close and love her night and morning and at midday, too, in the Fijian sunshine, he would have left her no energy to seek another man.

He swallowed the bile in his throat and thought of lucky Bernard, with his good marriage. What could Kit tell his own father, who so wanted Camilla for a daughter? He would say nothing.

He played over the awful scene again in his mind. She'd fallen upon the man and held him so oddly, without moving, almost as if she feared the little Scot was dead. The savage commands to get out came hissing from her petal-pink mouth that so recently had kissed his whole body. Had hatred for him grown from her love?

He caught the next train down to Glasgow where he would change for Edinburgh. At Leith, he would find a ship to anywhere, as long as it was far away. One more sight of Camilla would undo him and destroy his resolution. Kit had a compartment on the train all to himself. He drew the curtains on the aisle side, turned his back on the forests rushing by, and bowed his head.

Then the tears came in profusion.

Chapter 15

On the fourteenth of April, Camilla stared listlessly from dockside at the mighty ship *Hawkshead*, a vessel of the Peninsular and Orient Line.

She could not think, nor did she wish to remember. She looked at the thick blue waters of the English Channel, and willed herself to be uncaring, like a stolid animal. She would be like those cattle, pigs, and sheep transported with them to be slaughtered for their dinners at sea.

Beside her stood a bright-faced emigrant who was going out to meet her husband in Victoria. The woman refused to stop talking, but Cammy found her a good distraction.

"Everyone's rich in Victoria. Mutton's not four pence the pound. Why, they eat a hot meal two times a day, and the sheep! There's two dozen sheep in that land for every man, woman, and child."

Camilla nodded, pretending she knew nothing of the colony where she'd been born. It was easier to let the woman explain everything to her.

"Birds like you can't imagine, my son tells me, and all those gum trees, and hot weather over the century mark. This is autumn down there, not spring, and at Christmas, instead of burnin' a Yule log, you need cold compresses on your head!

"All the animals hop and skip, and black men eat you up!" She ran out of breath, grinning, so delighted to be gone from her shack in Harwich. "There, you're never warm, and you see red meat not once a fortnight!"

"The change will be lovely for you," Camilla said, playing the role of listener. She wasn't as good at this part as she'd been in the role of heartless slut.

"They've palms and parrots and fern trees ten feet tall."

"Imagine!" Cammy kept turning around to look behind her. If only a tall, eager, handsome young man would come rushing toward the wharf. She would run to him and explain everything.

"They've got huge birds walking about," the woman continued, "laying eggs the size of your head. And do you know, bears hang in the trees!"

"Will you please excuse me?" said a deep voice behind Cammy. She knew without looking it was her father, come to fetch her away from the steerage passengers with whom she stood. Undoubtedly, he didn't think they were fit company. Thank heavens Letty and her parents were here! It had long been her hope to sail back to Victoria with Letty and the Shraders, wrapped in their warm love. But, of course, that was before, when she'd thought Kit to be in Victoria or Fiji.

That was before she knew such delights of body and soul, before she'd fallen even more desperately in love with that dear, fine man. Kit was all perfect things, until he failed to see that her dalliance with another man was only a charade.

Of course, she had wanted Kit to believe her fickle and vile. Believing a lie, he was saved. It seemed impossible that he would believe it, but he had. Did this prove he'd doubted her all along?

She'd never know that. And now, ironically, she might be pregnant with his child.

Letty and her parents were not her only acquaintances on the voyage. The Van Beeks were sailing as well, and her father was, too.

"Father?" She found it difficult to call him by that name anymore. If only she were the daughter of someone else, an adopted child, perhaps, of a poor but merciful soul. Any man would be more merciful than Edgar Cochran—any man in the world.

Her thoughts flew back to Kit again, in spite of the agony it caused her to think of the dreadful scene. She could still see his wretchedly miserable face as he violently tore the man away from her. She'd been holding him down, pressing her body hard against him, to keep the cold pistol between her breasts. Then Kit hit him, and the man fell to the floor, his hand no longer moving like some horrid, huge crab across her back, but now at his shirtfront, which was buttoned over the pistol holster. She'd fallen upon him then, lain upon the man and his gun, gripping the man's arms to his sides, screaming at Kit to go. Ah, how effective an act to destroy Kit's love!

She could still hear Kit's boots rattling down the stairs while she lay weeping on the Scotsman's chest.

Her father, emerging from the closet, had pulled her to her feet, praising her for an excellent performance.

"Now I shall no longer have to watch the doors and windows for that wretch to reappear and steal you," he said, as the Scotsman rose and handed him the pistol. Her father broke it open under her nose. It was empty.

"I would not have a dead man to answer for," he explained calmly, putting his coat around her, and leading her, barefoot and half out of her mind, back to her own room. The one she had shared with Kit for seventeen blissful days! Cochran then commanded her to clothe herself, and when he closed the door behind him, she could hear him haggling with the Scotsman over the amount of payment due for such service. He came back in, walked to the chiffonier, and picked up a thick pile of bank notes lying there. The money Kit had left her now belonged to her father. He pocketed most of it, and went outside again. The Scotsman thanked him, and she heard him leave.

Camilla had put on a gown, and lay on the bed while the man who called himself her father silently packed the cases that Kit had bought for her. He handled the gowns Kit had chosen to suit her coloring and shape. Then he lifted her up and hefted her bags.

She'd stood staring into the water basin, where several blue-purple crocuses were floating. How lovely they were! She knew, of course, that Kit had brought them to her as a gift. At least she knew how much he'd loved her.

One crocus lay crushed and dead in the center of the room. She understood Kit's message at once. It cut her to the quick. She had only a minute to pen him a secret message of explanation. Perhaps she could catch him at the train station and deliver it into his hand. "Father was there. I pretended, only to save you from prison. The man had a gun." He would read that, and everything would be right again.

She folded the paper inside her glove. As they left the hotel, Edgar Cochran showed her the policemen who were still watching, and in her presence, he told them that Kit was not to be found.

Kit was safe. Father had kept his word. How honorable, thought Cammy, bitterly.

She walked stiffly beside her father, her eyes still wet, her breasts moving against the moist, soft petals of the surviving crocuses that she'd quickly stuffed into her bodice. Once out of view of the policemen, she wept so passionately that she could not see or walk steadily.

For once, Edgar Cochran had the grace to say nothing. They traveled by train south to the port, bypassing Salisbury. She was permitted a farewell note to Bernard and Beatrice, but she was forced to write it in her father's presence and hand it to him, so she could say little.

She pressed one of the crocuses between tissue papers in her prayerbook at the marriage ceremony page. The dried flower would forever be a reminder of her wasted love, of the man who had once been everything to her. Love was not a garden of delights; but a rocky field of thorns.

As the *Hawkshead* set sail, she dreaded the terrible seasickness of her voyage out, but Letty had come prepared with a potion from a London physician. Though it made Camilla feel sleepy and even sadder, it proved an excellent preventive.

She spared Letty the sorrow of her dreadful story. Let her friends dwell in happy ignorance, thinking she was sailing back to her lover and not away from him. She discovered that Hans and his father knew nothing of what had occurred in Scotland. Edgar Cochran had informed them that she'd been visiting friends there. So her sorrow was all her own.

She walked the heaving decks and leaned over the rail at the stern, watching the wake of the ship stretching white far behind them. Above the roiled water seabirds were poised, watching for something edible to be cast overboard. Camilla admired them. They hung in the wind, dove, and rose energetically into the air again to poise, hovering. When the birds disappeared, flying back toward England, she felt bereft. Cammy was at a loss for what to do. And yet, there had to be some answer, some way out of her situation.

She hastened to the stairs leading her toward the first-class quarters. Under the poop deck were two rows of staterooms lining the corridors. Between lay the long saloon with its fluted pillars and carved pilasters, an attractive place to dine, write, converse, and while away the weeks of voyaging. The spacious stateroom she shared with Letty had clever beds that pulled out of the wall, with brass fittings on the mahogany paneling. A comfortable sofa padded with leather, a cabinet for the wash bowl, and a basket chair and rocker made up the furniture. Wall racks were hung to hold small items. There was one large porthole set low enough so that Cammy could peer through it while seated. Beneath the seat was their chest of drawers with stops to fasten the drawers shut. They had been informed by a steward upon boarding the ship that a large bathroom with hot and cold water was located on their deck; and she might summon him by tugging on a bellpull in the stateroom, just as she would in a house on shore.

As soon as they were out of the English Channel, she began her lessons in the Shraders' sign system. They were very enthusiastic about her idea for a school in Victoria for children who could not hear. If Papa would allow it, she'd start work at once, as soon as they'd docked. She'd go mad, otherwise.

She needed a goal, something outside her own self. The traditional goal for a young woman was matrimony, and the requirements for that were making oneself as pretty as possible, learning piano playing, stitchery, and house management. If one seemed demure and pure and pretty, the goal would be achieved.

She was pretty, but no longer pure, and too sore at heart from all the blows she had taken to act demure. Therefore, she needed a life's work. Father could not live forever, commanding her to cater to his wishes at Blue Downs.

For young ladies of Camilla's station on board ship, there was dinner at the captain's table, musical entertainments in a modish music room, and dancing in the evenings. Nothing was lacking. The ship was just like an excellent hotel, with its potted palms, curved staircases, and Persian carpets. Cammy was expected to dress for dinner and wear jewels. A hairdresser was aboard, and a physician, and chefs to create eight-course dinners.

Below decks, in steerage, hordes of new settlers bound for the colonies did not live nearly so well. They shared tiny cubicles made of stacked bunks, and did their own cooking and washing in the areas where they also slept. Cammy pitied them at first when she heard of their conditions, but the cheerful shouts and songs that wafted up to the levels reserved for the wealthy reassured her.

"Camilla, we are just astonished at your skill!" Letty shook her gray head in delight.

Cammy sat in the Shraders' stateroom, in second class, bracing her feet against the tilting floor as she watched her own hands mimicking Katherine Shrader's.

"I really enjoy learning," she said with a smile. "If I'd had this to occupy me, I'd have suffered less during the voyage to England with Letty."

"And this trip is so different from the other," her dear companion noted. "Back then, you were sailing away from your lad, as I told me mum and dad. Now you're returnin' to him. Both of you will be the better for the separation, mark my words!"

Cammy tried to smile, but it seemed more like a grimace of pain. There was little which gave her enjoyment these days. But oddly enough, she had gained her father's approval in one respect. He liked to see her practicing the sign system.

"If you are sober and obedient, Camilla," he told her one day, "I shall ask Rina to depart, and make you sole mistress of Blue Downs. You shall concern yourself with the welfare of the women and children of the environs as your mother never did. You shall live quietly and soberly and do good deeds. Of course, no man would court you after this abominable escapade. I would send you to a convent, but the Church would probably not accept you, either." He sighed. "You must find good deeds to occupy you. All your mother ever wanted was to be smiled at and to amuse herself. But you will be different."

Camilla did not argue. The description of Mama angered her until she had the leisure to reminisce, and then she saw a sliver of truth in his words. When had Mama, for all her love of company and generosity to her guests and her children, ever bothered her head about abandoned wives living in the small bark houses along the roads? There were hungry children there, too. If Cammy had Father's wealth to spend on the poor, then that would keep her mind off Kit.

She was lying to herself, of course. Nothing on earth would prevent her from thinking of Kit all day and dreaming of him at night.

She forced her mind back to little colonial children who were deaf. They'd have no way to understand their teachers or their playmates. They'd lose the use of their voices and never learn to read and write. "We could save them," she said to the Shraders, and for an instant, she felt a surge of joy. "Just one or two. Maybe three or four if we work hard." Then she extended her hands to the Shraders and added, "Father owns houses all over Blue Downs, and you have no place to lay your heads in Victoria, so perhaps—"

But she could not do this if her belly were swelling with a child of her own. The scandal would rock the parish, which was still gossiping about Edgar Cochran's wife having run off. Now his youngest child had again disgraced the family name.

She shook her head. The best she could do for herself was to work on the sign system and try to avoid Hans Van Beek, his father, and her own.

Chapter 16

Eventually, her coldness toward Hans lessened. After all, he was totally ignorant of the suffering that his persistence had caused. The young Dutchman followed Camilla over the windy decks, sorrowfully polite and eager for attention. The only other man with whom she spoke was Mr. Shrader, and luckily, those were silent and private conversations.

In the saloon and other places where the stylish gathered for amusement during the long weeks afloat, men often sat beside her, cleared their throats, and smiled hopefully. Shooting out their cuffs, they let her glimpse the gold links, and murmured of the great wealth awaiting them in the Australian colonies. At least Hans, for all his passionate interest, did not boast about his wealth.

"My father wishes to see many grandsons with his name," he confided to her one afternoon as they sat in the lee of one of the lifeboats, wrapped in their cloaks. She had warned Hans that as long as he acted like a brother, she would not run from him. But now she dearly wished to avoid becoming his confidante.

"I go home to Java, and never again will I see your face, Camilla," he grieved.

"You're a fine gentleman," she said, trying to soothe him.

"You are strikingly handsome, and well spoken in two languages. I'm sure you will prosper."

"But what ladies can I find? In Java there are none. In the Netherlands there are too many. They push upon me, they want my father's money, but you—"

"I'm sailing to Victoria," she promptly cut him off.

"I am sorry. I apologize. I must not speak truth."

She gazed into the crystal green and blue water throwing up spray along the ship's hull, as white spray danced in the air. She had no idea what to say to this poor, sad boy.

"Strange to feel the cold air," Hans went on mournfully. "In my country, there is no difference. In Java, spring, summer, autumn, winter—all are hot." Then, quickly, he added, "But it is beautiful, so fertile and green. Your land, they say, goes brown and dry, and catches fire, but in my land come rains, and there are beautiful flowers . . ."

Cammy understood why he wished to paint her a lovely picture of Java. If she married Hans, she would be a rich, beloved wife with battalions of gentle Asian servants and a dozen children.

To Cammy's mind, even Blue Downs with Father was preferable, at least for the four remaining years until she turned twenty-one.

They passed the Suez, crossing the hot Red Sea. She had bought sari clothes in an Indian bazaar, and she and Letty and the Shraders filled their staterooms with the scent of rare woods and spices. Hans accompanied her ashore when she did not slip away from him. The women in India were dressed far more lightly and colorfully than in the Arab ports, where only dark eyes were visible amid mounds of shroudlike wrappings. Camilla felt alien in her tight-laced corset and the heavy skirts that impeded her progress.

One afternoon, a violent storm broke. The sky went gray, then purple, then sooty black. Everyone headed for their staterooms or cubicles to find a safe corner and hold on. The rise and fall of the enormous ship on huge swells was a hideous experience. The storm continued for hours, causing the floor to slant this way and then that way under one's feet.

Camilla's stomach knotted, and she felt her skin become damp with fright. They were surely about to capsize. Their floating hotel was flung from side to side, canted further over each time, so one moment she could look through the porthole into the dark sea, and the next moment the horizon would sweep by and the porthole was pointed toward the thunderous sky.

She lay in her railed bed with all her clothes on to brace herself as instructed for storms, but she was too small to reach from head to foot. The fact that she was forced to suffer alone made it worse. Letty had run off to be with her parents in second class, and Father's stateroom was on the other side of the ship. He seldom stepped outside its door, and she never wished to go in.

In less than an hour by her fob watch, the door to her stateroom burst open, and Hans swept in. He was promptly thrown against the far wall, and the next roll of the ship projected him into her bed, where he immediately grasped Camilla to his chest.

"Oh, Hans! Hans!" she cried in gratitude. "I'm terrified!"

"My Cammy, pretend it is a game," he laughed. "I will keep you safe!"

Oddly enough, even though there was nothing he could do to prevent their ultimate destruction, she'd never heard him more full of confidence. Her own had totally fled.

Of course, he had traveled more extensively than she and was accustomed to such storms. He vowed that he'd felt much worse. She gripped him around the neck, crying, "We shall die. The ship will list too far!" How could the helmsman stand at the wheel? she wondered. What of the tall sails? Were they furled and lashed down? Waves blasted the porthole with spray, then blacked it with seawater.

Hans lay down on his side and put his arms around her. He braced his boots against the foot of the bedstead, encouraging her to bury her head against his chest.

Repeatedly, he assured her that this was nothing. He knew of other storms and other ships that had pitched far more violently than this one was now doing. Masts had splintered and water had poured into the passengers' quarters. She wept in terror at hearing this.

"My father said you would be frightened," Hans told her. "Your father, though, he does not care. He said you are with Mrs. Finch," he added indignantly, holding her tight.

Cammy sighed. Hans was her friend, and if she died, she'd never see Kit again.

That realization opened the floodgates. Left alive, she could try to reach Kit and explain. Dead, she would go wherever God might send her, leaving no one on earth to tell Kit she was sorry . . . that she loved him and had never betrayed him.

"Don't cry so much," Hans said so tenderly that she held him even closer. He had to speak loudly now, for the storm was creating a racket around them.

They lay packed into the bunk for an hour, touching chest to chest and cheek to cheek. After a while, Cammy realized that Hans had placed his hand upon her hip, and his mouth was moving against her temple.

Fear of the storm and gratitude for his comforting left her limp and unresisting, though she loosened her grasp on his neck and brought her arms down to try to shield herself from his further advances.

"I kiss you now, Camilla," Hans said as soon as she moved. His lips gently touched her brow. Then he tipped her chin up and kissed her lips quickly but firmly.

She'd been kissed by only one man, and had vowed that he would be the only one. This was exceedingly distressing.

"Hans, you mustn't," Cammy protested, acutely aware of the pitching ship as it rolled her half onto his body, then sent his body half onto hers. She grasped his hand and moved it away.

"Hans, don't touch me so."

"I wish to be your lover," he said gently. "If you will not marry me. Let me love you, Camilla. I will learn to be good to you."

"I know you would be kind, but I don't wish—"

Again his seeking lips covered hers.

The snug embrace, the warmth of his body, and his yearning tone could never convince her. Cammy groaned. "Oh, please leave me!"

He hesitantly slid his fingers into the loose sleeve of her gown so that he could caress her arm. To respond, to feel the familiar shiverings that Kit had aroused in her was betrayal. But how could she really betray him any longer? Kit was gone, as good as dead to her.

"Let me touch you, lovely, beauteous . . ."

Where did he find such charming words and smiles? He seemed unmindful of the plunging ship that pitched from stem to stern. She could bear this motion better then the previous one, for he did not roll upon her now. He only prevented her from slipping up and down the bed. She gripped the lapels of his coat, and put her head against his collar to remove her lips from the vicinity of his.

As she moved abruptly, the top buttons of her bodice slid out of their buttonholes, and Hans began to toy with the exposed lace.

He told her how tiny and soft and dear she was, and how he felt. "I am all in a fever, Camilla. I am full of wonder!"

"You must leave me," she said, pushing at him.

But he ignored her. She was glad that she was wearing so many petticoats and that her skirts were heavy and gored. The layered, pleated costume swaddled her and made it impossible for him to prove his manhood any further. No matter how much gratitude she felt for his presence this afternoon, she could allow him no further liberties.

"Leave me, *please!*" she cried, after a kiss in which he held her head and parted her lips. His efforts were growing more inspired. He eased himself half over her, intermeshing the fingers of both their hands, and pinning her hands beside her head. As he bent his platinum head against her chin, she felt his rapid breathing in the hollow between her breasts, and then his lips sought her throat.

"Oh, Hans!" If only someone would come! But her cries would never be heard over the roaring wind and water.

"I will never hurt you. I will make you my wife."

"I can't. Oh, I can't!"

But she knew that Hans and his father could regain her father's permission if they so chose.

"No!" she cried, struggling harder. "You've taken advantage of my fear, and that's unkind. You should find another lady, one who cares for you."

"Don't struggle," he cautioned her. She knew now how very strong he was. "That drives me madly. Girls have kissed me, but not one ever struggled away. This makes me want to catch and hold you. Oh, Cammy, you are so sweet! You smell of sunlight and flowers."

Their grappling continued in the small bed. Hans' mouth consumed hers. His tongue felt invasive and unwelcome, but she could not scream even if she dared to.

What if the stateroom door flew open and her father entered? She'd be forced to marry Hans, as certainly as she'd been prevented from wedding Kit. That could not happen! She did not want Hans. They did not think and speak and dream alike, and catch fire at the same instant, as she and Kit used to.

Hans would soon be under her skirts, for he had the strength to force this to happen. She had to do something to prevent it.

"Do not ravish me!" she begged, a sob catching in her throat.

To her great relief, he drew back, flushed, shaking his head incredulously. He was still like a naive little boy.

"You think I would—? Oh, Cammy, I would never harm a hair of your body. But your heart goes so fast, close by my lips."

She straightened the front of her gown, and he rolled over on his side, releasing her.

"I will marry you, my beauteous darling. Oh, I love you so! Forgive me for my forwardness. I shall not act so with you again till we are wed."

She felt bruised, filled with regretful anxiety that was close to fear. She looked into Hans' desperate face and pitied him. He'd never before been overcome with passion, nor had he ever kissed a young lady's form and face. Hastily she did up her buttons.

Hans sat upon the bed and stroked her arm, kissed her hand, pressing her palm against his lips, his eyes closed in rapture. The storm was abating outside, but in Cammy's heart, it was yet growing.

Chapter 17

They had been steaming for several days in sight of land, the islands of the archipelago north of Sumatra and Java. As far as she could see, there was green wet jungle over white beaches. Camilla would not weep to see the last of Herr Van Beek, although he remained pleasant and attentive. Evidently, he had no knowledge of his son's behavior in her stateroom during the storm.

Docking at Batavia, the passengers were given the day and night to rest in port, and they poured down the gangway into the equatorial heat. They sweltered in their corsets, waistcoats, neckcloths, and crinolines. The natives here wore very little, the men bare-chested and the women lightly gowned. Camilla envied them their freedom of motion. To her way of thinking, their smooth golden limbs looked no more naked than did the legs of finely turned oak tables.

Hans was hollow-cheeked and vacant-eyed, the perfect model of a spurned swain, as they left the ship. The *Hawkshead* was scheduled to take on supplies, lose and gain passengers, and sail the next morning, so Herr Van Beek issued an invitation. Would they travel to his plantation for dinner so that they could enjoy a night in beds that did not pitch and sway?

Edgar Cochran accepted immediately. When Camilla looked upset about these arrangements, he sent her a look that commanded her not to object.

"I shall probably fall ill from the lack of motion," he said, surprising her with his levity. She could not recall when she had last heard him jest.

Letty was not permitted to go with her. Edgar Cochran handed the woman a gift of money and told her to spend it in the market at Batavia. At the same time, he told Cammy to dress very nicely and be ready to go ashore at three.

She chose her watered silk gown in blue and gold, with tucks all the way up the front. It was the coolest costume she owned, but that was small comfort in this torrid climate. She squinted at the glittering sky and hoped for a rainstorm to turn the heavy air into cool silver torrents.

"This shall be a sad parting," said her father on their way up the winding road to the Van Beeks' coffee plantation. They rode in an open carriage behind a Javanese driver facing their host and his son on the opposite side. Camilla mused upon another father and another son on another island, but she dared not mention them to her father.

They drove through endless rows of coffee trees. Camilla fanned herself with a palm-leaf fan, gazing at the brilliant sky, the simmering clay road, and the workers in broad-brimmed hats who bowed toward the carriage as it squeaked past. Workers farther off, who were trimming the small trees, stood, wiped their brows, and watched with great curiosity the white people ride by.

Hans' stiff white collar did not wilt, nor did moisture appear upon his brow. He was used to the heat. Edgar Cochran was not, however, and he was forced to wipe his bald head repeatedly with a handkerchief. Camilla wished she didn't have to wear white gloves and silk stockings. Victoria was never like this.

The Van Beeks' attractive house was constructed for maximum coolness. It stood well above the ground so that air could pass beneath it, and was flanked on each side by a deep veranda supported by white cast-iron work. The rooms had twelve-foot ceilings, Venetian blinds on every window, rush matting, and light-colored walls and furniture. Camilla was very impressed with the unusual decor, but she was surprised that the lady of the house did not come to greet them. Hans' mother had died years ago, and Mr. Van Beek had taken a Javanese wife.

"My wife, I learn, is in the south of the island," said Herr Van Beek, when Camilla asked politely about Mrs. Van Beek. "She is visiting our daughters there."

Upstairs in her bedchamber under the long, shady over-hang of roof, Camilla disrobed and bathed in tepid water, dreaming of a Fijian lagoon and a blue-eyed man with brown hair curling 'round his ears and temples, standing in the green shadows under mangrove branches. He would lie beside her in the shallows, naked, caressing her. She could not prevent the tears from coming then. Biting her lip, she spoke to herself sternly, and rose out of the water, stretching her arms above her head. Her body was beaded with droplets, just like the tears that would not cease. Now, Camilla, she told herself, you have only one evening to be polite to Hans and tolerate his father, and then back to Blue Downs. Back to her prison home.

She had been on the sea for so many weeks that the earth rolled beneath her like a ship. She wished the floor did not slant, since she was obliged to walk with her feet widely spaced. When she leaned forward to lift out her fresh gown for the dinner party, the room did acrobatics, and she had to hug the bedpost for support. So much for sailors' sea legs and the promised calm night upon firm ground!

That evening they ate a curried dinner. Everything was curried, from the beef to the rice and jellied fruit, but lightly so. She could bear the unusual flavors, but still, perspiration sprang out on her back and her lip, and she drank quantities of tea. Throughout the whole meal, Hans kept his wistful eyes upon her. She knew he pictured her as mistress of this house, or of one much like it. The voices of their parents droned on and on softly as they sat close together at the far end of the table. She wished to be kind to Hans tonight and to say farewell gracefully.

The humming of mosquitoes outside the clever netting tent that softly enfolded the area around the table began to lull her, as did the smell of the burning incense. Her head nodded. When her father noticed this, he suggested they end their desultory conversation and go up to their rooms. By candlelight they made the ascent. Father went first, Camilla next, and Hans followed after, carrying a hooded candle. He caught at her hand and pressed it to his lips.

"Will you not reconsider?" he pleaded, standing two steps below her on the spiral stairs that hung in midair over the polished hardwood floor. "Can you not relent? Can we not be wed? I promise I shall love you as you deserve."

Camilla had finished the leisurely repast with fruited spirits, which made her tongue perhaps looser than it might have been. She swayed on the winding stair, and the room seemed to rock beneath her. At this point, confession would be wise, she thought. How could she let the poor lad break his heart over someone who was not what he believed her to be? She was not the pristine, untouched virgin of his dreams.

She heard her father's door open and then close on the upper floor. In the dimness of the staircase, between the upper and lower floors of the cavernous house, she paused, and Hans moved nearer.

It was near midnight, and the temperature was dropping at last. Her lace sleeve, transparent in the candlelight, was so close to the flame that she feared if he moved closer, she would ignite and burn up like a blue moth in a puff of smoke. But the time was right to speak.

"Hans," she began, swaying and clinging, with one hand, to the slender bannister behind her, "I must confide in you. You wouldn't seek me for a wife if you understood, because I'm not as I seem. But I do pity you and grieve that you love me, so I wish to tell you the truth."

"What is that, Camilla?" he asked earnestly.

"That I love another man, have always loved him, and I always will. What you do not suspect is that . . . I have lain with him and he is truly my husband. If I never see him again, I shall live as his faithful widow. Now," she said, wincing to see how Hans' boyish face changed when she spoke, and grew sober, "now, you will not want me. You will find an untouched young bride to make you happy."

"You are married, then?"

"Not in the eyes of the law."

He looked at her dazedly. The house was silent but for his sharp intake of breath.

"You . . . are not pure?"

"In my heart I am. I have loved one man only. We would have been wed half a year ago, but Father prevented it."

"Where is this man?"

She sighed and shook her head. "I do not know. I hope and

pray I shall find him again. Things are—we are prevented
from seeing each other by terrible circumstances."

"What means that? He loves you?"

"I . . . I—" she dropped her gaze. "He shall love me again
if he understands my situation."

It was good to say the truth for once. She'd never confessed
a word of this to Letty or to the Shraders or to Mama, not by
word or sign or letter. By being honest, though, she could
ease Hans' pain and hers as well. He above all others would
know her heart, though he might come to despise her.

"How did this happen, Camilla?"

"He lives in the Fiji Isles, but he and his father used to visit
us in Victoria. One night over a year ago, I went to his room.
He did not impose himself upon me. My own folly is to
blame. Did my father not hint to you . . . about my condition?"

"No. Never."

"My father hates the fact that the episode occurred under
his very roof. Else, we would be married by now. I'm only
seventeen, though, and cannot be wed without parental
permission."

She'd had her birthday quietly on board the ship. She had
donned the pretty necklace Letty gave her and wept at the
toast proposed by Mr. Shrader with sweet port wine. Four
more birthdays. It seemed an eternity.

"Now, Hans, you see why you must not regret our parting." She put a hand upon his sleeve. She could feel the heat
of his arm through the linen fabric of his short Asian jacket.
She withdrew her hand and waited for a reaction, but still he
was silent. She should leave it at that, she thought, and run up
the last spiral of the stairs to her chamber. But there was one
last thing she needed to say.

"I admire you as a good friend, Hans," she whispered, and
she meant it.

"Now, Camilla, you go upstairs and sleep well," he said, in
a deep voice that she'd never before heard him use. Though
his eyes shone with hurt and pride, he'd accepted his loss.

She hastened up the remainder of the staircase as lightly as
a fluttering moth. Her heart was light as well, and she knew
that now she would be able to go on with her life.

Chapter 18

After the ship pulled out of Batavia, Camilla kept to the decks. She walked for hours each day, gazing at the changing waters and the shorelines of the tropics, as they made their way through the last weeks of their voyage around the continent to Victoria.

Letty never asked about Cammy's visit at the Van Beeks' plantation. She merely tucked Camilla in her bed with sassafras tea, and clucked over her, saying, "Java's no place for Christian English people. He was a handsome boy, so tall and fine, but the one you love is back in the colony of Victoria, isn't he? How romantic your life is, Camilla! First it's the boy you loved before leaving Melbourne, and now it's a Dutchman who must've wanted to keep you with him in Java. Ah, but with that face of yours, and the curls, and your dear little figure—who'd be surprised?"

When bad weather or darkness necessitated their staying indoors, Cammy worked diligently to absorb every hand sign that the Shraders could teach her. Until she was free of her father, she would occupy her mind and her fingers with something useful. With four fingertips touching and pointing forward she created a ship, which she sailed over imaginary waves, and Mrs. Shrader smiled at her progress. Then

Cammy's right hand arched gently to the right and dropped down to make the word "home," and then, touching thumb and fingertip together, she rocked her hand in the sign for "soon." Soon, their ship would bring them to her home and Letty's, and now the Shraders' as well.

Before they touched port at Adelaide, she approached her father on one of his rare outings from his cabin.

"After the indignities of being dragged home from Scotland, after that unspeakable thing you did to Kit . . . and to me," she said to her father, "I deserve to visit my mother. Since we are near her home, I insist upon seeing her," she added forcefully.

"We will not be in port long enough, daughter."

"Certainly we shall. I would need only two hours to go and return. You know there'll be enough ship's business to keep us there for several times that long."

He shrugged. "Well, I suppose an hour or so can do no harm. But I have nothing to say to her. Give her no message from me."

Cammy expected no more than that, but she was secretly surprised and delighted that her father had allowed her out of his sight.

Why could she not remain in pretty Adelaide with all its elegantly laid out squares and botanical gardens? she thought, as soon as she was off the ship. Mama meant far more to her than her father.

Hiring a buggy, she directed the driver to the address that was on Mama's last letter. There had been no way she could have written or telegraphed in advance of her coming, so she would have to descend upon Mama and Stephen without warning.

The small detached dwelling with "Plaskett" written on the gate was set below the footpath. A fern tree shaded the door. Camilla paused for a moment and then knocked.

Minnie Cochran opened the door. Her gray curls peeked out from under her cap. Her spectacles were sliding down her nose, but to Cammy, she was absolutely beautiful.

When Minnie Cochran saw her daughter standing there, she shrieked. Tears sprang into her clear blue eyes, and embracing her daughter, she called over her shoulder, "Stephen! Stephen, come! It's Cammy! My Cammy is here!"

Once inside, Cammy looked at the low ceilings and the

nondescript furnishings, and saw the house the way her mother must have seen it—a love nest better than any palace.

Pale, loose-jointed Stephen in his leather carpenter's apron, his sleeves rolled up and his hair tangled, came into the house from the shop, and taking Cammy's hand, joined Minnie in welcoming her.

"And how did you like England?" Stephen asked, as Cammy detected a trace of homesickness in his voice.

But Minnie did not give her time to answer. "Bernard! How is my dear Bernard, Cammy?" she demanded. "Did you like his wife? Is there a little baby yet?"

Cammy told them all she knew, glad that she hadn't mentioned Kit before she sailed to England. This was no time to tell about Scotland and the near marriage. Mother was so excited, she seemed like a new bride rather than a woman waiting for her divorce. She looked younger now than she had at Blue Downs, like a girl on her honeymoon. Even Stephen seemed younger than Cammy remembered him on his visit to their home. His long, horsy face was permanently creased in a grin.

Stephen had done well in moving from England to Australia, because he possessed skills that were badly needed in the colonies. Though he had been employed as a clerk in Leeds, Stephen Plaskett knew how to fashion furniture from the years when he was apprentice in his father's shop. When Mama wrote Cammy, she often spoke of the fresh smell of wood in their house, and the wood curls and sawdust underfoot in his shop adjoining the kitchen. Now, seeing them together, Cammy understood the reason for her mother's happiness. This man appreciated her mother, as Edgar Cochran never had. Cammy did not speak of her father except to say that he was on the ship, waiting for her.

"I wish I could remain with you, Mama," she said mournfully. But looking at the tiny house with no place for a third person to sleep, she knew that her suggestion was impossible. In summer she might sleep under a tree in the back garden, but now winter was coming.

"You seem so much older, my precious angel," her mother told her, patting Cammy's hair and examining her costume with astonished eyes. "When I last saw you, you were a mere child. Now, although you're no taller, you seem at least twenty. Even your voice is different. You no longer pipe like a little bird. How wonderful what travel will do! It *is* very broadening."

They asked more about Bernard, and Cammy could not tell them that Papa had thrown Bernard out of his fine house. Was the print shop lost as well? Cammy wondered, trying to keep up a cheerful face for her mother's sake.

"You'll soon be safely wed, looking as pretty as you do!" her mother cried, holding Cammy at arm's length and leaning back to admire her. "You must already be besieged with suitors, are you not? Take care, darling. Choose carefully. From my example, you'll know not to wed a man much older, hmm?"

"I understand, Mama," Camilla said, fidgeting with her hands. She so longed to tell her mother everything, but she didn't wish to spoil her happiness.

"Nor one cross and sour," her mother went on. "I took the first proposal made to me, I was such a silly ninny. Charlotte has written me that she is so very happy in her marriage. It's a pity you cannot see her. We'll try to make her visit here. Edgar isn't as harsh to his daughters as he is to his sons, but I'm sure she has no wish to visit Blue Downs ever again."

Cammy hid a sigh, but it was difficult to keep up her brave front. Stephen sensed something and smiled faintly at her in sympathy.

"Now Jock, I think, is buying more property adjoining his place. We must all go some day to Richard in New Zealand," her mother continued. "It has mountains as sheer as the Alps. As for Michael, his studies are going well, and Edgar sends him money, although not nearly enough. On the other hand, a boy of nineteen might take on wild ways if he had lots of money to spare. I don't expect you'll see Michael at Blue Downs for many a day. There is no love lost between Michael and Edgar." She coughed and looked away.

"I miss my brothers and sister, Mama."

"I miss them dreadfully, too, my dear. We are so happy here, Stephen and I, except for that. When your father finally divorces me, we can then wed and our relations with the others will be easier." At that moment, the teakettle began to whistle, and Minnie rushed off to answer its call. Cammy and Stephen stood looking at each other.

Her mother returned, laden with tea things on a tray. The ceremony must be properly performed. The hot milk and hot tea mixed, the sugar added, just as always. Just as Cammy remembered her mother doing it years ago.

"Do you still take two full spoons of sugar, as I do, Cammy?"

Her daughter nodded.

"Always eat sugar to make yourself more sweet, I say."

Cammy drank the sweet, milky brew as she looked out the window admiring the carefully tended autumn blossoms in the pocket-size back garden. The cat appeared from Stephen's shop and wound itself around her skirts.

For a few moments, all three of them were silent until Minnie said, "Forgive me if I don't go to the ship, dearest angel. Seeing Edgar would be rather difficult, don't you know?"

Camilla agreed. "Mama—" she began, wishing to have a moment of privacy when she could draw her mother aside. "I'd like to ask you—"

Dear Stephen understood and withdrew, stumbling into his woodshop with comical haste. Camilla froze for several seconds before blurting out the appalling question. "Mama, who is my father?"

"What? Whatever do you mean? Of course—"

Minnie Cochran's color did change markedly. She turned pink, and Cammy wondered if her question had hit home.

"Father is angry at you now, of course. And I make him angry as well. We seem so different, he and I. I have been hoping that, well, perhaps you had adopted me."

"Don't be foolish," Minnie retorted. "Just look at you! You can see Edgar's features, some of them at any rate, in your face!"

"But everyone says that I look like you."

"One cannot tell by faces. Why, I—Cammy, what a preposterous idea!"

"I feared it was, Mama," she said, embracing the woman who was just her size. "But I was really hoping you'd say a kinder man had fathered me. Then maybe I could get away from Blue Downs. You understand? I just had hopes. I would so love to escape him."

Her mother shook her head sadly. "What can I tell you, dearest Cammy? To have patience? I tried for many years, and I suffered for it. I stayed with your father far longer than I should have because I pitied him. He'd had a difficult time of it, you know. Did I ever tell you that he was orphaned at a very early age? And without any family, he was brought up by foster parents who were none too kind to him. He began to believe that all people were untrustworthy, and that life was a hard row to hoe. I tried to be understanding, and to forgive him his many cruelties. Eventually, I found it impossible. I should have left him in the first year of our marriage, but then the children started coming, and then I was tied to an existence . . ." She looked at Cammy, her eyes shining with tears.

"The cruel laws don't permit me to aid you at all, Camilla, you know that. Why, even if a father does horrid things to his family, even if he abandons them, he still has control of all his minor children."

"I ask you, am I accurate in calling Edgar Cochran 'father'?" Cammy persisted, grasping her mother by the arm. "If not, it's improper for me to live with him."

"He'd be your stepfather, nonetheless," Minnie corrected her. "And you cannot escape him until you're twenty-one." Her eyes filled with tears. "I cannot help you, my poor Cammy."

That was the most Cammy was able to learn. She spent many hours afterward, remembering each question and each answer, or *evasion* of an answer. Had she hurt her mother by this suggestion? Did she want to be a child of Edgar Cochran's or an orphan? At least she had a name, and an honest one. But then she began to wonder, had there been a lover before Stephen? It was certainly possible, given the lack of feeling Minnie had for Edgar. Who was that man, if indeed he existed? And why had her mother become so agitated when she asked? It seemed as though her reaction was more than shock at Cammy's accusation.

I cannot condemn my mother, thought Cammy Who am I to think ill of her?

The rest of her visit had been spent in pleasant conversation. Neither of them brought up any unpleasantness. After all, they did not know when they next would meet. Each moment together was precious.

In June, they finally made their way across the harbor of Port Phillip and docked at Sandridge, in sight of Melbourne. Letty assisted her sea-weary parents from the ship, excitedly pointing out all the sights. The Shraders seemed delighted with the modernity and cleanliness of their new land, and exclaimed about one thing or another at every corner they passed, the words fairly flying off their eager fingers.

Mr. Cochran was gracious enough to make space for them all in a hansom cab that took them to the same hotel. As they stepped down, Cammy drew her father aside.

"I should like to see Letty and the Shraders installed in one of your empty houses, Father," she said, trying to ask nicely. She stared at him intently, comparing their hands, their hairlines, and their ears. Were there really any traces of him imprinted upon her? She doubted it.

He took a long time considering her proposal. Just as she thought he was about to refuse, she added, "You said that I must occupy myself with community matters. I can still be a good hostess. Mama said I seemed quite adult now, as a matter of fact. The Shraders want to teach deaf children, Father, and for that they need a house. I could help, for as you see, I am becoming quite adept in their language. I can run after children as they cannot. May I, Father?" She finished in a strong voice.

"It would have to be near Blue Downs. I would not permit you to be out of my house more than an hour or two a day."

"That would certainly suffice," Cammy said calmly, wanting to jump for joy because he was being reasonable. Was he possibly becoming senile? But then, she corrected herself, why shouldn't he be agreeable? He'd stolen her twice from Kit, and now he had no fear that her lover would ever return. Her lover was her enemy now, as far as her father was concerned. Her goals would have to be different, and she was most fortunate to have an occupation that other ladies did not share. She was going to teach the hand language to children who would benefit from it. Ironic, she thought suddenly, that if she had been able to speak with her hands a season ago, and Kit could have understood her, her clever fingers would have saved them. She would have told him silently to feign anger, to go away, to meet her somewhere. Father could not hear a finger's flicker. But that was all in the past. There was nothing she could do about it now.

Things happened much faster than she could have hoped. Aunt Rina, who had been looking after Blue Downs in their absence, was sent away immediately after her first dispute with Edgar. Camilla saw why her father preferred an obedient daughter as mistress of his home rather than a disputative older sister. Rina was a spinster and a scold. Camilla, considered by all their neighbors to be a demure young maiden, comforting a father whose wife deserted him, was a perfect companion. She took instruction from the cook, the housekeeper, and the gardener in becoming mistress of a country estate. The old servants who knew her story had all been sent away and new ones hired from distant places, so she had no allies.

Father evicted a slovenly family from one of his houses in the nearby settlement, and had it fumigated, all in the period of three weeks. Then he himself invited the Shraders and Letty to occupy it.

A new institution for deaf children had just opened in the Praha district of Melbourne, so theirs would not be the first such asylum. The large Praha school, however, was overcrowded with seventy-five children. It would take none under seven years old, and turned away some over seven who seemed particularly troublesome. The Shraders' small shelter for children of tender years would certainly prove a boon. There was a definite need for what they had to offer.

By August, Letty was delighted to have gathered four waifs, one boy and three girls, ranging in age from four to nine. They slept in freshly built miniature beds in Edgar Cochran's renovated cottage, and they kept the Shraders very busy.

Like magic, the children began to imitate the gestures their teachers showed them. They all found signing so much easier than merely guessing at mouthed words. Camilla fell in love with each of the students and found, to her surprise, that she was a rather good teacher. Her father, upon inspection of the school, lifted an eyebrow and went away muttering that this at least was a better place for the unfortunate than the gutters or the coolie camps. Although at first there were incidents of bed-wetting, the Shraders and Cammy worked patiently to transform the children by precept and example into obedient little scholars. Reading and writing lessons would come later. First, the children needed an alternative way of listening—by eye, not ear—and they had to be persuaded to continue speaking, no matter how it sounded, for the benefit of those who were not deaf.

The shelter at first attracted suspicion in the settlement. The neighbors assumed that these odd children might be a danger to their gardens. Would their fruit be stolen, their houses defaced, women passersby offended by such peculiar voices? they demanded to know.

The answer was "no." The children were all perfectly behaved, and two more little boys were added three months later. These grew as gentle and alert as the first four, following their example. Teachers visited from the Victoria School to be sure that the Shraders were well qualified. They went away pleased.

Camilla's days were full and rewarding. She was constantly on her knees in the common room, hugging and consoling children for scratches, buttoning up their clothing. She loved all of them, the ones who had been deaf for a long time and had trouble speaking as well as the victims of high fevers who did not know why their world had suddenly gone silent.

This was not an expensive form of charity for Edgar Cochran, because each child performed useful tasks, ate relatively little, and only one servant was required. The Shraders seemed to grow younger and happier in this warm clime. They were stern disciplinarians, but they were also loving. The children, realizing that their teachers also could not hear, would look at them in awe.

"I could do this all my life," mused Camilla aloud one day, as she watched a group of little ones eating their suppers. "Now I needn't marry to have children of my own. I have these." She made the appropriate signs, asking little Betsy and Mary to bring her their empty plates for the washing up. Then she set them to stitching designs she drew on scraps of cloth, offering advice periodically to these apprentice seamstresses. She kissed each of them and smiled her approval when they were done. "Wonderful girls," her hands and lips said. "I'm very proud of you both."

She felt mature and responsible, although she was just five months past her seventeenth birthday. Oddly enough, she found that she was happier than she'd ever been. Although her heart would forever mourn her lover, she knew now that she was capable and could manage on her own.

The only difficult time for her was spring, the season of their anniversary. When that dreaded day arrived in Victoria, bringing with it blue-purple crocuses, she could not help herself. She opened her prayer book to the marriage ceremony and kissed the pale, pressed blossom lying there, the blossom that once had lain in Kit's hand in Scotland.

She filled vases with crocuses of every color, and set them all around the children's home, but she did not let her father see the blue ones—the ones she carried to her bedchamber.

Chapter 19

She was playing with the children one afternoon, her curls falling in her eyes, the front of her white apron dusty from kneeling upon the floor. The aged wooden floors sloped, which made the sport of rolling balls across a room even more fun.

"Look! The ball came back to me!" they'd sign, faces full of surprised merriment. Then they'd shriek with perfectly normal voices and start the ball in the opposite direction.

Camilla heard the knock at the door, and then heard Letty trot down the freshly scrubbed passageway to answer it. Probably a neighbor bringing a freshly baked loaf of bread to the children, or perhaps Father come to check that she did not outstay her daily three-hour stint. When he had guests, she was obliged to stay home and pour tea and look pleasant. Of course, he seldom had any guests.

She heard a masculine voice ask a question, and in a moment, Letty's boots rattled through the passageway toward her.

"Cammy, you've a caller at the door."

Cammy rose from her knees, and brushed off the gingham apron she wore over her brown poplin skirt.

"I'll tend the kiddies. You go." Letty gave her the strangest look, her face an odd map of warring emotions. If Camilla did not know better, she would have said that Hans Van Beek had come to see her. But he was safely home in Batavia.

The man standing in the doorway was not recognizable with the bright daylight behind him. She could see that the clothes covered a form any man would be proud of, but his face was shadowed as he had not removed his hat.

"Sir?" Cammy said, smoothing down her apron.

He said nothing but stood there quietly. As she narrowed her focus on him, her eyes grew accustomed to the noontime light and she could see his face. She scanned his form from head to foot, and only her fist pressed against her mouth prevented her from screaming aloud. Hoarsely, she whispered, "Kit? Is it you? Is it . . . my Kit?"

Suddenly, Letty appeared at her elbow saying, "Ah, you got to the door, then, Cammy. We've just laid a table for tea. Why don't we ask the gentleman in?"

The contrast of light and dark in the entryway was so severe that she was nearly blinded. At one and the same time, she was fighting tears, hysteria, and resisting rushing into his arms, arms that might very well strike her away. She was too dazed to indicate that she knew the visitor, and grateful for Letty's proposal, as it would give her more time to think.

Camilla trailed after Letty to the small drawing room reserved for guests where no children were admitted, and Kit was right behind her. She didn't turn to look at him for fear that he might vanish. What if the light were playing tricks, and the man was not Kit at all? Why didn't he speak to her? It was true that she herself had been struck dumb after seeing him, so maybe the problem was mutual.

The tea tray was laid, and sandwiches had been set out for a light luncheon. Letty snatched another cup and saucer from the breakfront, explaining that her parents would eat afterwards. The tea began.

Camilla took the precaution of never looking at the man. She busied herself with the milk pitcher and napkins, bending, turning, keeping as busy as she could. But Kit was like a burning tree behind and beside her. She knew where he was by a sort of aura, like heat on the road.

Letty noticed nothing, or at least did not let on so. After a year could Letty recall Cammy's tearful descriptions of her lost love? Had she said Kit's hair was brown, curling at the nape and sideburns? Had she told his height, the width of his shoulders, the exact color of his rich, deeply tanned skin?

Letty sat calmly at the table, and Camilla perched on a high stool as far as possible from Kit. She steadied her cup as Letty poured tea, and kept the edge of it against her lip while it cooled, so she could look into it fixedly, hiding her face.

Kit seemed as uncomfortable as she, for she noticed, when she stole a side glance at him, that he, too, bent forward intently over his cup without raising his eyes.

"And now," began Letty, watching them both with enormous curiosity, "we've not had leisure, sir, to inquire your name or your errand."

"I wished only to see the home," he said in his cultured Cambridge-bred voice with its odd Fiji accent. He did not risk giving his name.

His face was more tan than ever, and he was close-shaven. Every plane of it was imprinted upon her lips and her fingertips. She knew that face so well, and yet she could read nothing in it. For once he wore a mask she could not pierce.

Cammy made a fleeting sign that he would not understand, but Letty picked up the word "shy." Letty smiled and nodded. Then, with one hand out of Kit's view, Cammy rapidly spelled, "My lost love. Say nothing."

The tea party continued, but in silence. Letty looked astounded, her eyes opened wide. At last Kit looked up and focused his attention on Camilla. She sat back, conscious of her poor uniform of poplin and muslin. At least she did not wear a dust cap, as Letty did.

In an attempt to ease the tension, Letty finally launched into an explanation of the children's needs and their daily activities. Everything was so polite, so neatly handled, and Camilla valued the precious moments Letty afforded them. Soon the teapot would be empty and Letty would leave them and Kit would then unleash the full extent of his wrath.

Suddenly, Letty cocked her head, saying she heard a child in distress, and almost overturned the china in her haste to get away.

Kit stood up as the older woman left the room, and Camilla was terrified. All the words she'd been assembling like beads strung together slipped away and scattered. "I . . . I did it to save you," she stammered.

"Did what?" His voice was icy cold.

"Father was hiding in that room. The man was paid and he

had a pistol in case you became violent. That's why I was holding him down."

"I could hardly believe that if the Queen herself said it."

Words now rushed from her as swiftly as she'd ever spoken before in her life. "Kit, when you hit him, he might have shot you. I made you go to save you! Father made me put on an act. There were policemen standing outside! I never saw that man before. Father said I would have to make you hate me or he would have had you arrested for kidnapping. Surely you saw my face! Didn't anything make you suspect? Oh, Kit, those crocuses in the basin that you'd brought to me, they were so lovely they broke my heart!"

"How I wish I could believe you," he said wearily. He looked much older. She noticed lines on his face as he said, "You've had a long time to invent that story, Camilla."

"Come home with me and see your crocus pressed in my prayer book between the pages of the marriage service! Look in the children's room. There are vases full of blue crocuses to remind me."

They stood staring at each other. He did not know what to believe or how to respond. She was distraught. How could she take him home to Blue Downs to Father?

"If you hate me still, why did you come, Kit?"

He did not answer, but kept his eyes on her face, searching for the truth.

"My father followed us to Scotland, Kit," Cammy persisted. "He found me and dragged me into the next room. He planned the performance with that hired man. Why can't you believe me?"

"Then why didn't you write to me?" He was consumed with doubt, wanting desperately to believe her but still suspicious.

"I didn't know where you were. I didn't know where to start explaining everything. The task seemed impossible, although I should have tried."

"I find no other woman desirable after you, Camilla," he said slowly.

"You have enjoyed other women, then?" She tried to keep her voice calm.

"Of course not. How could I?"

"You haven't?"

She devoured him with her eyes. Her hands ached to divest him of his clothes so that she might kiss and hold him. The conflict in his face cut her to her very soul. He'd aged five years since last she'd seen him, but he was more striking as a man than he had been as a boy.

"It's not jealousy," he said despairingly. "I don't call it that. How can I make my feelings clear?"

The sound of the children at play was loud, but the loudest sound in the room was that of her own heart beating. She waited, in a frenzy of suspense, for his next words.

"Camilla—" he said at last. "Cammy, if you loved me, somehow you'd have sent me a signal. A wink of the eye, a mouthed word, a gesture, even in the midst of your 'performance' as you call it."

"If you'd only known the sign system!" she cried in exasperation. "How do you think I felt, with no way to warn you? Had you glanced toward the wardrobe where Father was hiding, or had you spoken a word, you would have been put in jail. I wanted you to think me a slut! I wanted you to leave me, furiously angry, since nothing else was safe for you. Believe me! The police were waiting!"

"I . . . I'm trying to—"

"You don't even inquire if I was left pregnant by you!"

He looked aghast at her slim form.

"No," she muttered. "I didn't conceive a child, Kit."

She could not bear to stand there arguing with the man she adored. Should she hide her adoration or express it? Each instant she was pulled in an opposing direction. If only she dared strike him and then kiss away the pain. But this older, restrained, suffering Kit allowed her only the meager comfort of words.

"Then what is my standing with you, Kit Westcott?" she asked earnestly. "You came here to see me, so please speak your piece."

"I had to be with you again and read your face, Camilla. This Children's Home—" he shrugged. "It is the last place I expected to find you."

"Not what one expects of a loose woman, eh?"

"Please bear with me. At least you *knew* I loved you, but you led me to think you *hated* me!"

"Don't you think that grieves me?" She was shocked. "The only important thing to me, Kit, was that you did not lie rotting in an English prison."

He was silent for a moment. Then he asked, "What of your father? How does he treat you now?"

"He permits me to work here, for he thinks you will never come for me again. I'm not even permitted to go to Melbourne, although I've vowed not to run away. If I do, he'll close this place and throw the children and Letty and her parents into the street."

"I see." There was deep admiration in his face for this woman of such strong principles.

"I'd ask you to go to him to see if I lied, but he'd set the police on you. Then you'd believe me, but it would be too late."

He kept staring at her, and Cammy knew he was willing himself to believe her and trust her again. If only she could persuade him!

"Bernard lost his house over us. Father burns his letters unread. I'm a virtual slave at home. All of us have suffered, Kit. Except you!"

"Except me?" he cried incredulously. "Camilla! I was left believing that the love of my life despised me, that she considered my devotion worthless! I followed you halfway 'round the world. My duties in Fiji are enormous, but my heart's not there. Oh, Camilla, listen to me! Your father would delight to see us now. What an actress he made of you, when only an hour before we had made love."

"Indeed, I have talents . . . undreamed of," she said bleakly.

"Frightening ones," he said, but she could see that he did not blame her for elements of her life over which she had no control. He put out his hands. "Camilla, may we begin again?"

"Do you mean that?" she asked with a sharp intake of breath. "With what you believe of me?"

"Even if I believed the worst, still you are a fascinating, elusive creature. If you speak the truth, then I am mortified and do not deserve to kiss the hem of your garment . . . in penance."

They moved toward each other very slowly, like swimmers treading water. She did not drop her gaze from his face.

"Kit . . . Kit," she said between clenched teeth, not daring to believe that he was reaching out to embrace her.

Then, holding her by the shoulders, bending over her, he kissed her softly, his lips slightly parted, his mouth so warm on hers. The tips of their tongues renewed acquaintance, like small animals hesitantly touching noses before commencing to play.

"Cammy," he groaned, and one arm dropped to loop under her bustle and lift her. She lay against him and clasped her hands around his neck, kissing him on the mouth, the cheek, the brow, the eyelids. What matter who might see them?

"Kit!" she gasped, pulling away briefly. "We must be alone to talk. For just an hour!"

He put her feet on the ground but holding her still pressed against him, he scooped up his wide-brimmed hat from the table. They walked out the door together and down the path to his tethered horse. He vaulted onto the beast's back, and took her hands, swinging her up behind him. Then he drew her arms tightly around his waist.

"Now you shall ride holding *me*," he said with a smile.

So still he remembered that ride half a year ago with Hans. Well, what difference did that make? She had Kit now, and she'd never let him go.

Kit pressed his heels into the horse's flanks and off they flew.

Cammy sat sideways behind him, her skirts blowing back, and her seat very unsure on the broad rump of the horse. She'd never cantered like this, and she held Kit desperately close, her cheek against his back so she could feel his powerful muscles. She could hardly believe that this was happening. She was holding her Kit! He was hers again; because he loved her and could not have left her forever without knowing the truth. She cried a little as she thought of this, and dampened a spot on his coat. Kit put one hand over her linked hands on his waist to make sure her grip did not loosen. His very touch was reassurance.

Where were they bound? she wondered. Not toward Blue Downs, that was certain. When carts and men on foot appeared in the road ahead of them, Kit swerved the horse into a narrow lane among yellow wattle bushes. Masses of tiny golden blossoms brushed her skirt and caught in its folds. Their featherlike foliage surrounded them, tickling her cheeks and stroking her hair. She could not remember when she'd been happier.

Kit's hand pushed her linked hands lower than his waist, so she could learn how amorous he was, and a shiver of delight coursed up and down her back. She loved him. He loved her. All would be right from now on. Father had had his chance and failed to destroy their love. He could do no more damage, because together, they were far stronger than he. They had been joined in a kind of holy matrimony and no man, least of all Edgar Cochran, could put them asunder.

Kit slowed the horse in the endless bouquet of yellow flowers, but he did not speak. It was so quiet in this glen that each could hear the other breathe. Camilla sighed, resting her face against his back, and she cuddled her body closer as Kit used both arms to lift branches aside so that the horse could make his way through the shrubbery. She kept her hands cupped over his manhood, and was pleased at her effect. She was slight and small, but at her mere touch, he squirmed in the saddle and gasped for breath.

"You shall pay for this, dearest," he murmured mischievously. "Be warned."

"Let us bury each other in blossoms," she suggested, delighted at his eagerness.

"There is a clearing somewhere near," he said, and then, as he pulled another branch aside, they saw the smooth grassy space.

The wattle was higher than Kit's head, and no sound except the cries of parrots came to their ears. Half in sun, half in shifting shadows, Kit drew Camilla off the saddle and slid to the ground, looping the horse's reins around a tree limb.

They kissed, then she leaned back to look at him again. She could not look enough, and she sighed as she traced his features with her fingertips. Then she kissed him once more.

His fingers, meeting no resistance, unfastened the neck of her gown. He had his warm hand in her bodice, freeing her breasts as she reclined in his arms, arching her back in pleasure.

This was a dream from which she wished never to awaken. Kit was hers again, and was making sweet love to her! The gentle horse stood patiently a distance away, shifting from leg to leg, cropping the grass under the tall wattle bushes, but Cammy was unaware of anything but the man beside her and the soft ground beneath her.

When Kit wished for more than her bosom to be fondled, he eased her upright again, and lifted one of her knees so she sat facing him astride his thighs. They kissed deeply, holding onto one another for dear life. They both were starved, frantic for release, after half a year without love.

He pushed aside Cammy's long, white apron so that the brown poplin skirt was pleated between them like a Venetian blind. She held Kit 'round the neck, hardly giving him room to take off his coat. In the tickling leaves and flowers, he did not doff his shirt, but helped her to pull her gown down to her elbows and slip off her chemise. In the shelter of his taller, wider physique, she could sit thus disrobed.

"Oh," Kit murmured hoarsely in his throat. "My love, my bride, soon you will truly be my bride!" He freed her from her pantaloons, freed himself from belt buckle and buttons, and hoisted her against him, putting her silk-stockinged legs around him. In a haze of blossoms, Kit forced their eager flesh to meet and meld, as Camilla cried out her pleasure.

He said no words, nor could she speak. Little cries of joy rose half strangled from their throats when they were not hungrily kissing. Camilla locked her arms 'round Kit's neck and rose upon his tensed legs as if posting on a horse, her slipper soles pressing against the calves of his legs. He held himself still, urging her on with little sounds, and she joyfully rode him, prolonging their wild ecstasy.

Wattle blossoms covered her curls, captured by the tangles of their hair, and they fell like golden snowflakes upon their shoulders. The sun filtered through blossoms, kissing the bodies that had become one. Kit's hands cupped her quivering hips and lifted her almost off him so that he could dip his head to her breasts. Then he let her down, plunging deep in her. She churned over him, groaning and sighing.

When the end came, Kit's face contorted and at the same moment she felt herself arising to a summit such as she had never known. As she gained her own sweet joy, she collapsed against him, panting.

Finally, Kit pulled her gently up and leaned her against him, still joined to him. Her legs hung limp upon his and her head lolled back upon his shoulder as he played with her soft breasts, their tips still firm under his touch.

"Shall we mount the horse and ride into town this way?" he teased. "Then every man in sight would want you, Camilla."

She flinched at the hint of bitterness in his voice. If only he could see into her heart and mind and understand her passion for him!

Reluctantly, he parted from her and pulled her bodice up to cover her white breasts. Then he untethered the horse and got astride, pulling her up in front of him. Urging the horse on and clucking to him briskly, he reached forward under her flowing skirts. She moaned with pleasure.

"Shall we ride like this?" he said in her ear. Her eyes were shut in a stupor, and she could not will her arms to move from her sides. Kit urged the horse, which burst out of the wattle, and they rode across an unfenced plain. She was nearly blinded by the sudden brightness of the day, the emerald grass and the golden sun and the blue sky. Triumphantly, Kit rode holding her before him, as if he dared anyone to see the girl he loved, her skirts over their tangled legs. His arm crooked around her waist, holding her safe.

She dreamed herself a Tartar's bride on the steppes of Russia, without a duty in the world but to receive her lover, resting helpless in his powerful arms.

"Husband," she said to him, turning her head to see his flushed face and brilliant eyes. "We must never be parted again."

"I love you," he said, expressing his trust. Spontaneously, she responded, "I love you."

Only then did she realize that her gown and apron were hopelessly rumpled, her pantaloons gone, her stockings had been torn by the branches, and one shoe had fallen off somewhere. She'd never be able to comb all the tiny golden flowers from her hair before she arrived home.

She looked back at the wattle, which made a wall on the crest of a hill behind them. They would never find the path they came by, and she was not even sure of the direction back to Blue Downs. Was her father waiting there for her now? And what about Letty? She had run off from her duties at the home without so much as a by-your-leave!

Well, Letty could be handled, but how would she get back? She'd have to ride through the settlement in this condition. Anyone would think she'd been ravished. Kit had managed to keep his coat, but his hat was lost.

"If you want to ruin me again," she jested, "set me down on the edge of town like this, and let me limp shoeless back to the house."

"I will fetch you fresh clothing," he said. "And shoes, of course. I won't have people seeing you like this. I did not realize how fragile girls' garments can be."

"When there's an amorous lover on a horse," she pointed out.

"And too many prickling shrubs and blossoms." He was pulling flowers from her hair, vainly trying to arrange it neatly. But in a minute or so, he gave up.

"It's no use. I shall leave you here, and ride to Letty for something with which to cover you. I suspect she knows something about us. Am I correct?"

"I told her all about our first sad encounter," Cammy admitted. "But I didn't tell anyone about Scotland. It was too tragic to remember."

They rode on until they came to a place where the grass was high and soft under a stand of white barked gums beside a meandering stream. Kit dismounted and lifted her off the horse. She sat in the grass, arranging her skirts.

"Will you feel safe if I leave you for a while?" He looked concerned.

"I'll be out of sight here," she said, reclining happily in the tall grass, not caring a whit how undignified she looked. She thought this must be like drunkenness, though she'd not had a drop.

"Be careful," she called after him when he had mounted again. "Anyone but Letty could betray us to Father."

Then he was gone, riding off across the sun-dappled grass. Cammy hoped he had chosen the right direction. The sea of golden wattle was huge and had confused them.

Camilla, sighing with contentedness, stretched her limbs and smiled. She felt warm all over, head to toe, inside and out, like a cat basking in the sun.

Discarding any possible fear for the future, she lay back again. As smoothly as a platypus into a pond, she slid into sleep which closed over her gently.

Chapter 20

When Camilla awoke, she quickly became aware of a familiar sound, grasses against fabric or leather. Someone was coming, probably Kit, returning with her clothing. She rolled over and opened one eye. Sweet Kit come back to kiss her from her slumber? How delicious!

A form stood over her, his arms crossed over his chest, the sun shining behind his head. It was like looking up at a black column, a tower shaped like a man. She raised herself on one elbow, jolted fully awake. It was not Kit, but a smaller man, well dressed. As he moved out of the sun's pathway, she could clearly see his bald head.

"Oh, Father!" Camilla groaned, falling back into the soft grass and turning away from him.

"Get up," he growled, prodding her with the loop of his carriage whip. "On your feet immediately, or I shall give you reason to moan in earnest."

She was glad that she'd covered herself with her skirts, and she quickly whipped her one stocking foot under the folds of her gown. Her fingers flew to the buttons of her bodice and did them up rapidly.

There was nothing she could do with her flower-flecked hair, the coiffure of a wood nymph.

"I visited the children's residence," he said, watching her closely. "I asked after you, and was told in a very peculiar and halting manner by that Finch woman that you had gone out. She did not say where. Get up!" he commanded, reaching down and jerking her to her feet by one elbow. "Despicable!" he hissed.

She could see her father's gig standing on a carriage track not far off, the black horse hanging its head as if ashamed to have drawn him here to witness his daughter's shame. He dragged her toward it.

"In driving home, I was passed by a horseman riding rapidly toward the hamlet. Something about him seemed familiar, so I was curious. I tracked him backward from this spot," he said, indicating with the whipstock the edge of the road where hoofprints appeared.

He would not release her elbow, but pressed it tightly in his grip. "That was Christopher Westcott, was it not?" His voice had a strange, evil intensity about it. "Get into the carriage. We shall see what interesting company awaits us at the haven for deaf children. Have you already made it a bordello?"

She flung up her head in sudden fury. "How dare you speak so of the only place in the parish that you own where love and kindness, instead of harsh cruelty, prevails," she retorted.

He did not respond, but pushed her into the gig ahead of him. His glare of hatred was more forceful than any words.

"Drive me home, Father. I am quite ill. Truly I am."

Naturally, he had no intention of doing that. He wheeled the horse around abruptly and whipped it back to the hamlet toward the children's home.

If only Letty had been able to warn Kit! If he'd recognized Edgar Cochran and knew enough to flee! But undoubtedly he hadn't seen her father, or he would have halted. The only thing on his mind had been their recent ecstasy and the desire to return to his love as soon as possible.

Cammy gripped her crossed arms over her front, and tucked her chin into her collar. The lovely spring day had lost its beauty. She shivered, although it was warm. Now she smelled no meadow grass, heard no breeze in the gum tree branches arching over the road. Such a feeling befitted a prisoner being whisked along by the silent, triumphant jailer beside her. He laid the whip on the horse, as he probably wished to lay it on her own back.

Only for the sake of the poor horse, she was relieved when they reached their destination. But she was dismayed to see Kit's big mount tied to a post before the door.

"Get out. Get into that house!" Her father's face was white.

She had no choice but to obey him. She climbed down and stumbled out in her one shoe. Edgar Cochran pushed her through the entrance and shoved her into the dim passageway, slamming the door shut behind them.

"Come out, Westcott!" He stormed into the first room. It was empty. Then he marched her down the corridor until he came to the first open door.

Kit stood in the playroom with a woman's dress draped over his arm and a pair of slippers in his hand. Guilt could not have been more obvious. Letty was beside him, her hand on Kit's sleeve, her eyes dark with fright. Mr. Shrader was there, holding a child on his hip. Cammy was too blind with tears to see the expression on his face.

"So you are in league with this libertine, this child-snatching, indecent felon!" her father roared at Letty and Mr. Shrader.

Letty quickly interpreted for her father, who set down the wide-eyed boy very slowly and gently as he watched her. Cammy looked at him, unable to look at her beloved.

"This is the end of this so-called charity, this benevolent asylum for deaf brats!" Edgar Cochran hissed. The expression on his face was truly loathsome. The lowered brows, the curled lip, and the icy glare made him a monster. Mr. Shrader put up one hand to object and somehow, he produced the words, "No. No. Wrong!" The sounds were clear and resonant, music to Cammy's ears.

"Our love has nothing to do with the children here," Kit interrupted. He dropped the clothing in his arms and came forward. "I've come back to marry Camilla. Your wiles and wickedness are finished. Get away from her."

Two more children wandered into the room just then, and no sooner had they stepped inside than they halted, open-mouthed. Without any translation from Letty, they could see that something terrible was happening. Mr. Shrader was giving Letty a message.

"My father says, 'In the name of God's mercy, let the young lovers go,' " Letty said in a shaky voice. "Can't you recognize true and constant love?"

"Your father can go to hell," Cochran stated flatly. "He is a meddling fool and should be on the street corner begging. This girl is a slut. As for Westcott—"

Little William Cross made a dash for Camilla and hid his face in her skirts. Emboldened by his courage, Mary and Jane followed suit. Then Jane turned and looked up at Edgar Cochran. She made a few quick, emphatic formations with her tiny hands.

"What is that?" he snarled, staring at the child.

"Jane says you are acting hateful," whispered Letty.

"These children should not see such a bold display of ill manners," Kit noted. "A child knows injustice when she sees it."

Edgar Cochran was silent for a moment, and Camilla could see something new behind his crafty eyes. When he spoke, his voice lost its edge, and he regarded his daughter sadly. Then he said to Kit, "If you could only have kept her for your own in Scotland, Westcott, this would not be happening now. It is true that I tried to prevent her running away with you, but once the act was done, I prayed that I'd see you two wed, instead of perpetually sinning."

"What?" cried Cammy and Kit together. She could tell he was about to fabricate another lie.

"When you came running home to Salisbury from Scotland, once Kit had found out your habitual vices, Camilla, I thought you were lost, indeed. And even after that, on the ship sailing home, you cavorted with Hans Van Beek shockingly. Westcott, she is unfit to be any man's wife."

"Father!" she cried. "You yourself were in Scotland! You are inventing this! You were in that room, forcing me to . . . And I rejected poor Hans. You know I did!"

"I believe you, Cammy," said Kit at once. "Do not let him think he can sway my mind ever again."

"Have you heard any such story, Mrs. Finch? About the episode in Scotland, or on the ship, for that matter?" asked Edgar Cochran. "And she tells you everything, does she not? She is like a daughter to you. You are her confidante."

"No, I have not, but she . . . but I know my Cammy is absolutely good. She is not a talker, she keeps her feelings to herself."

"We shall marry, Camilla and I," said Kit resolutely.

Cammy adored his trust. She would have run to him, but the three children still held her in place, clinging to her hands.

"I should have let you wed a year ago, Christopher, but now, knowing she has run off from you and will whore with anyone, I cannot permit you to disgrace your family name with such a wife."

She stared at Edgar Cochran, a man she no longer could think of as her father. She instantly disowned him, and this gave her sudden strength. She was alone, but she was no longer bound in her mind to this monster. She sucked in her breath. This was a nightmare! The worst of it was that Letty was still interpreting for her father, and the expression of disgust on Lawrence Shrader's face told her how accurately Letty reported. The children were watching, too, until Cammy bent and cupped their heads in her hands to turn their faces away.

Although she was in the right, she could not speak to defend herself. Whatever she said would be twisted by that man to fit his tissue of lies. He dared to look at her wistfully, pretending compassion for her.

"Kit, you do not believe him, do you?" she whispered.

"Of course not," he said, staunchly.

"Are you finished?" Letty interjected in a bold, loud voice.

Mr. Shrader rose from his seat and faced Edgar Cochran, signing angrily at him.

"We have work here," Letty said for her father. "Will you please leave off tormenting these two and let us get on with our teaching?"

Edgar Cochran turned red. Never had Cammy heard any other tenant of his so bravely chide this man, and she trembled to think what his reaction would be.

But he did not scream at Mr. Shrader or threaten to evict him. He sent him a withering glance and then strode over to Camilla, seizing her wrist, tearing her hand away from the child she was caressing. It was William Cross, who could speak clearly, although he could not hear. He stared up at Edgar Cochran, scowling in indignation.

"You let go!" he insisted, and slapped at Edgar's hand.

"Oh, don't," Cammy cautioned the seven-year-old.

The man pulled back an arm as if to strike William, and Cammy had a flash of memory to when she was five. Her brother Michael! Father had struck him repeatedly one night. She never knew why.

But at that instant, Letty and Lawrence Shrader suddenly leaped into motion, placing their bodies between the man and the child. Kit grasped Edgar Cochran by the arm and whirled him around.

"This is between you and me," he said fiercely. "Leave the boy alone and let us talk in privacy."

"Camilla is coming with me," Cochran retorted, pulling at Cammy's arm.

"Please, stay here," Cammy told her dear friends over her shoulder, still trying to extricate herself from Mary's grasp. "Go play," she signed with one free hand. "I shall be safe," she lied.

"He is hateful," Mary signed back to her. "He will hurt you bad."

She had no chance to answer because Edgar Cochran was dragging her from the playroom as though she were a rag doll. Kit stood in front of them, holding the door open.

They walked in silence to the parlor, a lovely room that was now golden with late afternoon sunlight the color of wattle blossoms.

"Now," Cochran began breathlessly. "I shall be extremely generous. Especially considering that you seduced my daughter and then had the audacity to come to England and kidnap her across a border. That, I need not mention, is a felony. Depart and never return again, and I shall not press charges."

"I will risk any legal action, sir," stated Kit. "I think you have no case here in the colonies, and if you did, well, I can hire lawyers as well as you can."

Her father stopped, unable to reply. His tactic had been unsuccessful and he seemed at a loss.

"Let us be, Father," Camilla begged, daring to pull free of his grasp. "Let us wed and we will never trouble your mind again. In Fiji, we shall be out of your sight, and—"

"You shall be my hostess at Blue Downs for the rest of my life or of yours, whichever is the shorter."

Kit shook his head, his blue eyes flashing with intensity. "When she is of age you can no longer command her, sir." He made the "sir" hiss like the snap of a whiplash.

"Of course. You have a point." Cochran turned to Cammy and smiled weakly. "I shall tell you something. I do not like these impudent deaf and dumb creatures you have saddled me with—"

"Do not use that terrible term!" she cried. "They are not dumb or mute or stupid!"

He nodded at her hot defense. "Ah, I thought that would

bring a response. Now you listen to me carefully. This child-snatcher of yours shall go back to his islands and forget you, and you shall be my dutiful daughter and mistress of Blue Downs. Either that, or I shall close this house at once. The brats and the mutes will be thrown out on the street, and I shall make sure that no one else in this colony will take them in. No one will touch them when I testify that they contributed to the corruption of my minor daughter."

"They did not!" Kit exclaimed, and Cammy gave a small cry of pain.

"Who will believe them? To whom can they appeal to make themselves understood? The Finch woman was my hired servant once, and without a character reference from me, no one would hire her again. They will all starve, and deservedly so."

"You are beneath contempt, sir," Kit softly remarked.

By the despair in his voice, Cammy knew that he had no solution. They were beaten. Another suitor might have had little concern for the Children's Home, but not Kit. He could not doom these children, as he could not abandon Katherine and Lawrence and Letty.

Cammy hung her head, misery covering her like a cloud.

"Do you surrender, daughter?" Cochran muttered.

She did not lift her head. Kit was silent.

"Well, then, just remember. Engrave it upon your mind, Westcott. One word from you, one visit, one letter to my daughter, and there will be suffering in this house. The brats will be spilled onto the countryside to fend for themselves. The meddling old man and the women will never work again. Do you understand?"

"Very well," Kit said, unable to fight this cruel and unusual threat.

"Well!" Edgar Cochran exclaimed. "I think that concludes this meeting." He pulled Camilla's hand through his arm. "We are going home now. Westcott, you are defeated."

Kit could utter no word of objection. Not with the Shraders and Letty and the children under a roof owned by Edgar Cochran.

Camilla desperately wished to say something to Kit, but her father's presence would pollute any such communication. They gazed hungrily at each other as the man ushered Kit through the door ahead of them. Kit walked down the path to his tethered horse, turned, and sent Cammy such an agonized look of futility and despair that she could no longer keep back the tears.

This was blackmail! He had extorted from them a promise they hated, but how could they break their unsaid vow? They must not meet or even correspond. And if they dared to send their letters through Letty, her parents and the children would be in grave danger!

She knew from his face that Kit brooded on these same thoughts.

"I will kiss him goodbye," she sobbed to her father. "I love him!"

"You shall not, daughter." He pulled her roughly into the gig, and slapped the reins on the back of the horse.

Kit would see this vision of his love forever: her hair still entrapping wattle blossoms like a net full of tiny golden butterflies, her face white, a fist pressed to her lips. Camilla was driven past him, out of his life. He stood by his horse, still as a statue, his face rigid and his eyes glassy with unshed tears. He raised his hand in a silent salute and formed the words, "I'll always love you."

She could read his message on his lips and in his blue eyes.

Her lips and hands replied, "I love you."

Then the gig turned a corner, and he was gone from view.

Book II

Chapter 21
1873

"We are having a house guest, Camilla," said Edgar Cochran, putting down his newspaper as soon as she came in from her day's work, shedding mantle, gloves, and hat. This year he'd let her work at the Children's Home again, as many as three hours each day. She'd been in such a decline, had grown so thin and wan during her months in the house that he admitted fear for her life and relented. The work did wonders for her. Within a month of starting again, her thin frame filled, and, as her father put it, "she got her nasty temper back."

"Who's coming to stay with us?" Cammy asked, mildly curious. At least it was not a suitor. He had kept his word in that regard. Whether or not he believed his own lies about her, he did not want her married. She was a much more malleable mistress of Blue Downs than his sister, Rina, would be.

Two years of waiting for freedom from her father lay behind her, AnDtwo YEAPq lay ahead. But the work with Letty and the Shraders helped a great deal. Several of their first children had now graduated to the big Victoria School, and new little ones started their course of training.

If only she could move to Victoria to teach! If only she could move anywhere that was far from her father.

Edgar Cochran glared at her and said, "It is my old friend Mr. Torandor, the gentleman I visited in London. Did I ever tell you about him? He's of German-Spanish paternity, with an English mother. Quite a hybrid, but very talented. And he has a fortune."

Her father went on explaining that the Torandors were immensely wealthy. Riclef's father had manufactured some sort of steam engine, and Riclef himself was now set for life. He required no occupation but spent his time in travel and diversion. He had often dwelt apart from his wife, who had died some years ago, childless. Mr. Torandor's travels took him from the British Isles to all the colonies several times a year. Now he sought a quiet country house with blossoming gardens in which to spend a pleasant spring.

"When does he arrive?" she asked, merely to be polite. Camilla and her father conversed very little, since so many topics were closed to them. The infrequent house guests who came to stay talked only of sheep and bush fires, diseases of wheat, and the apportionment of Crown lands. They were the dullest subjects, and she was not interested in the men at all.

"Mr. Torandor is in his middle years, about forty-three, I should say. It is cold in England in September, as you no doubt recall, and therefore he's decided to come out for our springtime."

Everything happened in the spring, Cammy remembered with a rush of sadness. One year, she had enjoyed two springtimes, but that was eons ago. That lovely spring in Scotland.

She wondered for months about her brother's fate and had sent a letter to be posted by Letty. It was true, she discovered. Father *had* demanded payment for the Salisbury house, but Bernard and Beatrice, despite their now meager surroundings, felt little bitterness. Beatrice had borne a son and was expecting another child.

"Our humble cottage has made me fertile," she jested in a reply to Camilla, which was sent via Letty's address. Cammy was delighted at the news about the children as well as their happy parents. At least the print shop was paid for.

Cammy wrote back, but she did not disturb them with any appeal for aid. She would be ashamed to tell her beloved brother and sister-in-law how awful her life had turned out.

She did not even tell her mother, not wishing to upset Minnie's happiness. A letter early in the year informed

Cammy that the divorce was final, and Mother had immediately wed Stephen Plaskett as soon as she received the papers. Every two months now, Cammy would receive a letter from her mother. Father handed them to her still sealed.

"I need no longer read your mail, Camilla," he said. "I know you are striving to reform. When you are thirty, perhaps you will be fit to entertain gentlemen again, and even perhaps to marry. I may be gone by then, and your filial duties ended."

She didn't hear much from the rest of her family, so she couldn't confide in anyone.

Michael wrote describing his studies in Sydney. He hoped to qualify for the bar in the summer and then practice law. "I'd prefer to practice in Melbourne, Cammy," he wrote, "for you are there, but so is Father. Need I say more?"

Not one word arrived from Christopher Wain Westcott.

And so her life proceeded. She spent truly pleasant hours with the deaf children. All were older than seven, but the Victoria School was full this season, with seventy-five scholars. Until their new section was completed, the Shraders' cottage school, the Children's Home, filled a real need.

Cammy had grown skilled in the manual signing method, and the deaf children's insatiable hunger for conversation, hugs, and kisses warmed her. She cosseted and cuddled them, and fetched and carried for the Shraders. Mr. Shrader, who had grown a long white beard that the children loved to tug upon and stroke, was nicknamed "St. Nicholas." His wife, recovering from a broken hip, sat in a bath chair, and Letty had to push her around. Aside from this inconvenience, the old woman was more alert and busy than ever. She might have communicated without her hands, her wonderful face was so expressive.

Cammy dragged herself back to the house each afternoon, wishing she could stay and live in the back of the home with Letty. Letty had forgiven her at once, after Cammy explained the real events of that terrible afternoon and of the time in Scotland. Letty had nodded when Cammy talked about her father and had said, "Yes, if that is so, he is a truly horrid man."

"Consider us your parents, Camilla," Mr. Shrader insisted when he heard the story. "We are a bit too old and failing fast, but we do love and trust you."

She held nothing back from them, though they were distraught to hear some of the truth. Katherine and Lawrence Shrader said that faces cannot lie and that hers was honest.

At home she puttered in the gardens and went out walking, but never very far. Father no longer kept a horse for her, as if he feared she might ride away to Melbourne. The worst threat hanging over her head was that the Children's Home would cease to exist if she ceased to obey him in all things.

Exhausted by emotion, she no longer beat her wings against the bars. In May of 1875 she'd turn twenty-one. Then she'd be able to leave him, and somehow she'd protect the Children's Home from closure, regardless of what Father did.

No man she saw in the settlement or faced across a Blue Downs tea table appealed to her. Some were naive like Hans Van Beek. More were cynical, even coarse, and they ogled her rudely. Handsome men were proud of their appearance, and plain ones never seemed cheerful. She did not fancy spending her life with any man less intelligent than she, or one who'd gorge and grow fat, or one who'd prove a tyrant like Edgar Cochran. Knowing Father made her very cautious. Knowing Kit made her doubt that she'd ever love another man again.

"I see that he is coming," was Edgar Cochran's excited report that Saturday evening just at dusk.

Mr. Torandor had come up their front steps from his shiny landau, while a richly clad footman hovered just behind him. The dark, tall gentleman swept through their door in his traveling cape, greeted Father, and then spun on his heel to take Camilla's hand. He stared down at her for a long time before speaking, which gave her the opportunity to examine him with equal curiosity.

He was an imposing figure of a man, not so much in height, but in coloring and personal presence. His hair and beard were so dark they were nearly blue-black in hue. The beard was short, shovel-shaped, and flecked with white, although the hair on his head was gray only at the temples.

His elegant long coat bespoke wealth and a fine tailor, and it hugged his narrow waist. His countenance was striking: deeply tanned and marked with grooved lines beside the mouth that ran down his cheeks and disappeared into his beard almost like long dimples. He studied her with his deep-set dark eyes.

"Miss Cochran," he murmured in a resonant voice, bending lower and almost kissing her hand. He kept those eyes on her face, as he whispered so her father could not hear, "I knew your mother. I come to help you, Camilla."

She looked up startled, but she had no time to reply. Father had walked ahead into the drawing room where they would offer their guest a light repast. With a glance at Camilla, whose face still mirrored shock, Mr. Torandor swept into the drawing room, his cloak swirling behind him. She came along in his wake, very much intrigued. Mother? Did she really know this man? Had she sent him to aid her daughter?

Camilla listened to the dinner conversation between the two old friends with great interest. Mr. Torandor spoke of his harrowing voyage, the many storms at sea. Then he expressed admiration for their house. Camilla noted that his tone shifted constantly when he spoke to her father. One moment it was cold, the next moment almost teasingly intimate. But Edgar Cochran did not notice.

This inclined her to believe that Mr. Torandor was indeed an old friend of Mama's. Perhaps her mother had told him all Father's faults. That was likely, since Mama never kept any secrets, another reason that Camilla had been reluctant to confide in her mother about her miserable agonies involving Kit.

The following evening her father left the house on a weak pretext, with the result that Cammy found herself alone with Mr. Torandor in the fern-filled south parlor.

The parlor doors stood open into the hallway, and a servant intruded every half hour to inquire if anything was wanted. Mr. Torandor sat stretched out in a chaise lounge in the bay window that gave him a view across the lawns toward Port Phillip. Melbourne lay in that direction. He kept a brown plaid rug over his legs, like a man in a deck chair on a ship.

Camilla's chair was drawn up close to the chaise, at his request, and she was to read aloud to him. He had told her that his eyes were not good for close study in the evening, and that he would be most appreciative if his "new young friend" would oblige him with some poetry.

Often he drew attention to his age, which seemed curious in such a vigorous man. Of course, he was more than twice her age.

The south parlor was lit by four blue-shaded banquet lamps

that turned the draperies, pillows, and carpeting into pools and hills of midnight-blue velvet, with no sharp outlines. Camilla held the heavy book in the circle of light from the nearest lamp, glancing up every once in a while to see that faraway glow through the windows which was the lights of Melbourne.

She could not forget another man who had chosen Blue Downs as a retreat, that golden-skinned islander who had come here each spring to hunt deer and kangaroo, who had taken her as his love and left his mark in her so deep she could still feel it. She told herself to stop fantasizing, to give up the past.

She began to read to Mr. Torandor from Sir Walter Scott.

"Do you prefer something more appropriate to a young lady?" he interrupted after a few pages. "I do not know what you would enjoy."

"I very much enjoy reading anything at all," she said. "I teach children who cannot hear, so it is pleasurable to read aloud, I assure you."

Neither had mentioned his whispered confidence of the previous day in regard to her mother. Camilla was waiting for him to speak first, and he seemed to be daring her to mention it. Sir Walter Scott, in any event, was just a means to fill the time.

She wished he would not stare so intently at her. How did his wife die? she wondered. It was sad that he had no children. Men require heirs, rich men especially. She tried to picture him as some young woman's husband and shivered.

"Will you not one time permit yourself to smile, Camilla?" he asked suddenly. "I have never seen a young lady so solemn, outside of church."

Her lips flickered upward, but it was an embarrassed grimace rather than a smile.

"I don't often smile, because I was once a silly child with too much laughter and folly."

"Extraordinary," he remarked. "But I would expect Edgar Esterbrook Cochran to rear at least one extraordinary child. He married an extraordinary woman of whom I am most fond."

"Oh," Camilla said with curiosity, letting her book fall to her lap. "Indeed?"

"May I speak of your absent mother?" he asked. "I have

not seen her for so many years. You see, I never visited here after your birth, because certain duties kept me away. Do you never visit your mother?"

"No. I'm not permitted. I last saw my mother only for an hour or so two years ago, when our ship stopped in Adelaide. That was before she was divorced."

"I know that. I have written to Minnie."

"I don't go down even to Melbourne. I live a quiet life here," she said, thinking suddenly that her mother's life was far more active than her own.

She lowered her gaze, and her shoulders rose and fell very slightly. Riclef Torandor seemed not to miss a move or the faintest change in her complexion. Sadly, he clucked his tongue. "If I were younger, Camilla, I might court you myself. As it is, I fear I am dull company, and too old for such a young lady."

"On the contrary, Mr. Torandor. I welcome every visitor who brings news of the world outside. Books of verse and novels can be dull companions after a while."

Camilla enjoyed talking with him and fully intended to keep theirs a friendly relationship. She believed she was perfectly in control. Therefore, she was quite startled when his big hand reached out and captured hers; hers vanished into his like a small white rabbit down a brown clay burrow. Before she could even tug away, the book on her lap slid to the floor.

"Miss Camilla, if you yearn for news of the world, how would you like to see that world? To travel away from Blue Downs?"

Her eyes brightened with excitement. "Is there any way? Might I leave here . . . and not have Father be angry? He's threatened to close the Children's Home if I go—"

"He would have no reason to do that if he willingly let you depart. On the strength of our long friendship, I don't see why he would not."

"Oh, I'd love to go away under such circumstances!" A smile lit up her face.

He noticed it at once. His arched brows rose. "So you are indeed walled up in a castle and want a prince to come free you. Unfortunately, I resemble a dragon more than a prince, but I am a friendly old dragon, you may be sure. I can offer you honest employment, a pleasant situation, outside this colony."

"What are you saying? I do not understand."

"Hush." He looked around, fearful of being overheard. "Your mother advised me to come and help you get away. Your father has described to me in detail the exact reasons he is keeping you here."

When she recoiled in shock, he added a comforting observation. "Most men would overlook a childish indiscretion in one so young and lovely as you. But they would also fault their prospective father-in-law for being so righteous, a true monster of virtue."

"Oh!" she exclaimed, delighted to see that Torandor was willing to be her advocate.

"Do you understand me? I am perhaps disloyal to speak ill of my own host, but your mother mentioned your sad circumstances—"

"But Mama knows nothing of my . . . unhappy love," she said. "I shielded her from knowing, for she can do nothing, and I wanted her to be happy."

"You are a kind child. She senses only that you'd love to live with her, or would be happier with Charlotte than with your father. I personally am of the opinion that you would be happier anywhere."

She stared at him in amazement. He seemed like a kindly and merciful judge on the highest court of appeal. Unaccustomed to trust from few men since Bernard, she was tempted to believe that they were all suspicious.

"Let me explain," he said. "A very dear friend of mine recently died. On his deathbed he asked me to discover whether his little son was being properly cared for. The child lives with a simple couple who might not have the means to train the boy to his fullest potential. I have ascertained that the boy now requires a governess."

"Governess," she echoed numbly. "And you're asking me to assume the position? Is the child deaf?"

"Oh, no. You see, I thought of you because you appear to be a good judge of humanity. I am charged with the task of learning if he prospers, but I myself do not wish to investigate. It might be taken amiss."

"He's an orphan, then?" She was still confused.

"I wish to place a sensitive, sensible young woman in that home to discover how the boy is doing . . . someone who would be a discreet emissary. Would you stoop to playing governess?"

"Oh, yes!" she cried. "But Father surely wouldn't permit it. He's informed me that I am to remain at Blue Downs forever." She scarcely noted any longer that Riclef was still gripping her hand in his.

Now he pressed it earnestly. "I think that I can persuade him if I do not tell him the complete truth, perhaps."

"Where is this child?" she whispered.

"Outside Victoria. Look there, where the lights make a haze on the horizon. See the moon on the black water? Do you know what lies over that wide strait?"

"The Bass Strait? Why, the colony of Tasmania!"

"Once called Van Dieman's Land, in the wicked old days."

Since childhood, the name had always sounded to her like "demons' land." "Yes, go on!"

"Have you ever voyaged to Tasmania?"

"No, never."

"My dear friend's son is but five years old, and it seems that you would be a perfect companion and teacher for him."

Camilla tried to keep back the tears, but failed. She felt such pity for the child and enormous gratitude to Mr. Torandor for offering her a way out of Blue Downs.

"I wished first to learn your feelings on the matter. Now I shall attempt to bring your father around."

"Oh, do!" she pleaded. If anyone could convince Father, it would have to be Riclef Torandor.

He was caressing her hand, but she was not offended. Such a good friend! He was quick-witted and kind and tolerant of her past. He knew and cared for her mother. The touch of his hand was at the same time reassuring and a trifle frightening, since no man but Kit had ever caressed her. Hans Van Beek had been only a foolish boy.

For some reason, she trusted Mr. Torandor. He would aid his friend's child and free her from Father. Camilla felt excited hope and a twinge of fear.

As for romantic notions, she had none. Father had long since drummed them out of her.

Chapter 22

During the next four seemingly endless days, Father did not mention Mr. Torandor's proposal. Camilla spent most of her spare time reading aloud to her new friend or sitting nearby, embroidering, while he told yarns of his world travels and worldly life. In comparison with him, she felt like a provincial, not a daring adventuress at all.

"It is hard to wait for my father's response." She sighed in the midst of one of their reading sessions.

"I must warn you, Camilla, that what I said to you about this mission and what I had to tell your father differ. Please don't be alarmed, but to bring him 'round I had to make mention of marriage."

"Marriage? Whose?" A knot formed in the pit of her stomach.

"Yours. To me." His lips trembled in a small smile.

"But Father wishes to keep me a spinster as punishment!"

"Not really. He seemed to encourage my suit."

"Why would he?" she asked, and then suddenly saw that she'd hurt him. "I mean, why would he vow that he would never permit me to marry, but would always keep me with him as mistress of Blue Downs, and the next time—"

But she suddenly fell silent. He'd vowed once before that she'd not wed, and then he forced Hans Van Beek on her. And now this man, because both of them were wealthy, very wealthy. Her devoted father was willing to sell her to a high bidder.

"Which of course," Mr. Torandor continued, "does not mean that you must wed me! But it is your only means of escape, my dear. I have your best interests at heart, believe me."

Her anxious impatience ended on the sixth day of Mr. Torandor's stay. Her head began spinning when her father approached her in the sitting room and said, "My dear daughter, our guest has broached the subject of matrimony."

"Oh?" she said, trying to seem nonplussed.

"He has not proposed immediate marriage, for there's such a disparity in your ages and experience. He wishes you to visit relatives of his in Hobart, Tasmania. If you fit in with his family and do not offend them, then we will proceed with arrangements for your wedding."

Edgar looked self-satisfied in his morning coat with padded shoulders and his shiny boots. He was being cozened, but she did not care. Her only response was a small look away from him.

"I made an error in regard to your previous suitor, Camilla. I hid the matter of your impurity. That was dishonest. Therefore, in Mr. Torandor's case, I have revealed everything. You might have had a younger man, but this man is even more . . . comfortably provided for." He gave her a thin-lipped smile. "Prepare to depart next week."

Father's smile was so unlike Mr. Torandor's, which was cynical but good-natured. Kit's was glorious, the most beautiful smile she had ever seen.

Why did she dream of Christopher Westcott now, her lost love? Because her father was speaking of marriage for the first time in two years, and because a man looked tenderly upon her, though she did not favor him. Certainly not as a husband! She put the thought out of her head. This was a means to an end, that was all.

Only a week hence she packed up her best summer gowns and her Bible and her prayer book and her copy of Keats. What were the styles in the colony of Tasmania? What was the climate like? What clothing should she bring?

"You'll remain here with Father, of course?" she asked Mr. Torandor.

"Exactly. I remain behind, and you go as my spy. There are good spies and bad spies, my dear. You shall be an angel in disguise."

"I do hope I shall accomplish this mission to your satisfaction," she said, looking down at the dark man sitting in his chair. He watched her with his sharp eyes, stroking his well-trimmed short beard.

"Come perch for a while, Camilla," he said, patting the arm of the chair. "I cannot talk to you when you flit about like a little bird."

"A bird soon to fly from a cage!" she pointed out.

"Camilla, listen to me very carefully," he said in a suddenly grave voice that brought her quickly to a halt.

"You do not, I hope, confide much in your father?"

"No, I dare not. We talk very little."

"Excellent. Then I shall share a secret with you. In Tasmania, you shall be governess to the son of my friend, a barrister, a highly cultured man. But," he paused and pinched his lower lip, watching her closely, "his mother used to be a chambermaid."

"I . . . see," she said, wondering what he was getting at.

"I have learned that she has become an honest woman, and married a draper, an upstanding tradesman who is generally believed to be the father of the child. Her past is cloaked from general knowledge. You know the weaknesses of the most sensible young servants, and my friend was thoughtless!"

"That's why you chose me!" Cammy gasped. "Because of my—"

"You would not be likely to sneer, that is so. But it also works the other way, my dear. I cannot simply carry you off. This is the only way I am able to get your freedom. Unless I married you, of course, and that is not yet in the cards."

She sat down, staring straight ahead of her, feeling suddenly sobered.

"My friend made sure that the former chambermaid was provided for, Camilla. She and her legal spouse have a fine house, one that is comfortable and respectable. My friend saw to that the year before he died when he first discovered that he had a natural son who was living in poverty."

"Does she know?"

"She knows nothing. Howard—I shall not give you his full

name for discretion's sake—furnished the funds through a supposed bequest from an unknown aunt of the husband. It was arranged that Janet, the mother, would believe her husband had been left a large inheritance and not see any connection between her husband's sudden good fortune and her own misbegotten child. Do you understand?"

Camilla nodded solemnly, then rested her chin on her fist and tried to follow his explanation.

"My friend Howard would be devastated to find that the boy had food and clothing but insufficient love. How is one to judge the quality of love in a home? And care and training?"

"That will be my task," she said.

"Exactly. And you are exactly right for it because you would never cast stones."

He extended his hand to her, and she put hers into his. A manly handshake, firm and abrupt, sealed their bargain.

Preparations were well underway for her journey to Tasmania, to freedom, when one evening Father requested her presence in the library. He was standing talking to Mr. Torandor when she entered the room.

The library had a sober, judicial air. A piano, silent since Mama left, stood among bookcases towering to the ceiling. The carpet that muffled all sound was so deep that Cammy's slippers sank out of sight in it. But she was not concerned in this lugubrious setting because her mood was light. She and Mr. Torandor had already agreed on what would be said in front of father. The rest was a secret between them. He had promised her that she would be able to remain in Tasmania as long as they could make it credible for her father. When he became suspicious, they would think of some other scheme to keep her away from Blue Downs until her twenty-first birthday. "I owe that to your mother," Mr. Torandor had assured her. "I will make sure that you are not kept here, a miserable prisoner. No matter what happens, we'll not give you back to your father, Camilla."

So as she stood before them both in the library, there was not a shred of doubt remaining in her mind.

"Camilla," Father began without any preliminary greeting, "I must object to your traveling to Tasmania."

His words were like rapid blows to her body, and she actually bent slightly forward, breathless.

Mr. Torandor was standing slightly behind her father, and

therefore he was able to send her visual clues. He would shake his head or raise an eyebrow. Taking note of that, Camilla took heart.

"In Tasmania," her father went on, "you will be unprotected and out of my sight. No loving father would allow such an arrangement involving a minor child. I have decided that there is one condition under which I may permit you to depart."

"What's that, Father?" she asked anxiously. She would meet any condition at all if it assured her escape.

"Mr. Torandor will first marry you."

A cry coming from the depths of her soul rang out. "Oh, no! He shall not!"

"Although I am sincere in my desire to wed her, I feared this would seem too hasty to your daughter, Edgar," Torandor cut in quickly. "Therefore, I propose an interim plan. We shall give notice to the Deputy Registrar before we leave this colony of our intention to marry. The waiting period is no less than twenty-one days. If my family and Camilla do not get on together, no harm is done. We would then reconsider marrying."

Camilla listened in amazement at his smooth deception.

"Is that agreeable, Edgar?"

Her father glared, shifted his feet, and did not answer.

"If this is not suitable, I do not see how I can ever marry your daughter, Edgar. She must meet with the approval of the only kinfolk I have on this side of the globe. Then, and only then, can we wed. But that is not to say that arrangements couldn't be started beforehand."

Her father had to agree. He was not a man who would let this slip from his fingers. Her friend signaled Cammy for acquiescence, and she felt like a puppet on strings, jerked this way and that as she smiled and nodded. There was no mention of church or the reading of banns on three successive Sundays. Her father might consider her unfit for a church wedding, but no matter. She would not be marrying Mr. Torandor. Not in a thousand years!

Her conscience was clear as she glided from the room, leaving the men to smoke and drink brandy and congratulate themselves. How rich to be playing a trick on Father just like the wicked tricks he had played on Kit. Her father deserved retribution, and he would meet it at the hands of Mr. Torandor.

She went to sleep happy, assured of her escape from Blue Downs. Letty would miss her, but there would not be a great deal of work with the Children's Home temporarily empty. The Victoria School had agreed to admit all their little scholars at the end of October. If and when there was need for their country shelter again, Cammy would give the Shraders the pin money she had saved these two years and that could pay for her replacement. She would need no funds of her own or of Father's in her new situation, since Mr. Torandor was very rich and would pay her well.

At last the day arrived. Mr. Torandor and Father accompanied her as far as Melbourne and stayed only long enough for their visit to the Deputy Registrar's office. There she watched her supposed intended husband, and coconspirator, record their names giving notice of their intention to marry. She tried not to think about Kit.

Mr. Torandor announced to the Registrar that they intended to wed in this office, in Melbourne, in little more than twenty-one days. If this date passed and no marriage had taken place, a new notice would have to be written in the Marriage Notice Book, and another waiting period of twenty-one days would ensue.

Riclef Torandor was a widower, he wrote down, and she, a spinster. He was of full age, and she, a minor. There was nothing to make their marriage improper, not residency requirements, not the lack of parental permission. Father certified that his daughter might marry Mr. Torandor. Then he and her friend bid her adieu, without a kiss or a handshake, and made their way back to Blue Downs.

She was at last free. Free! For the first time in her life Camilla could be her own self, out of sight of Father or any other master.

Chapter 23

It was spring again, September in Melbourne. Kit had not returned to Victoria during these two years, and for good reason. To think he could visit Melbourne and not hire a horse to ride straight north to Blue Downs was ludicrous. He could not have stopped himself, in spite of the fact that Camilla had not answered any of his letters. He'd written to her about everything and nothing.

His duties in Fiji were gratifyingly hard and kept his mind off her. When the War of Secession had ended in the United States, American cotton was exported to England again, and the Fiji cotton market plummeted. Quickly, other planters also converted their plantations to sugar cane as the West-cotts had done. But Kit's father was often away. He spent half his time in the capital, Levuka, as adviser to the beleaguered black King Thakombau. Kit was also needed on Viti Levu, the big island, to supervise the business. No longer did he have time to lie upon the beach or in the warm shallows inside the reef, teased by the giggling girls he had known in his youth. Anyway, they were decent matrons now, married and with children. It would not have mattered to him if they'd been available. He had no taste for anyone after Camilla.

Why did she not answer his letters? Would Edgar Cochran keep them from her? Kit kept his words restrained and polite, suspecting that her father might read the letters first. He sent her news of his life in Fiji and of the Fijian troubles with American debt and cannibal forays on Ovalau and Viti Levu. She'd loved to hear of the Fiji heathen customs and their unusual *wangaa*, the great canoes. The last time he'd talked to Camilla of those customs, they had lain entwined in each other's arms, far away in chilly Scotland.

He was now returning from England, en route back to Fiji after an expedition to talk with colonial office functionaries and sugar buyers in London. The sugar mill recently built at Suva was a portent of things to come. If the Westcotts built a mill, they might well capture the sugar market in England. The trip home afforded him the time to consider and to plan, but not only in regard to business.

Before arriving in Victoria, the ship was due to stop in Batavia for one day. He recalled that Camilla's ship also had docked at Batavia. A man still dwelt there, Kit hoped, who could set him right. He had to talk with Hans Van Beek.

It was maddening. He'd never own his own heart or body as long as Camilla haunted him. If she wed another, if she told him outright to his face that she despised him, he would find another girl to marry. But he did not want another girl. He'd met Cammy when she was ten years old, and for all their years together, he did not know her. And yet, they thought alike, wished for the same things, and in bed . . . He could not allow himself to remember that. But it was harder not to remember. Particularly when he was in England, everything reminded him of Cammy. He remembered the Scottish inn, the delight of playing chess with Cammy when it poured and rain streaked the windowpanes. She'd read to him, and he to her. And then they'd fall into bed again.

He'd brought up scones and cream and butter from the landlady's kitchen, and he'd poured honey on her bread and on Camilla.

She'd perched on his knee one evening, while he undid her gown. When she was cuddled, all white and soft against him, he'd reached out to the pot of honey, and stuck his finger in it. He'd teasingly offered that confection to his darling, and watched with fascination as she held his wrist and licked the finger clean. The small pink tongue darting, curling, sliding upon his finger, her mouth sucking it while her eyes danced with amusement. In short order they were on the bed, and he was holding the honey pot above her lovely, bare body.

"I shall write my name on you in honey, Camilla. To brand you as my bride."

" 'Kit' should not be too difficult," she giggled to him.

"No. 'Christopher.' "

Slowly, with consummate skill, he'd written his name with a thin golden thread of honey, begging her all the while to lie still. And then he licked it all off, from the "C" to the "R," and took his time about it, savoring in particular the "O" that he had traced around her little navel. It was a very sweet repast.

Camilla, though in a frenzied state, would not be still until he let her sign her name upon his body. She wanted him to turn over on his face, but he refused. "Just as I did it, or not at all, Camilla. And write your whole name."

She proceeded with the task, taking her time. His ecstasy had never been greater when she at last licked him clean of the honey.

He shook his head to clear it of memory. They were steaming into the port of Batavia now, but Kit was still back in Scotland with the woman he loved. No! He must forget all that. He would forget the honey-gold wattle blossoms in her red-gold hair as they lay in the grass in Victoria. He would forget everything and go to find Hans Van Beek.

A white-blond Dutch bride named Katrina, who was Cammy's height but had none of her vivacity, answered the door. When Kit introduced himself, she went to get her husband at once. Hans entered the room looking pale, and Kit gave him a look that he hoped would indicate his desire to talk alone. Katrina, whom Hans had wed recently in Rotterdam, did not speak much English, but she gazed at her bridegroom with tenderness when he asked her to leave the room. She lingered a moment longer, reluctant to tear her eyes from her husband.

"My father has died," Hans began. "His heart was no good. I have the plantation now."

Kit expressed his sympathies and then asked about the business. They spoke of coffee and of sugar. Hans was first to come to the point. "Now, you had questions, Mr. Westcott?"

"I need to know all you can tell me about Miss Camilla Cochran," he said, holding Hans' eyes with an earnest stare.

"We have had a serious misunderstanding. I want the truth from you. Nothing you can say would worsen my relationship with her, and perhaps you may help to improve it. I bear you no ill will, even if you were once Camilla's lover."

"I was not her lover!" Van Beek instantly retorted, his blue eyes registering dismay. "Oh, my dear sir, would that I was, and her husband as well, but she would not!"

"She never . . . succumbed to your affections?"

"My marriage owes much to Miss Cochran," he said. "I would not be married now without having met Camilla. Excuse me for using her given name, but I had great regard for her."

Kit was impressed by the man's honesty.

"She was very kind to me in England, and I hoped for her love, but she had given it away. Always I seek her heart—I do not tell this to my bride, Katrina—but she refused, saying we must be friends only."

"Her father, he suspected that you and Camilla—" Kit stopped himself, not wishing to cast aspersions on this kind man.

"Her father, he is a man who sees only what he wishes to see. He was concerned only for my family's money." Hans then added, "I know very shortly after I met Camilla that I shall not have her for wife. I was so sad. Our fathers both want that I marry Camilla. I want it, too. She did not say about you, her love. She tells me about you on the very last night, at this house, standing upon those stairs."

Kit looked up, wished with all his heart that Camilla still poised upon those spiral stairs, that he could rush to her and take her in his arms. Hans studied his face as if he knew Kit's heart.

"I tell you, too, that her father is not a nice man. He made with my father a pact, but her father lied."

"I thank you," said Kit, well able to imagine what the young man hinted at. So Edgar Cochran had wanted her wed to Hans!

He got away from the Van Beek house, thanking Hans for his gentlemanly deportment.

"I hope that you find her and marry her," said Hans with deep feeling.

Kit believed him. This man could not have lied if his life depended on it.

* * *

Now, at five o'clock on a late September morning, he was riding northward in Victoria, his face set in a grim mask of determination. He did not deserve to find her, for once in Scotland he had doubted her love. If there was justice in the world, he would not find Camilla. But, he reminded himself, there was also mercy in the world.

He rode to Blue Downs as swiftly as he could, cantering until the horse flagged and stopping only once to water the beast. He needed to see her as he never had needed her before.

In sight of the big white house standing among its gum trees in the early morning sunshine, he reined in, pushed his hat back on his head, and considered. Should he go to the servants' entrance and try for admittance? But no one would know him now. The old servants had been dismissed and new ones hired. He'd have to risk the front door. If his love was walled up in this silent house, he'd find a way to reach her.

He brushed off the dirt of the road from his coat and took a cloth to his boots before he left the horse tied to a gum tree, and walked up the pebbled drive. His heels sounded loud in the quiet garden.

When he gave the maid at the door his card, she looked at him with curiosity and scurried away. Yes, the master was at home. Kit had meant to ask after "the young mistress," but his mouth suddenly went dry and he could not form the word.

He was left standing in the library, fidgeting, fighting dizziness like oncoming heat prostration when Edgar Cochran walked into the room. He looked far older than Kit remembered him. Why had Hans Van Beek's father died and not this beast? Kit found himself looking down into the man's narrowed, small eyes, set in his scowling face, and suddenly wanted to commit murder. So much pain had come to Camilla from this self-righteous tiny man!

"My daughter has departed," Cochran said with a smile before Kit could get one word out. "She no longer lives here. She is already wed."

"Wed? To whom?" Kit cried, not totally believing it, but not quite sure that it was a lie. He wished he were wild enough or drunk enough to strangle the appalling man.

"It is none of your concern, Westcott. Why are you here?"

"Why did she not answer my letters?"

There was a brief pause, long enough to make Kit absolutely sure of the fate of his letters. "You didn't allow her to receive them!" he exclaimed. "I desisted for an entire year, and then wrote, but you wouldn't permit even an innocent note!"

"You are very fortunate I was merciful. I should have been wiser to keep my word and close the Children's Home the moment the first forbidden letter arrived in my hands."

"You are incredibly vengeful!" Kit cried, striking his hand upon his thigh in disbelief. How had he been so stupid? No letter would find its way to or from Camilla past this insect of a man.

Cochran had the gall to take out his watch and consult it. As if he had anything useful to occupy his time! The place was a well-appointed tomb, and Cochran was its guardian.

"Mr. Cochran," Kit said, swiftly speaking the words he had memorized. "I know what happened in Scotland. I found the man you hired. The one who pretended to be Camilla's lover. He told me everything."

The man's eyes bulged. "You couldn't have! You never found that same man! I paid him well enough to disappear and keep his mouth shut!"

"Thank you," Kit said. "I thought so. You were hiding in the room, weren't you? And to think I would trust your story and disbelieve Cammy!"

Kit heard his own indignant voice, amazed at his control. Inside he was writhing with rage at his cruelty. He did not deserve Camilla, not after what he'd believed.

"You can do nothing about it," Cochran said in a steely voice. "She's married to a rich and powerful man far better than you. You'll never see her again. She'll never become a Westcott now!" He spat out the name.

"We'll see about that!" Kit nodded, more confidently than he might. "I shall find her." The kernel of hope growing inside him had been planted. Perhaps she was not yet wed to this man. Perhaps there was no man at all. Cochran was a notorious liar.

"You'll get no help from me. Beat your head against the walls, but they'll never tell you anything."

Kit walked out of the room and quickly left Blue Downs, stamping down the steps in a state of exhilaration. Camilla had always been truthful to him. As he considered this, his mood changed, and the next moment he was plunged into depression. Wed to a rich and powerful man? Could this be so? Why not? She'd been bereft and abused for two long years. Kit groaned, thinking of the letters. Her father had burned them all, but he could not destroy their love, no matter what he said or did. They would vanquish him.

He mounted his horse and headed at a gallop for the settlement. Letty Finch! She would know where Camilla had gone.

Chapter 24

The twenty-four-hour voyage across the Bass Strait was nothing compared to Camilla's journeys to England and back. She spent the time listening to Mrs. Mullen, her new chaperone, describe the island colony.

"Abel Tasman, the old Dutch explorer who also found the Fiji Islands, named it after his beloved, Marie Van Dieman," she said. "And then later it was used for the wicked . . . you know, the prisoners over from England. It's called by Tasman's own name, now the convicts aren't kept there any longer."

Camilla sat in a deck chair under a rug and smiled, not really listening. She was free! She was going off to see the world! Torandor was her protector. He would see to it that she remained free.

The pleasant, elderly woman went on about Tasmania's black natives, all dead now, and about its history. The island had a terrible past, with its felons and cruel punishments. But now Tasmania raised fruit and mutton, and holiday travelers came to see its seals and its landscapes. When heat struck Victoria, many would travel to its southern neighbor for the cool climate, reminiscent of England. Tasmania was populated by only a hundred thousand souls living among a million and a half sheep. "Sleepy Hollow," as it was called, was always losing men to the continental gold fields, and it boasted more women and girls than any other colony.

They docked in Launceston, a delightful town in the north, and Cammy helped her companion collect their luggage. The Royal Mail Coach, done up in the scarlet and gold of the royal livery, took them south toward Hobart. Snug, sturdily built towns on the wide highway were surrounded with daffodils and rhododendron, mountains bordered the right side of the road. Cammy was thrilled as always on seeing a new place. A pity Letty was not her companion, but Father no longer trusted Letty. At any rate, she was making a visit to Sydney now. Cammy had asked her to look up Michael there. That way she'd hear from two people she loved.

The coach passed hedgerows and walls and rolling green meadows inhabited by sheep, as well as lakes and ponds unusual on the drier, flatter continent. Yes, indeed, Tasmania did resemble the English lake country, through which she'd fled with Kit to Scotland. But she had to stop thinking about Kit. He was lost to her.

One hundred and twenty miles south lay the great River Derwent, crossed by a hand-hewn stone causeway a mile long. When they had gone over it, they were in Hobart Town, now called Hobart. To the east lay Port Arthur, and Mt. Wellington towered over the city. As Cammy looked up at it, she noted that it was snowcapped and surrounded with wispy clouds.

The Ruyell house where Cammy was to be governess was named Sweet Orchards, and it stood among larches and apple trees just showing their new leaves. Sandy Bay Road ran between the river and stately homes that were decorated with fantastic gables, protected balconies, wide verandas, and steep, slate roofs. Pretty houses with pretty names drew her eyes to the right. On the left she saw the flutter of white sails upon the Derwent. Fresh salt breezes blew off the ocean.

Sweet Orchards, built of gray free-stone, sat beyond a lush green lawn. A painted wagon stood in the drive. Mrs. Mullen saw her to the door, and then bid her farewell. She was bound for a hotel in the city, and Camilla was left at this fine house in Sandy Bay, with its mistress—the mother of the bastard of Riclef's friend.

Janet was not at all what Cammy expected. She was short and round, her face as innocent as a babe's. Her breasts were like small round apples upon the trunk of her body. The solid woman invited Camilla across the threshold with a smile and a dip of the knee that told Cammy Riclef Torandor had not lied when he said Janet was a former chambermaid. It was evident from the way she treated Cammy as one of her betters.

"I'm Janet, to you, Miss Cochran," she insisted, ushering her into the drawing room. It was a spotless, tastefully furnished room with a shiny highboy and a low table, a love seat, and sofa. From hanging pots and slender stands trailed ferns and creepers, giving the room a vernal atmosphere that sent Cammy's memory back to Bernard's conservatory in England. She felt happy to be in this lovely setting and said so.

She would never feel ashamed to labor in this house, though it did occur to her that Father would be apoplectic if he ever learned that she came to Tasmania as hired help, and not as an honored guest of Mr. Torandor's phantom family. But this room was superb! The beadwork, the Tiffany lamp, the rolltop desk were all above reproach.

Janet's husband, Mr. Ruyell, came in straightaway, wearing fresh linen and a soft country coat, unbuttoned. He looked considerably older than Janet, and his thinning hair was brushed over his shiny, freckled scalp. He walked with the swinging gait of a laborer, and he smiled warmly as he approached her, rubbing his hands.

"We are most honored havin' you with us, Miss Cochran," he said, thrusting out his hand to her. "Our little boy, Jason, he'll be keen to meet you. Just call me George, and don't stand on ceremony."

Cammy was served tea and soon began to feel that she was a guest rather than an employee. Janet moved around the room smoothly as if there were wheels, not legs, beneath her skirt. Her hands seemed always busy, whether they were brushing a fern frond out of Camilla's path, straightening an antimacassar, or touching the teapot to see if it was still hot. Janet refused to be seated, even though the maid could just as easily have served. But the mistress pushed the tea cart around by herself, offering cakes and cups to her husband and Camilla.

"I've a shop in Walpole Street," George said. "Walpole's Drapers. It's not large, miss, but it serves."

"He's ever so fine a businessman," Janet added. "Now I'll go fetch our little chap."

Camilla was enormously puzzled. How could such a cozy, conventional, plain girl as Janet have brought a bastard into the world? It even seemed odd that she had attracted the eye of a friend of Riclef's, a man of considerable social standing. And the other startling thing was that Janet was surely no more than nineteen. It would be lovely to work for a girl of her own age. They would almost be like friends. But the boy was five years old, Riclef had said. How could that be?

The child came into the room hesitantly, dressed in short trousers and black stockings, and a loose, pale blue shirt with a tiny necktie. His cheeks were rose-red in a shining, alert, eager face. His hair was straight and he had brown eyes.

Camilla looked from George to Janet to Jason.

Seldom had any child, she thought to herself, so little resembled its mother's husband. But then, why should he?

In a week, she had discovered what Riclef had sent her to learn. Jason was beloved. He was honored and adored, and he was a wonderful child. He asked questions tirelessly, seeking and demanding to be taught. It was clear that he did require a governess.

In her severe gray housedress under an apron, dressed in the same fashion as she had in the Children's Home, Cammy went about the house, seeing to the child's well-being. One moment, she was guiding Jason's transit down the polished bannister. The next, she was sitting on the veranda swing, reading to him about hot-air balloons. There was his cat to feed and visits to make to the carriage horse in her stable. Jason read to her from the daily *Mercury* about shipwrecks and a desert expedition, sounding out the letters. He needed only a little assistance with the harder constructions, and his vocabulary was astonishingly large, amazing in a child only five years old who had never been to school.

"I shall one day sail on a great ship, Miss Milla," he said. "I shall be captain, and me mum shall hang down like the lady on the front."

"What lady, Jason?"

"On the ships! The wooden ladies in their nightdresses!"

"Oh!" she laughed, understanding that he meant the figureheads. He must have haunted the docks and seen them on many brigs and barks. How she wished to sail away with him on one of those boats! To Fiji, perhaps . . . No. It was better to sit with the child at a cricket match, to purchase sweets and toys for him than to dream of a place where she could not go. She could be a child again with Jason. She'd grown up too fast with Kit.

She made Jason a large calendar. On each square, which stood for one day, she had the boy paste paper clouds and suns to represent the appropriate weather. This taught him to be observant. She knew no French or Latin, but she taught him some of the sign system, which he picked up even faster than she had. He loved communicating with her silently in front of his parents, because this was their own secret code.

She wondered about correcting his English when he spoke like his unlettered parents. That was a serious problem. Could she explain to him that what they said was fine, but that he should know two ways to speak? Soon he would learn to write, and she wanted him to do it properly.

She sat down on her ninth day in Sandy Bay and penned a long, thoughtful, and detailed letter to Mr. Torandor at Blue Downs. She described Jason's environment exactly, quoted the boy's clever remarks, praised his parents, and thanked Mr. Torandor profusely for sending her here.

She'd warned her friend before she left to try to meet the postman at the door before her father got the letters. That was often hard to do, but she doubted that even Edgar Cochran would censor the mail of his respected house guest.

Camilla tried to describe Janet Ruyell to Mr. Torandor, but it was difficult to be objective about this lovely woman who had already become her friend. Any notion that Janet had once been a loose woman, hopping into bed with a gentleman in some country house, was beyond belief. Of course, she'd been a mere child then and hadn't known better.

"I was but fourteen when it started, just a baby meself," Janet conceded one afternoon when they were sewing together in the drawing room. "It should not 'ave happened, but it's not uncommon."

"Jason's true father must have been a handsome and brilliant man," Camilla sighed, "but I am surprised that he would victimize a girl of fourteen."

"You're not blamin' me, then, Camilla?"

"I care nothing about your origins, Janet," Camilla responded firmly. "I am glad to find a friend. Why, at sixteen I was so brainless that I—" But she did not finish the sentence. She had been fortunate not to conceive. What would have happened to her then? She looked at Janet, this naive child who, only five years before, had been a plain, lumpish girl with chaff-colored hair. How could a man friend of Riclef Torandor's abuse a little girl?

"Jason's a marvel, ain't he? Comin' from a creature like me!" Janet laughed at herself. "I look at him," she went on, shaking her head, "and I wonder how did I make a boy so beautiful? It's a miracle. He was born in New South Wales in me mother's shack. I weren't married then, as you might guess. I weren't reared in no house like this one, miss. It was only after George inherited that money . . . that and a discovery of gold is the only way humble settlers can rise like sky rockets in the colonies. You can see for yourself, I was a lucky girl."

Camilla smiled at her friend, so eager to confide in one with a willing ear and a tolerant heart. "What happened to you happens to a lot of girls," she told Janet. "And not all of them poor ones."

She might have herself a child or two by now if her luck hadn't held. But she didn't want to think of Kit or a child. To ask for more than she now had would seem devilishly ungrateful. She had a kind protector who stayed home and kept an eye on Father, and the Ruyells were a precious pair, as was Jason. She managed not to dwell on the fact that her name and Riclef Torandor's were inscribed in the Registrar's Marriage Book in Melbourne and that tomorrow only ten days would be left of the required waiting period before a marriage was legal.

"George married me when Jason was one year old," Janet was saying. "I wasn't pure, but he took me anyhow, and Jason, too."

"Well, George has himself a treasure, and he's been a good husband and father, anyone can see that," Camilla said.

"Me mister and me, *we* didn't read books when *we* was five years old, nor cipher, nor talk to grown folks! What's Jason to become? He's freeborn of free parents, and there's ticket-of-leave men even in the legislatures, and women sent out here for stealin' a handkerchief have 'ad governors' wives to tea."

"He might become anything," Cammy sighed, putting down her needlework. "He has his whole life ahead of him."

The next day she borrowed the Ruyell gig and drove into town to get new books for Jason. The child had fairly devoured the ones he had at home. Jason had wanted to go, too, but his mother objected. "He's not goin' out in the rain, the little donkey!" she exclaimed.

"I ain't a donkey!" retorted the boy, and he romped around the room, prancing, snorting, and tossing his head, "I'm a pretty pony!"

Camilla scooped him up and kissed him. It was a blessing to have Jason ease her sorrow. She truly missed the deaf children she had left at home, but this clever lad made up for them.

She drove the gig slowly, attempting to accustom herself to the horse and the blustery winds off the river. The high, two-wheeled vehicle seemed very precarious. Along Sandy Bay Road she spun, and into the city of Hobart. By the time she reached Franklin Square, it was shimmery with raindrops in the emerging sunshine, and birds flitted through pale green leaves. This was a lovely small city, compact and very English. On one side of the square was the St. David's Cathedral, and on the other, a ship at the end of the dock. Because of the angle, it looked as if it were moored right in town.

In her golden serge gown under a brown velvet mantle, Camilla knew she looked fine, and she actually felt happy. Her broken heart, not healed after two years, was something she had simply learned to live with. As she strolled around, she wondered what to buy in the Elizabeth Street bookshop for Jason. Did a boy of five with the mind of an eight-year-old want stories about ships and trains, or about bushrangers and kangaroos?

She was in the shop leafing through a variety of tales when she became aware of a man standing opposite her, across the book-filled table, rudely staring at her.

She caught her breath in exquisite anxiety when he removed his rain-streaked hat and she saw his bearded face. It was Mr. Torandor. She had just posted a letter to him in Victoria! What had possessed him to come down here? He'd sworn he would remain at Blue Downs and take care of Father!

"I see you are perplexed, Camilla."

"I certainly am!"

"May I say you look lovely today? Here, let us walk out. I was watching for you to leave Sweet Orchards, and I followed you."

He was as poised and calm as could be, so she tried to put down her rising sense of dread and distrust. She walked along beside him, keeping pace with his longer legs, and they continued in silence until he stopped in the square to turn and face her.

"Can you guess why I am here, Camilla? Your father is not pleasant company, I must say. I soon tired of his inquiries into my financial affairs, my family. Therefore, I left, told him I might look in on you. How is Jason Ruyell?"

"I wrote to you, but you are not there to receive my letter. Father is bound to open it and discover—"

"He is not that deceitful, is he?"

"Most certainly, he is," she brooded, biting her lip. "Oh, what if he demands I come home, or comes here to get me? Can you keep me away from him, Mr. Torandor?"

His dark eyes studied her, and she suddenly became uneasy.

"There is but one sure way, Camilla—to make you my wife. I doubt you have considered that possibility seriously."

"We are ill matched, as you once said, sir," she responded promptly. Then she quickly changed the subject. "Jason is as well loved as any child I have ever seen. Janet is a dear. The house is beautifully kept, and I fear there is no reason for me to remain here in Hobart, but I do enjoy it very much, and I would like to stay."

"Then you shall, Camilla," he said enthusiastically. "The next task I have for you is to bring the boy to me at Riven Oak. I have leased the house for this month."

"Bring him to you?" She looked at him curiously.

"It doesn't seem discreet for me to come knocking at the door, does it? I simply want to meet my dear friend's son, since you say he is a pleasant child."

"Pleasant? He is *brilliant!* He is reading at the age of five, having taught himself. He is handsome and charming. His speech is not exactly that of a cultured person, but he's a fine mimic, so that will correct itself, I think."

"A fine recommendation! Now I wish even more devoutly to meet him. Tomorrow, say at two in the afternoon. You can manage to drive out with the boy. Just say I am a kinsman of

yours come briefly to town and that you would like to bring
Jason for a visit."

"I suppose I could."

"Certainly you can, Camilla. And in advance I thank you."
He took her hand and impulsively raised it to his lips. As he
kissed the back of her gloved hand, she felt a shiver run
through her.

Chapter 25

Camilla did as she was bidden. What else could she do? The following day she proposed taking Jason to see a distant cousin of hers she'd coincidentally met in Hobart. She thought that Janet might be offended when she was not invited to accompany them, but Janet, subservient and unassuming, never even expected to be invited.

It was a brilliant cool day without a trace of smoke or mist in the air. Cammy wore green, and Jason sat beside her in his very best visiting costume, a brown woolen jacket and knickers.

She was approaching Glenorchy when she saw the first signpost, and she turned off the main road full of surreys and hansoms, milk carts, and drays hauling lumber. At the second turning she drove the gig under trees that reminded her of those at Blue Downs. They were pale, white-barked trees with sparkling leaves like silver pieces. The horse walked through a patch of dead gum leaves beside box hedges. A large house lay behind the tall, wrought iron fence.

At the entrance she reined in beside a gatehouse, and a workman stumbled out to unlock the gate for her. She felt an urge then to turn the horse and fly back to Sandy Bay, but it was too late. The man was already leading the horse into the grounds.

This estate had probably belonged to one of the first settlers of Van Dieman's Land, for it was low and weathered, the roof was covered with moss, and every stone bore the marks of convicts' chisels.

Riclef Torandor came down the steps at a trot, bare-headed, and with no tie. His coat hung open and he was smiling broadly. He could not take his eyes off the child.

" 'Ribbon' Oak?" said Jason, reading the signpost, Riven Oak. "I still don't see no ribbons."

"I'm delighted you've come to call," said Mr. Torandor, sweeping Jason out of the gig and turning toward the house. The gatekeeper handed Camilla down, and she picked up her skirts and hastened after them. When she caught up to them at the front door, Jason was contemplating the new face so close to his, staring at Riclef Torandor who was staring right back.

"Isn't Mr. Torandor kind to invite us?" Camilla asked nervously. He had not even greeted her and he ignored her now. He led the boy deeper into the old house, and she followed. It was a sparsely decorated place, with only a few pieces of early colonial furniture. The house faced north, and they walked straight through to the sunny side, which looked out on a garden of tulips against a wall of golden wattle.

From the limb of a tree hung a child's swing.

"Will you eat some cakes with me?" Torandor asked Jason. "And sit and tell me all about you?"

She hadn't seen Jason shy before, but receiving such undivided attention from such a large and hairy-faced man probably stunned him. He ducked his head and glanced over at her.

They all sat down and Riclef ordered tea to be served.

"Does Jason remind you of anyone?" she asked cautiously.

"Oh, yes, he certainly does. He reminds me of the closest friend I ever had."

That was safe. Anyone might say that regardless of the situation. Then they talked of other things, of life in Tasmania and in other countries. Jason perked up when Riclef told him about sailing from Europe around Africa, and the boy was particularly impressed when he described the snapping and straining of the ship's great sails. Then Torandor gave Jason a small ivory elephant carved in India, and when the tea table was brought in, he pressed frosted cakes upon them. Jason sat propped up on pillows in a big chair, across from his new friend, and he leaned his elbows on the table as he told Riclef about Maggie the horse, and the cat, Bamboo, and the new house where he had his very own room, which he had not had when they lived in the city over a shop.

"I would very much like to see your room, Jason."

Camilla drew her breath in sharply. Surely he would not go there. Riclef wasn't as bold as that!

"When we goin' home?" Jason suddenly asked her. He seemed bored or nervous, she wasn't sure which, but as he asked the question, she saw disappointment in Riclef's face.

"You have not seen the swing I have for good boys," he said, trying to buy a few more minutes. "It is new. Just for you."

That won the boy instantly. "Can I swing, please? I haven't done it in ever so long."

"It is 'may I,' Jason," Cammy corrected him.

"May I swing, sir? Please?"

They went down into the garden, and Riclef led Jason to the tree where he helped him to climb into the swing. As he carefully swung the boy in a shallow arc, and Jason squealed, Camilla wondered whether George thought of some other man, a person he had never met, when he pushed the boy in a swing. After Riclef showed Jason how to pump the swing himself, he came back to Camilla, out of the boy's earshot. They sat on a garden seat, and he began speaking to her in a low and earnest voice.

"Camilla, I wish to reveal something to you. You may have suspected it, but after hearing your father rail against supposed enemies, I think I should verify it."

"And what is that?"

"The man who helped your mother to leave Blue Downs, who paid for Stephen Plaskett's passage from England, that was I."

"You! But I thought—" This was what he meant when he said he was a friend of her mother's!

"Your father had a serpent in his bosom, and did not know it. Someday I shall enjoy enlightening him, when it will harm no one except himself."

"You must have been very close to my mother," she said.

He shifted in his seat and did not look at her. "Is there anyone who does not love Minnie Cochran?" he asked in a faraway voice.

"But you aided her, and now you rescue me as well. What can you expect me to think?"

"That you are alike. Love one, love the other."

"Tell me what Mother was to you," she bravely persisted. "Surely more than an object of admiration and pity. Father has said repeatedly that she—" Camilla stopped, trying to think of the best way to phrase this. "He has suggested that Stephen Plaskett was not my mother's first lover. And I have often wished that perhaps I was someone else's child."

He threw back his large head and laughed out loud. "What are you asking, Camilla? You think that I am your father?" He shook his head. "Look at us, Camilla. You are tiny and fair. I am big and dark and heavy-featured. Camilla, even if the mother were Minnie Cochran, a daughter of mine would be twice your size and far darker."

"Did you," she persisted stonily, "take part in the War in the Crimea?"

"Good heavens, what sort of question is that?"

"Please tell me." She had been born in May of 1854. The Crimean War had begun about nine months before that.

"No, I did not. I saw many good friends go out of England and die in the Turkish muck, but I was not there. Why do you ask?"

"When were you in Victoria, then?"

"I recall that I missed the opening of the Great Exhibition, the Crystal Palace of Prince Albert. That was May of 1851. I was back in England the following summer. Then I came out twice in the 'sixties, but Minnie felt it best that I not call. She was a saint, your mother. She said she intended to rear all her children before she gave a thought to her own happiness."

"And you were then married," Camilla remarked.

"Yes, I was. And I myself was no saint, but I did not desert my wife. She had a fine house in London and was equally happy to see me arrive or to bid me adieu."

Camilla sighed as she realized with relief that Riclef could not possibly be her father.

"Now that you know I am no relation," he said, still with repressed amusement, "I shall be bold to ask you a question. Camilla, our names are already inscribed in the book in

Melbourne. In a few days we can legally marry. Will you have me?"

She gasped, unable to answer. She never imagined that it would come to this.

"We could be very happy, my little golden-haired wren. I shall love you better than any man ever has, and give you fine children, and be a good father. Oh, Camilla, would it not be worth it, to be free of your father? And besides, I am falling in love with you."

"I thought all that about the marriage arrangements," she stammered, stunned beyond belief, "was . . . a ruse . . . to trick my father. I never, never . . . dreamed . . ."

"It was a ruse, the only one that would succeed. And I honestly did not think of you as a wife until now. I saw you with that lovely child and I suddenly became very domestic. If only Howard might have lived to see Jason! I want you to give me a son like that. I would like us to have many sons and daughters."

"I . . . I am honored, but regretfully I must decline." She knew her refusal sounded overly polite and stiff, but she had no idea what else to say.

"Need I play the young swain and confess my love for you upon my knee? I do love you and I want to keep you safe. Suppose I do not succeed in keeping you away from Blue Downs? Do you wish to remain your father's prisoner?"

"Are you threatening me?"

"Not at all. But every good thing has its price."

"My price is very high, then. I shall marry only a man I love, and I do not love you, Mr. Torandor. I am grateful for your kindness to me. Your admiration is a compliment. I owe you much, but not so much as my own self in matrimony."

He seized her hand again, and held it helpless in both of his. The back of his sun-browned hand was marked like a map with veins and tendons, but the palm was smooth as a boy's. It did not bear the calluses built by years of pulling on a horse's reins, like Kit's hand.

Suddenly, too quickly for her to dodge away, he bent over and touched his lips to hers. Then, with an abrupt nod, he got up and went to play with Jason Ruyell.

While she sat and considered her dilemma, Riclef twisted the ropes above Jason's head, and wound him into a wild spin. The child squealed even louder with delight. Then

Riclef squatted upon his haunches, stopping the swing's action. He talked to Jason, touching the boy's nose and cheeks, tousling his hair. Camilla felt her eyes fill with tears. Poor, lonely man. If she relented and wed him, and gave him a pretty little boy with brown hair, he would surely be a doting father. The child would be his whole life and enjoy every advantage of travel, education, security, love. But what of her own life, and her poor tormented heart?

He came to her, leading Jason, his face lit up with affection for the boy. "I want to see him in his home, Camilla," he said softly. "Then I shall rest satisfied."

On the way back to Sweet Orchards with Jason, she turned into Battery Point, and the buggy slowly rolled around Arthur's Circus with its quaint, doll-like houses, and their gardens all in bloom. She looked down Kelly's Steps and chose Runnymede Street to reach Salamanca Place. The neighborhood was full of pretty trees and antique buildings, and the salt breeze whipped them as they drove. She had never seen such a clean city.

"Did you have a good time?" asked Jason, startling her out of deep brooding. "I did," the child went on proudly. "He likes me. He said so. I like him, too."

"I could see that, dear," she responded, not knowing why she felt so sad.

When they arrived home, Jason told his mother about the "nice man with a hairy face who let me swing."

"We shall hang a swing for ye, Jason, me boy," said George Ruyell instantly.

Camilla did not look up from her dinner. She was acutely aware of this man's determination to be a good surrogate father.

"It's good luck you've got a cousin here, so close by," said Janet. "You'll have to invite him here. Or is he too much the toff to dine with the likes of us?"

"You must not put yourself below other people," Camilla chided her, avoiding the issue of the invitation.

"Is he a married man, Camilla? Is he old or young? I hope he's a far-distant cousin, so you might—" she giggled. "I mean, you're nineteen now, and gracious, that's plenty old enough to marry."

"I do not propose to marry him," she said softly. She had never confided in her dear friend about Kit. How could she ever explain the depth of her feeling, the love that had lasted so many years?

That night she did not sleep well. She was suffused with passion for Kit. When she did sleep, she dreamed of two men, Kit and Riclef, hovering over her. She writhed under the covers, arching her back, tossing her head. No good girl should know at age sixteen the joys of the flesh, the feel of a man lying upon her. And since she had felt need at sixteen, how much more did she yearn for release now at nineteen years and five months of age! But her desire was not for a dark, middle-aged man, who wished to claim her as his wife and the mother of his future children. It was for only one man, and she would have him or no other.

Chapter 26

Janet came down the stairs several days later with a secret to impart to her new friend.

"I'm tellin' you, Camilla, before I'm tellin' George," she confided, "'cause I want to have you see his face when he hears. And now it's time to tell him, as I'm startin' to show."

Cammy gasped and clapped her hands together. "Oh, Janet! Are you going to have another child?"

"I'm the proper age for it now, ain't I?" she said hopefully. "I've not told George, as I had a hard time in the first months," she said. "This baby was dropped down, 'cause of my havin' a bad struggle to birth Jason. I was too young with him they told me, and it like to tore me apart. But now, this one, he's big enough to lay like he's supposed to, and I'm feelin' fit again."

"Will you tell Jason, too?"

"You think it's proper to do that? I'd like to, for sure, but I don't know that he's old enough."

"He seems quite grown up to me," Cammy smiled. "Why don't you try it?"

That evening at the supper table, when Janet told her husband and small son that she was to have a baby, both of them rushed to hug the pregnant woman. Jason demanded that it be a sister. As for George, his face was a true mirror of his happy heart as he looked upon the slight bulge that was his own child. Camilla, feeling very much the outsider, excused herself and left the table.

George was such a dear man! And Janet, so well meaning, did not have to try to measure up to impress their well-born governess! If she only knew Cammy's own story!

The following week, Camilla came upon Riclef Torandor strolling behind Sweet Orchards. He begged her to come to Riven Oak with him, which she reluctantly agreed to do, for only an hour. The poor man seemed so lonely. She had no sooner removed her mantle when, without any warning, he dropped to the floor on one knee and grasped her hands.

"Marry me, Camilla. Give me a child like Jason."

"Please," she said, "I cannot!"

His eyes were pleading and the lines fell away from his uptilted face, so that he might have been a man in his thirties. She felt great compassion for him, but that was all.

"All your worries in life end with one little word, Camilla. Say 'yes.'"

He put his lips upon her bosom, in the opening between the lapels of her jacket. She felt the warmth of his lips and began to struggle as his arms tightened about her. She gingerly touched his hair and then his broad shoulders. She almost wished she could be borne away on a tide of passion, which would make everything so much easier. But she felt no passion. He was foreign to her mind and to her life. He offered to give her safe harbor, but that was not enough to win her.

"Wait," she said as his lips moved toward her throat. "Oh, please do not kiss me!"

Could this man teach her to love him? It would take a long time, and even then, she doubted that her feelings would be true.

The fading day turned the green foliage outside the windows to a faint blue. The sky was suffused with a pink glow. Slowly, he rose, kissing her throat and her unresponsive lips, pulling her closer against him. But he did it gently, as one handles a bird that has stunned itself against a window and must be stroked back to sensibility.

"I wish to visit Sweet Orchards, Camilla," he said when she would clearly have no more of him. She extricated herself from his arms.

"I see," she said, combing her hair with her fingers. Turning away from him, she wondered what she should do.

"Your duties at Sweet Orchards seem to be ending," he said. "The boy is so bright that he requires a tutor in Latin and mathematics, and you are not proficient in either, Camilla, are you?"

"No. I'm not."

"So . . . what shall I do with you, my dearest child?" He chuckled without mirth. "Were you mine, Camilla, I would tear you out of Edgar Cochran's grasp in a moment, and take you to Europe to be tutored yourself. You would be polished and garbed in fine clothes. I would do that for a young wife. Would you prefer to live in Paris or London, Camilla? The twenty-one days are nearly passed, so we can wed. Then as we stand in the Registrar's office, I will reveal to Edgar that it was I who aided Minnie's escape, and cozened him in regard to you. You deserve the pleasure of seeing your father foiled, made to realize his wickedness toward his family and especially toward you."

She stood unmoving before him, trying to fathom a way out. All she could do was delay him until she had a solution.

But she did agree to let him see Jason in the Ruyell home, feeling that this would appease him and take his attention off her. She asked Janet to invite him. Mrs. Ruyell was delighted to oblige.

Janet looked lovely in a plum-colored velveteen gown with pearl buttons down the front. Camilla stood beside George, who had a silver pin in his tie tonight, and had polished his shoes until they shone brilliantly. It would be a candlelight dinner. The greenery that spilled over from the drawing room into the dining room in the dimness cast shadows on the walls that seemed mysterious and exotic. The flickering flames obscured their faces, and Cammy was glad of that, since she felt rather anxious, especially when she saw the landau turn into the Sweet Orchards drive. Why did Riclef feel such great loyalty to the deceased Howard? They'd been university friends, he'd said, and that tie was sometimes very close. Michael used to tell her that, and so had Kit.

Why did everything make her think of Kit Westcott? When she dreamed of Kit, afterward she would remember her innocent childhood, before sin and duty, guilt and subterfuge entered her life. No wonder adults developed lines in their faces, not to mention white hair.

When Riclef walked through the door, a tall hat covering his head, Janet greeted him at once, but she was too shy to look him in the eyes.

"Oh, this must be the fine man Jason prattled of!" she exclaimed. She could tell that Riclef was middle-aged, but not too old to be a suitable husband for a well-born young lady. He moved like a youth, his eyes bright with eager curiosity.

George was shy with him, smaller and less elegantly attired than their guest, but Riclef treated him as an equal. He put on a bland, pleasant face as he bowed over his host's handshake. Cammy was glad to see that things were going well.

Janet curtsied, flushed, and immediately blurted out that dinner would straightaway be served. "We are so honored by your visit. We love Camilla, your cousin, and are delighted to meet a kinsman of hers," she said.

Camilla winced. Riclef smiled.

After a few pleasantries about the room and its vernal atmosphere, with the flickering candlelight for effect, Riclef asked, "Where is the young lad? He is to dine with us, is he not?"

"We thought not," said George, "bein' that he's a child. It's not the custom for kiddies to dine formal like with their elders, now is it? 'Course the other child, the one that's comin' nigh on a few months, he'll have to stay where he is." George laughed at his little joke, and Janet blushed at the mention of her pregnancy. Cammy noticed Riclef suddenly became very pensive.

"I do hope you shall permit Jason to come down now," he said, his voice suddenly tinged with an edge of annoyance. "I do not care for most children, but yours seems extraordinary."

He was staring down at Janet as if he could look straight through her and view the new baby within her body. Still, even as she felt his scrutiny, Janet was too embarrassed to meet his gaze.

"Shall we have the boy summoned?" Riclef said authoritatively.

"Why certainly, if that is your wish, sir," Janet responded. She summoned the maid, who went straight upstairs to fetch Jason.

He came down with the maid several minutes later, dressed nicely with a bow under his chin and a pleated gray coat, striped stockings, and tiny polished boots. He broke into a trot when he saw their visitor, and ran to Riclef, yelling "It's Mr. Torandor!"

Riclef restrained himself from crouching to greet Jason, and from lifting the boy in his arms, although Camilla could see that it pained him not to do so. He merely tousled the neatly combed little head and withdrew his hand abruptly.

Cammy was on edge throughout the first course, though she told herself there was no reason for fear. Six years had passed, and surely Janet had never met this friend of her seducer. She would never suspect that he had known Howard, and therefore knew her circumstances. No, Riclef was going to carry this off superbly, making the Ruyells feel comfortable and worthy. He invented stories about Camilla's family to keep the dinner conversation lively, speaking of virtues she was too modest, as he put it, to admit.

At this, Janet replied, "The best I'd wish for any young lady is a husband like my George, and a son like Jason." She was slightly nervous herself, but only because she was unsure of which fork to use for which course.

"Jason's to become a brother, as I've said," George interjected, rendered more voluble by the wine. The men then launched into a discussion of family size and the desirable mix of boys and girls. There was no way to know, from George's enthusiastic chatter, that Jason was not his own son.

There was a dish of capons in cream and a course of beef with mushrooms and a number of side dishes excellently prepared by their cook. Naturally, they wanted Riclef to think Jason ate such fare on Irish linen every day.

Jason, however, behaved less like a fine gentleman than Camilla would have wished. He picked up a capon leg and gnawed upon it, then he sucked his fingers noisily. Eventually, Cammy thrust a napkin at him, which he took, but did not use. "It's awful good, Mum," he chortled. "D'you like carrots, Mr. Torandor? I don't and I won't eat 'em. I give 'em to Maggie."

"His horse," Camilla murmured.

"Where do you plan to educate Master Ruyell?" Riclef asked the boy's parents.

"We've not thought of that, bein' he's so little," said George.

"There's a fine grammar school outside Melbourne," Riclef remarked, "and when he's ready and old enough, I'm sure he could be sent abroad to Cambridge or Oxford."

Janet's eyes widened. "Oh, lands, we couldn't part with 'im to some place like that!" she exclaimed. "Them's in England, ain't they? But that's not necessary. There's schools fit for a duke right out here in the colonies."

George nodded his agreement. "We don't want the kiddie puttin' on airs."

"Your boy is exceptional," Riclef objected heatedly. "He should have the very best education. When Miss Cochran leaves you, I hope you shall immediately obtain an English tutor who has several languages. It is never too early to begin Latin."

"And what would he be needin' Latin for?" asked George suspiciously. Although the light was dim, Cammy knew he was frowning.

"He may wish to go into the church, to read law, to be a scholar. Latin and Greek are the bases for—"

"There's employment enough for 'im among people who speaks the King's English," George interrupted, "though I should leave out the King in respect to me missus' family bein' from Ireland. I mean, sir," he said, catching a glimpse of Cammy's worried face, "we're beholdin' to you fer bein' so concerned for the lad, but we don't see why he needs Latin in Tasmania."

"I'm sure you do not want to hold Jason back from the highest he might attain," murmured Riclef solemnly.

Suddenly, Janet put her fork down and cleared her throat. "I thank you for your advice, sir. Now let us speak of something else!"

Cammy's head jerked around when she heard Janet's tone. She never spoke this way, surely not to a guest! The woman was staring fixedly at Riclef, and her hand shot out to seize Jason's. Cammy intentionally dropped a spoon. "Pardon me! Look at my carelessness." She coughed to make everyone turn to her, but Janet did not remove her gaze from Riclef's face.

The boy who was playing with the remnants of food on his plate, pulled his left hand out of his mother's grip and resumed chattering to Riclef. Cammy felt terrified for no known reason. Something was happening here. If only she knew what it was! Why did Janet look so strange?

"You're white as a sheet," whispered Cammy to Janet. "I fear it is your condition—"

Janet did not even glance at her, but rose from the table, letting her napkin slide to the carpet. "I am going up," she said coldly, and reached for Jason.

"I haven't had my sweet yet!" he howled.

"Go with your mother. I shall bring it up to you," Cammy said rapidly. "Behave, Jason!"

Reluctantly, Jason went with his mother, muttering all the way to the stairs, tugging away from his mother. But she stolidly marched on and did not stop until she reached the next floor.

"The baby," said Cammy. "I think perhaps she—"

"Somethin' must have disagreed with her innards," commented George. "Hope you'll pardon them leavin'. Now let's have the sweet served us," George said to the maid. "It's chocolate, so I've been told."

"I think I'll go see if she's all right." Cammy jerked her chair back and ran up the stairs, her heart in her throat.

Janet and Jason were on the upper floor now, walking quickly. Cammy heard Jason whining about having to leave his new friend. At that moment, Janet bent down and slapped the boy hard across the seat of his pants. Jason shrieked in pain and humiliation.

Something was terribly wrong! Cammy had never seen his mother strike him before. Then she whirled around to face Cammy with an expression of hatred and fear.

"I'll put 'im to bed myself," she said. "With me!"

She closed the door to her chamber in Cammy's face with a cry of rage.

Chapter 27

During the remainder of Riclef's visit, George showed him around the garden, carrying a lantern to illuminate the shrubs and flowers. The men puffed on Riclef's slender cigars, and thin plumes of smoke rose in the still air above them.

Camilla tagged along after them, feeling responsible for the evening's unpleasantness, and ill with anxiety. George was not familiar with the custom of gentlemen sipping brandy and smoking in the library while the ladies chatter in another room, and so he made no objection to her company. He had been only a laborer before Jason's father set him up as a draper by leaving him a shop as a "bequest."

Riclef was very quiet and seemed annoyed at Janet's sudden exit. Camilla knew the reason for his visit was seeing Jason, and he wanted more conversation with the child.

In another hour, after Riclef had departed, brushing a kiss on Camilla's cheek that George did not notice, Cammy ran straight upstairs to Janet's room. She knocked at the door, but there was no response.

"Janet, are you awake? Are you well?" Cammy whispered.

There was no sound.

She tried the knob. The door was unlocked, and she walked

into the room. A short candle nubbin was almost guttering out on the mantelpiece, and Camilla used it to light one of the oil lamps. As the flame grew higher, she could make out a bulge under the covers of the bed.

Janet was half sitting, half lying in bed, still dressed. Jason dozed in her arms. She huddled over her child protectively, as her haunted eyes accused the young woman standing before her.

Camilla came across the room to sit hesitantly on the edge of Janet's bed. "Are you overtired? Was Jason overexcited?" She had no idea how to begin. "May I fetch you a draught of cordial?"

Janet said nothing. Jason sighed in his sleep and burrowed deeper into his mother's bosom. "I don't want no cordial," she muttered, her face contorting with suspicion. "That man down below is kin to you? You been truthful to me, Camilla?"

"What . . . what do you mean?"

"I asked is he your true cousin?"

Cammy bit her lip, chagrined at the ruse. "He is a longtime friend of my mother's, but no kin. I said that only so you would not think me bold when I visited his home without a chaperone. He's the man who found me this situation with you. My father treated me badly, and he offered me a way out." She watched Janet's face and saw clearly that all this was irrelevant.

Camilla looked away, gathering all her courage. Then she asked, "Janet, tell me what is amiss?"

"He's the man!" Janet breathed, her eyes enormous.

"Mr. Torandor? What are you talking about?"

"Jason's father, that's who," she whispered, so softly that Camilla had to lean forward to be sure she understood. She blinked in astonished horror. His father? Riclef? But Howard was the father!

Janet folded the blanket carefully up over Jason's ear. When she spoke again, her breathless whisper was almost inaudible.

"You knew," Janet hissed. Her brows and mouth were drawn down, aging her girlish face.

"I did not know *that!*" Cammy replied.

"You're his person! His helper."

"Janet, I love you!" Camilla exclaimed, reaching for her friend's hand. Janet shook it off. "I do, Janet. I'd never harm you! He asked me to come and teach the son of his dead friend. Then he insisted on seeing Jason himself."

"It's not his friend. It's him."

"Didn't you—You never knew the man's name, Janet?"

She shook her head. "I never heard his name. Papa had debts. He owed money. We was like to starvin'—"

"You mean, your father—?"

"Men likes to have girls the first time, and they thought I'd not make a baby, being I was only fourteen. That man paid Papa lots—"

"Are you saying that a man bought you? That your own father sold you?" Cammy cried, aghast.

"It's done often enough," Janet nodded grimly. "Ladies like you don't hear about the likes of us who's poor. Me mum was the one got the money."

"But you were just a baby yourself!"

Janet looked down and stroked her son's soft hair. "He's gonna take Jason away. He's come to get 'im," she whimpered.

"He cannot! Oh, dear one, he cannot take away your son!"

"He took me, didn't he?" Her voice was harsh and unfeeling. "Them with money, they can do anything they pleases. I always feared he'd find me and take my boy."

"But why didn't you know his face, Janet? When he walked in here tonight, you were so—"

"He didn't have no beard, back then, six years past. And he'd not say his name, not to me," she said, scowling. Cammy felt ripples of ice run along her backbone. "Tonight, we was all fancy, with the candles for dinner. You don't see so good by candlelight," Janet murmured.

"Are you sure he's the same man?" Cammy asked hopelessly.

"I know 'is eyes. He's come here and wants to see Jason and touch him, and see to 'is education. Who's he, if not the same man?" She wiped her nose and choked back a sob. "Look at 'em. Him and my boy. They look just alike!"

Cammy had seen it without understanding the resemblance. Jason's hair was brown, not black, but Janet's was lint-colored. Jason was still small like his mother, but his big feet and hands, like a puppy's, promised growth. The snapping dark eyes of the boy, the keen intelligence! Camilla had actually pictured the boy's dead father as someone very much like Riclef, a brilliant and handsome aristocrat. Why hadn't she admitted to herself what she'd unconsciously suspected? She might have run off immediately that day when he suddenly appeared at the bookstore, telling her he'd come to stay at Riven Oak. But where would she have run? Back to Papa to be shamed and scorned? She had no place else to go.

"Janet," she said, daring to slide an arm around the shoulders of her friend, "what does George know?"

"He knows the reason Mum got that money to go off and get us a house. She took in laundry and all eleven of us helped, especially after Dad died.

"Then I got a big belly, and near to died havin' Jason, but George, he married me just the same. And then we got that letter saying George's aunt died, the one he didn't know he had, leavin' to us money of our own, and more to spare."

Camilla knew by now that Riclef was responsible for that bequest, but she did not mention it.

"You won't tell George about Mr. Torandor, will you? Please, Janet. It would crush him, and Mr. Torandor means you no harm. He's just visiting Jason, that's all. He wants . . . he wants to marry me and have children of his own. We'll fix this, Janet. I shall leave here immediately, and draw the man away."

"He was gentle with me, though," Janet mused, softly touching her son's dark, wavy locks. "He gave me a drink so it hurt hardly at all. It was the birthin' that was hard."

"He was a monster!" Camilla exclaimed fiercely, wondering how she could ever have liked Riclef Torandor.

"Worse things happen, though ladies don't hear 'em. I'd rather it was a strange man, since he went straight away after, than me own dad who had me. That happens y'know."

Camilla gasped, sickened by the thought. She could not imagine any such horror. How shielded she'd been! She, who'd often eavesdropped upon adult conversations as a child and read books not meant for young eyes. And she thought of herself as an experienced woman!

"You never heard from him again?" she asked. "He didn't find out—"

"I got from him a beautiful brilliant boy," Janet said solemnly. "This new baby," she went on, patting her stomach, "George's baby, will be a dear, the love of my heart. We're hopin' for a little girl."

Cammy stared at her friend, wishing she had Janet's

resilience. "I'll be leaving immediately, Janet," she repeated. "You mustn't have any more shocks like this."

She wanted to assure Janet that Riclef had no intention of taking Jason away, but she couldn't be sure any more. She remembered the man's intense face gazing at Jason when they first met. She hadn't understood then, but now she knew how much his own son meant to him. And having met him, how could he now let him go?

Her last week at Sweet Orchards was agony for Camilla.

Only George was blithely unaware, speaking proudly of their fine dinner guest, and saying how much he'd like to invite him again. Obviously, Janet had revealed nothing to her husband, and Jason had slept soundly through all their whispered midnight confidences.

Camilla worried that Janet would soon come to some correct conclusions about their wealth. She might want to return the "inheritance," mortified that her own despoiler, not George's "aunt," had lifted them so high in the world. Janet was distant and thoughtful, and was cold to Camilla.

Jason, deprived of his exciting admirer, pouted for two days, continually asking when he might see his new friend again. Each time Camilla looked at Jason she saw what she'd previously refused to see, that he was unquestionably Riclef's son. Every feature was a mirror of his father's.

Camilla couldn't help thinking about her own part in this. Her mission had seemed harmless, even beneficent. Suppose Jason had been neglected and abused by an ignorant mother and an indifferent stepfather? It was Riclef's right to learn the facts. But now he should go away and never look back. Just because he was the child's natural father didn't make him an omnipotent god! No longer did Edgar Cochran seem to Camilla to be the worst father in the world, not now when she considered a father who would sell his child. Yet brides were often sold to the highest bidder, some of them unwillingly.

At midweek, she returned alone to Riven Oak. She walked into Riclef's house unannounced, without a glance at the caretaker who guarded the place, and marched straight in past the fluttery maid.

She found Riclef writing in the library, and she glared at him from the doorway.

"I am appalled that you would gull me, gull Janet! And

when she told me of your crime—" The words poured from her, and she was unable to control her rage.

He stood up and considered her with a pale face. He did not speak.

"You were monstrous!" she accused him. "And you were no lad then. You were a grown man of thirty-seven! To abuse a mere baby, a child of fourteen—"

"I am sorry you had to learn that." He was somber, and seemed truly contrite.

"I wish to leave here immediately," she said stolidly. "I trust you will not try to detain me."

"Where will you go, Camilla?" he asked gently.

She whirled away from him, about to go, but she could not resist a confrontation. She turned to face him again.

"You deny nothing? You bought a child and used her?" she spat out, hoping to hurt him.

He sighed, lifting his hands in a gesture of apology. "I paid her mother enough money to free her from servitude. Then I paid George Ruyell for that house of theirs, and for a drapery shop. What do I have to show for it? I do not have my son, and I have earned your scorn."

"You deserve it!" Then she moved a step closer. "Jason is Janet's! He is Janet's and George's child, not yours!"

"He is mine, and you know very well that no one could prevent my taking him."

Camilla shook her head, unable again to utter a word of protest.

"I did a vile thing once, yes, Camilla. But have you never sinned?"

"My sin did not ruin the life of a little maiden!"

"You were once a little maiden, and it did ruin your life, Cammy." His voice was so tender that she took a step backward, pierced to the soul by the truth of his words. "Your lovemaking broke your heart, and even now you are scarcely past childhood," he pointed out. Then he came toward her.

"I love you, Cammy. This indignation you display makes me value you more, for I see that your heart is good. Marry me, Camilla, and share your love with me. God, for how many years was I wed to an unloving, barren wife! My sins were many, and now I am found out, so that I no longer have anything to hide. Marry me and make me a good man, Cammy!"

"I don't love you," she said, sick at heart. Then there was silence between them. She knew exactly what was coming, and was powerless to stop it.

"If I cannot have the woman I adore, Camilla, I must have Jason. Give me a son, and Janet will keep Jason. Otherwise, I cannot answer for what I might do."

"You would ravish me, next?" she hissed, furious at the alternative he presented.

"Never. I would not harm a hair of your glorious head," he vowed. "I want a wife, Camilla. And another son. I acknowledge all my failings and pray that you will forgive them, Camilla." He rubbed a hand over his beard, and shook his head as if some terrible pain tormented him.

"If you love Jason, give him what he wishes, not what you so selfishly want," she pleaded.

"Jason is too young to know what is best for him."

"But Janet is not too young to know. She's terrified that in your high-handed way you'll commit a second crime. You're like some medieval lord, claiming his right to the maidenhead of any female vassal and any promising child who was the issue of his union."

"Even when you abuse me," he said softly, "I admire your perceptiveness. You have an acute mind and you read me well. I shall take you back to Melbourne three days hence. Pack your things and bid Janet adieu. I tell you, Camilla, if you marry me, I will no longer covet Jason."

"I will consider it," she whispered, knowing she would have to deceive him and then warn Janet.

"Consider wisely."

She turned to leave and then stopped at the door. "If Janet confides in George, he may try to kill you."

"I can do nothing about that, unless you advise me to go armed! Let us be gone, Camilla. I shall send a carriage for you Friday morning."

The next three days were torture for Camilla. On Thursday afternoon, however, she warned Janet of the danger.

"Will he take away our boy?" the woman asked, clasping her hands together. "He's bound to, I know it."

"I've led him to think I'll marry him when we arrive in Melbourne, Janet, so that will content him for a while. You must use that time to hide yourself and Jason."

Janet stood staring into her friend's eyes, unable to speak.

"I have caused you such heartache, Janet. All I can do is to give you time to vanish. You must go far away and cover your tracks. Tell George the reason only after we have departed."

"George would die 'afore he'd lose Jason. He's reared 'im like he was his own. Jason's more to 'im than life itself."

"You can sell a few possessions to finance a new beginning, Janet. I love you, dear heart. I could happily dwell with you and George and your darling boy forever. How I wish I could remain with you!"

"Take care," the woman said, then she kissed Camilla. Camilla did not know that Janet's thoughts were to advise her not to wed Riclef Torandor, but no mother in Janet's situation could be so self-sacrificing as that.

Chapter 28

On Monday morning, after the overnight voyage, Camilla preceded Riclef off the ship at Melbourne. He was smiling as he had been for the past day, and referred to her as "my bride."

Spinning up the broad avenues of the city, through kaleidoscopic crowds of scurrying people, men in top hats, and ladies carrying fashionable parasols, they made for the Menzies Hotel in Bourke Street. The moment they walked into the lounge, a small man in a black suit rose to greet them. Camilla was face to face with Edgar Cochran.

"Couldn't you have told me?" she spat at Riclef. She glared at her father, but said not one word.

"I am gratified beyond measure, daughter, that the gentleman of my choice will become my son-in-law—today. Your dear aunt, who has taken your place at Blue Downs, is not well, and unfortunately could not join us for the ceremony."

"This is not—" she began.

"This is the twenty-third day, and today you can legally be wed. There's no reason for delay. Let us be off to the Registrar's office," he insisted.

She needed time to think. To go back to Blue Downs with Father and Aunt Rina, to see him close the Children's

Home—Was marrying Riclef much worse a prospect than that? And if she did go through with this wedding, she'd redeem herself for bringing Jason into range of Riclef Torandor's power.

She tried to figure the safety factor. Only five days ago Janet had learned of the necessity to hide Jason from her ravisher. How long would it take her to break the news to George and then find a place for the three of them to go? Riclef would need another three days' travel time if he decided to return to Hobart for the boy.

In the midst of her pondering, Camilla was sent upstairs to the suite Father had reserved for her adjoining his, and told to dress well for the occasion.

She chose a visiting gown of cashmere and silk in two shades of blue, with ruchings and fringe of magenta and a blue striped underskirt. Inside the palisades of so many layers of skirt, she somehow felt safer, protected from prying eyes. Ladies dressed to attract men, but also to shut them out.

In the carriage on the way to the office, she sat beside Riclef, taking no comfort from the grasp of his large gloved hand upon hers under a fold of her gown. Their alliance against Father was still secret, but Father and Riclef today were allied against her in the matter of this unwelcome wedding. She was totally alone.

The only thing that prevented her from swooning with sorrow and fear was the thought of the Ruyells and their dangers. Janet was so fatalistic about Jason, so intimidated by her lofty gentleman abuser, that she might not flee, after all. If Riclef came back and George resisted his taking Jason, the man might end in prison. He might be hanged! And what of the child himself? Would he survive a kidnapping? His mother petted and spoiled him, usually allowing him a great deal of freedom. Riclef, on the other hand, would clap him into laced boots and stiff collars and put him under a stern tutor armed with a cane. One careless word, one lesson unprepared, and poor Jason would have his palm or his bottom beaten or his mouth washed out with soap.

No, she could not picture that life for Jason. What right did Riclef have to tear him from his parents? He merely loved the boy, and had contributed half Jason's inheritance of looks and mind, but that was all.

"Camilla, smile. This is your wedding day."

Her father interrupted her reverie and displayed one of his

frigid, brief smirks. Riclef pressed her hand and bowed his head over hers protectively. If only Riclef were another man . . . the lost and lovely man she mourned for. . . .

As they drew near the government building where three weeks ago they had inscribed their names in the Marriage Book, Camilla went cold as death. If there was only herself to consider, she could easily refuse Riclef Torandor and last out the remaining two years at Blue Downs. But suppose her refusal sent the man straight to Hobart, and he snatched Jason away?

While Father was paying the driver, she drew Riclef aside to speak with him. He looked resplendent in his black wedding suit, although the garment was far too warm for this spring afternoon in the busy city.

"Riclef," she whispered, hanging onto his arm. He had to bend forward to hear her. "Suppose Father knew you had aided Mama, and . . . that you loved her. He would never allow me to wed you."

"The moment we are safely wed, Camilla, I intend to tell him all. You deserve to see his rage and miserable impotence."

"Must you wait until we are wed?" she cajoled, thinking furiously. Perhaps there still was a way out!

The expression on his face clearly said she must be more foolish than he thought. He made no reply and her hopes fell.

They went inside to do their business. In short order, the license was granted and the document saying she was free to marry Riclef Torandor was signed. And, because of her age, she also had her father's permission to wed this man.

"Shall we have the thing done immediately?" asked Edgar Cochran strutting with conceit and self-importance. Everyone in the office was smiling and peering at them. Since there were few well-born ladies in this land, such a match was not frequently seen.

"Where will you wish to hold the ceremony?" asked the Registrar, a gruff man with a bristling mustache.

"Right here, and right now," said Father.

"I shall see if that is possible," said the frowning functionary. "We have a great deal of work to be done, it being the beginning of a new week, and with no notice in advance . . ." He clucked his tongue in annoyance.

"I am sure it can be managed," Riclef murmured, pressing close to Camilla and taking her hand.

Was it really going to happen then? And after the ceremony, when they retired to their room, would he then . . . ? She would indeed fall ill if she thought about it, she felt so faint now. She had to lean against a counter for support.

"We should have both Westcotts here as witnesses," said Cochran arrogantly. "Wouldn't they be pleased to see my Camilla married so far above them?"

She turned away her face, too ashamed to cry, and Riclef moved between her and her father. "It is not appropriate, Edgar," he muttered in a low voice, "to torment this fragile, precious victim of your endless—"

He cut himself off, and Cammy shot him a glance. If only he'd gone on! If he spoke of his feelings for Minnie, this wedding would never take place. But at that instant, the clerk came back. "I fear that the press of business will not permit a marriage ceremony this afternoon," he said. "It is close to four o'clock, and that, of course, is the very latest hour permitted by law."

Riclef sighed audibly and shrugged, taking her arm. Father was muttering about bureaucratic inefficiency, but Cammy wasn't really listening. She must control herself and say absolutely nothing. She had been granted one more night! That was something to be thankful for.

Be calm, she told herself. They walked toward the doors. Behind them, the whole office was buzzing with regret. Her father gave the clerk the name of their hotel, saying they would return in the morning, and then he joined them at the door. Stepping in front of them, he led the way out of the building.

"A night of waiting will be hard, we've come so far already," Camilla's fiancé said. Her father scowled and said nothing, but his eyes spoke worlds to her. She knew they feared she might bolt, and they'd never let her out of their sight all evening long.

When they had arrived at the hotel, and Riclef stood with her in the lobby while her father saw to their luggage, he whispered, "How much is this acquiescence because of Jason, and how much can I hope that you care for me?"

"Brides learn to care for their husbands after the wedding," she said with false evenness. Actually, had he not been clinging to her arm, she would have rushed for the door, the street, and vanished into the crowd.

They ate in the hotel dining room. She could tell that Riclef was just barely holding himself in check. He was fairly vibrating with hatred for the man opposite them, who was so pompously boasting about his virtue and accomplishments. Edgar Cochran had been difficult to take before, but now, with his daughter about to marry a wealthy man, he was impossible.

Cammy remembered another night in another fine hotel in Salisbury, Wiltshire. That night she had dined with her father and the Van Beeks. Kit had seen them and decided that she loved Hans, but at least he had been there! No such lucky chance tonight. Kit was in Fiji and had forgotten her completely, or if not, he realized it would be far too dangerous to contact her until her twenty-first birthday. Yet, tomorrow morning she would be joined to Riclef Torandor for life.

She let her eyes sweep the dimly lit dining room. The two men seemed to be enjoying their food, but Camilla could not eat. She sat up taller and examined the diners.

There were several tables of large, noisy parties, a few quiet couples, and only a few men sitting alone. She stared at one of them.

He did not look much like Kit, though he was curly-haired. The man had a dark mustache, and his chin was sunk into his coat collar. When she looked up at him a second time, his eyes burned into hers. His hair was brushed down to his brows, unlike Kit's, but what now riveted her attention was his hand. The knuckles supported his chin, and the fingers now formed the letter *K* from the one-handed French manual alphabet. Was he really signing to her, or was it her wild imagination?

She gaped, trying to hide her emotion from her dinner companions. Then she stared at him again. Only a few experts in the hand language knew that alphabet, like Letty Finch and her parents. The man's attention was still directed at her, and the *K* had vanished. Now the little finger was straight, and the other four were folded down into a fist. She heard nothing of the noisy dining room, so deafened was she by the thundering of her own heart. The fingers slowly, carefully moved again. The thumb now bisected the index finger.

It was a *T*. He had spelled *Kit!*

It was he! Kit had somehow miraculously come for her!

She tore her gaze away from Kit just before Riclef raised his head and commented upon the excellence of the food. She agreed with him, smiling, and tried to eat while at the same time she watched Kit's hand silently communicating to her across the room. She must arouse no suspicion. She must not cry. She must simply remain here until she learned what he wanted and responded to him in the same alphabet. This French system was so small, so subtle. He was still supporting his chin on his knuckles as he pushed his food around his plate. When had he come into the room? Surely after they were seated so he could situate himself behind Riclef and Father and in front of her.

Now his eyes held hers again, and his hand moved slowly. She had shown by her face that she knew him, though she dared not attempt the slightest nod. She put a forkful of food into her mouth, almost choked on it, and smothered her cough.

"Are you all right, dear?" asked Riclef solicitously.

She nodded yes, so emphatically that Kit knew the affirmative to be meant for him as well.

His fingers moved more swiftly from one letter to the next. *I will come tonight. Where?*

She sent him a panicked *Wed tomorrow*, pausing between the words to be sure he could decipher the meaning.

Thank heavens Katherine Shrader had given her instruction in this other alphabet. By using it carefully, she would only seem to be straightening the dangling curls on one side of her face.

Save me, she added in her message to her beloved.

"I cannot say when I've had a better meal," said Edgar Cochran. "Your last supper as a spinster, eh, Camilla? Will it do?"

"What?" Her startled face made the old man twist himself around to see what she was looking at, but Kit was sipping wine now, and seemed to be just another unconcerned diner.

Father would not suspect that curly-haired young man. He knew Kit was far away in Fiji.

"Father," she said, pushing her plate away, "I'm too excited to finish all of my dinner, as you see, but you must order a sweet. I adore sweets, and I promise I'll eat that."

She had to delay as long as possible. Kit could not say much very fast with this system, and she had a dozen questions for him.

She quickly signed her room number to Kit: *245*. Even a novice could read those numbers on a hand.

"I plan to forgo the sweet," complained her father. "I am weary. It has been a long and troublesome day, and I prefer to rise with the sun. It is positively degenerate to retire late and rise late, you know," he added with a short laugh.

"A topic on which you would be expert, Edgar," said Riclef acidly.

Her father was vaguely aware that he had just been insulted, but he did not want to risk calling his future son-in-law on the comment. He pretended nothing was amiss.

Save me, she spelled again toward Kit. *Room 245.*

She saw his eyes flicker from Riclef to Father and back to her, though he did not raise his head, then signed that he would come to her tonight.

How much did he know about her awful situation? She wanted to spell *I love you,* but she dared not.

She was pretending to eat her dessert when Kit rose, folded his napkin, and left the table without a sign of goodbye. She stared after him so openly that Riclef turned to see what she was looking at. But Kit was gone. When Riclef asked her with his eyes what was amiss, she simply smiled. Evidently, he was not willing to alert her father to his own concern. Camilla took a small sip of her tea and complimented the raspberry torte.

"I think we shall go up now, Edgar," said Riclef abruptly. Then he looked behind him again.

"But I'm not finished!" she objected.

"Then please excuse me for a moment," he said, springing up from the table.

"Whatever is wrong?" she demanded. "That's not civil, Riclef! Can't you wait until I finish? I'm almost done."

Her father frowned at her insistence, but Riclef did not respond. He stood in the center of the crowded dining room, staring after Kit. He turned to Cammy again, and asked with his eyes, as plain as day, "Who was that man?"

Camilla hid her anxiety, pretending not to see his questioning gaze, and attempted to look right through him. Riclef sat down again, but he was on the edge of his chair, ready to leave. He tapped his fingernails on the tablecloth, and she ate faster. She forced the torte down although it nearly gagged her. No desperate plotter can eat, so she would relish the food and deceive them both. Had Father noticed Riclef's fretful curiosity or his attention to Kit?

When she could dawdle no longer over her dessert, she

allowed her fiancé to pull out her chair and assist her to her
feet. They followed her father out of the dining room, Riclef
holding her arm very high, pressing his knuckles into the side
of her breast.

"Camilla, I do not like this behavior," he hissed in her ear.
"What are you doing?"

She decided on the safest course. She would play the young
bride, very anxious and concerned. She said, "I am afraid to
wed you, Riclef. Will you be kind to me? You are so much my
elder, so experienced, so different. Don't you think it could
be an error? I must admit that I am afraid of you."

"Is that all? You do not plan to run away?"

"How could I? Where would I go, but to Blue Downs? No,
thank you."

He seemed halfway satisfied, but still he frowned and
looked carefully around the lobby.

"I wish to retire immediately," said Edgar Cochran when
they reached the staircase.

Camilla would have to go up when her father did, so Riclef
escorted her, grim-faced and quiet. They climbed the stairs,
and the two men walked her to her door. After they waited
for Edgar to retreat into his own room, Riclef fixed her with
an intense gaze. His dark eyes searched her very mind and
heart.

"Would that this night I possessed you, Camilla, body and
soul. You seem like quicksilver. I fear you will slip through
my fingers."

"I shall be more steady in the morning," she promised
nervously.

"I would like to steady you in my arms all night long."

"I made that sort of error once before, remember?" she
said. "Father would know, just as he knew then. Don't
encourage me to ruin myself tonight, again." When would he
leave? When would Kit come for her?

"Kiss me, then, my bride-to-be."

She lifted her face to him, and his kiss was harsh and
hungry. She let her arms hang at her sides passively. What if
Kit were nearby, watching?

"Now, go," she said, pushing him away.

"I do not wish to go."

"But you must!" Her smile was lopsided and less than
merry. Her lips still stung from his rough kiss.

"At Riven Oak, I was the complete decorous gentleman,

and you're no maiden, Camilla, so let's not hear you complain."

"We are in a public corridor, Riclef," she reminded him. "Do be decent, and please leave. I shall need my sleep tonight."

At last he was persuaded. He released her, and stepped away from her. "I am tempted to sleep right outside your door, my sweet temptress," he cautioned her, "like a guard dog. I do not know exactly why, but I swear, I fear your flight."

"Your fears are unfounded," she stated flatly, closing the door in his face.

Chapter 29

She locked the door behind her and leaned against it, breathing very deeply. She felt ill and her whole body shook. She had a sudden, violent compulsion to pack and run. Even if someone came in and saw her, it would not appear suspicious. If she was to be wed and carried away in the morning, certainly she'd need to be packed, so why not do it now?

She ran to the wardrobe and pulled out two gowns. She would not undress, but would sleep in her costume. Where was Riclef's room? Why had she not thought to ask? Was he on this floor? She listened against the wall of her father's room, but there was no sound. Was he in bed by now, or listening to her at the very same wall? Could he hear if her door was opened? She twisted her hands together and strode around the room, trying to think clearly. Oh, it must be only a cruel, cruel punishment of fate that she'd glimpsed Kit in the dining room. A glimpse of paradise before the jailer-father or the jailer-bridegroom slams shut the door.

How long was it now since Kit had left the dining room? How long would it take for Father to fall asleep, and for suspicious Riclef to retire? She had to admire his perceptiveness in knowing just what she wanted to do, but at the same time she dreaded it.

Impulsively, she shed the evening slippers she was wearing and donned her stout walking shoes instead.

It was growing late. If Kit was not coming, then she would find him!

Her heart thudding, she hauled her two smaller cases off the carpet and started for the door. She'd have to forgo the large portmanteau, with her finer gowns and mantles, but that didn't matter. She couldn't walk far with this weight, but she'd have to try. It was ten o'clock already and pitch dark out. She donned her cloak and hat.

Panting, she wrested the suitcases to the door and quietly turned the key. There was still no sound from Father's room. She eased the knob around very slowly and pulled on the door. She had no idea why both men dared to leave her alone, but it was truly a blessing. She went out, closed the door behind her, and picked up the cases. Her arms ached already. Oh, why did she not have the strong arms of a boy or of a farmwife, who could harvest grain and lift large stones from the path of a plow? She prayed that her determination to reach Kit would give her strength.

We are already wed, Kit and I, she told herself to keep from screaming at the pain in her shoulders and back. It would be illegal to marry Riclef. It was imperative that she run and hide from him. Then suddenly she thought of Jason and Janet Ruyell. Would they hide in time?

She approached the carpeted stairs, gritting her teeth against the agony in her mind and her back.

"May I assist you, miss?" A voice came out of nowhere. She whirled around and saw a middle-aged man. "Or shall we call a porter?" he asked. "Do you travel alone at this hour?"

"I must," she said hurriedly. "Yes, if you would be so kind, I would appreciate some assistance."

She pulled up the collar of her cloak and pulled down the brim of her hat so that only a little of her face was visible. She didn't want him to be able to describe her if he was questioned later.

The man saw her to the bottom of the stairs, but when he raised his hand for a porter, she stopped him.

"This is quite sufficient, sir. I thank you. I am . . . meeting friends here." The man nodded and walked away.

But as she spoke, she turned around and gasped at the sight of two men deep in conversation, standing in the center of the lobby. It was Riclef Torandor and Kit Vestcott!

She left her cases behind and fled toward the nearest potted palm, concealing herself behind it.

How could she get to the door without passing by them? And what would she do if she left? Did she really wish to go out into the black Melbourne night alone? She was riveted to the spot, watching them. Why were they speaking to each other?

If either man had seen her leap out of sight, neither betrayed her to the other, or made a sign to her. Kit had bent his head and was rubbing that odd mustache. Riclef had his fists on his hips. His coat was pushed back so it hung down in folds. Two handsome, tall men, one fair and one dark, with a world of difference between them.

She had a wild, insane urge to march straight past them and see if either followed. Then she thought about throwing a fit, falling on the carpet and frothing at the mouth. She fought back tears. I want Kit and I must be strong, she counseled herself.

She was still clinging to her beaded handbag. She stuck a hand into it, and her fingers closed around shillings and half crowns among the paper money. Suddenly, she had an impulse.

She pulled out all her silver coins, and flung the coins toward the chandelier near the two men. Then she darted from behind the concealing palm fronds and made for the door.

All heads turned toward the source of the loud tinkling and clattering. Camilla ran through the hotel's front doors, unseen, as the crystal chandelier was suddenly raining silver pieces.

Outside on the street, she hailed a hansom. The little money she had left would not take her far, and she had no idea where to go. Leaving Kit behind would be worse than waiting for him in vain.

She sat in the hansom, and told the driver not to move. Leaning forward, safely out of sight, she could watch through the space between the tied-back curtains.

Suddenly, a tall figure was silhouetted in the doorway. Was it Kit? She couldn't be certain. He looked from left to right up and down the street. When he started to stride away up the footpath, she put her hand against the window and rapped sharply.

"Kit!"

Her hoarse whisper was penetrating. He peered at the carriage, and recognizing the face within, sprang toward her. Flinging the door open, he leaped into the hansom.

Camilla was sobbing with joy and anxiety. "Let's hurry, Kit! Oh, I saw you standing in there talking to him. Why?"

"I had to hold him there and find out. Oh, damn! Driver, move on!"

As the hansom left the curb, he looked back in dismay. She twisted around and saw another dark silhouette on the steps of the hotel. Riclef ran down the steps trying to hail their hansom. When he failed, he raised his arm and summoned the cab right behind them.

"Outrun him!" ordered Kit to the driver. "Lose him! It'll be worth a lot of money to you, old man."

Settling back on the seat beside Camilla, without a word he embraced her with ferocious eagerness, crushing her to his chest, kissing her face. His fingers tangled in her soft hair.

She held him close, unable to speak.

"Cammy, you precious, clever angel!" he murmured when at last he drew back to take a breath. "Thank God I found you in time!"

"Just hold me, Kit, and tell me how it is you came here. I am astounded that you are not in Fiji. When did you learn the manual alphabet? Oh, tell me everything!" Her words ran together in excitement.

"I sought you at Blue Downs, and your father told me you were gone. He told me a pack of lies, of course, and I knew enough not to believe a one of them."

"You visited him? He never breathed a word to me."

"Of course he wouldn't. If you knew I was so close by, you never would have cooperated with those two, and never would have rushed off to Tasmania with Torandor."

"But go on," she insisted. "What happened between you and my father?"

"I trapped him into admitting that he was present at our hotel in Scotland, and that he'd staged that scene with the man. I learned then that he'd never given you my letters."

"Letters? Then you dared to write to me despite his threats!" There were tears of joy in her eyes.

"Perhaps I was foolish, but I did send them. Letty said no harm was done to her or the children."

"That was because Father saw how weak and ill I became when he kept me away from the Shraders' school. He was forced to keep the project going just to keep me alive. You see, in a sense I blackmailed him into it. So you saw the Shraders?"

"Yes. They taught me to sign. I thought it might be useful when next I saw you, and I was right!"

"Oh, Kit. Then everything will really work out?"

"I should have come back for you sooner," he said ruefully, "but I had business in England, and it was unavoidable since my father couldn't leave the islands. I stopped in Batavia on my way home and visited Hans Van Beek. He is married now, you will be interested to know."

Cammy breathed a sigh of relief. "Yes, indeed. That does please me," she said softly.

"He swore that you repulsed his every advance. Perhaps you'll believe in my terrible shame that I doubted you in Scotland," he finished, hanging his head. His voice was low and husky.

She embraced him then, covering his mouth and face with kisses as light as a butterfly's wing. "Oh, I do believe you! Kit, we have suffered so much, and we have triumphed. This is proof of the strength of our love!"

But at that moment, the hansom jolted over the rough stones, and they were passed by a second carriage. Cammy drew him back into the shadows.

"Riclef is pursuing us. Does he know you are my—?"

"This time, my darling, I'm armed." Kit took her hand and placed it on the lump under his breast pocket. "I've learned," he said grimly, "I must play rough with your captors!"

"You cannot!" she said, terrified of the consequences should there really be a fight.

"If he catches up to us, I shall put him in hospital or in the morgue. I won't give you up again."

"Kit, oh, Kit." She held him and mourned their years apart. But she also mourned the future she saw for them. Would they always be forced to run and hide? Would there always be loss and grieving? "I can't bear any more heartbreak!" she cried.

"Nor shall you. I am angry, bitterly angry, Cammy, and will put up with no more delay."

"Riclef has not harmed me. He is troubled, not wicked like my father. But even he, bad as he is, does not deserve death. There is no sin worse than—"

"There is no sin worse than parting two who are destined to be man and wife."

She had found Kit aged when last she met him at the Children's Home. Now, two years later, his heavier chest and stronger jaw marked him as a man near thirty, and the intensity of his gaze clearly showed the mark that life had left on him. He tore off the false mustache as the hansom cab rattled down the avenue.

Would they truly be together now? She kept looking back for Riclef. There were many hansoms on the road, and she did not know which one held her pursuer.

"Torandor saw me chase after you," said Kit. "He's a highly intelligent man. I engaged him in casual conversation and he boasted of his lovely young bride, but I sensed he knew the bride was unwilling. He was obviously stationed there to guard the stairs, afraid she'd flee."

"I could not believe it when I saw you signing to me in that dining room!" she sighed, leaning against Kit.

"Letty told me of this marriage scheme, and I feared Torandor would try to make you go through with it. So I hired a man in the Registrar's office when the twenty-one days were passed. He was the one who delayed the ceremony yesterday. I would have lodged an objection to the marriage at dawn today, but my man discovered your hotel as well through your father, and that made everything easier."

"I love you!"

"Not so much as I love you, my dearest."

Their hands were gripped together, and they clung to one another as if they would never let go. The hansom rushed on. Kit leaned from the window and gave an address to the driver. There was no way to tell in the dark night if they were still being followed. Cammy thanked heaven that the hansoms all looked alike. Perhaps they had lost Riclef in the crowd.

"He was suspicious of me in the dining room, Kit," she told him. "He knew I was watching someone, and when you left I was so agitated that he arose and almost went after you."

"Unfortunate," Kit muttered, sitting back heavily in his seat. "Then I was foolish to talk with him, even though I did give him a false name and occupation. Cammy, I have friends here in Melbourne who have taken Letty and her parents in as their guests. That's where we'll hide for the night. The home is empty now, all the little ones go on to the Victoria School, and the Shraders swore they'd rather come with me than remain in your father's quarters."

She hugged him to her, filled with yet another joy at the knowledge that she would see her dear friends again in just a few moments. Everything was perfect now, except for the fact that she'd neglected to explain her relationship with Riclef to Kit. She knew that he loved her, since he'd never questioned why she had allowed herself to come so close to wedding Riclef Torandor the previous afternoon.

"I am yours and always have been," she whispered. "I want you to know that. Mr. Torandor held the fate of an innocent child over my head, or I never would have cooperated as far as I did. Oh, Kit, the dear child is in danger and I cannot think how to protect him."

"Think of yourself for once, dearest." Kit stroked her face, drinking in her beauty.

"If I did not marry him, he said the boy who is his natural son would be stolen from its mother. He wanted me to give him children in exchange for this son in Tasmania."

"And if you did not cooperate, you would again be the prisoner of your father," Kit added.

The opposition seemed allied against them, far stronger and more powerful than they. Cammy collapsed against Kit's hard, muscled chest, and they sat holding each other in silence like infant koalas in a swaying, storm-swept gum tree. Kit's heartfelt tears spilled onto Cammy's cheeks, mingling with her own.

Chapter 30

The rest of the rapid flight through the city was passed in silence. Their arms and bodies entwined, they kissed away each other's tears, and relished each other's warmth.

The hansom drew to the curb, stopping before a fine freestone house, with gaslights outside and tethering posts and sculptured columns. No second hansom followed them.

Kit paid the driver with a handful of notes, and whisked Cammy inside. They were both extremely anxious until the door closed behind them, but they had not seen any pursuer. Their hansom driver clucked to his horse and vanished down the street.

Letty ran to the door and seized Cammy in her arms without a word. Her old parents, in wrappers and night-clothes, came rushing in after her, signaling their amazement at this rescue. Cammy was exhausted, but she wanted to hear everything, and everyone talked and signed at once to give her the true story.

The most startling news was that Kit had sent a courier to Minnie Cochran in Adelaide as soon as Letty had informed him about Tasmania and Riclef Torandor. The new Mrs. Plaskett would know the man's character and intentions,

Letty had said. The courier had returned with a letter for Kit and another one, sealed, for Camilla.

"Your mother wrote me that Torandor is the man that your father should really hate," Kit marveled. "It does seem sad that the man who aided Minnie and got you away from Blue Downs so cleverly is not my friend, but my foe, challenging me for your hand."

"He is not a bad man, Kit. He's simply desperate to have his son, and he can't have him. He . . . he once loved my mother. I don't condemn him or her."

"Nor do I, after seeing your father for what he is!"

At this point, the Shraders excused themselves, bidding everyone goodnight. They had let her know they were safe and contented, soon moving to a cottage of their own. She suspected who must have financed that. It had to be her generous Kit. How Father must rage and rail to find all his victims fled! He had no weapon left to him. Riclef, however, did hold a weapon. And that was Jason Ruyell.

After they had said their goodnights to Letty, Kit drew Cammy into his own bedchamber and softly closed the door, locking it behind them.

"It has been so long, my darling," he said with a shy smile. "It is tragic how little of each other we have had. The last time we had only half a day together, mostly spent riding on that horse. At least that is the part of the day I remember and cherish."

"I love you, Kit," she sighed, as he kissed her. "But first I must read my mother's letter," Cammy gasped, coming up for air. "It may contain very vital information."

"Your mother didn't know I love you," Kit said incredulously. "You spared her the tales of our sad separations and battles with your father?"

She nodded, tearing at the envelope, while his hands glided over her silk-stockinged legs. Her skirts were up, her bodice unfastened. She arched her back, overcome with desire and relief. Mother's letter would have to wait just a little while longer. Her tongue found Kit's ear and caressed it, as his hands fondled her hips and thighs. He would pause for an instant and tear off another of his garments, then fall to their love play again. The letter lay on the pillow above them, and in a moment, her hand flying up brushed it to the floor.

One moment Cammy was suckling a starved, precious one at her breasts, and the next was borne down by a tenderly lusting lover. Nothing on earth should cheat them of this delight. They had been deprived for years, and deserved this. Nothing in the world would ever part them again.

Somehow, in the back of her head, thoughts of another parting intruded on their passion. No, it could not wait.

Camilla half fell out of the bed to retrieve the letter she dropped, and she hastily withdrew it from the envelope. Kit, love besotted and groggy with desire, tried to restrain her. "Oh, let me love you well and now, my precious."

"Of course, but after I read this. There is something I must know, dearest, that I cannot explain. Mama possibly has written me the answer to my question."

She unfolded the paper and began reading.

"My Sweet Angel," the letter began. Kit was out of the circle of candlelight and could not read the letter over her shoulder. He continued to stroke her slim and lovely form, but what she read quelled the sweet sensations. "I was terribly shocked to learn that you hope to wed Kit Westcott, but that you may be forced to wed Riclef Torandor.

"I did not suspect that you and Kit were enamored of each other, and Riclef never said he was drawn to you. I had thought him only a kind friend come to rescue you from Edgar's unkindnesses. I hasten to write and pray with all my heart that this will reach you before it is too late. Had I known, I would have spoken out before. In Adelaide you asked me an important question, Camilla, but I was so ashamed!"

Camilla clasped a hand upon her breasts. She had had a suspicion of what her mother would say. The letter was scribbled in Mama's undisciplined hand, crumpled at the edges and bespattered with tears. Camilla could just barely make out the next words.

"Riclef Torandor is more to us than I have told you, dearest. I beg you not to condemn me. Please, please forgive and believe me. This is the truth."

Camilla made a small frightened sound, and Kit moved toward her. She thrust out her arm to keep him away, pressing the letter to her.

"You cannot read this!" she cried.

"Would you keep anything secret from me?" he asked sadly.

She nodded without raising her eyes to his and went on reading.

"Riclef was once my lover, Camilla." Camilla knew that already. She'd guessed it only recently and she'd forgiven her mother.

"For years I hoped that my sin had no lasting effect, that it ended when Riclef went back to England, after a week of the greatest happiness I had ever known. We did not meet again, and seldom corresponded. Stephen does not even know the degree of our closeness, and I think you already are aware that Stephen owes everything to Riclef.

"But my darling, there was a baby born of that love, and this is the second reason you must not wed Riclef. That he was your mother's lover is sufficient reason. But what I am about to tell you will convince you beyond all possible doubt."

Camilla blinked hard, still picturing her mother and Riclef together. But a child! Who was it? She read on.

"Cammy, this must never be revealed to anyone, not to Riclef, nor to Edgar, nor to any other person, certainly not to your brother himself—Michael. Riclef is the true father of Michael."

"Oh, no! Oh, please, no!" Camilla whimpered, muffling the words behind her clenched fist. But her heart nearly burst with relief.

"I could not be sure of it until Michael was three or four years of age," the letter went on. "By then, Riclef was far away. The physical resemblance became clear only then."

Michael was the tallest and the darkest of all her brothers! Michael! Dear, unknowing, beautiful, dark Michael! Who'd never loved Edgar Cochran.

"Michael would have been harmed to know the truth," her mother continued. "He was just a lad and could not keep his own counsel. Edgar surely would have disowned him, and thrown us both upon the streets. You may recall that he never spared the rod when Michael misbehaved. Perhaps, unconsciously, he felt that this son was no kin to him. I was not sure Riclef would come to our rescue, and the damage to Michael by then would have been significant. He is still not of age until next month, nor is he yet established in the law. He depends upon your father's financial support—"

"He would not accept that support if he knew," Cammy muttered to herself.

"No one must know this, Camilla, but I say to you now that you cannot become the wife of your own brother's father."

So that was the total of her mother's sins! She had taken a lover and borne his child, and allowed Edgar Cochran to claim him. Of course, she herself was Edgar's child. She shared his height and coloring as did Bernard, Jock, Charlotte, and Richard. But Michael, on the other hand, was a Jason grown tall, brilliant, animated, charming. He would undoubtedly enjoy Riclef Torandor. And why shouldn't he? They were father and son.

No, she could not ethically or morally wed the father of her brother, nor her mother's lover. The case was closed. But then the implications of this knowledge began to make themselves clear to her. Riclef loved Jason, his son, and wanted to own him. But he did not know that he already had a son. He had a right to know the truth, and so did Michael. But Mother must not suffer shame or scandal. What would happen if the truth came out? Would Stephen leave her? Would Edgar trumpet the news far and wide? Could she safely tell Kit? And what of Michael? Would this revelation affect his career?

She pressed her fingertips to her temples, her head throbbing. She was still bent over the letter, but without looking up she knew that Kit was studying her as she sat on the bed. She felt so confused, so alone.

Finally, Kit drew his breath in sharply and came near, laying his hand on her hair. It was such a delicate, gentle touch. She caught hold of his hand and kissed it, but even this sweetness could distract her for only an instant.

She pondered her horrible dilemma. She was on her honor not to betray Mama. Yet was there anything she could do about this that would not hurt her mother? If she told her father, naturally he would prevent her marriage to Riclef, but she'd surely lose Kit. Riclef would kidnap Jason for revenge so that he'd have the son he craved.

If she told Riclef she could not wed her brother's father, then her mother and Michael would suffer. Michael, more than any of them, was innocent. Each had sinned in some way, except Michael. And Jason, of course, and kindly, trusting George Ruyell.

Kit could not hold his tongue any longer, watching her agonized expression. "Is your mother terribly sick, Cammy?" he finally asked. "What else would cause you to become so quiet? Can't you confide in me?"

"I can't, no," she said dully. "Not now."

She stayed there, lost in thought, and Kit sat on the bed. Slowly, meeting no resistance, he drew off her chemise and continued to disrobe her. She was weeping now, and he had to pause every once in a while to kiss away tears, shaking his head over his own dread and confusion. He did not press her to speak.

As gentle as a nanny, he removed her last garments and her stockings, and rubbed her back until she slid face down in his bed, nude.

"I shall take you away to Fiji with me tomorrow," he promised. "If there is no last-minute space free on some ship of the Steam Navigation Company, then we'll find a schooner or a frigate. Any vessel bound for Fiji. When you are ready to tell me your sorrows, Cammy, I shall aid you any way I can."

Her mind was whirling. Where was Michael now? She'd thought about him so little in the four years since she'd seen him when he left Blue Downs forever. Michael worshiped Kit. What had he just said? That he'd take her away to Fiji? Truly?

"May I sleep beside you, dearest?" Kit asked softly. "I will not disturb your rest, if you prefer. You seem so upset."

"Touch me. Hold me," she begged, turning toward him and opening her arms to him. This was her own precious Kit, and no one could take her from him.

This time she felt rather than saw his velvet smooth torso, all a flawless golden brown, silken skin over firm muscles. She hid her face in his neck, as Kit slid closer until their bodies touched. He pulled the muslin sheet lightly over them and settled himself against her, sighing. His pity and worry were palpable. She knew exactly what concerned him. Did her sorrow have to do with him? With illness, death, or scandal? How did it involve him, and why couldn't he hear the truth?

She said nothing, but only cuddled nearer, thankful for his presence. Cammy flung her arm around his chest, and passed her hand down the valley of his spine, between the two rows of muscles. A ripple of pleasure and caring passed over him, and he said under his breath, "Oh, my darling, I love you!"

She said nothing, but touched his lips with hers.

"I'm not worthy to lie beside you, but I'll keep you warm 'til morning, dearest."

She could not have that, because it had been too long for them to remain celibate. His bronzed body lay beside her to be cherished and loved, his heart a diamond. She could not think of the life that animated him without rejoicing and holding him tight.

She made love to Kit.

She kissed the soft eyelids. She moved up the bed and fed him her breasts, and his hands tightened around her slim waist. He touched her until she was weak with longing. She rolled him over, and slid on top of him, so much warmer a resting place than the cool bedclothes, and she felt his heart quaking underneath hers. He rose to meet her, and she held him, drawing him up and in, and she moaned in happiness as they gave each other such sweet joy.

He held himself back until she feared he would burst, and then she brought him over the edge, and went with him.

Afterward, she held him, and they slept. Soon they'd sail to his islands, the wonderful place that she'd never seen but that he had so lovingly described to her.

She and Kit would be together forever. But for her mother's secret, everything would be perfect.

Chapter 31

Camilla was awakened from her heaving bunk by the unfamiliar sound of surf pounding on a coral reef. They'd reached the Cannibal Isles. From her porthole she could see the leaping blue-green waves crash white upon a red coral reef that shielded the lagoon. Beyond it was a small town of thatched and wooden houses. Behind the town were green mountains.

"Where are we, Kit?" she cried as he walked through the cabin doorway. "Where have you been?"

"Up before you, lazy lady," he chided. "I hoped you'd awaken to see your new home, but I couldn't rouse you no matter what I tried."

"But you gave me little time for sleeping," she pointed out, contentedly smiling and stretching like a cat. "Home? Home already! Is that Suva?"

"It is. Suva on Viti Levu. The island that will be your sanctuary."

She rested her arms on the slope of the porthole and stared. The rigging above them that had creaked and screamed during their trip was now silent. Cammy remembered how the ropes screeched and the blocks rapped when their schooner bore down on Norfolk Island and then made for the eastern archipelago. Now they were home.

The sea wind during their voyage had not blown away all her worries by any means. Kit would find her on deck each day, silently staring out to sea. In bed, in his arms, she was fierce and ardent. She drowned in smothering kisses and sank beneath Kit's eager body as he plumbed her depths again and again, all during the long nights at sea. Still, thoughts of Mama and Jason and Michael and Riclef would surface, and Kit could not get past her silent pain. They'd sent Letty to Hobart to warn the Ruyells, and she'd promised to send news as soon as she could. Even Kit's words and caresses could not soothe Cammy.

He called her his little bird, *tikivili,* and his tiger moth, *kumukumure,* and he promised that they would not speak of sorrows back in Australia, but only of love and Fiji. He teased her about her red-gold hair, telling her it would cause a sensation there. Native women occasionally put coral lime and the juice of wild lemons on their hair to dye it gold, but they could never achieve so rich a color as hers. She did not wear tattoos on her lips or her chin, done with shaddock thorns as the island women did to make themselves beautiful.

"I'll garb you in red, the sacred color *kula,*" he said. "And you'll wear scarlet feathers from the breast of the parakeet. They are valued more highly here than gold."

"Some would dress me in red for my sin," she said with a sigh.

Kit was quick to cover his tactlessness. "You are my wife, if any woman ever was wife to a man. There's no sin between us, Cammy." He kissed her fiercely, and asked quietly, "Do you wish for a baby, Camilla?"

"I do. If we had a child, then no one could part us. Father might actually let us be, if we presented him with a grandchild. Oh, I want your baby. It would be such a loved child, because it would be the issue of two who love each other dearly."

Holding one another close, they left the cabin and went to stand at the rail, where they watched the helmsman make for the narrow passage through the reef into the still lagoon at Suva.

The water was green and transparent as it ran over the coral, but it was rough. The high seas began to fling their light craft sideways, as if to break it on the coral spines. Cammy shut her eyes to block out the sight, but when she opened them, she saw that the bow was still aimed toward the grass houses. Above the town, on the horizon, reared a tall peak. Kit said it was Rama, the "thumb" of the devil according to local legend.

Everything here seemed two things at once—good and evil, beautiful and frightening. There was the translucent sea pounding over murderous reefs. There were good Christian natives called *lotu*, and the heathen *tevoro*, or "devil men," who came out of the mountains to slaughter and eat their converted neighbors. Christians "put on the cloth," the skirtlike *sulu*, but they might "throw off the cloth" and run in groin straps as cannibals again if they were so inclined. "There are so many factions," Kit explained. "Christians against cannibals, Wesleyans against Catholics, settlers against natives. But it will come right eventually, when Britain makes us a law-abiding, peaceful colony."

"I pray that it shall," she said.

Surely in Fiji she'd be safe from Riclef and Father under the protection of Kit and Mr. Westcott, who was now an adviser to the renowned Thakombau, King of Fiji.

When at last they were close enough to Suva and the schooner could go no farther, small boats were paddled out to pick them up from the white coral strand. They were hollowed log boats, twin hulled or with outriggers, full of smiling natives, evidently delighted to greet them. Kit shouted and waved and was met with excited familiarity in an unfamiliar language.

As she listened to him call to his friends, she could distinguish the famous pidgin Kit spoke lyrically, as he grinned and pointed to her. The boatmen smiled and nodded at his explanation and informed their girlfriends, their lovely, broad-faced companions. All of these people were either former cannibals or the offspring of cannibals, but were now Methodists, who, Kit assured her, had forsaken human flesh and fleshly sins and observed the sabbath faithfully.

The schooner's crew unloaded many parcels while the passengers who had reached their destination were ferried to the beach on the backs of Fijians. It was a shallow harbor, and one either had to wade ashore or be carried.

Camilla and Kit clambered down into one of the ship's boats to be rowed to the shallows. When the boat scraped bottom, Camilla was gently carried on the seat that Kit and a crewman created by holding each other's wrists. Kit had removed his boots and stockings and rolled up his trousers to the knee in order to wade ashore. He always went barefoot at home. Even knighted English gentlemen and government officials, he explained, adopted "island kit." The standard dress was all white costumes and no shoes.

Camilla was a trifle disconcerted when she saw the half-naked, tall brown men wielding sixteen-inch knives. But were it not for them, they would never have been able to proceed through the jungles. The men hacked a path clear of under-growth, and she and Kit followed some distance overland to a curve in a river. A dozen carriers trotted behind them, bringing luggage and goods from the mainland.

"We are *vavalang-i*," Kit told her. "That is, whites, come here to save souls, make money, or escape our fates. Mission-aries, mercenaries, or misfits, as one man put it. Which do you think we shall be?"

"As for myself, why I don't know yet, but you are Fiji-born. You cannot be classed so narrowly," she objected.

"With such a staunch defender," Kit said, grinning, "I should soon find more friends than enemies around me!"

She walked beside him now, gripping his arm, her skirts brushing through fronds of bracken and club moss as she ducked under trailing lianas. She gazed up at vines that wound themselves 'round the trunks of tall trees, festooning them with shiny leaves. In their high canopy, parrots darted about, showing their jeweled breasts. There were buzzing, armored insects she'd never seen before. The native carriers behind them chatted and laughed as they walked. All of them were craggy-faced, straight-nosed men, wide-footed and agile. They wore the decent cloth skirts that labeled them *lotu*, or converted natives.

"My father will be enormously pleased to see you," said Kit. "But he may not return for some time from Levuka, the capital on Ovalau. That's sixty miles off, by sea."

"He won't be shocked that we are not yet married?"

Kit gave her a wry look. "Customs are not so strict in this land. And let me remind you, our love is perfection itself, Camilla, here or anywhere."

When they had reached the river, the entire company boarded slender canoes, called *takia*, with one steadying single outrigger. Holding onto Kit, she perched on a small bamboo platform under a flimsy roof. Branches of huge trees spanned the whole river, throwing dappled shade and sun-shine on their silent, skillful oarsman. By the time they disembarked, Camilla had decided her costume was totally unfit for this land. She would have to adapt.

She'd stitch thin, simple skirts from her linen petticoats, and decorate some vests and camisoles to use as bodices. Her heavy silks and velvets could serve as drapes or covers in their house, or perhaps the native children would enjoy them as amusing costumes. Kit promised that he would make her a plaited hat from the pandanus palm, half as large as a sunshade.

Suddenly, a cry sounded from a village sitting to one side of the trail ahead of them. Camilla could make out a horde of brown children pelting down the trail past the Fijians. The small ones were naked, the larger ones wore small cloth *sulus* or a fringe of grass around their middles. Seeing her pale skin, the children grew shy and fell back, stumbling into one another with tentative smiles and staring eyes.

Kit spoke to them in Fijian, and they all squealed in delight. He reached out and touched their curly heads and tweaked their ears, pointing at Camilla as he did so. In giggling, whispering groups, the children conveyed them toward the village.

"I told them you belong to me," Kit explained as they walked along. "They have decided you are most beautiful of all the *vavalang-i* they have seen."

"Oh, that's lovely," she said, very moved. "Tell them thank-you for me."

Kit, as merry as she'd ever seen him, strode along with a rolling gait. "Say *vinaka*," he instructed her. "It means thank-you."

"*Vinaka*," she echoed.

"There! Your first Fijian word. But pidgin is far easier. You'll be speaking that within a fortnight." He put his arm 'round her waist, to the giggling delight of the observant children. "But they only speak the truth, my darling. You are extremely beautiful. I agree wholeheartedly with the children."

At last they reached the thatched village. The adults were waiting for them, all smiling, holding out their hands to Kit. He told her that they could not leave that village until the *yangona* ceremony was performed.

Under a thatched roof supported by palm trunk posts, she and Kit were shown to piles of mats. She gathered her bulky skirts around her so that she could sit low to the ground. Kit sat cross-legged. A semicircle of village elders sat on each side of them. One young man set a wide bowl on legs in the cleared space before Kit and Camilla.

Cammy stared in deepest interest, her hand in Kit's. Tall men with blackened faces and grass skirts sank to their haunches around the bowl. Another man fastened a thick cord of fiber decorated with white sea shells to the bowl and extended the other end of the cord toward Kit.

Kit leaned toward her and murmured quickly, "This ceremony is in honor of our arrival. That's the *tanoa* bowl with *yangona* from the pepper tree." Then he fell silent, not wishing to disturb the spell of the solemn ritual.

She might have been in an English church, celebrating the Eucharist, so seriously did her love and her new neighbors take this ceremony. Camilla folded her hands in rapt attention.

One man repeatedly drew a bundle of bark through the liquid poured into the wide, shallow bowl. It was important that the *yangona* be stirred. The big man squatting behind the bowl, facing the lovers, immersed his arms up to the elbows in the bowl in order to strain the cloudy mixture through his fingers. When he seemed satisfied, he indicated that he was ready to a slender man carrying a shiny small bowl that might have been half a coconut shell. This was the *tanoa*-keeper, who, resplendent in his shell necklaces and leafy skirt, bare-chested, filled the shell. He then turned, and in a half-squatting position, he proceeded toward Kit, holding the cup raised in the air. He presented his offering at arm's length to Kit, who accepted it, drained it at a single draught, and sent it spinning along the ground. The crowd called out, "*Mathaa!*" and struck their palms together.

The next cupful went to the man Kit identified as the chief of this village, and then there was a pause. No one seemed to know what to do about the *vavalang-i* lady. Perhaps none but she had visited here. She wanted so much to partake, but she didn't know if it would be proper. She looked questioningly at Kit, and he nodded slightly. Everyone smiled. The cup-bearer performed his presentation to Camilla, and when she extended her hands for the coconut cup, she felt as honored as if she were taking tea in the Royal Court in London.

"Drink all of it," Kit murmured, watching her.

She put it to her lips, expecting a throatful of fiery spirits or a blast of pepper, or at least a drink as strong as Communion wine. To her amazement, it tasted like very dilute magnesia, with a flavoring of cinnamon. It was mild, milky, and vaguely pleasant. She smiled as she attempted to spin the cup away from her as Kit had done. It skittered across the matting. Scores of Fijian hands clapped solemnly. *"Mathaa!"* they called in unison.

"It is emptied," Kit translated for her.

Another Fijian drank from the cup, and then the lead carrier, and then another villager. Not a word was spoken. No one moved. Camilla was fascinated. The discipline and formality of these *lotu* were clear indications that even before the missionaries, there had been order and honor.

After these rituals done in honor of *Ra* Christopher and *Andi* Camilla, as they were called, they were at last able to continue to the Westcott plantation. They left the ceremonial hut and passed through the green central square, or *rara,* of the village, followed by their carriers.

Kit forbade another *yangona* ceremony at the plantation, insisting that his lady needed time to recover. Indeed, Cammy had trouble walking, and her mouth was slightly numb because *yangona* was a mild soporific. That and the return to land after weeks at sea made her sleepy and off balance.

After steering them through a crowd of hand-shakers, Kit managed to bring Camilla to his house, which was situated near his father's. But her mouth dropped open when she saw where he lived. His house had a steep roof, with a log threaded through the long top knot of the thatch. The brown roof capped a square house ten fathoms in length. The walls were woven in a basketwork pattern in shades of tan and brown. Bamboo alternated with dark fibers in intricate designs.

Inside, the house had proper windows with shutters, and the floor was made of split bamboo and covered with plaited mats. Among the tables and chairs hung partitions made of beaten mulberry bark, *masi* cloth, which was dyed in fantastic patterns. The sunshine penetrated the airy dwelling in ripples.

"It is perfectly lovely!" she cried, clapping her hands in delight. "So bright, and clean, and cool!"

"Would you have preferred a colonial house made of lumber with a tin roof?"

"Most certainly not! Why, it's twenty degrees cooler inside, and so airy and bright!"

The bed was draped with netting to keep away mosquitoes at night, and neat cabinets made of reeds held books, linens, and wine bottles.

Then there were the flowers! The lane leading up to the house was lined with double pink hibiscus blooms. No red carpet could be more welcoming than these detached blossoms making a path for them. Inside, blossoms festooned the head of the bed, the columns supporting the ceiling beam, and the corners of each window. Bright coleus and croton leaves peeked in at the windows. Amaranths and heliotrope grew all about and stood in vases in the house.

The plantation people had been alerted to Cammy's arrival and had decked the house like a honeymoon suite.

"They knew I was coming!" she called to Kit, who was making sure all her suitcases had been correctly selected from the piles of baggage off their ship.

"I suspect they did. If I'm away for a year, I don't find flowers like this to greet me. I do get lots of *yangona* and *dalo* and a pig, though. You'll get the pig, too, roasted whole, and I trust you'll have an appetite for it by night."

There was no question about it. She was ravenous by the time it turned dark. She sat wide-eyed on the porch of the larger house, belonging to the absent Mr. Westcott, and watched Kit's workers and foremen and their families carry in bowls of *dalo*, yams, leafy greens, coconut meat, coconut milk, breadfruit, mangoes, and finally the mighty boar with an apple in its mouth, its eyes glazed and its skin crisped brown. Triumphantly, it was paraded before her. Torches everywhere lit up the banquet area.

"Fijians love feasting, and there will be a *meke* afterward, mark my words," Kit said, reluctantly taking his hand from hers to eat.

"They adore you," Cammy said, noticing the expressions on all the neighbors' faces. "And for that I love them."

"Not everyone adores us," he muttered.

She recalled his stories about the gin-swillers and beachcombers cast upon these shores. No, the whites who stole land and kept Fijians as slaves would not like a white man who earned such loyalty and love. "You are never in danger of . . . assassination, Kit?" she asked hesitantly. She wished to know the worst at the very start.

"No more than I'm in danger of being eaten by the other side, my love," he said lightly.

The feasters cleared away the wooden bowls and wiped their bare fingers. Even Cammy did without cutlery and licked her fingertips. Men now appeared in grass skirts and shells, armed with spears. Lines of men posed, pretending to threaten each other and Kit and Camilla, feinting with their spears. Others beat on wooden drums and clacked sticks. The leaping, crouching, spinning war dances excited her. The rhythmic expression of restrained violence, the excellent, strongly muscled, half-naked bodies shook her to the base of her spine and made her legs tingle.

"I want to love you," she whispered to Kit, who seemed loath to sit through the ladies' *meke*, the gentle line dance of women in bright *sulus*.

"Then shall we retire?" he said, smiling wickedly.

Bamboo and reed torches flared in the dark around the grassy *rara*, picking out the bright colors of *masi* cloth, feathers, and shells. Painted faces shone red, black, and white, and white teeth glittered in false ferocity. Cammy swayed with pleasant weariness as she rose and walked from the circle of dancers. Kit's arm curved around her, warm and strong, and she tipped her head back upon his shoulder.

"You will grow to love my people," he whispered. "They are generous and they always say what they mean."

"I think I already do. But I love you most of all."

He closed both her eyes with kisses without a moment's hesitation.

She'd come home at last.

Chapter 32

After ten days on Viti Levu, Cammy could say ten sentences in pidgin and could understand twice that many messages in return. Not every Fijian spoke pidgin, what they liked to call "business" English.

She was feasted more than once, and the exotic foods became familiar to her. She decided that she liked all the dishes but the gluey purple *dalo* pudding, which reminded her of swamp ooze. She and Kit slept between crisp linen sheets that were washed in the river and dried in the sun. She was *Marama* Camilla, and he, *Saka* Christopher.

"I began as *Andi*, and you were *Ra*."

"Those titles are a bit too lofty for us yet," he laughed. "Wait until I am knighted for service to Her Majesty."

She was at last gaining some sense of his role here. The Westcotts were not merely entrepreneurs come to make their fortunes. They might employ labor and produce cotton or sugar, but they were also politically involved. They were diplomats, and that meant being tightrope walkers in Fiji. She could not think more highly of Kit than before, but she was certainly impressed. Thank heaven she'd had sense enough to understand and to forgive. This man did not exist merely to be her love. He was risking his life making a haven out of a

241

troubled and divided island. She prayed that she could be an
inspiration to him, and that she herself might find some good
deeds to perform. What could she contribute? What could
she give, besides her appreciation and her thanks? Were there
any deaf children living nearby whom she could help?

Although word had been sent to Henry Westcott in Levuka
that Kit was home, and Camilla with him, the King had need
of Henry in these perilous times, and he could not leave. The
government was remaining in power by less than constitution-
al means, but the alternative was chaos. The least slackening
of vigilance might tilt the islands into chaos.

Kit was run ragged. After his four-month absence abroad,
there was much work to catch up on. He had to deal with the
planters, confer with the missionaries. He rowed out to the
British men-of-war in Suva harbor so that he might keep the
naval officers apprised of the situation. They were constantly
reassessing their view of the emergency government that
sustained the King in power against throngs of unruly settlers.
The future belonged to the Fijians, but at least for the
moment, skilled white settlers were vital to the economy.

"Badfella go 'long home," said Rebecca, the overseer's
wife, to Cammy one day. "Go 'long *Melevani*, go 'long
Sereni." Waving her hand away from her with a grimace, she
dismissed undesired invaders.

"Me come 'long *Melevani*," Camilla faltered, trying to
explain that not everyone from Melbourne was evil. "*Melevani* true goodfella place." Her arrival from there was
already known far and wide in Fiji, and she was the gold-
haired darling of the people who knew Kit. They enjoyed
taking care of her. She washed her hair in a basin brought her
by a pair of girls in orange-flowered dresses, and agile fingers
spun fresh curls from the wet mass.

During the day when Kit was at work, she walked the
perimeter of the settlement, investigating the neat, fertile
gardens of the village and of resident plantation workers. The
overseer's family joined her for Bible readings and hymns in
the afternoon and on Sundays, for there was no mission
church nearby. When she coupled her small pidgin with
animated hand gestures, she could easily communicate with
the Fijians.

Her big, plaited sun hat materialized on her second day at
the plantation, as well as necklaces of cowrie shells and palm
seeds, reverently dropped 'round her neck by maidens who

then darted away in fits of shyness. A deputation from the village presented her with the *tambua*, a carved whale's tooth of great value. Kit said she should keep it with her always.

"It's worth more than sterling, even more than gold. It's a traditional symbol, you see, almost something to conjure with. As a betrothal gift, too. It's high time you had a *tambua* from me. Again, I have been outdone by my dark friends."

They toasted the occasion of her receiving the *tambua* with a claret wine, and kissed.

She had the curved, ivory tooth strung on a gold chain from her jewel casket, and she wore it beneath her bodice, lying between her breasts. An old woman had advised her to keep an oiled stone, "the *tambua's* mother" with the *tambua* so it would not be lonely and cry. She promised to do so. The earnestness of the woman touched her heart. These people were lovely and loving. But now she could understand why Kit and his father had come to Melbourne each spring for a rest. To deal with tribal peoples from several islands was a difficult balancing act. Laborers were largely from the New Hebrides. They were indentured but paid a good wage by Mr. Westcott. Lovoni families from Ovalau, former cannibals captured in wars, were employed here, too. Whenever any unpleasantness occurred, Henry Westcott made sure that judgment was swift and fair, and the punishment severe enough to be dreaded. The Westcotts' command of the two chief languages and culture gave them power as well as respect.

The Kit she had loved and lain beside years ago seemed different in this setting. His new maturity was good for both of them. They made love nearly every night, but it was coupled with a deeper affection.

One morning before he set off for the fields and village, she said, "I think, Kit darling, that at last something is going to happen. Something I once feared."

He froze and turned toward her, his belt half buckled. "Camilla!"

"See how my breasts have swelled? It is not only from your loving care," she teased. "There is no doubt of it any longer."

"We're going to have a child?" He was beside her on the bed in an instant, his face close to hers. Then with great tenderness, he placed his hands on her shoulders, on her hair, and on her swelling breasts.

"Children seem to be much loved here," she said, smiling.

"Camilla, I am so glad! Oh, you do want it, don't you?"

"Of course I want it! This is so splendid! We shall be able to marry legally a year from next June!"

As she thought of a wedding that had not taken place, a picture of Jason Ruyell formed in her mind. How awful, at a moment like this, to think of danger and unfinished business! She and Kit could not return to the colonies before they were married, and she had no idea what transpired there. If only Letty would write!

"I'm glad we are not Fijians," Kit was saying, still delicately fondling her breasts, which gave her pleasure beyond all past experience. "Then I would have reason to grieve, as well as to rejoice."

"Why?" she asked, startled.

"There is a custom here that a man may not touch his wife for three or four years after the birth of each child!"

"What an idea!"

"That allows the child to suckle, and the mother to regather her strength. It is indecent here to have one child following quickly upon the other."

"Well," Cammy said thoughtfully, "that's hard enough upon a loving wife, but what of the men's pain?"

"Men who have not converted to Christianity have three or four wives, my dear, so it is not such a trial."

"You shan't have more wives than just me!" she insisted in a shocked voice. "I shall not allow it, Kit! You shall not throw off the cloth and turn *tevoro* and marry other women!"

"And grow my hair in a great mass and wear war paint and boars' tusks? No. I think not, my darling. Even holes in my ears would offend you, am I right?"

"Cut holes in your ears, and I shall have my face tattooed!"

They laughed and held each other very tightly, listening to the music of faraway drums in the mountains. She heard them often, but never asked what they meant, knowing Kit would not tell her. He would not say whether they meant raiding parties or celebrations, circumcision rituals or war, or the eating of human captives. She was frankly glad to be spared that information.

When Kit went about his business during the day, she lazed in the sunshine, which turned her arms and ankles and face golden against the white of her hidden legs and torso. Kit came back to her at night, and enjoyed tracing the clear outlines of her sleeves and skirts on her body. They would laugh and kiss in the lantern light. She felt heavy and slow these days and very contented. Thankfully, she was not at all ill, either from any tropical fever or nausea from their baby, but she did not wish to move about or talk much or even to think. Her father became a dull, dark cloud upon her past, and Riclef a jagged bolt of lightning out of that cloud. She had not risked writing to her mother, for fear of saying too much or not enough.

After several long weeks, Letty's letter finally came. She said that the Ruyells stubbornly refused to leave Sweet Orchards and hide. At least they had had no word from Riclef, not yet at any rate. This news relieved Camilla somewhat.

She stirred herself to action only in the evenings and mornings, when she lay in bed with her Kit discovering all the things that hands and lips and limbs could do. Her condition made her skin and her insides far more sensitive. She persuaded him not to hesitate or hold back, though they did give up some of the rougher play they had once enjoyed. They would sit in bed, Kit with his back against the headboard, and Cammy between his outstretched legs, leaning against him, holding a book they read together.

Tonight, she leaned against the firm contours of his torso, listening to the wind and rain pounding upon the thatch. The little house shook with it, and it was hard to distinguish the sound of thunder from that of drums echoing in the mountains. She tried to read aloud over the noise, while he traced the curves of her breasts and lifted them to ease their aching. To stare down upon his busy hands and feel his breath quicken upon her temple made her shiver. What quiet ecstasy! The slightest squirming of her hips aroused him. She sat so close against him, she could tell his exact state.

"Do you still want to read, or shall I fill your arms, my dear, and all the spaces you wish filled?"

"I think that I should read," she answered pertly, but still she snuggled against him. "This story is delightful. I like hearing island history and reading of the earliest *turang-a ni drau ni kau,* 'the gentlemen of the leaves of trees,' and the *turang-a tuki vatu,* 'the gentlemen who hammered rocks.'"

"Splendid names for botanists and geologists, eh?" He reached around her. He knew his mind and picked up the book, pinching it closed and almost catching her fingers in the pages. "But that is heavy reading for such a stormy night."

Even as they talked, he continued stroking her, and she was ready and eager. When he gently came into her, she sighed and gritted her teeth so that she might prolong the pleasure, and not explode in instant ecstasy. The man she loved touched the mouth of her womb with the same gentleness with which he had kissed her lips. Deeply he caressed her, and for a long time. But eventually, she could bear it no longer, and she begged him to make an end to it or she would perish.

"Perish?" he asked her, murmuring into her soft curls. "What an idea! Then we should have to die together, precious!"

Together they did not die, but danced, in a sudden, gripping, plunging rhythm of passion. Then they were still so weary that without a word of goodnight, they peacefully fell asleep.

Chapter 33

The next day Kit had to take the government cutter along the coast to plead with planters to cease resisting the customs duty on gin, and to ask them to pay their taxes. If they didn't, the government would be starved out of existence. No one was making money working to establish Fiji as a Crown colony. His father, for example, got not a penny for his work, which in any colony would be almost full-time service to the Crown.

Cammy had been on the Westcott plantation for nearly a month. She tried to make herself useful, but it was difficult to summon up the energy these days. She loved to watch the boys scramble up towering palm trees, their ankles bound a hand span apart, their soles pressed firmly against the trunks. She savored the tangy taste of green coconut milk, as well as the taste of sweet, ripe coconut meat. She could stay here forever, she thought lazily.

But Kit had promised her a busy life in Levuka when he replaced his father in government service. Loyalists like the Westcotts would eventually get some reward, he vowed. After all, they deserved recompense for the risks they took.

In a week, another letter from Victoria arrived saying that the Shraders had been hired at the Melbourne Deaf School.

Letty lived with them. In a postscript she asked if Cammy and
Kit were married. Cammy read the letter over many times,
relishing the meager contact she had with the outside world.

One afternoon, a boy ran in to tell her she had a visitor.

"For me? Someone Kit sent?"

The young Fijian did not know. He was hot from running,
his brown chest beaded with sweat. He bowed after his
announcement and hastily retreated. It was almost Novem-
ber, three o'clock in the afternoon of a sunny day. Feeling
very curious about her guest, she quickly turned to check on
the front "parlor" half of the house, which was screened off
from the bedroom space by hanging woven panels. Was it
neat enough? When she heard the sound of boots coming up
the path to the door, she turned around to greet the visitor.
As soon as she saw him, she clapped a hand to her mouth,
muffling a shriek.

There stood Riclef Torandor.

Shuddering, and hugging her thin shoulders with her
hands, she whispered, "Why have you come here?"

He was out of breath and sweating in his black coat and
neckcloth. He held his white Panama hat in his hand.
"Camilla, I've come to take you away from here. This is no
place for a white lady. Pack a bag at once!"

"I most certainly will not!" Her first impulse was to slap his
face, but she noticed how ill he looked. He was hollow-eyed,
and his skin was tinged with yellow. He seemed a very sick
man, and an exhausted one.

"This is my home now," she said more calmly. "I am Kit's.
Coming here was foolish of you." How she wished she might
have said "wife" but it was not yet so.

"You will marry me," he told her, reading her thoughts.
"You cannot have legally wed Westcott, unless by some
native law, and that would be invalid in any civilized court. I
have our license here." He patted his vest. "It is signed and
sealed. You are bound to me, Camilla."

"I'm going to have Kit's child," she spat at him.

That statement stunned him, but he recovered quickly.
"Oh, Camilla, you cannot be! You are saying that just to put
me off!"

"I can't prove it to you," she said, "but I assure you it is so.
We've been living as man and wife ever since I last saw you. If
I were not with child, it would be amazing."

He stared at her oddly, as though he wished to hurt her. "I have Jason with me," he announced.

She gasped. "Oh, you haven't! You couldn't do such a horrible—"

"I told you my choices. Camilla as my wife, or Jason as my son."

"He'd be your son even if he lives with Janet," she cried. "And that's where he should be. What a wicked thing to do, to take him away!"

Two of Kit's workers, who had been outside the house, were drawn by the sound of loud voices. They walked into the front parlor and stood close to Riclef, one on each side.

"Do they know English?" Riclef asked of Arum and Samisoni, her volunteer bodyguards. They had masses of flowers braided into their hair in traditional fashion.

"No, they don't," she said. They moved closer to Riclef and eyed her questioningly. The stranger's tone of voice and her consternation were undoubtedly troubling the two men. Much as she wanted to be rid of Riclef, Jason's safety was at stake. She must not let them harm Riclef.

"Give me proof that you have him," she said clearly but with a sinking heart. "Where is he?"

Riclef presented her with a folded piece of paper, and she opened it quickly. It was a page from one of Jason's favorite books, the one about balloon flight. So he'd told the truth.

"I had Janet pack up his books and toys," he explained. "I did not snatch him away by night, or by violence."

"What about George?" Cammy demanded. "Didn't he offer to fight you?"

"Luckily, he had been called away to measure some windows for draperies. I visited in his absence."

"Indeed lucky, for you!" she snapped sarcastically, blinking away tears. "He might have killed you."

"And then he would have been hanged, and Jason would have no father at all."

"Jason must be terrified. Where is he?"

"He is asking for you, Camilla. I told him we were sailing to visit you. You know how he loves ships and the sea."

She prayed that the boy's spirit would not be destroyed by this abduction. There was no doubt in her mind that she was to blame for leading Riclef to Jason. Now she was determined to get the child back to his mother.

"I want you to bring Jason to me," she said cautiously, wondering if she could fool Riclef.

"I cannot. Westcott is no friend of mine. Your people would take Jason from me." He glanced nervously at the tall, fierce Fijians.

"Then what do you suggest?" she demanded.

"You come with me to see him. He is on a sloop anchored off the mouth of your river. Take your bodyguards for safety if you distrust me."

She sighed and looked away. What else could she do? If she didn't go, he might take Jason away forever. She had to see him.

"I must go with this man," she began in English to the two men. They followed her when she stepped out the door. Her pale green skirts were dappled by the leaves of fig and breadfruit limbs high overhead. It was hot and there was no trace of a breeze.

"Me go 'long boat, 'long this fella man," she stammered in her clumsy pidgin.

Her face more than her words communicated her feelings. Her bodyguards moved in on Riclef, their bare shoulders touching his coat. Riclef glanced from side to side, backing away from her. Suddenly, a third man appeared like a shadow and stood behind Riclef, completing the blockade. Despite Riclef's height, he was dwarfed by their combined natural massiveness.

Kit would not approve, she said to herself, but there was no way to stall her visitor until Kit came back. Then she turned to Riclef. "How can you do this thing?"

"I plan to sail to Europe with him. If you join me, you and I will go instead, and I will return Jason straightaway to Hobart, to his mother."

"I am pregnant, Riclef."

He shrugged, glancing down at her stomach.

"Then Jason must be mine, and I shall seek another bride someday. When my heart is healed," he said mournfully.

She put her hands to her temples and rubbed them despairingly, a gesture that did not reassure her silent friends.

But Riclef was not frightened any more. He lifted his head, and his mouth tightened in the neat circle of his black beard. "I'm waiting, Camilla."

"Let me gather some things," she said. She needed time to think.

For the first time in her life, she wished for a pistol to protect herself and Jason. She might have a Sheffield knife somewhere in the house, a gift from one of her Fijian friends, but she knew she never could stick a blade in another human being. Kit's rifles were in his father's house, and they were far too heavy for her. As she walked to the back of the house, she could see Arum and Samisoni and Mosese still hemming Riclef in, without touching him. Through the window, she noticed that all of them were facing forward, like four soldiers. Riclef was calm. He did not move, but it was clear from his stance that he felt relaxed, a sign to the Fijians that he was rather courageous. Maybe the cannibals, the *tevoro*, would catch Riclef and eat him, she thought, but the next minute she was appalled by her imagination. Riclef was tormented, a driven man. And she had helped to lead him to this extremity. Now she must act alone to get the boy back.

She gathered up her beaded purse, a shawl, her hat, and her leather shoes, which she hadn't worn since coming to Fiji and putting on woven sandals. Always, it seemed, she was hurriedly packing for survival, continually fleeing from one place to another!

When she had everything, she looked around the lovely room once before going out to face Riclef.

"Me go 'long *Saka* Christopher?" asked Mosese, wise man that he was. She told him yes, and thanked him.

Then Samisoni asked her if she wished both of the other men to accompany her as well, and she nodded, knowing he knew she had little choice.

"Twofella," she whispered. Then she added the word meaning "thanks," *vinaka*.

"Just for a little while, long enough to see Jason and comfort him," said Riclef, as she accompanied him down the path. The large Fijian men flanked them, but they did not ease Camilla's fear.

Bitterness rose within her. Why couldn't he have left her alone in her island paradise? How could he be so monstrous as to take Jason away from his mother? And how would the lad be affected by this experience, mentally and morally?

She walked between Samisoni and Arum, who assisted her whenever she had to step high over a root in the path. They moved quickly through the village, Samisoni clearing their way with curt commands to the townspeople in Fijian. What must these gentle new friends think? She had no idea how to explain in her few pidgin phrases or graphic hand signs.

When they finally got to the river, a ship's dinghy was waiting for them. A white man with a gizzled beard, wearing sailor's togs and carrying a pistol on his belt, stood in the stern, watching as they boarded.

"Who is this?" she demanded.

"Mr. Terrence Livermore," said Riclef. "He has property here, and is well acquainted with the Westcotts."

She read the expression on the man's face at once. He and Riclef evidently shared an unfavorable opinion of the Westcotts, as well as of taxes and of duty on gin and of Loyalists.

At least Livermore knew pidgin. He spoke rapidly to her friends, but the two Fijians stood their ground, replying in unfriendly mutters. Samisoni clutched at the long knife hanging by his side. The conversation went back and forth for a while, and finally Riclef said irritably, "We cannot carry along both these giants in this small boat. Not with Miss Cochran and myself and you as well."

"I shan't be left behind in their tender care, y'may be sure," the man said. Camilla noticed that he had an East London accent.

She stood wrapped in her shawl, and her plaited hat sheltered half her face. She did not speak, but simply waited through all the negotiations. Eventually, a compromise was found. The dinghy would take her, Riclef, and Samisoni to the lagoon, with Livermore at the tiller. Arum would stay behind.

Then they started off. The current took them swiftly toward the sea, and Camilla watched Arum disappear in the tangle of vines along the shore. She hoped he would not swim down the river, for sharks were commonplace here. Would he tell Kit? She sat and glanced from Livermore's pistol to Samisoni's keen knife blade, and shook all bad thoughts from her head. The only important thing now was Jason's need for her comforting.

What condition would the child be in after so long a voyage to so foreign a land?

When they arrived at Livermore's sloop, outside the mangrove-fringed mouth of the river, she got her answer. Riclef caught hold of the ladder on the side of the ship and assisted her over the gunwale.

Jason ran to meet her at once, his arms outstretched, his

face pink with weeping and speckled with tears. "Miss Milla!" he cried. He was neatly dressed in blue trousers and black stockings, and his little white shirt stuck to him in the grueling heat. It was so much hotter here than in her shady basket house!

She nearly fell getting all her skirts into the sloop and throwing her arms around the boy. He clung to her neck, pressing as close as he could get.

"Jason, dearest, it is all right!" she said. "I'm so glad you came over the sea to visit me. Did you have a nice voyage?"

She was thinking very fast while she gaily talked on. She would be calm and show no fear. She tried to seem delighted. Think of Jason, she kept telling herself.

"I've got you now and I won't leave you," she soothed him. "You'll be fine from now on. Miss Milla missed you."

Jason responded promptly with a long list of complaints. He'd been sick in a storm at sea, and he wanted his mum and his dad. "I didn't want to come on this trip," he confided, looking earnestly into her eyes as she crouched holding him and smoothing his hair. "I wanna go back right now! It's hot here and I miss my friends. I miss everybody!" he wailed.

"You'll go home soon," she promised, trying not to be specific. "But we want to have a little visit first." Riclef was a monster. He had no feelings at all! Suddenly, she heard the anchor chain rattle. The sail was run up, and the lines snapped taut. But Samisoni had not come aboard!

"Hey!" she cried to Livermore, who was now forward, standing at the wheel. "My friend is coming with us. You cannot—What are you doing? I must disembark, and the boy with me!"

She went to the rail and saw that the dinghy was now tied to the stern. Samisoni was swimming toward them. The wind came up and filled the sails, sending them out to sea. They were easily outdistancing the swimmer.

"I want him with me," she cried uselessly. "Turn around. Samisoni has to come with me!"

Riclef, standing on the other side of the sloop, was also shouting at Livermore to halt the ship and go back. Jason clung to her waist so that she could move neither forward nor back. At that moment, the sloop tilted and nearly threw her down. But the crew had the ship swiftly underway, and the winds, unfortunately, were cooperating. Along the mangrove-shielded shore they flew, past beaches and palm trees. Samisoni had turned around and was stroking hard for the shore now. He was a mere dot, just a head and splashing arms. She hoped there were no sharks.

"You'll be sent to prison for kidnapping!" she threatened Livermore. "I'm a minor, under the Westcotts' protection here." But she kept her voice level. The five-year-old was very perceptive, and she did not want to frighten him. She would make this a game, a glorious adventure.

"We are sailing fast," she said to him in a falsely jolly voice. "What do you think we shall see next? Flying fish and pelicans?"

"I want me mum," whined Jason, hiding his face in her skirts.

She clutched him to her, thinking that she wanted Kit above all else. What was she to do?

Chapter 34

Inside the reef, the water was still as glass. Mr. Livermore kept out of sight at the wheel, and Riclef guided Cammy and Jason into a small deckhouse where he sat them down facing him.

"Livermore says we're bound for Levuka. I can do nothing against five men on this craft. He must be doing this to spite Westcott. Honestly, I had no idea. But I'm unarmed."

She indicated the boy who was glowering at Riclef. "You must not, in any case, disturb his equanimity," she warned.

"I have said that I feel like a father to him. We have had a fine journey, like father and son."

"I want me dad," Jason sulked. "Me real dad. And Mum, and me cat and horse."

Riclef leaned toward him, stretching out his hands. "Do you remember when you rode on my swing?"

"Oh, hush," Cammy commanded him. She found his wistfulness unbearable. It was so unfair to use the child this way.

"Go out on deck, Jason," Riclef suggested with a sigh. "But take care."

The boy jumped up and bolted through the cabin door.

"Will he be safe?" she asked, looking after him. "If he's alone—"

"He has learned some seamanship during many dull weeks on the ocean. We sailed endlessly through storms, both of us sick and feverish. The boy was little better off than I. I will not give this boy up, Camilla. I will protect you, somehow send you back to your Christopher, but—"

"If ever I had liked you, I would hate you now for stealing that child," she spat at him in disgust. "He will never forgive you for this."

"He is only five years old," Riclef shrugged. "He will find much joy in the life I can offer him."

"Children abandoned or kidnapped are marked for life. I know it!" She shouted at him, rising to her feet. "My father was orphaned and he never became a true human being. He has no heart. Do you wish to see Jason grow up like him, embittered, always striking out at the world? The reason Edgar Cochran is the way he is is because he was stricken so young!"

Riclef listened with a pained face, as if her words had hit home. "But I mean him no harm!"

Before she could answer, he sprang up and left the cabin. She saw him pacing the deck, head down, blindly marching past Jason, who rushed inside again now that Riclef was not there. He settled down on the padded bench, leaning against Camilla wearily.

"I wanna go home," he repeated. "I don't want to go to England. That one, he don't smile anymore. He says I must call him 'Father,' and I shan't. Take me home, Miss Milla."

"We'll see to that," she consoled him, her head spinning. How stupid of her not to have left a note for Kit! How would he ever find her now? Mosese and Samisoni were capable of describing Riclef to Kit. The Fijians knew she'd gone reluctantly. But had Samisoni survived his long swim, and had Mosese found Kit? He was not due back from his errands until tomorrow.

Evening came. After supper she persuaded Jason to lie down with his head in her lap. She would not close an eye. Riclef was still pacing. To his credit, he did not want her or Jason to be harmed. If she resented him less, she might even pity him. He had no wife to give him a child, like the one curled within her, or the boy resting close against her side. Of course he did have another child, now a lawyer living in Sydney.

Mr. Livermore came into the cabin just as it was getting dark and sat down opposite Camilla, stretching out his arms on the table between them.

"How dare you drag me off to Levuka!" she demanded without any preliminaries.

"You've picked the most hated men in Fiji, lady," the bearded and foul-smelling man said by way of explanation. "The lousy Westcotts, father and son. Take my advice, you'll stick with this gentleman here—" He motioned toward Riclef, standing on the deck. "You'd best clear out o' these islands before a war starts and they begin the feasts of long pig. I'm just makin' it easy for you to go off with Mr. Torandor."

"Long pig?"

"Humans," he grunted. "And them which eats it will get their deserts, meanin' be wiped off the face of the earth. Nobody's gonna stand for thieving of their hard-earned profits by a so-called 'king' who strangled his own mum to death."

"What?" she cried, too loudly. The noise roused Jason, who whimpered and rolled up tighter against her, his thumb in his mouth. Livermore seemed to enjoy telling her this. His lip curled as he spat out each shocking word.

"Old Cockaboo, we call 'im, that's Thakombau, 'til recently was a cannibal swingin' a club. His dad was a man-eater like none ever seen on these islands, King of Mbau, he was. Why, when he died, his five widows got ceremoniously strangled. Thakombau, he had the privilege of doin' in his own mum, out of the five." Livermore chuckled, and then sat back to watch her reaction.

"But he is now a Christian," she offered weakly, sickened by the information.

"Sometimes they bury folks alive. Didn't yer dear Westcott lad tell you? When they build houses, they plant a live man in each post hole. They launch them war canoes over rollers which really are livin' men."

She shook her head, grimacing.

"They kill babies, too, and eat 'em."

"In the old days," she murmured.

"Not so long ago. Why, only last February, a white family

by the name of Burns were killed and eaten on the Mba River. You know how they'd slaughter that small boy there if they got hold of 'im?"

"I'd rather not know." She turned her head away, but Livermore went on gleefully.

"They'd grab 'im by the heels and smash 'is head against the post of a veranda, that's how."

"Stop it!" She covered her ears. Jason still slept peacefully.

"You want the likes of them rulin' over you?"

"The King's a Christian now," she insisted, "the ruling chiefs, too, Kit told me. Fiji will soon be a Crown Colony."

"Ha! Eatin' people, brainin' children, cuttin', tatooin'. There's no good in 'em. All of 'em needs killin', the *lotu* as well, them so-called converts."

"I suppose you belong to the Ku Klux Klan," she said sharply.

"It's the British Subjects Society and Volunteer Corps, miss. That's its name, and our motto is 'an eye for an eye.' Don't you be misled. The Queen don't want Fiji."

"She is almost persuaded," Cammy said staunchly.

"You'd make one sweet puddin' for a horde of painted cannibals, miss," he said, leering at her nastily. "You and the little lad both. They'd cook you in spinach leaves and eat you with a special fork they got just for human flesh." His eyes glittered in the dim light. "Finish you off right proper and all the time the death drums poundin'!"

"Stop it!" she commanded, her shout bringing Riclef on the run. "He's been abusing me," she explained, pointing shakily at Livermore.

"Get out!" Riclef shouted at the man. At that, Jason woke up. He looked around him and began to weep bitterly.

"Don't you come near Camilla again!" Riclef was still incensed.

Livermore turned around and shook a finger at the three of them in admonition. "Just you watch your tongues, Lord and Lady Whatever. This is my ship, and you're here at my not-real-eager invitation. If you got objections, then you just take a walk over that gun'le there, and keep on walkin'. You'll get a mite wet, I think." Grinning broadly, he walked out of the cabin.

Riclef stood staring at Cammy. There was no need to speak. They both felt the same in regard to their captor.

Riclef rubbed a hand over his face and sighed, shaking his head in defeat. "This is a terrible thing, Camilla."

She nodded numbly. When she made no reply, he edged slowly out of the door, evidently preferring the night wind to her accusing eyes.

The night was so black, and who knows how far they'd gone, en route to where? She could no longer see land.

Finally, after an hour or so of thinking, after Jason had fallen back to sleep on her lap, she rested her head on her arm on the table top. She dozed off only to be awakened, stiff and groggy, by the grinding of the sloop's hull against something. It was the reef! She heard the thud of feet running up and down the decks, and she went to the porthole, straining to see something in the mist. There were shouts, then shots.

Jason stumbled over to her. By reflex she covered his ears and hugged him, desperate to give some reassurance, however small. Carrying him to the door of the deckhouse, she saw nothing in the black sky flaunting the white banner of the Milky Way. The sails of the ship had gone slack and flopped over the mast. But where was Riclef, Livermore, and the crew?

She did not want to risk going to the gunwale to look over the side. But she still felt the unmistakable rocking motion, which meant that they were not stuck upon a coral reef.

"What is—?" Jason began, but she interrupted him.

"Hush, now," she said, and hushed her own whimper of dread against the boy's silken locks. Conquering some of her fear, she stepped out on deck, and as she bore down, she felt something pliable but hard under the arch of her foot.

It was a man's wrist!

She lunged back, gasping. When she bent over the man to investigate, she saw that it was one of the crew sprawled senseless. Jason fastened onto her neck and waist, clinging, monkeylike, and she found it impossible to straighten up.

But suddenly the boy was lifted from her, screaming and kicking. She whirled around to attack whoever dared to touch this child.

"Jason! Jason! Give him back! Let go!"

Hysteria overtook her. She plunged after Jason, and felt herself mauled by hands she could not see. Though she fought with fists and nails and elbows, it did no good. She was hoisted effortlessly off the deck. Now she was sure she'd be thrown overboard, have her brains smashed out! Where was Jason? She screamed his name again.

A torch flared, and in the glow she saw their captors. They were tall, black-faced, painted *tevoro*. She knew them by their giant mops of hair, though never had she seen one. These were the cannibals. They wore no *sulu* skirts and were naked but for their curved groin straps and white boars' tusks hanging 'round their necks like spikes.

She was set on her feet, and the first thing she saw was Jason, scared senseless, in a cannibal's arms. She forced herself to speak.

"Me true *Andi* Camilla belong *Ra* Christopher Westcott," she blurted out. "Onefella Samisoni friend true belong me."

There was no response, and then she recalled that highland cannibals speak no pidgin. Her few Fijian words came spluttering forth, but the men did not move.

"*Ni sam mbula,*" she breathed. That was a greeting. Would they admire politeness? "*O thei? Veitau?*" Who were they? Friends? What a foolish hope.

The men remained silent, staring at the small, defiant woman. Jason was crying harder now. One man took Cammy around the waist and lifted her over the railing. She hung for a moment from his arms, and then, just before he dropped her, hands rose up from beneath and captured her kicking legs. Then she was passed from this one to the others, and in a moment, she found herself in a rocking native canoe on the platform between the two hulls. The men holding her in place were huge. Their faces were painted black and they were decorated with feathers. Jason was dropped like a bundle of old clothes into her lap. She held him as ferociously tight as he held her.

Other men with torches left the white sloop and left it floating there. She feared they would set it on fire and let it burn to the water line, incinerating anyone left alive inside. Where was Riclef?

"Goodfella man?" she began, but the oarsmen raised their paddles and with dazzlingly rapid strokes, they went skimming away from the sloop. Camilla was in one twin-hulled canoe, made of hollowed logs, and another followed behind them. But mountain cannibals had no canoes. Did that mean the canoers were Christian *lotu*? What a foolish hope!

She prayed that their deaths would be quick, that they would be buried and not consumed by savages. Her only regret was that she had not said farewell to her love, her Kit, whom she would never see again.

"See the pretty torches?" she asked Jason, dread tightening her face into a grimace she hoped he might take for a smile. "Isn't this an exciting surprise?"

Jason hung on her neck, half strangling her, but he managed to nod. He was so manly for his age.

"We're just going for a nice boat ride. A nice surprise," she croaked as the canoes moved toward shore, leaving the sloop behind. Its light grew fainter as they proceeded. Were all the men still on board dead? Poor Riclef! They paddled for home.

The canoes slid onto the beach, and she knew they would now either be taken to a village or killed on the spot. She bound her shawl across her breasts and over one shoulder in a sort of hammock like a Fijian mother, and encased Jason in it. Kissing him softly, she waited for a summons to disembark. When one of the natives tugged on her arm, she rose and stepped over the hollowed log. The men were silent. They had not hurt her yet.

Camilla was led up the beach by one wrist. She walked carefully, hugging Jason, but she accidentally trod on the hem of her skirt, and fell. Shiny black faces with swirls of red and white paint bent over her, and their eyes and teeth glinted in the torchlight. Their remarks to each other were inaudible and incomprehensible.

"I am with child," she said softly, although she knew they couldn't understand her. "And this child is only five years old. Please have mercy. They are innocent."

At the line of the palm trees, she was forced down onto a pile of mats, half reclining and trying to protect Jason with her body.

Then the litter on which they reclined rose straight up in the air, lifted at each corner by four tall men. She was hoisted as high as the men's shoulders. She and Jason were carried swiftly into the rain forest. Jason's eyes were all she could see, since the torch was on a level with her face. He huddled against her, and she could feel his little heart racing.

"Isn't this exactly like a magic flying carpet?" she said to him, keeping her voice steady. They sank lower in the sling of fibers. What had they done with Riclef and Mr. Livermore? Had they killed them? Cammy wondered whether the crew had given any resistance to the boarding party.

She could tell that they were climbing now. Shifted from shoulder to shoulder, they were jarred and swung about. Jason whispered to her that he was frightened. So was she.

Their bearers never turned their faces up to look at her, crouched in the litter with Jason. Think of the child, not of yourself, she admonished herself. These people may be known as savages, but their *yangona* ceremony was as formal as a ballet and as solemn as the Mass. And how could she be harmed? She had a *tambua,* the curved whale's tooth, inside her clothing, warmed between her breasts. She prayed that its magical powers were as strong as Kit had said they were. Otherwise, she and Jason were doomed.

Chapter 35

How she slept at all during that long night trek, Cammy did not know. But oddly enough, they both dozed off, and had to be shaken awake. It was dawn when she felt herself lowered from the men's shoulders. She carefully looked around. The sky was black overhead, a storm was coming. They were in a fenced, moated village of thatched houses set around a square and closed in by giant rain forest trees. When she awoke, she found that she was still sitting on the pile of mats upon the litter. She was terribly thirsty. All around her were mostly naked Fijians, staring at these white people who had just entered their village.

Women with bare breasts and blue tattooed faces clustered around her, touching her garments, picking at the lace and gauze and ribbons in awe. Jason's clothing also entranced them, especially the tiny pearl buttons down his shirt. They stroked his pale skin and looked into his wide eyes as if they had never seen such a sight before.

"Talk pidgin?" Cammy asked hopefully, but she got no response.

A tiny old woman, smaller than she, took Cammy's hand and drew her to her feet. She led her and Jason into one of the biggest houses, and the minute they were inside, rain started pelting down. The house was a shabbier, smaller version of her own clean and airy basket house. But any shelter was welcome now, for the packed clay outside would soon become mud.

Camilla put Jason on his feet, took off her shawl, and examined the faces of the women surrounding them. She mimed lifting a glass to her lips, then when that didn't work, she mimed scooping handfuls of water. One girl, who seemed to understand, leaped up and ran outside in the rain, returning with a thick section of bamboo, filled with fresh water. Cammy gratefully tilted the hollow tube first to Jason's lips and then to her own. But she was still parched, and it was refilled for them two times before they were satisfied. The village seemed clean, although the house smelled of smoke and oils she could not identify. Were they here to be fattened for a feast?

She looked around the room for any large bones and saw none. There were no skulls, either. As she was determining what sort of people these really were, one of the women gestured for her to sit down, and she did so.

"I wonder where this is?" said Jason loudly, as she pulled him down beside her. Their female audience seemed very interested.

"It's a nice house," she reassured him.

When an old man entered, stooping through the doorway, the women and girls surged back against the walls either in fear or reverence, Cammy couldn't tell which. The man wore fibers between his legs and flowers in his hair, and his shell necklaces clattered when he squatted before her. He studied her and Jason for a moment, and then spoke something that sounded like Fijian.

She didn't recognize one word, but his inflection communicated an emotion she didn't expect. It was sympathy. She shivered in the dank air, listening to rain patter on the thatch overhead and rattle the bamboo walls. He motioned with his hand, and one of the women came near and draped a long piece of *masi* cloth over Camilla's shoulders. It felt stiff, but snug when she drew it around herself and Jason.

Another woman blew upon a pile of coals buried in a central firebox. The house had no chimney, of course, and the smoke stung Camilla's eyes, but she still welcomed the bright orange flames and the heat against her face on this wet morning.

"Look, Jason, a bonfire. Right inside the house!"

Jason sat up in her lap and stared, then he studied the old man's face. He seemed quite calm and very interested. At least he would be cheerful until the end, Cammy mused philosophically.

These people were not *lotu*. Why were they sitting around her as if she were a sacred icon? In a flash of inspiration, she reeled in the golden chain hanging beneath her bodice, and proffered her *tambua* respectfully to the old man with both hands. She had seen Fijians do this when they begged a large service from Kit Westcott, or when sealing a pact between themselves.

The old man's eyes widened. She dared not take the chain from her neck. A *tambua* was something to conjure with.

"Belong *Ra* Christopher Westcott," she said adamantly. Should she stake her life on her relationship to the Westcotts? She wracked her mind for stories Kit had told her about customs and beliefs. She recalled that paler-skinned people from the more eastern of the Pacific islands were taken as divine and made Fijian leaders in the olden days. She remembered, too, that the Fijians admired magic and loud noises from machines unfamiliar to them. They marveled at a tin of fish that exploded when put on the fire.

What had she with her that might produce a good effect? Only the clothes she wore, and the bead purse still dangling from her arm. She reached into it, grasping for anything that would be unfamiliar to these people. In the bottom she found a vial of perfume hardly bigger than her thumb. She uncorked it and held it out to the old man, who seemed loathe to touch it. He gazed at it quizzically, tilting his head away, and then his nostrils flared and he jerked his head back.

Numb, but guided by instinct rather than reason, she dabbed some perfume behind her ears, then leaned forward and motioned for the old man to come closer. Frowning uneasily, he did so. She moistened her fingertip on top of the vial and touched it to his forehead. He eyed her nervously and seemed unsure of what to do to counteract this.

Taking her fate in her hands, Camilla rose to her feet as gracefully as she could, bade Jason stay seated, and carried the tiny vial over to the cluster of women. She repeatedly inverted it over her fingertip and then bent to anoint each of the women in the center of her forehead. When several of them tried to get up to run away, a barked command from the old man kept them in their places.

She tried to work from the eldest women to the youngest girls because Kit had told her that Fijians are in awe of rank and dignity. With each touch of her perfumed finger on a woman's forehead, she intoned, "I want to be your friend. I want to be your friend."

The fire colored her gown golden as she went from one woman to the next, applying the scent. Soon the whole house was redolent with the smell of lilacs. She had never seen lilacs growing in Fiji, so that was another unfamiliar element in her favor.

Jason sat perfectly still and watched her. She had but one half drop for him when she was finished with the group. She anointed him under each ear, as she had done to herself.

Then she sat down beside the boy, shaking with anxiety. No one moved. The old man stared at her and at the vial, contemplating the strange ritual. If they now believed that she had mystical powers, she prayed they'd see her as a kind spirit, one to love, not to fear. Not one to put to death and devour! An eternity passed.

She looped her arm tightly around Jason, and she felt two little lumps in his pocket. Reaching in, she retrieved a pair of glass marbles and asked Jason if she might have them. Transfixed, he nodded.

"This will be such a nice gift from you to the chief," she said, referring to the aged man.

The marbles picked up the firelight, glowing gold and crystal as she rolled them between her fingers. As though they were jewels to buy their freedom, Cammy offered them to the fascinated old man.

He took the glass balls with grave curiosity, holding each one up to the fire to examine. He sniffed them. They had passed through her perfumed hands and were also lilac-scented. As an afterthought, she gave him the empty perfume vial as well, smiling and nodding. He nodded back. "*Vinaka*," he said politely. It was the word she knew for thank-you.

Then he arose, backed away from her, and went outside. The rain had ceased, and a dim light now filtered through the lattice.

"I want to go out and play," complained Jason, who seemed bored now that the gift-giving was over. What would happen next? Cammy's racing heart half smothered her. But she was glad that she had thought to create her magic ceremony. So far, the charm had worked.

The women and girls, freed from the spell of the old man, began whispering and murmuring among themselves. Camilla arose and took Jason firmly by the hand. With as much dignity as she could muster, she walked through the low doorway and stood on the wet stoop outside. The Fijians in the village square stopped in their tracks, every head turning toward her, though she had not made a sound. No one approached her this time. A few girls smiled and then hid their faces, hurrying away in their tiny grass fringes.

It struck Camilla that perhaps this village had never before seen a white woman. White men had probably visited here, but no green-eyed, golden-haired female in a diaphanous gown.

Jason released his hand from hers and walked toward a group of children, calling back over his shoulder, "They don't wear no clothes at all!"

"That's because it's so hot here," she explained, and more heads turned to her. "Jason, it's fine. Don't show disapproval. Be mannerly."

"Can I take off my clothes? I'm hot, too."

He kicked off his shoes before she could answer, and then sat down in the mud so he could tug off his black stockings. When he unbuttoned his shirt and handed it to her, she didn't object at all, although removing his trousers seemed a bit much. Still, Jason would earn acceptance being like the other children.

Looking startlingly white, he sidled over to a pair of boys his size. Camilla was distracted by two women who came over to her and took her hands, smiling and leading her toward a smaller thatched house. When she looked back, she saw Jason rubbing mud onto his chest and stomach while the Fijian boys watched in amazement. Naturally, he wanted to turn himself their color.

The women led her inside a house full of flowers, with fresh mats on the floor and bowls of *dalo* and yams set out for her to eat. This was evidently to be her house.

She ate a little of the food offered her, and put some of the waxy blossoms in her bodice. Their scent, though faint, was preferable to the bottled scent of lilac. Jason seemed to be happily occupied, so she tried not to worry about him.

One of the women came toward her holding out a long-handled, giant wooden comb. It was clear that they wished to handle her strange hair. No fear remained in her, only exhaustion, so she bent her head and gave herself over to their ministrations.

They clucked over the springiness of her big curls, so different from their own small, tight ones. They sniffed her hair and examined the small pearls in her ears. Working with gentleness and intense concentration, they left her hair smooth and bedecked with flowers.

Cammy was suddenly overcome with emotion. Unbidden tears sprang to her eyes. Their shy tenderness, the little house that seemed to be hers, the soft mats under her, the happy laughter of Jason at play! She had never felt so grateful to be alive. Quietly, she wept at her good fortune.

She held her stomach and rocked herself and her unborn child as she cried. Her companions watched in silent consternation.

By way of explanation she rocked her phantom baby in her arms. When they nodded, understanding, she pointed to her belly. Murmurs of interest and sympathy rose around her. Then she outlined the waves of the sea, and lifted her shoulders in a question. Where? she motioned, looking all around. Her hands formed a ship, rode it over the sea, and again made signs of interrogation.

No one answered, but one woman got up and left the house. She returned with a tall man, who squatted in front of Cammy and studied her. He was handsome and decorated much as the old man had been.

"I cannot stay here," Cammy cried to the young man. "Take us to Levuka. To the island of Ovalau where your King lives. Thakombau!" she added. He must surely know that name.

The rain started up again, pattering like mice upon the thatch. A woman walked in leading a brown child, and it took Cammy a moment to realize that this was Jason, patterned with hand prints. His little friends had helped smear him with mud so he would match them in color.

The man frowned in thought, spoke to her incomprehensibly, and finally nodded. The woman came back with a bowl of water, and she briskly swabbed Jason white again, which he endured as if she were his nanny. Then the man rose and quietly departed.

Jason ran after him, frisking in rain that completed the washing of his body. Thanks be to heaven that he was happy, for now, with friends.

Camilla lay down on her side, pillowed her cheek on her hands, and the women gathered around her solicitously. Suddenly, she felt terribly sick to her stomach, as she had not yet been from her pregnancy. What was she to do? How long must they stay here? For life? Would Kit's child be born in this mountain village?

The day dragged on, and they were given more of the tasteless root vegetables to eat, and a bit of meat she felt sure was some kind of bird. It was not pig, and surely . . . surely, it was not—

Jason, happily weary, came in, slept, and went out again to frolic with his naked peers. He'd spent weeks without seeing other children on the sea, and now he delighted in having these companions. They did not need spoken language to communicate.

That night, wrapped in mats against the mountains' evening chill, with Jason cuddled against her, Cammy slept fitfully. She awoke to find her lashes stuck closed with tears.

"I must do something. I have to try to get us down to the shore," she said, but Jason simply ran away from her out the door without bothering to put on his garments. The women appeared soon and methodically combed her hair. She bathed her arms and face in a wooden bowl of water they had brought her.

The sun broke through at noon, and she sat in the doorway, watching the stick-and-coconut game of one white boy and a dozen brown ones. Large, well-groomed pigs marched through the square, snuffling the ground, and thin dogs rooted out anything edible. Camilla was curious to see women coming from the gardens with bulging cloth bags. Others sat nearby nursing babies or pounding roots to paste. The young men were undoubtedly out hunting anything that would fit in the cook pots.

It must have been midafternoon when the commotion started. A lone dog began barking first. Children rushed around madly, women gathered up their tools and babies and retreated toward their houses. Camilla, not knowing what else to do, remained numbly seated in the sunshine, hugging her knees.

Animated warriors came through the gateway to the village. The dogs' barking was now frantic. In the midst of the spear-armed escort, a white shirt flashed.

She leaped to her feet, hiking her skirts up, and ran, choking back screams of relief.

"Kit! Kit! Oh, Kit!"

He caught her to him, and she kissed his flushed, scratched face. Then as she pulled back, smiling, she saw how exhausted he looked. Samisoni, standing beside him, took Cammy's hand, muttering his own emotional greeting.

"Thank God they didn't harm you," Kit cried. "Oh, precious one, you're unhurt? The baby is all right? And Jason?" He embraced her again, gasping for breath.

"The baby's fine, my dearest. Jason's playing with his new friends. How did you find me? Did they kill everyone else?"

"Samisoni arranged it. He was responsible for these people getting you taken off that sloop, before we lost you forever! Mosese came for me and brought me here."

"Are they truly cannibals? They were kind and peaceful."

Kit smiled ruefully, not wishing to malign these good people. "The chief says he's too old to convert, so the village doesn't, either. But they do trade with Suva."

"But where's Riclef? Is he alive? Tell me, Kit," she insisted.

"Just a bit the worse for wear, that's all. He put up a fight, as I understand."

"He was defending me," she said, aware that Kit cared very little for the man. "Kit, I have to explain. Riclef didn't kidnap me. The only bad thing he did was steal Jason, his own child. Livermore is the real villain."

She gripped his arm. "Where are we? Are we far up in the high mountains? It took us all night to get here. Tell me everything."

"They chose a roundabout route to evade trackers. You're not over fifteen hundred feet up, and not fifteen miles inland from Suva. We must get you out of here and show everyone that you're well and happy, before the Ku Klux Klan gets here with rifles and slaughters every soul in this village. Livermore escaped in spite of his wounds. He rushed off to collect vigilantes 'to save a white lady.' "

"Oh, that's terrible! Kit, I've been their guest, and so well treated."

"Samisoni dared not use our own village people to rescue you. They'd be dead by now because of vigilante 'justice.' And that's why he sent out an appeal to hill people, offered payment for the task. Then he came to find Mosese and me."

Camilla, relieved and grateful, rose on tiptoe to give Samisoni a kiss.

"I need a bath," Kit sighed, "and a bit of rest before we go down." He picked at his sweat-soaked shirt. He'd come up the trail barefoot, and his feet and ankles were lacerated with scratches and cuts.

It was only at this point that Jason tore himself away from his friends to come over to them. Kit looked down at him and chuckled. "This is your small Tasmanian boy, Camilla? He's dark as any Fiji lad!" He bent and scooped Jason up in his arms, much to the child's delight. "He needs a wash worse than I do!" At this, Jason made a face.

The sun appeared and shone brightly, as if to celebrate Kit's arrival. While they were standing there in conversation, a village woman came hastening to them with Jason's garments, all clean and dry.

"All you need is a bit of brushing off," Kit said to Camilla with a loving glance. "Let's go to the river. We'll let Samisoni give Jason a wash, but much farther downstream."

She understood, and strolled beside Kit, her hand clutching his. When they got to the clear pool, he stripped in an instant, plunged in, and held out his arms to her.

She did not need a second invitation to wriggle out of her bodice and skirt and pantaloons. Jumping in, nearly on top of him, she pressed her wet body to his, stroking his broad shoulders and his hard chest as he covered her mouth with his.

After they had frolicked together, he scrubbed his shirt and trousers and spread them on flat stones by the water, above the line of green moss.

"Oh, my darling. If I'd lost you!" he mourned, stroking her lovely face. "If that wretch had taken you to Victoria—"

"I never would have let him marry me, but that does not stop him from refusing to give Jason back. We must return him to his mother, Kit! I know he seems happy in this setting, but that's just his good nature and a child's love of adventure. On the ship, he was weeping hysterically for her. Riclef could not persuade him to love a new father when he had one at home he missed so desperately."

"We have much to do, Cammy," Kit said solemnly after they had been silent for some time. "We must go down, and stop the reaction Terrence Livermore has managed to put in motion. We must make sure no Fijian is murdered because of this."

She knew they had to, but she was reluctant to pull herself from his arms. "Your garments are still drying," she said, pressing the water out his hair and down his back in streams as he tried to do the same for her sodden curls.

"They'll dry on my body," he said, easing himself out of the pool and putting on his white cottons again.

He dried her nude body with caresses. It was still very hot, and the silver droplets rose from her flesh in steamy clouds. Finally, she put on her rumpled clothes, and took his hand again. They walked toward the village, savoring every minute they could spend alone together.

Chapter 36

The direct route back to Suva was steep but so well trodden that Cammy insisted on walking herself rather than being carried in another high, swaying litter. Jason rode happily on Samisoni's shoulders, scrubbed and immaculate. No one would ever have suspected that this child had spent a day in muddy frolic with cannibals!

"You were never in danger of being eaten, Cammy," Kit reassured her after they were far from the village, "but I never dreamed you could charm them so thoroughly. They call you, 'Lady of the Sweet Fragrance.' Now they consider that you belong to them. Your recovery will cost me dearly."

"Are you teasing, Kit?" she laughed, pleased at herself for thinking of the perfume ceremony.

"Not at all. Samisoni promised two dozen pigs for your rescue and safekeeping, but now they have asked me for a bride price, as well." He was unable to stop grinning.

"A bride price?" she gasped.

"As if you were a girl of their tribe. I have no choice. I must give twenty pigs, a dozen good knives, and ten *tambua*. You're worth twice that, so I consider it a bargain!"

"Kit!" she cried, hastening to keep up with his long strides, so she could reach up for a kiss. But then she thought of

something and quickly sobered. "I may never be your bride,
Kit. Riclef will not try to wed me now, but I am still a 'minor'
according to the law. He is sure to tell Father where I am, and
he could take me away from you for nearly two years. I would
die in that time, Kit."

"He'll never touch you again, or even see you," Kit replied
gravely. "I'm taking you away from here at once, since
Torandor has found us. My father must be back at the
plantation by now. He was due home from Levuka today. I
left a message for him just before I rushed off to find you. We
shall see him first and then take the first ship out of Suva or
Levuka."

"Where will we go?"

"Anywhere."

"But what about Jason?"

"We'll take him along with us, if you insist."

"He must go back to his mother in Hobart, immediately."

"But that's not a safe place for you to go, Camilla," he
retorted. "Neither Victoria nor Tasmania. I would not even
risk taking you to Bernard in England now that he has felt
your father's wrath."

They walked down the mountain, Cammy slipping and
sliding on the sudden drops in the path. It was so distressing
to realize that she had no home, no refuge. But when she
stumbled into Kit's strong body and he caught her, she was
righted again, and when he kissed her, she knew that her
home was wherever this man led her. Jason, swaying high up
over Samisoni's head, batted vines and branches out of both
their faces, chattering about the village and the ship Camilla
promised would take him back to Mama.

When they arrived in Suva, it was packed with armed men.

Kit, Camilla, Samisoni, and Jason walked into the little
town and went directly to the native church that stood in its
coconut grove over a pond. The missionary there could best
quell the stirrings of violence now palpable around them.

When the townspeople saw Kit, the name "Westcott" was
murmured, and not in a friendly fashion.

Cammy picked up Jason in her arms as Kit hastened into
the church. When several armed white townsmen caught up
to her, she whirled to face them, determination shining in her
eyes.

"The white lady you seek is safe!" she said loudly. "Please
tell everyone that I am completely unharmed."

The word was passed around the crowd, and other men and women were summoned to bear witness. Angry, excited citizens surrounded her. Because she was smaller than everyone save the children, she decided to step up onto a horizontal coconut trunk so that she would be seen. Then she pulled Jason up to stand beside her.

"*Tevoro?*" cried one voice. "Stolen from a sloop!" "Livermore told us. Where is he? He was going on about them thieving cannibals."

"But I am all right!" she insisted. "I tell you they were my friends!"

"Kill the bloody savages!"

"They are my friends!" she shouted. "I was on Livermore's sloop against my will. This boy was kidnapped from his parents by a white man. You listen to me!"

Those who were not muttering did listen, but they didn't seem happy about what Cammy had to tell them.

"We are getting up a rescue party," somebody yelled.

"There is no one to rescue!" she insisted. "Stop this! This is insanity!"

A man burst through the crowd and fought his way to her. He was busy scribbling down everything she said in a notebook. "*Fiji Times,*" he told her. "You're saying that you're Miss Camilla Cochran, stolen from the *Bluefin?*"

"Yes. Mr. Livermore was taking me away from Viti Levu when I did not wish to go. My good Fijian friends saved me and this child."

He wrote frantically, and when the crowd's murmurs and protests grew deafening, he turned around and shouted for silence.

Just then, Kit emerged from the church with two men. As they stood staring in disbelief at her audience, she shook her head, trying to signal that he should stay out of this. It was clear that many in the crowd disliked the Westcotts, and she did not want Kit dragged into this dispute over Riclef, Jason, and herself.

"Livermore?" one vigilante was yelling. "Terrence Livermore stole her? What a thing! Whose boy is this? We've volunteers and guns!"

When they brandished rifles, the journalist jumped up on the log beside her and waved angrily at them. "Let the lady speak! Put your guns down! Can't you see she's unharmed?"

"If you want an excuse to murder Fijians," she said boldly

to the crowd, "then look elsewhere. Savage cannibals do not shelter and feed people!"

The muttering subsided, and some women in the crowd called, "Let's hear her!" Everyone was frowning and gaping at Jason. The journalist, a young, carrot-haired man wearing thick spectacles, remained beside her. Eventually, the men lowered their rifles and put them out of sight against their legs. Livermore was nowhere to be seen.

"You may print in the *Fiji Times*," she said to the journalist loud enough for the crowd to hear, "that if any punitive expedition is mounted against my Fijian hosts, I shall bring charges against Mr. Livermore. This beautiful island should not be marred by one man's evil intentions." She looked around for a reaction and then added, "Let us all be good subjects of King Thakombau."

There was another angry ripple in the group, and a few men spat on the ground in disgust. Seeing that she was in trouble again, she commanded Jason, "Wave to the people. Please wave."

He did as he was told and then, quickly, hid his face against her neck. But at least his gesture recovered a modicum of good feeling for her, as the crowd saw that he was unharmed.

She descended from her improvised podium, and as soon as she was on the ground, she felt a hand under her elbow. It was Kit's. Dragging Jason, she glided along the path opened for them by staring onlookers.

Camilla could only hope she had sounded thoroughly convincing. If only she could help her Fijian friends, and Kit as well.

"Miss Cochran!" The friendly man from the *Fiji Times* was tagging after them. "What errand brings you here? Is the boy—?"

"He's the son of a friend of mine, and now he's going straight back to his mother. You see, there's been a rather sad misunderstanding I would rather not discuss." She felt it would be best to leave Riclef's name out of this muddle.

Kit shook hands with the journalist, verified that he was the famous Henry Westcott's son, and closed the interview. He whisked her away down the street, and Jason clung to her hand for dear life.

"He's new. I've not met him before, but he seems open-minded," Kit remarked. "Now we have to get going. The missionary told me that Father has come through Suva, and he's bound for the plantation. He's not very well. He overtired himself trying to help put out the brushfire of this uprising."

"Oh, I am so sorry, Kit," she said. "I never wanted to cause him such sorrow."

"Don't worry, he'll recover. He'll want to see you and Jason, so come on."

She pulled back and he looked at her questioningly.

"I must see Riclef first. I want to know how he is."

Kit threw up his hands. "Are you mad, Camilla? He abducted Jason, and carried you off as well. Why should you care what happens to him? He's a sick man, and the missionary said he'd been injured."

"That settles it. I shall not have his death on my conscience, Kit. He means nothing to me, but he is a tormented man who must be dissuaded. Otherwise, if Jason reaches home, he'll only be kidnapped once again!"

Kit sighed, realizing it was useless to argue. "He's in the infirmary. I'll accompany you."

They left Jason with Samisoni, who was sitting on the beach near the canoe, waiting to take them all home. They assured him they'd be back and then took a path into the town, among thatched houses and a few European boxlike structures, past the Suva Hotel, the Polynesia Company office. At last they arrived at the house of the doctor who kept a small infirmary next to his surgery.

Cammy told him to wait outside, but Kit refused. When she went to see Riclef, her chin was held high but her insides contracted in dread. Kit was one short step behind her. They climbed the stairs to the veranda, and there he was.

Riclef Torandor lay on a bed with his chest bare, a bandage bound across it. One arm was hanging in a sling, and sticking plaster covered one side of his face. Camilla stood before him and studied him for some moments, totally silent.

"Camilla?" murmured Riclef, starting as soon as he opened his eyes. "I feared you were dead!"

"I was well treated. Far better than you, I am sorry to see. Kit, Christopher Westcott, brought me down the mountain."

"We have met," said Riclef tonelessly, inclining his head very slightly to the other man. Their eyes locked.

"I regret your injuries, Riclef," Camilla said, "but you had no right to lead me to that sloop or take Jason."

"I relinquish any claim on you, Camilla," Riclef said in a

frail voice. "My error, Westcott, was to fall in love with this lady when her heart was already given to you."

Cammy gave a large sigh of relief. She hadn't wanted them to come to blows or to speak bitter words. But as she gazed down at him, she saw that Riclef was in no condition for the former. How severe was his head wound?

"As for my son," he went on, "I cannot give him up. I told Camilla that if I could not make her my wife, I would keep my natural son. He is all I have in the world." He glanced down at Camilla's stomach, and made a wry face at Kit, adding, "You would not give your own child to another father to rear, Westcott, and neither will I. When I depart these shores, I take my son with me. Try to prevent that, and you shall surely regret it."

"You're in no position to make threats," said Kit softly. "You're totally incapacitated, and you're a stranger here. No one will help you."

"In a month or two, it is possible no one will help you, either. Camilla's figure may scandalize the good citizens of Fiji," Riclef continued. "Will your career in the Fijian government, about which I hear so much, survive the birth of a bastard child, Westcott?" Riclef's tone was dispassionate, merely that of an interested onlooker. "You need to marry very promptly. I offer you a way."

"What can you mean?" exclaimed Camilla.

"I have a license to marry Camilla, and all the other required papers, signed and sealed. I shouldn't think it would be difficult to remove one name and write in another," he said slowly, with an odd expression on his face. "Who would question the word of the son of a King's adviser?"

"You'd do that for us?" Camilla asked.

"I'd do it in exchange for my son. On the understanding that he sails with me to London."

"That license is not worth Jason's whole future life!" said Camilla instantly. A moment later, Kit echoed her. "That is not a bargain I could make, sir," he said firmly. "We shall make do, and Jason is going back to his mother."

She would have flung herself on Kit and kissed him for making such a sacrifice, but this was not the time or the place for a display of emotion.

They bid Riclef a curt goodbye. Departing via the surgeon's office, Kit asked that Mr. Torandor be given all the sedatives he'd accept and that he not be encouraged to leave.

Kit and Cammy walked out into the waning afternoon and stood to watch the sun touch the Pacific, far beyond the sheltering reef. Tall, curving palm trees shook green and silver fronds over their heads.

"I love you," Cammy said, so quietly that he nearly missed it.

"I love the both of you," said Kit. "You and the child who will soon be born."

"But, Kit . . ." She turned and touched his arm. "What are we going to do about Jason?"

"I don't know. As you say, if we return Jason or send him back to his home with friends of mine, Riclef will only come after him again. How much of that can a small child suffer?"

They wended their way slowly back to the plantation. Old Henry Westcott was waiting to greet them and embraced Cammy warmly. He was overjoyed to see her and took the news of the coming grandchild with hardly a grimace. He kissed Camilla and wished her well, adding, "I would like the baby to have our name when it comes, my daughter. We will see to that. But in the meantime, you have to hear some very bad news, I'm afraid."

"What is it?" she gasped. "Has anyone else been hurt because of my journey to the mountains?"

"No, I wish it were only that! You yourself stand in danger now, my dear. Edgar Cochran disembarked at Levuka just as I started out for Suva yesterday."

"What?" Kit cried. "Are you saying the man is here? Did you talk to him?"

Mr. Westcott shook his head. "I thought it unwise. He was standing at the dock, asking for lodgings for one or two nights. That's what I overheard. We shall shelter you, Camilla, do not fear. You must not go back with him."

"Of course not!" she moaned. "Oh, but does he have a legal right to drag me away?"

"The child," said Kit softly. "He would never let either of us see our child!"

She sat down, hugging herself, blind with tears of fright and fury.

Samisoni brought Jason in at that moment, and that ended any futher discussion. Mr. Westcott sat down heavily in his armchair and propped up his sandaled feet, encouraging Jason to come sit in his lap. "I'm too old for such crises," he sighed. "It's bad enough with politics, but to involve innocent children—" He indicated 'he boy in his lap and stroked Jason's head lovingly.

"I so hate to distress you," Camilla said. Already she was furiously thinking of what she must do. She had to save their baby from Father, and save Jason from Riclef. Her own welfare and Kit's were farther down the list. She could not disgrace him or draw him away from Fiji. The King needed Kit now, more than ever.

That night, she retired early, leaving Kit to catch up on the news with his father. She slept in Kit's bed, cradling Jason in the curve of her body. When Kit came in at last, he lifted the sleeping child tenderly and placed him in a little bed prepared on the other side of a *masi* screen.

She woke up then and reached for him. "My father can force me to go home with him," she told Kit, when at last he held her in his arms. "He can have me hunted down if I try to hide in the mountains again. Those armed men will assemble and innocent people will be killed. I cannot draw you away now. Kit, your father can't divide his time between the plantation and the capital, and do your own work, as well."

Kit's silence was all the confirmation she needed. It was true. He was tied here by duty. If he left, she would never forgive herself. But if she were taken back to Blue Downs, he would never see his own child, nor its mother. Cammy was exhausted. She had no solutions left.

She and Kit silently labored over each other's bodies as if this were the last time they would ever make love. Afterward, he lay so still for such a long time, she was sure he had fallen asleep. But then he spoke in the darkness. "I shall arrange for the pigs," he murmured, "and then I shall take you away."

"What? What are you talking about?"

"The reward and the bride price. I have to do it to keep the peace, and my honor. We'll have good fat pigs imported from New Zealand to improve the stock. Father can see to their delivery."

"And Jason?" she whispered.

"We'll take him with us. Eventually, when we get to Hobart, we'll leave him there. That's all I can think of until we discover a way to keep him safe from Torandor. Now get some sleep, Camilla. We will sail out of Suva on some cutter or some trading vessel, and then find space on a steamer. It doesn't matter where we go as long as it's away from Torandor and from your wretched father."

She knew exactly what this pledge cost him, and she loved him for it.

"I won't let you leave Fiji, Kit," she said. "I intend to leave the islands with Jason, but I won't let you accompany us."

"Cammy, I can't let you go. You are carrying my child!"

"It is mine. As Jason is Janet's."

He sat up in the bed and looked down at her. His body, faint in the moonlight, was rigid with shock and indignation. "It is our baby, Camilla. A child conceived in love and trust. We were wed in the little church in England, remember? I am your husband."

"I'll never deny that, Kit, but now I must follow my own conscience. I can escape alone and hide, and then when it's safe, I'll come back to you."

"Absolutely not. Never. I'm going with you!"

He held her tightly and said no more, but the fierceness of his embrace told her he was resolute. She would not have him ruin his life. There was only one way out.

When she was sure that Kit and Jason were asleep, she got up, dressed silently in an earth-colored gown, and put a cloth over her vivid red-gold hair. Then she stole out of their house, away to the village right by the river, the river that ran to the sea.

Chapter 37

Each Saturday, women went to the Suva market, laden with large hemp bags of vegetables and fruit. Camilla figured that if she smeared clay on her cheeks and on the backs of her white hands, she could mix with the women and get away before Kit could stop her. She had a task to perform.

The village women welcomed Camilla's company when she joined them. Smiling broadly, refusing to let her carry even a few shelled coconuts or an infant to lighten someone's load, they drew her into the midst of their group. Although they asked no questions, they sensed she wanted anonymity. Why else the drab clothing, head scarf, and tinted face?

There were eleven of them all together walking down the river. She was tired and flushed with the exertion of the trip when they finally reached Suva. In the market square, they joined other women, children, and a few old men.

Pouring out their produce onto small rugs, the women prepared to sell or barter their bright oranges, lemons, green and ripe coconuts, leafy vegetables, and naked pale roots. The market was a profusion of all these and wooden combs and dishes and necklaces of seeds and sea shells. An ideal place for a white woman in disguise, since all eyes were riveted on the goods for sale!

Before she could leave the market, however, she felt a tap on her shoulder. She whirled around with a gasp. A small white woman was smiling at her from a sunbonnet.

"Miss Cochran? You are the lady who stayed in the village?"

"Who are you?" Cammy rudely demanded. After seeing the behavior of the white people of Suva toward the Westcotts, she was suspicious of them all.

"The missionary's wife," the woman said. "Ellen Brown. My husband talked to Mr. Westcott yesterday. I have news for you, my dear."

Cammy was worried about anyone else recognizing her.

"A *tevoro* visited us last evening. He came to talk about you."

"About me?"

"He's the son of the old chief of your village. He said that his father was most struck by your good nature and the sweet boy you had with you. In some way, you gave the village a blessing, though he wasn't clear about what kind."

"I . . . all I did was share a little scent with the chief and some ladies. I had nothing better to give, as a mark of friendship."

The woman grasped her hands in sincere appreciation. "You did more than you guessed. My husband has been invited to the village tomorrow, and we may soon see a massive conversion. That would be twoscore souls saved, and a cessation of their ancient habits—the eating of human flesh and infanticide and killing widows."

Cammy smiled with relief. "Oh, do you think so?" she exclaimed.

"Well, the Lord works in mysterious ways, His wonders to perform," Mrs. Brown said, shaking her head. "Do come to tea with us at your earliest convenience, dear, and bring your Kit. He is a fine, forthright young man. He will be a minister in the government some day, mark my words."

Camilla thanked the woman for the information and made her excuses before rushing off. She had to go or Kit might catch up to her. It seemed so impossible! Were man-eaters and widow-killers those kindly people who sheltered her? She was awestruck but she had no time now to consider this revelation. She had work to do. It was vital that she get to Riclef before he learned of Edgar Cochran's arrival in Levuka. After all, Riclef hated Edgar Cochran. As she ran up the steps of the infirmary, she went through all her options in her mind. There were very few.

Riclef was on the veranda, sitting up in a chair. The sticking plaster on his head was gone, and she could see the barely healed wound. He had obviously been clubbed. When he saw her, he bowed coldly over the sling that half covered his shirtfront. "How kind of you to visit again. Have you gone to see that Livermore wretch as well? It seems he's mended more quickly than I."

"He has avoided me. I called his bluff yesterday. He'd best not show his face around Suva," she declared.

"What a fright you look! Here, take this napkin and wipe the mud from your own face," he said with surprising tenderness. "Where is my son?"

"I'll tell you all that later," she said impatiently. "But first, have you yet heard who has come?"

"No. I want to hear about Jason, Camilla."

"My father is in Fiji! He's come to fetch me home!"

She dropped onto a chair, facing him. She said nothing more, but scrubbed at her face and hands with a cloth dampened in his water carafe.

He looked at her intently. "Is this an appeal for my aid? When you have my son? I want to see him."

"He is well, Riclef. He is in a fine house, with all the comforts. Riclef, I can flee my father if I know you'll give up Jason forever. We want to take him back to Janet. Oh, please relent!"

He didn't answer, but stared at her for a long moment. "Is it true that you are carrying Westcott's child, Camilla?"

She nodded.

"I no longer know, these days, whose word to trust."

"I might say the same thing, Riclef," she countered.

"You swore to wed me, and you ran away," he said.

"I didn't want to hurt you. I was running from an impossible dilemma."

"I don't see how I can help," he shrugged. "Your father will deal with you severely, far more severely than I would, Camilla. Were you safely wed to me, I could protect you. I would spit upon that horrible man and deprive him of his vengeance."

He gazed at her mournfully, but she wouldn't back down. No matter what tactic he used.

"Riclef, you can visit Jason when he's grown. When he

chooses to acknowledge who you are to him, it still won't be too late. You can finance his education, perhaps take him traveling with you, if you do not make him hate you now. Surely, when he's fifteen or sixteen, he'd want to get to know you. Even now, Janet could be persuaded to trust you later."

"I am forty-three years old," he said grimly. "When he is fifteen, I might be dead, Camilla." He got up and walked around the veranda, evidently disturbed.

Camilla watched him in an agony of indecision. "Do you want to see my father capture me, when he has caused such pain to me and to my mother?"

"At a moment like this," he said, "I hate him most, merely for having two daughters and four sons. He does not have to threaten and beg to have his sole child given back to him."

"You may have more sons than Jason," she blurted out.

"No, Camilla," he laughed shortly. "I have not been an angel, but apparently I have been more cautious with ladies than I remembered being. There are no other children that I know of."

Cammy was desperate to persuade him, and time was getting short. Each second that Riclef hesitated, her father might be getting closer.

"Riclef," she said, wondering which ploy would sway him. "Riclef, if Father takes me back, he will snatch Kit's child away. I will never see it nor will Kit. He will roam the world over, seeking me and his lost child!"

"Just as I have sought Jason. Now you can understand my pain, Camilla."

"But what of mine? Of a mother who will give birth to a baby and then lose it?"

He gazed at her, and his face filled with concern and care. "By God, child, I will come to you when the baby is near to arriving, and take you away from Blue Downs. I vow it. You shall keep your baby!"

"You see!" Cammy exclaimed. "You have sympathy for me, but not for Janet Ruyell! Think how she is suffering right now, Riclef. She has not lost an infant, but a boy she's reared for five whole years. A person in his own right with a formed character, one who can be ruined for life if he's frightened and lonely for his mother."

She ran out of breath and stopped suddenly, hoping she had been persuasive enough. Riclef put his head in his hand, torn by his own wants and needs and his desire for the child's welfare. She felt pity for him. There was no way she could hold back now. Perhaps it was all for the best.

"Riclef," she cried, getting up and going to him. She put a hand on his arm, "Riclef, you do have another son."

His head jerked up, and he whipped around to face her. "What? What are you saying?"

"Didn't you pay court to my mother years ago?"

"Everyone who's met your mother loves her."

"Yes, and with that sort of tender love, you helped her leave Blue Downs. You made sure she had a good husband in Stephen. But before that, did you not love her even more deeply many years before?"

"She had six children," he murmured, his eyes wide and unfocused. "You were the last. I was . . . I was not there between—"

His face was a mask of pain, and she could nearly see the years of memory pass before his eyes. Then he reached out and seized her hand, pulling her closer. "Tell me, Camilla. What are you hiding?"

"You do have another son, Riclef. Oh, I intended to keep it secret, but I can't! Kit doesn't even know. No one does except my mother, and now me. I have to betray her trust and tell you. It's important that you learn the truth."

"Tell me," he whispered. "What son? Tell me his name!"

"Let Jason go, Riclef! Swear you'll let him go until he's grown. Promise me! Then I'll tell you."

"How do I know you'll tell me the truth?"

"He is the image of you. If you ever see your older son, you'll know in an instant." Then she spat the words out. "If Mother knew the stakes, she would tell you herself. She had your child, Riclef! My brother Michael!"

"My God!" he shuddered violently, and she thought for a moment that he would lose his footing. Then he shook his bowed head and wiped his face with his palm. "Oh, my God! Minnie had a—that wretch reared my son?"

"My dear, handsome, brilliant brother survived it. He is the very image of you, Riclef, and he's just come of age. He is a lawyer."

"I have never seen Michael Cochran." Riclef still could not believe it.

"Mother thought you'd take him from her, or tell Father, and Michael would be disowned. She would have been thrown out on the street. I swear to you, Michael has never loved my father."

"To think I might have gone to my grave without knowing my own grown son!" He could hardly speak. He began pacing the veranda. "I want to see him. I don't have to tell—"

"Yes, think carefully, Riclef. Michael doesn't know."

"Wouldn't he prefer any father to the one he's had?" he asked, whirling on her. "The tormentor of his mother and sister?"

"He would be a child of shame instead of the son of a legal marriage, but he could love you, Riclef, if you are worthy. If you don't destroy another family."

She was finished. This was the point to which she had to bring him. Now there was nothing more she could do.

"Minnie never told me about him. I can give a son so much! I can make him trust me and like me. I know it. Michael! Michael and Jason."

"Relinquish Jason, Riclef. I have done a terrible thing, revealing this to you. Now you make it right. Give up Jason."

He was silent, debating the issues with his conscience.

"When Jason is Michael's age, even before, you can become his friend," Cammy promised. "If he doesn't think badly of you for what you once did to him, that is."

His face told her that this had never occurred to him.

"I must go into the fresh air," he said. "Come with me."

She walked beside him, and he put a hand on her shoulder. She felt strangely content to help him and steady him.

"Riclef, my father will soon be here," she reminded him. "With police, most likely."

He was her last chance. And yet she still could not be sure if he would help her and defy her father.

On the beach they found a fallen palm, and she brushed off a place for them both to sit down. Riclef was not strong enough to walk farther. He eased himself down beside her and sat leaning forward, his chin in his good hand. He seemed so far away. She knew he was thinking of her mother. And Jason and Michael. But all Cammy could think of was Edgar Cochran, whom no one loved.

Chapter 38

A Fijian boy of fifteen or sixteen came over to them after they had been sitting there for perhaps half an hour.

The boy asked, *"Silini?* Got work?"

"He wants to know if he can do anything," she told Riclef, "for a shilling."

She looked out to the sailing canoes on the bay, with their triangular brown mat sails. A storm was coming up. It might be hard for a ship to come in if the rain clouds broke open.

"Here," she told the boy, "suppose you lookim onefella man. Man come in ship, quick-time. Lik-lik man no got grass belong head."

Riclef managed a startled smile. "What is 'grass'?"

"That's how they say 'bald,'" Cammy explained.

"You think he's coming to shore here, today?"

"I can feel it in my bones."

The boy was already pushing his tiny outrigger canoe into the water. He paddled swiftly toward the ships anchored out in the shallow lagoon.

"That boy is probably mission-educated and speaks excellent English. I hope I haven't insulted him," she said, looking out toward the ships. She was already tired of waiting. Either way, it would be terrible. Kit would come, or Edgar Cochran

288

would come. She had no strength left to try to run back to the plantation alone. Riclef was her only chance for freedom, but she had no idea if she could trust him.

"Riclef, say the words to me. 'I relinquish Jason.'"

She wondered what his reaction would be. After all, he'd never seen Michael, that tall, dark young man. Jason was the only thing he could really count on.

"I relinquish Jason Ruyell."

When he gave the boy's entire name, she was convinced. He clearly meant what he said.

"Thank you," she said, and pressed his hand. "Oh, thank you. You won't be sorry, especially when you meet my brother."

"My son," he said slowly. "Minnie's son and mine."

The two of them watched the Fijian boy paddling from ship to ship for the next half hour. As yet, he'd found nothing. Cammy kept her eyes trained on the outrigger, telling herself all the while she was stupid to sit here like a sacrificial lamb. But then a flash of white appeared in her line of vision. Before she could even look around, she was caught by strong arms that pulled her from her seat.

"Kit!"

"You ran off from me! What's the matter with you, Cammy? We have to get away." He hardly even glanced at Riclef. "What is happening between—?"

"Oh, Kit, he's promised to relinquish Jason," she said excitedly.

"Do you trust him?" Kit frowned.

"I have been convinced," Riclef assured him. "Now go on, you two. I shall take Jason back to Janet myself, so she will know I am not an evil man. We shall be reconciled, Janet and I."

It was Kit's turn to be surprised. He stood there, studying Riclef's face. "Dare we leave the boy to him?" he asked Cammy.

"Yes," she nodded. "I have complete faith in him now."

They were so engrossed, they did not see the boy approaching from the water. He was smiling.

"*Silini*," he said. "*Silini*, missus," holding out his hand for payment. "Little man with no hair, he's coming. Out there!" He pointed. "Thank you, sar," he added when Riclef gave him a shilling. Then he was off, frisking away toward the trade store.

The boy had not been far in advance of Edgar Cochran, as it happened.

There were three other men in the little boat with him. Kit and Cammy stood there hand in hand, and Riclef sat, watching. They were rooted to the spot, realizing he would see them at once. Several Fijians waded into the shallows to offer the men transport to shore.

They could see two Fijians, in *sulus*, stepping into the knee-deep water. Another, in dark European garb, was struggling with his boots in preparation to do the same. The bald man was complaining loudly about the indignity of having to ride piggyback, but the strong Fijian simply lifted him out of the boat and paid no attention to his protests.

Another time, this might have seemed comical, but not one of the three watchers on shore was smiling.

"Two constables," murmured Kit.

She turned to him with a frightened gasp. "Coming for you? Oh, Kit! They can't! Your father's in the government and he—"

"I snatched an underage girl," he said dully.

Riclef stood up, his face livid. "They can't—" he began.

But the old man and the two Fijian constables, one of whom was carrying a rifle, were almost upon them. The expression on Edgar Cochran's face was one of evil pleasure.

At that instant, with a cry of pain, Kit plucked a small object from his pocket and held it out to Riclef.

"Will you save her from what you've led her into, Torandor? Take this and use it. It's already been blessed by a priest."

Riclef and Camilla both looked down upon the ring in Kit's hand. It was a wide, golden band.

What loving madness was this? Cammy reached for her beloved, but before she knew what was happening, Riclef picked up her left hand and thrust the ring instantly onto her third finger. Then he led her out onto the beach, in view of her father.

The stout Fijians flanking him blocked her view of the fourth man who'd come with them in their boat. Cammy was numb with fright, and the sound of Riclef's voice greeting her father seemed to come from miles away.

"Why have you followed me here, Edgar?" He put a falsely exuberant tone to his voice. "Foolish of you to come out—"

"Arrest that child-snatcher!" demanded Edgar Cochran, pointing at Kit.

"Of what child do you speak?" demanded Riclef crossly. "Camilla is my bride. She saw the error of her ways, Edgar. And I will not permit you to lay a hand on Westcott. He has done the honorable thing and given her over to me."

Her father stared at the three of them, his hands on his hips. "Married? But she fled from you with Westcott! How can this—?"

"I hate to cheat you of your revenge, Edgar, but it seems that you have no complaint against anyone here."

"Cammy, are you happy? With this older man?" said a voice behind them.

She whirled around, tearing her eyes from Riclef's fierce profile to look at the tall young man coming toward them.

"Michael!" she screamed, heading toward her brother.

Cammy felt faint, but she forced herself to move. Kit, Riclef, Father, and now, as if come out of the thin air, Michael.

"Mother sent me," he explained, taking her into his arms. "She said you needed me, and when I heard that, I had to come. We sailed on the same ship, Father and I, merely by chance. But she told me you wished to wed Kit!"

"Michael!" She pressed her face against the nap of his rough-textured coat, touching him to make sure he was no phantom. "Oh, Michael, I am so glad to see you!"

Then, on impulse, she turned to look at Riclef. His face was chalk-white. Had he entertained any doubt of her words, that doubt now fled. He'd seen Michael, and he knew his son at a glance.

"I don't understand. Why was I not informed?" stormed Edgar Cochran.

Michael walked slowly toward Kit, leaving Cammy alone. He gripped his friend's hand, speechless, his face a study in consternation. He had once loved Kit like an elder brother, and he was distraught to hear that his sister had rejected him. Cammy came to his side at once.

"You will understand later. Say nothing," she whispered to her perplexed brother.

Then she turned to her father. "There is nothing for you to do here."

Michael's eyes narrowed, and he looked around the circle, stopping at Riclef.

Then Edgar Cochran began to laugh. He puffed out his chest and took a step toward Kit. "Perhaps the voyage was worth it, to see your face this moment. To see you forever and hopelessly defeated, Westcott!"

Cammy shut her eyes, praying that Kit wouldn't strike the man, or roar out the truth. But he held his peace, as did Riclef, whose eyes remained fixed on Michael.

The Fijian constables moved off, perhaps understanding that they weren't needed.

"Well . . ." Cochran cleared his throat. "You came to your senses at last, daughter. Be grateful that this fine man will have you, regardless of your past. Tell me, where will you make your home, Torandor?"

"In England, most likely," said Riclef without hesitation. "She certainly does not wish to dwell near you, Edgar. Nor do I." Riclef shifted his gaze to Michael again, and then back to her father. "I am glad to be of assistance to your sweet and blameless child, Edgar. She is like her precious mother, whom, I will now disclose, I was pleased to aid in years past. You never knew what I did for Minnie."

"What?" Cochran's eyes narrowed suspiciously.

"You gave up your daughter to your worst enemy."

"Explain yourself!" Cochran stormed. "This is insanity!"

"Put simply, it was I who made it possible for Stephen Plaskett to come out to Victoria, and I made it possible for Camilla, like her mother, to leave Blue Downs. I came only to help her and fell in love with her quite unexpectedly. She has been infinitely kind to me. Now you are the proud possessor of a son-in-law who owes you no respect and knows every one of your cruel machinations."

"I did not come across the ocean to be vilely insulted, sir!" Edgar cried. "Why, if you were not wed to Camilla, I would call you out!"

"Go back to Blue Downs," Riclef said jeeringly. "You've driven away a good wife and a good daughter. I am sorry, Michael," he said, suddenly turning to the young man, his voice hoarse. "You should not be torn between filial loyalty and facts that are common knowledge. Camilla can tell you what she's suffered at her father's hands. You do not know her whole story, and neither does her mother. Camilla shields everyone from knowing her pain."

"Enough!" cried her father. "I am sailing for Levuka

immediately. I swear, you shall have not a penny from me, Camilla! Nor is either of you ever again welcome at Blue Downs!" He whirled again to face her, his smile like acid. "I even doubt that you are mine, Camilla. The daughter of such a mother can never be sure of her paternity!"

Michael stood there speechless, his face white with shock. Riclef was consumed with rage. Kit visibly trembled, so hard was it for him to remain silent.

Cammy knew she had to speak before someone struck her father down. She took a deep breath.

"You cannot be sure, sir, that any one of your children is really yours!" she cried.

Edgar blanched. His lips moved, but no sound came forth, not a word or a scream. The arrogant man suddenly was deflated, and for once in his life he had no bitter rejoinder. Riclef and Kit watched him with fascination. Michael seemed greatly pained, and Camilla held his hand tightly, interlacing her fingers with his.

"I shan't stand for this," gasped Edgar Cochran at last in a breathy voice. He turned on his heel and walked unsteadily down the beach away from them. He raised his arm as a Fijian paddled by in a canoe. The constables murmured something apologetic to Kit.

"Stay, Michael. Stay with me," Camilla whispered. "Mother would wish it. I had to say that to him. He's a sick man who's done much harm to many people."

"Are you truly married to this man?" murmured Michael.

Her father was perched on an outrigger's platform, staring out to sea, being paddled swiftly back to the ship from which he'd just disembarked. He did not even look behind to see if Michael followed. He did not seem to care, or even to expect it.

Camilla did not glance up at Riclef. She did not need to, since she could feel the waves of intense emotion he was emitting. He still refrained from seizing Michael and embracing him.

"Tell me, Camilla," her brother demanded, grasping her by the shoulders. "All the truth!"

"No, we aren't wed. We deceived him to save me and our baby, Kit's and mine. Michael, I love Kit. I always have. I have struggled for three years to be with him. Please don't condemn us."

"Cochran prevented their marriage. I have tried to right his wrong, and my own," said Riclef. "Michael, I am glad finally to meet you. You seem like a fine young man."

Kit held out his hand to Riclef, palm up. He was very intense and unsmiling.

"Give it over," said Kit firmly, his eyes narrowed. "I want them now."

Riclef stared at him without comprehending.

"She's wearing my ring. Now I want those papers."

"Ah." The dark man's teeth flashed in a grin. "The signed and sealed papers. Yes, most certainly!" Cammy was delighted to see that Riclef was smiling, though it must have cost him dearly to do so. He reached into his coat and brought out a fat envelope.

"What's that?" asked Michael, stepping nearer.

"The license to wed," Kit told him. "A touch of lemon juice on his name," he said, glancing at Riclef, "and it's done. We'll simply substitute my name in its place. And so the deceiver is deceived."

"I must say I'm glad," said Michael. "No offense, Mr.—"

"Torandor. Riclef Torandor."

"Mr. Torandor, I admire your decision. My sister has been dear to my friend Kit since both of us were children. And I have always hoped they would wed," he confessed, looking at Cammy.

"I would like to remain their friend," Riclef told him, "and yours, as well. But I must be off soon, because I have a boy to deliver back to his mother in Hobart. Tell me, what plans have you, in this chaos of confrontations? I suppose you will remain here in Suva for a visit with your sister?"

"At least long enough to attend her wedding," said Michael staunchly. "I would like to give the bride away, Camilla, in our father's stead."

"Nothing would please me more," she said, pulling his arm around her.

Riclef examined his earnest face. "I understand you have qualified at the bar and are already a lawyer at your young age. I once wished to follow that profession myself."

But Michael was more occupied with Camilla and Kit than with this stranger. It pained Cammy to see how badly Riclef wanted to continue their conversation.

"You really will take Jason back to Hobart, Torandor?" Kit asked suddenly.

"Most certainly. Then I'll bid him goodbye and make my peace with his mother."

Michael looked curious about this interchange, but he was too well mannered to pry into this stranger's personal problems. Riclef nevertheless seemed anxious to bare his soul. "Jason Ruyell is my five-year-old natural son," he told Michael. "I wished to give him wealth and position and a father's love, but I see now that he will perish without his mother. Camilla persuaded me to do the honorable thing."

Michael blinked in surprise to hear this confession, but he said nothing.

"I have met your elder brothers and sister, Michael," Riclef continued. "They are all delightful. They were very small when last I saw them. And then when I returned, you had all left home, all except Camilla. At your mother's behest—"

"By subterfuge," Cammy cut in, "he got me away from Blue Downs and from Father. He was very kind."

At this point, Kit tugged her away from Riclef and Michael, and closed her lips with a kiss. "All right now, that's sufficient. They'll make each other's acquaintance in due time, Camilla." He fingered the precious marriage license and smiled down at her. "I'll perform the needed alteration on this, and have us wed within two days."

"Would you mind?" Cammy asked Michael. "Riclef is still weak from his wound. Would you be so kind as to help him back to the infirmary?"

Riclef nodded, and accepted the young man's assistance. High excitement had kept him on his feet for too long, and now his legs were quite unsteady. He begged Kit and Camilla to join him for tea at the hospital, and then he turned, leaning on his tall son's arm for the journey back into Suva.

"It strikes me as odd," said Kit, standing and looking after the pair, "I never really saw it until today, but Michael so little resembles your father." He stared at her quizzically. "And one might say that had Michael a beard . . ."

"Don't ask, Kit," she said, at the same time exultant at what he'd guessed.

Kit obeyed her command, but as he thought about it, he shook his head in awe. "So that's why," he murmured very softly, "that's why you trust him to relinquish Jason! Camilla, you're a miracle maker! At last I see what you've been about! I was so blind—"

"Hush!" She laid a hand over his lips. "In time it will all come clear to everyone. Now what do you say we gain a legal father for this tiny one that I'm nurturing?" She touched her stomach with gentle fingertips and then lifted her face to him. "Kiss me, husband."

He embraced her, standing in the coconut grove, where no one could see them, under the waving fronds. She reached up and smoothed his hair, still damply curled from the perspiration of his morning's efforts. She untied the head scarf she'd been wearing and used it to dry his temples and the nape of his neck.

"I love you," she murmured with a sigh that came from the depths of her being. "I love you, Kit. It has been so long and hard and hopeless, but now—"

"But now we have each other forever. There is no one to part us."

"And Fiji will be my land, too. Forever."

Epilogue
October 10, 1874
Levuka, Ovalau, Fiji

Three hundred Fijian chiefs and white settlers, and one small family, were present for the great occasion. King Thakombau, a gigantic man with a tremendous head of graying hair, clad in *masi* cloth, presided over the end of his reign and the delivery of his country to the United Kingdom. Exactly on the opposite side of the globe, England was taking Fiji as a colony of the Crown.

The King's regal face, his long, straight nose and keen eyes, his expanse of shining black skin, drew the rapt attention of the crowd.

Sir Hercules Robinson, Governor of New South Wales, signed and sealed the Deed of Cession directly above the seals of Fiji's twelve greatest hereditary chiefs, who were all former cannibals or the sons of cannibals. Hereby, Fiji was given, as the proclamation read, "unreservedly to the Queen of Britain, that she may rule us justly and affectionately, and that we may live in peace and prosperity."

A loud salute was fired by the massed warships crowding the harbor. The Royal Standard—a missionary's design of a dove holding an olive branch, embroidered in red and white calico—was lowered over the Royal Palace, and the Union Jack rose skyward in its place.

"The King is sending his war club, *Tutuvi*, the blood-bather, to Her Majesty in England as a humble tribute," whispered Kit Westcott.

"The dove and the club," sighed the white-haired man standing directly behind the younger image of himself. "Our island history in a few words!"

Between the two men stood a delicate, golden-haired beauty, her face flushed with excitement, her green eyes one moment flashing and the next glazed with tears. Half smiling, she murmured, "The King is giving up his throne to save his land reminds me of another man . . . who gave up his little son—"

"And gained another," Kit added, smiling. His arm tightened around Camilla's slim shoulders. He, too, could not forget the sight of Riclef Torandor climbing the gangway to the *Balaclutha*, bound for the Australian colonies, one son held high in his arms, and the other striding close behind him. After they left Jason in Hobart, Michael and Riclef planned to sail to London.

Kit's own child, Cammy's precious one, would be wanting a feeding soon. Janet Letitia Westcott was just past four months old.

"I wish Michael were here to see this," Cammy grieved, watching the pomp of the ceremony continue.

"He'll be back. We'll have need of his talents here in Levuka. A lawyer trained in Sydney and in London!" Kit spoke enthusiastically.

At least some of her family had been present for little Janet's baptism. Cammy stood there, remembering.

At four days old, the little girl had been named according to Fijian custom. The village people nearest Levuka had gathered 'round the open veranda where Camilla lay holding her child. Then they brought a large *yangona* bowl filled with live prawns and tiny fish, all swimming in a mass. Their baby was held over the bowl, sprinkled with water, and given her name. Afterward, the fish and prawns had been distributed among the village children to be cooked and eaten as a celebration of Janet Letitia's birth. This rite ensured that the infant would grow up to be generous and unselfish, traits preeminently desirable in Fijian tradition.

At three weeks old, their adored little Janet Letty had been baptized in a Wesleyan chapel by the missionary from Suva who had married them. Standing as godparents were Letty Finch and Bernard and Beatrice Cochran. Michael had even come back from London for the event and had introduced his father, Riclef Torandor, to Bernard and Beatrice with great pride.

Cammy was roused from her reverie by a hand on her arm. The long spectacle of Cession was now almost over, and Henry Westcott murmured, "I'm too old for many more of these occasions. The time is ripe for the new generation to step into my worn shoes."

She reached behind her and squeezed his hand. She was still so moved by the spirit of the day that tears came easily.

"You're a stronger man than you think, Father," she said earnestly. "You mustn't stay away long in other colonies. We want you back with us." She truly saw him as her own beloved father. "Kit told you, didn't he," she went on, "that I may have a useful task to perform soon?"

"It was that advertisement she placed in the *Times*," Kit chuckled, overhearing them. "She's at the beck and call of our own precious baby, but already she's found two little children who cannot hear."

"Kit says the summerhouse will do just fine, and maybe if our numbers grow, we can import Letty and her parents."

"I can see you intend to populate Levuka with your family and friends!" the old man exclaimed, tousling her curls. "But I must say I like everyone you've attracted here, and Michael, of course, will prove invaluable."

"Could you use a draper, do you think?" she teased.

"You are irrepressible, Cammy!" Kit said. "I knew it would only be a matter of time before you insisted on seeing Janet and George, not to mention Jason."

"You've guessed it. I also want to meet Mary Camilla Ruyell."

"She cannot be more beautiful than our daughter," Kit vowed, "though her name may help her grow like a blossom in Tasmania."

Mr. Westcott was busily shaking hands, bidding farewell to

the celebrants, and Kit and Camilla were left standing to one side of the crowd.

"I am so proud," Cammy said, meshing her fingers tightly with his. "So very happy."

"And so am I, my darling. Our dream at long last has come true." Very softly and gently, he bent his head and kissed her, oblivious to everything but their love.